SANTA MONTEFIORE

The Gypsy Madonna

HODDER

First published in Great Britain in 2006 by Hodder & Stoughton
A division of Hodder Headline
First published in paperback in 2006 by Hodder & Stoughton
A Hodder paperback

A Hodder paperback

4

A CIP catalogue record for this title is available from the British Library

ISBN 0 340 83654 7

Typeset in Plantin Light by Palimpsest Book Production Limited,
Grangemouth, Stirlingshire

Printed and bound by
Mackays of Chatham Ltd, Chatham, Kent

Hodder Headline's policy is to use papers that are natural, renewable
and recyclable products and made from wood grown in sustainable
forests. The logging and manufacturing processes are expected to
conform to the environmental regulations of the country of origin.

Hodder & Stoughton Ltd
A division of Hodder Headline
338 Euston Road
London NW1 3BH

For my sister, Tara,
with love

Out of all the books I have written, this one has posed the greatest challenge. However, thanks to my husband, Sebag, my trusty partner in crime, who helped me plot the adventure over a glass of rosé on our annual holiday in France, it turned out to be the most enjoyable. Two minds are better than one and I couldn't have written it without him.

When faced with the prospect of researching Bordeaux in the war, I turned to my dear friends Sue and Alan Johnson-Hill, who live in the most beautiful château and were incredibly kind to share their experiences, though I hasten to add that neither is old enough to have lived through the war! Alan was quick to correct my French and Sue was in constant touch by e-mail, making suggestions and answering my lists of questions. I thank them both.

I also want to thank my friend, Eric Villain, who grew up in Bordeaux. I needed a child's perspective so I took him out to lunch, poured him a large glass of wine – French, of course, and took out my notebook while he reminisced about his childhood. He was a deep well of information and very entertaining too. Thank you, Eric.

The book took me not only to Bordeaux, but to New York and Virginia as well. Naturally, I picked the most handsome American I know to help me with my research, Gordon Rainey. I thank you, Gordon, for all your help and amusing e-mails that have made doing business with you such fun.

Writing about the sudden appearance of a painting by

Titian, I sought help from the highest echelons of the National Gallery. I cannot thank enough both Colin McKenzie, Head of Development and David Jaffé, Senior Curator, for their advice, anecdotes, support, wit and exceedingly good company while researching *The Gypsy Madonna*. A part of the book I dreaded was made one of the most enjoyable thanks to them.

A girl must stay in shape while spending most of the day slumped in a chair in front of her laptop! Therefore, I would also like to thank my kickboxing trainer Stewart Taylor from Bodyarchitecture.co.uk, who has not only jabbed and ducked with me about the gym, but also been a good listener and sounding board as I shared the plot and its various characters in between punches.

I thank my parents, Charlie and Patty Palmer-Tomkinson, for their constant support and encouragement, especially my mother who read the first draft and made very useful additions. My parents-in-law, Stephen and April Sebag-Montefiore, who take such an interest in my books, their enthusiasm and praise giving me the impetus to write on.

Kate Rock always deserves my thanks for getting me started five years ago as does Jo Frank for selling my first book to Hodder & Stoughton. Hodder & Stoughton deserve an enormous thank you for now publishing my sixth and for signing me up for four more! God bless you!

Thank you Linda Shaughnessy, for selling my books all over the world.

Sheila Crowley, my literary agent, is the most dynamic, capable, positive person I know. Nothing is too great a challenge for her. Thank you so much for representing me and please stick around for the next four!

My gratitude also goes to my editor, Susan Fletcher, for working so hard and for being so patient. Your criticism is invaluable and your praise the fuel with which I am able to continue writing. Long may our very productive partnership continue.

The Gypsy Madonna

The Virgin and Child (also 'The Gypsy Madonna')
About 1511
Oil on panel, 65.8 x 83. 8cm
Metropolitan Museum, New York

Titian's young Virgin has traditionally been called the 'Gypsy' Madonna on account of her dusky complexion, dark hair and eyes. Mary, little more than a child herself, supports her infant son as he stands unsteadily on a parapet. Both mother and son seem lost in thought. However, their communication goes beyond words; with his left hand, in what is a very natural and engaging attitude for a young child, Christ plays with his mother's fingers while with his right, he toys with the gold-green fabric lining of her mantle.

PART ONE

As I walked out on the streets of Laredo
As I walked out on Laredo one day
I spied a young cowboy
A handsome young cowboy
All dressed in white linen
As cold as the clay

I see by your outfit
That you are a cowboy
These words he did say
As I boldly stepped by
Come sit down beside me
And hear my sad story
For I'm shot in the breast
And now I must die

Prologue

New York, 1985

I was as surprised as anyone when, shortly before her death, my mother gave away the Titian. At first it seemed the action of a woman not in control of her mind. My mother had grown increasingly stubborn with age. She gave the painting to the Metropolitan and flatly refused to talk about what she had done, even to me. That was my mother. She could be cold and brisk. She had that air of self-control, of haughtiness, so often associated with the French. But, if one persevered and won her trust, beneath the thorns she was a rare and fragile flower, like a briar rose. In spite of all their efforts, though, every journalist who approached her was rebuffed. Pressure mounted but she would not bend, not for a moment.

She was not mad, however, but maddened. I recognised, in those shiny, restless eyes, a deep and urgent need way beyond my comprehension. She was dying. She knew she had little time. The dying are often beset with the desire to tie up loose ends so they can die in peace, with a clear conscience. But my mother's desire was far greater than the simple sorting of one's affairs before embarking on a voyage. 'You don't understand, Mischa,' she had said and her voice had been strangely anguished. 'I *have* to give this painting back.' She was right, I didn't understand. How could I?

I was angry. We had shared everything, my mother and I. We were closer than other sons and mothers because we had lived through so much together, just the two of us. It was us against the world, *maman* and her little *chevalier*. And, as a child, I had dreamed of wielding a sword powerful enough to slay all her enemies. But she had never told me about the Titian.

Now she is dead, her lips forever sealed, her breath taken by the wind, her words whispers that come to me in dreams. One night she slipped away, taking with her all her secrets; or so I thought. It was only later that I discovered those secrets, one by one, as I walked back down the path of memory to my childhood; they were all there for me to find if I could only bear to walk through fire to reach them. On my journey I suffered both pain and joy but, most often, surprise. As a small boy I interpreted everything with my young, innocent mind. Now I am a man in my forties, with the wisdom gained from years of experience, I can see things as they really were. I expected to find the provenance of the Titian; I never expected to find myself.

I

It all began on a snowy January day. January is bleak in New York. The trees are bare, the festivities over, the Christmas tree lights taken down for another year. The wind that races down the streets is edged with ice. I walked briskly with my hands in my coat pockets. Head down, eyes to the ground, lost in thought: nothing particular, just the business of the day. I tried not to think of my mother. I am an avoider. If something gives me pain I don't think about it. If I don't think about it, it isn't happening. If I can't see it, it isn't there, right? My mother had been dead a week. The funeral was over. Only the journalists pestered like flies, determined to find out why an uncatalogued, unknown, Titian of such importance had only now come to light. Didn't they understand that I knew as little as they did? If they were grappling in the dark, I was floundering in space.

I reached my office. A red brick building in the West Village with an antique shop on the ground floor. Zebedee Hapstein, the eccentric clock-maker, toiled against a discordant orchestra of ticking in his workshop next door. I fumbled in my pocket for the key. My fingers were numb. I had forgotten to wear gloves. For a moment I looked at my reflection in the glass. The haunted face of a man, old beyond his years, stared grimly back at me. I shook off my grief and walked inside, brushing the snow from my shoulders. Stanley wasn't in yet, nor was Esther who answered the shop telephone and cleaned the place. With leaden feet I climbed the stairs. The building was dim and smelt of old wood and furniture polish. I opened the door to my office and stepped inside. There, sitting quietly on a chair, was a tramp.

I nearly jumped out of my skin. Angrily, I demanded to know what he was doing there and how he had got in. The window was closed and the front door had been locked. For an instant I was afraid. Then he turned to me, his mouth curling into a half smile. I was at once struck by the extraordinary colour of his eyes that shone out from his cracked and bearded face, like aquamarine set in rock. I had a sudden sense of *déjà vu* but it was gone as quickly as it had come. He wore a felt hat and sat hunched in a heavy coat. I noticed his shoes were dirty and scuffed with a hole wearing through at one toe. He looked me up and down appraisingly and I felt my fury mount at his impertinence.

'You've grown into a fine young man,' he mused, nodding appreciatively. I frowned at him, not knowing how to respond. 'You don't know who I am?' he asked and, behind his smile, I noticed a shadow of sorrow.

'Of course I don't. I think you should leave,' I replied.

He nodded and shrugged. 'Hell, there's no reason why you should remember. I hoped . . . Well, what does it matter? Do you mind if I have a smoke? It's mighty cold out there.' His accent was southern and there was something about it that caused my skin to goose-bump.

Before I could refuse his request he pulled out a Gauloise and struck a match to light it. The sudden smell of smoke sent my head into a spin. There was no way I could avoid the sudden arousal of memory. I gave him a long stare before dismissing the idea as preposterous. I took off my coat and hung it on the back of the door to hide my face and play for time, then sat down at my desk. The old man relaxed as he inhaled but he never took his eyes off me. Not for a moment.

'Who are you?' I asked, bracing myself for the answer. *It*

can't be, I thought. *Not after all this time*. I didn't want it to be, not like this, not smelling of stale tobacco and sweat. He smiled, blowing the smoke out of the side of his mouth.

'Does the name Jack Magellan mean anything to you?'

I hesitated, my mouth dry.

He raised a feathery eyebrow and leaned across the desk. 'Then perhaps the name Coyote might be more familiar, Junior?'

I felt my jaw loosen and fall. I searched his features for the man who had once held my love in the palm of his hand, but saw only a dark beard fringed with grey and deep crevices in thick, weatherbeaten skin. There was no evidence of his youth or his magic. The handsome American who had promised us the world had died long ago. Surely he had died, why else would he not have come back?

'What do you want?'

'I read about your mother in the papers. I came to see her.'

'She's dead,' I said brutally, watching for his reaction. I wanted to hurt him. I hoped he'd be sorry. I owed him nothing – he owed me an explanation and thirty years. I was glad to see his eyes fill with tears and sink into his head with sadness. He stared at me, horrified. I watched him watching me. I didn't endeavour to ignore his emotion. I simply left him like a fish struggling on the beach, gasping for air.

'Dead,' he said finally and his voice cracked. 'When?'

'Last week.'

'Last week,' he repeated, shaking his head. 'If only . . .'

He inhaled and the smoke that he blew out enveloped me once again in a miasma of memory. I fought it off with a scowl and turned away. In my mind's eye I saw long, green rows of vines, cypress trees and the sun-drenched, sandy stone of those *château* walls that had once been my home. The pale blue shutters were open, the scents of pine and jasmine blew in on the breeze and somewhere, at the very back of my thoughts, I heard a voice singing *Laredo*.

'Your mother was a unique woman,' he said sadly. 'I wish I had seen her before she died.'

I wanted to tell him that she had long clung to the hope that he would one day return. That, in the three decades since he had left, she had never doubted him. Only finally, when she reached the end of the road, had she resigned herself to the truth – that he was never coming back. I wanted to shout at him and haul him off the ground by the collar of his coat. But I did not. I remained calm. I simply stared back at him, my face devoid of expression.

'How did you find me?' I asked.

'I read about the Titian,' he replied. *Ah, the Titian,* I thought. *That's what he's after*. He stubbed out his cigarette and chuckled. 'I see she gave it to the city.'

'What's it to you?'

He shrugged. 'Worth a fortune that painting.'

'So that's why you're here. Money.'

Once again he leaned forward and fixed me with those hypnotic blue eyes of his. 'I'm not coming asking for money. I'm not looking for anything.' His voice was gruff with indignation. 'In fact, I'm an old fool. There's nothing left for me here.'

'Then why did you come?'

Now he smiled, revealing teeth blackened with decay. I felt uneasy, however, because his smile was more like the grimace of a man in pain. 'I'm chasing a rainbow, Junior, that's what it is. That's what it's always been, a rainbow. But you wouldn't understand.'

From the window I watched him limp down the street, his shoulders hunched against the cold, his hat pulled low over his head. I scratched my chin and felt bristles against my fingers. For a moment I was sure I heard him singing, his voice carried on the wind: '*As I walked out on the streets of Laredo.*'

It was all too much. I grabbed my coat and hurried down the stairs. As I reached the door, it opened and Stanley walked in. He looked surprised to see me. 'I'm going out,' I said and left without further explanation.

I ran into the road. The snow was now falling thick and heavy. I set off along the trail his footprints had made. I didn't know what I was going to say to him when I caught up with him. But I did know why my anger had been overridden by something almost visceral. You see, it's hard to explain, but he had given me a gift, a very special gift. A gift no one else could give me, not even my mother. And, in spite of all the pain he brought, ours was a bond that could never break.

I was able to follow his footsteps for a while, but soon the track was lost among the millions of faceless inhabitants of New York. I felt a sudden ache deep within my soul, a regret for something lost. I scanned the pavements, searching for the old man with the limp, but my heart yearned for someone different. He had been handsome, with sandy hair and piercing blue eyes, the colour of a tropical sea. When he smiled those eyes had twinkled with mischief, extending into long white crows' feet accentuated against the weathered brown of his skin. His mouth had turned up at the corners, even when he was solemn, as if a smile was his natural expression and it cost him to be serious. He bounced when he walked, his chin high, his shoulders square, exuding a wild and raffish charm powerful enough to soften the heart of the most determined cynic. That was the Coyote I knew. Not this old, malodorous vagabond who'd come like a vulture to peck at the remains of the woman who had loved him.

I stared bleakly into the snow, then turned and walked back. My footsteps had almost disappeared. And his? They had gone too. It was as if he had never existed.

2

'Oh, Diane, do look, here's that dear little boy again!'

Joy Springtoe bent down and gave my cheek a generous pinch. I breathed in the sweetness of her perfume and felt myself blush. She was the most beautiful woman I had ever seen. Her hair was a mass of blonde curls, her eyes the colour of the doves that cooed from the *château* roof, her skin soft and pale like suede. She was elegant in that overdone American way that French women consider brash, but I liked her. She was colourful. When she laughed you wanted to laugh with her; except I didn't, couldn't. I just smiled shyly and let her caress me, my young heart overflowing with gratitude.

'You're mighty handsome for a little boy. Why, you must be no more than six or seven? Hm? Where are your parents? I'd so like to meet them! Are they as handsome as you?'

Her friend walked over, looking anxious. She was stout like a teapot, with rosy cheeks and soft brown eyes. In spite of her red floral blouse she looked drab beside Joy, as if God had got carried away painting Joy and forgotten to give Diane any colour.

'His name is Mischa,' said Diane. 'He's French.'

'You don't look French, my little one. Not with all that blond hair and those pretty blue eyes. No, you don't look French at all.'

'His mother works in the hotel,' Diane added. Joy frowned an enquiry. 'I was curious, so I asked.' She shrugged and smiled down at me apologetically.

'Don't you go to school?' Joy asked. *Est-ce que tu ne vas pas à l'école?*

'He's mute, Joy.'

Joy straightened and looked at Diane in horror. When she turned back to me, her face had melted with sympathy.

'He doesn't speak?' she said, running her hand over my cheek. Her eyes glistened with compassion. 'Who stole your voice, my little one?'

At that moment, while I basked in the warmth of Joy's affection, Madame Duval strode around the corner. When she saw me her face darkened for an instant before she checked herself. '*Bonjour*,' she said to her guests. Her voice was light and sugary. I froze like a startled mouse with nowhere to run. 'I trust you had a pleasant night?'

Joy stood up and ran a hand through her hair. 'Oh, we did. It's so beautiful here. My window looks right out over the vines and this morning, in the sunshine, they simply sparkled.'

'I am pleased. Breakfast is now served in the dining-room.'

Joy glanced down at me. By the expression on her face she had registered my terror. She patted my head and winked, then she and Diane walked down the corridor towards the staircase. When they had gone, Madame Duval's expression hardened like water that is suddenly turned to ice.

'And you! What are you doing in this side of the house? Get away! Go on! Get away!' She shooed me off with a brisk wave of her hand. My heart, only a moment ago so open, now closed in on itself. I ran off before she could hit me.

I found my mother polishing silver in the pantry. She looked up anxiously when she saw me enter. 'Oh, Mischa!' she exclaimed, drawing me into her arms and kissing my temple. 'Are you all right? Did someone hurt you?' She looked down at my face and understood. 'Oh, my love, you mustn't go into the Private Side. This is a hotel now. It is not your home.' My tears soaked into her apron. 'I know it is hard for you to understand. But this is the way things are now. You must accept it and you must behave, for both our sakes. Madame Duval has been good to us.' I pulled away and shook my head angrily. To my shame the tears began to flow again. When she tried to embrace me I shook her off and stamped my foot. *I hate her, I hate her, I hate her*, I shouted. But she could not hear my inner voice.

'Come, my love. I understand. *Maman* understands you.' Unable to resist the warmth of her kisses I allowed myself to be won over and snuggled into her lap. I closed my eyes and breathed in the lemony scent of her skin. Her lips rested against my cheekbone so that I could feel her breath on my face. I sensed her love. It was fierce and unconditional and I drank it in with parched lips.

My mother was my best friend. However, that dreadful episode at the end of the war also brought me someone special, someone all my very own. His name was Pistou and no one could see him but me. He was about my age. Unlike me, he was dark with ruffled hair and olive skin and deep-set brown eyes. He heard my inner voice and I didn't have to explain, because he understood everything. For a little boy, he was very knowing.

The first time I saw him was at night. Since the end of the war I slept with my mother. We'd curl up together and she'd keep me snug and safe. I had nightmares, you see. Terrible dreams where I'd wake up crying with my mother stroking my brow and kissing me sleepily. I couldn't explain to her the nature of my dreams so I'd lie blinking into the darkness, afraid that, if I closed my eyes, the images would return and take me away from her. It was then that Pistou appeared. He sat on the bed and smiled at me. His face was so luminous, his expression so warm, I knew instantly that we'd be friends. From the look of compassion in his eyes I knew he saw my dreams as I did and that he understood my fears. While my mother slept, I lay awake with Pistou, until I could fight my tiredness no more and I, too, drifted off to sleep.

After those initial midnight encounters, he began to appear during the daytime. I soon realised that no one else could see him; they looked right through him. He'd run amongst them, playing pranks, pinching the old women's bottoms, tipping their hats with his fingers, sticking out his tongue right in front of them, but they did not see him. Even my mother rubbed her forehead and frowned when I played with him in our small room in the stable block. Of course, I couldn't tell her about Pistou, even if I had wanted to.

I didn't go to school. Not because I was mute, but because they wouldn't take me. My mother tried to teach me what she knew, but it was hard for her. She worked long hours in the *château* and would return in the evenings exhausted. However, in spite of having toiled all day, she managed to find time to teach me how to write. It was a frustrating process because of my inability to communicate, but we struggled on, the two of us. Always the two of us – and Pistou.

I knew it saddened her that I had no young friends to play with. I knew a lot that she didn't suspect me of knowing. You see, she often spoke her thoughts out loud, as if I were not only mute but deaf too. She'd sit at her dressing-table, brushing her long brown hair, staring at her solemn face in the mirror, while I pretended to sleep in the iron bed, listening to everything she said. 'Oh, I fear for you, Mischa,' she'd say. 'I brought you into the world and yet I cannot protect you from it. I do the best I can, but it is not enough.' Other times she'd lie beside me and whisper into my ear: 'You're all I have, my love. It's just the two of us. *Maman* and her little *chevalier.* I grew up with enemies all around. We were like an island in a shark-infested sea. But to me, no enemy was more fearful than Madame Duval.

It was because of her that we had to move out of the *château*, into the stable block. My mother said that she was good to us. She spoke to the old woman with deference, her words full of gratitude, as if we owed her our very lives. But Madame Duval never smiled or responded with kindness. She peered at my mother through reptilian eyes, with conde-scension. As for me, to her I was worse than the rats they set traps for in the *cave* beneath the *château*. I was vermin. The very sight of me alarmed her. When the hotel opened I strayed out to the front, captivated by the shiny cars that drew up on the gravel, chauffeured by solemn men in hats and gloves. She grabbed me by the ear and dragged me into the kitchen where she hit me so hard about the head that I fell to the floor. Her shrill voice attracted the attention of Yvette, the cook, and her small army of staff, who all crowded around to see what had happened. But none of them helped me. I cowered on the floor in fear, like I had done back then, for their faces were the same: full of hatred.

It was my mother who held me and her tears that proved again and again that against all the odds she loved me deeply.

Unable to communicate and fearful of the staff, I with-drew into myself and my secret world. Pistou and I played *cache-cache* for hours among the long rows of vines. He'd have a way of popping up out of nowhere, then laugh so hard he had to hold his belly. His shaking shoulders caused me enormous amusement, so I'd copy him, which would make him laugh all the more. We'd sit on the stone bridge and throw pebbles into the water. He could make them bounce, like the little rubber ball I carried about in my pocket.

That ball was very special to me. In fact, it was my most treasured possession because my father had given it to me and it was all I had left of him. We'd play catch with it and perform tricks like seals. Once, it fell into the water with an ominous plop. Unlike the stones we tossed in, the little rubber ball didn't sink but bobbed up and down, swept along by the current. In my haste, I jumped in after it, only remembering that I couldn't swim when I was waist-high in the water. Gasping with shock and terror, I grabbed my ball and struggled through the mud and weeds to reach the bank. Pistou wasn't concerned. He put his hands on his hips and laughed at my foolishness. I dragged myself up the bank. I had nearly drowned. But I got my ball. The relief gave me a delicious high. In celebration of my heroics we danced on the grass like a pair of Red Indians, waving our arms and stamping our feet. I held on to my ball and vowed never to be so careless again.

When the Duvals bought the *château* and turned it into a hotel, we began to spy on the guests. I knew the grounds better than anyone and certainly better than the Duvals. I had grown up there. It had been my home. I knew the places to hide, the doors to crouch behind, all the escape routes. Oh, I didn't hide from guests like Joy Springtoe; she knew how to keep a secret. I hid from Madame Duval and her coarse toad of a husband who smoked cigars and kissed the maids when his wife wasn't looking. Pistou disliked the Duvals, too. His favourite game was hiding things. He hid Monsieur Duval's cigars, Madame Duval's reading glasses, and we watched from our secret places while they bustled about irritably in search of them.

My fascination with Joy Springtoe overrode my fear of Madame Duval. I was only six and three-quarters, but I was in love. In my desire to see her, I risked everything. I'd sneak into the Private Side and hide behind the furniture and plants.

The *château* was full of narrow corridors and nooks and crannies perfect for a child of my size to hide in. During the day Madame Duval spent a lot of time in her office on the ground floor. They had laid an ugly blue and gold carpet there on top of the big square stones I had skidded across as a toddler. I hated that carpet. The hall was her lair and there she'd wait like a spider to welcome the guests who arrived from England and America with money in their pockets. While she spun her charm, so false to those like me who knew her true face, I crept along the corridors for a glimpse of Joy Springtoe.

From behind the upholstered chair that stood in the corner by the window, I saw the comings and goings of guests. It was morning. The pale light flooded the carpeted floor and white walls with summer. Outside, the birdsong was a loud clamour. First to appear were the Three Pheasants, as my mother called them – three elderly ladies from England who had come to paint. I liked foreigners. I hated the French, except for Jacques Reynard, who ran the vineyard; the only one who was kind to me. The Three Pheasants made me smile for they were always arguing. They had been in residence for weeks. I imagined their rooms stuffed full of paintings. The tall one was called Gertie, a pheasant with a long neck who tried to be a swan. She was white-haired with a thin, bony face and small black eyes. Her bosom was large, and wobbled as she walked, like soft-boiled eggs in muslin. Her waist was small, cinched in by a belt, before her body expanded as if all the fat from her waist had been squeezed into her bottom. She had long white fingers that played with the pearl necklace that hung down to her waist, and she was always the first to give an opinion.

Daphne was my favourite: Daphne with the feathers in her hair. Daphne was eccentric. Her dresses followed no recognisable code, some days covered in lace, others trimmed with what looked like the fringes on curtains. Her face was as round and pink as a ripe peach, her full lips always breaking into a smile as if she argued just for the fun of it. She carried a small, fluffy dog that she had smuggled into France. His pale brown fur obscured his face so I never knew which way he was facing. Once I waved a biscuit in front of him to find that what I thought was his face was his bottom. Daphne's voice was thick and smoky and she spoke slowly so that I understood, although I had grown up with English spoken around me. Best of all I liked her shoes. She seemed to have enough shoes to wear a different pair every day, and each one was more colourful than the last. There were pink velvet ones; purple satin ones; some had small heels; others were flat and pointed, turning up at the toes; one or two had straps around the ankles with beads or feathers hanging from the buckle. She was curvy and soft and her feet were very small.

Then there was Debo. She was languorous in thin, floral dresses. Her black hair was cut into a shiny bob that accentuated her sharp jaw, and her lips were always painted scarlet. Her eyes were wide and the palest shade of green. She was still beautiful. My mother said she dyed her hair, for a woman of that age would surely be grey. She also said that they all dressed from another era, but I was only six and three quarters so I didn't know of which era she spoke. They certainly didn't dress like anyone I had ever seen before. Not like Joy Springtoe, anyway. Debo smoked all the time. She'd suck through an ivory holder and the end of the cigarette would light up like a firefly. Then the smoke would either trail out of the side of her mouth or she'd puff it out like a train in one long stream. She never simply blew it out, but played with it as if it was a game that amused her. Unlike Daphne, her voice was brittle and her laughter a cackle. She talked as if her mouth were full, her jaw stiff and unmoving.

'Don't look behind the chair, girls,' said Daphne in a loud whisper. 'That dear little boy is hiding again.'

'He needn't hide from us,' said Debo, cackling softly. 'Hasn't someone told him, we don't bite?'

'He's hiding from "Mrs Danvers",' continued Daphne. 'And I don't blame him.'

'I think she's charming,' argued Gertie.

'You would,' Debo replied, her scarlet lips curling into a smile.

'You're always wrong about people, Gertie. She's a horror!' Daphne exclaimed and they disappeared around the corner.

After they had gone I waited for Joy Springtoe. A couple of men walked past, but they didn't see me. When I began to lose hope, she emerged from her room and came towards me. However, she didn't walk with her usual bounce and I noticed that she was crying. Moved by her tears I risked being caught by Madame Duval and stepped out from behind the chair.

'Oh, you startled me, Mischa,' she said, placing a hand on her chest. She managed a small smile and dabbed her eyes with a hanky. 'Were you waiting for *me*?' she asked. She looked down at me and frowned. 'Come, I want to show you something.' She took me by the hand and led me back to her room. My heart was racing with excitement. She had never held my hand before.

Her room smelt sweet. The windows were wide open, giving out on to the box garden and beyond to the fields of vines. The air that blew in was fresh and heavy with the scent of cut grass. On the large bed her pink silk nightdress was draped over the bedspread, the pillow still dented from where her head had lain. She closed the door behind me and walked over to the bedside table. She picked up a photograph in a frame and motioned for me to join her on the bed. I sat beside her shyly, my feet dangling over the edge. I had never sat in a woman's bedroom before, other than my mother's, and it filled me with fear, as if at any moment the door might open and I'd be caught, dragged off by the ear and beaten.

The photograph was of a man in uniform. 'This was my sweetheart, my little one.' She sighed and caressed his face with her eyes. 'I'd dreamed of marrying him and having a little boy like you.' She laughed to herself. 'I don't imagine you can understand what I'm saying, can you? The trouble is my French is very limited. It doesn't matter.' She put her arms around me and kissed my head. I felt my cheeks enflame and hoped she wouldn't see. 'He died here in Bordeaux at the end of the war. He was a brave man, my little one. I hope you don't ever have to go to war. It's a terrible thing for a man to do. To fight for his life, to lose everything. My Billy was killed in action, in a war that wasn't his. It makes me feel a little better, though, to think that his efforts might have preserved you. That if America hadn't entered the war the Germans might have won and then what would have become of you? Hm? I'd like to have a little boy like you one day – a handsome little boy with blond hair and blue eyes.' She ruffled my hair and sniffed. I felt her eyes on my face and I blushed all the more. This seemed to amuse her for she smiled. Even if I had had a voice, I would have been speech-less.

When she went downstairs to the dining-room, she was no longer crying. I returned to the stable block. It was Sunday, my mother didn't work on Sundays, she went to Mass instead and I went with her. As much as I hated it, I knew I had to go for her. The animosity of the villagers was such that if I let her go alone, I feared it would overwhelm her.

When I found her at her dressing-table, demure in a black dress and cardigan, her black hat placed carefully on her head, she smelt Joy Springtoe at once. She pulled me into her arms and sniffed my neck. 'You have another woman besides me?' she exclaimed in amusement. 'I'm jealous.' I grinned up at her. She sniffed me again, this time exagger-ating the noise. 'She's pretty. She smells of flowers. Gardenia,

I think. She's not French. She's . . .' She hesitated to tease me. 'She's American. Her eyes are grey, her hair blonde and she has a very infectious laugh. I think you are in love, Mischa.' I lowered my eyes, believing that I had indeed lost my heart in the way grown men do. 'Does she know?' I shrugged helplessly. 'Oh, the language of love far exceeds the need for words. I think she knows.' She placed her lips on my forehead. 'And I think she likes you too.'

As we walked down the path that cut through the fields to the town, my heart was so light it almost lifted me off the ground. Thoughts of Joy Springtoe vanquished my fear of going to Mass. I pictured her tear-stained face and knew that I had stopped her crying. My mother was right; she liked me too.

Small flies hovered on the hot air, their tiny wings catching the sunlight and sparkling. A light breeze blew playfully through the cypress trees, making their branches dance. I held a stick in my hand, hitting stones on the ground as I went. We walked in silence, listening to the birdsong and the rustling of the branches above us. The sky was clear, the sun bright but not yet too intense. Then I heard the doleful chiming of church bells, and the pink-tiled roofs of the town came into view. I took my mother's hand.

The church of St Vincent de Paul dominates the small town of Maurilliac. To me it was a fitting home for Père Abel-Louis, whose stern accusing eyes appeared in my nightmares, but not for God. If it was God's house, He had moved out long ago, leaving it vacant for Père Abel-Louis to move in like a cuckoo. The church was built of the same pale stone as the houses, with a pinky-orange tiled roof, bleached by the sun, and a tall, needle-thin spire. Below it was a square, the Place de l'Eglise, around which the town was built. There was the *boucherie*, with its red and white awning and shiny tiled floor, where long *saucissons* hung from the ceiling with other dry carcasses upon which fat flies settled. The *boulangerie patisserie*, smelling of freshly baked bread and cakes, enticingly displayed in the window. If I had been as other children, I would have skipped into town and spent what my mother gave me on *chocolatine* and *tourtière*. But I didn't, because I was not welcome there. Then there was the *pharmacie*, where my mother bought cream for my eczema, and a little café and restaurants that spilled out on to the pavement beneath awnings in the colours of the French *tricolore*. I'm sure the Pheasants lunched there on duck and *foie gras*, drinking fine wine from the *château*, and perhaps Joy Springtoe bought apple tart from the baker's; she looked like the sort of woman who liked sweet things.

We walked down the street, in the shade of the houses, as if my mother was keen not to be noticed. Her grip tightened around my hand as we entered the square. Although I kept my gaze to the ground, watching her black buckled shoes and white socks as she strode forward, I could feel the eyes of the town upon us. My throat constricted and not even thoughts of Joy Springtoe could assuage my fear. I moved closer to her and lifted my eyes to see that her chin was high, defiant, though her throat was tight and her breathing shallow.

In spite of the horror of it all, my mother had only missed one Sunday – the Sunday I had been taken ill with a fever. Otherwise, she had gone, as she had done before and during the war. She said she felt safe in the church and that nothing would stop her worshipping God. Didn't she know He wasn't there?

We strode over the checkerboard floor, past hostile congregants and unforgiving statues of the saints, and sat on our usual chairs at the front. My mother immediately sank to her knees, as she always did, and placed her head in her hands. I dared to look around. People were whispering, staring, the old ladies nodding their approval as if the right place for my mother was on her knees, asking forgiveness. One of them caught my eye. I looked away for their eyes stung like wasps.

Père Abel-Louis strode in and the whispering stopped. Draped in crimson robes he cast an awesome shadow. I winced for I knew that it was only a matter of time before his eyes would rest upon us and I would feel the full weight of his reproach. My mother sat down. Her movement among the still congregation would have caught his attention if it weren't for the fact that we sat in the same chairs every Sunday, watched over by a sombre statue of the Virgin Mary. Père Abel-Louis turned his burning eyes on us and spoke. I shuddered. Why couldn't my mother see that this church was no longer God's home?

I took my little rubber ball out of my pocket and played with it in my hands. It was the only way I could distract myself from my fear. As I rolled it around in my palm I thought of my father. If he were alive he would never permit me to be afraid. He'd have the priest strung up in the town square and punished for his evil ways. No one was more important than my father. Not even Père Abel-Louis who believed *he* was God. How I wished my father were there to protect us. I didn't dare look up in case the priest read my thoughts and, besides, the disgust in his eyes was something I would never get over. The trick was to avoid looking at him. If I didn't see him he couldn't hurt me. If I blocked my ears to his voice, I could almost pretend that he wasn't there. Almost.

Finally the clock chimed twelve and the priest invited the congregation to partake in communion. That was our cue to leave. I sprang up and followed my mother up the aisle. Her footsteps made loud tapping noises on the stone. I always wished she'd leave with more discretion. It was as if she wanted everyone to notice. I felt the priest's eyes burning into my back. I could smell his anger as if it were smoke in the air. But I followed my mother and I didn't look around. I kept my eyes on her ankles, on those white socks that made her look more like a girl than a woman.

On the way back I was like a dog let out into the fields after being locked in a dark cage. Mass was over for another week. I ran about chasing butterflies, kicking stones, jumping over the shadows cast by the towering cypress trees that lined our way. When finally, in all its magnificence, the *château* came into view my heart swelled with relief. Those sand-coloured walls, tall shiny windows and pale blue shutters were home to me. The imposing iron gate, upon whose pedestals sat watchful, silent lions, represented refuge from the unfriendly world outside. That house was all I had known.

3

Yvette was unpleasant to everyone. Her eyes were always clouded with fury, her wide forehead screwed into a frown and her thin, dry mouth a mean line carved into a face of dough. She was large, and dominated the kitchen with zealous determination to inflict on those who worked under her as much misery as possible. She shouted, and banged the table with her fist and huffed like an angry bull until smoke almost blew out of her nostrils. Only when Madame Duval entered her premises did she yield to the greater power. She would incline her head, wring her hands but she never smiled. Not ever. I was her favourite target and, being small, I was easy prey.

I didn't like to go into the kitchen, but often it was unavoidable. Madame Duval thought it inappropriate for a boy of my age to run wild about the grounds all day and ordered Yvette to find things for me to do in the kitchen. So, I was put to work. I scrubbed the flagstone floor on my hands and knees until my skin was raw and my knees bruised. I helped dry up, taking the greatest care not to break anything, for the force of Yvette's strong hand across the back of my head was far greater than Madame Duval's cold slap. I washed vegetables, peeled them and chopped them, collected eggs from the chickens in the yard and milked the cows. However, that summer I became indispensable for the most unlikely of reasons – a bane which became an unexpected boon.

It was a big kitchen with copper pots and pans and utensils

hanging from the ceiling and walls, and strings of onions and garlic and bunches of dried herbs. In order to reach them, Yvette had to fetch the ladder, for, in spite of her ferocity of character, she was short. It was a wonder the thing didn't break under her enormous weight. She was old – at least to me – and her joints creaked, and her thick ankles trembled even on the first step. She was fearful of heights and often ordered Armande or Pierre to do the job for her. But one day her eyes rested on me and suddenly glowed with a spark of inspiration. 'Come here, boy,' she called. I hurried over, afraid that the floor didn't shine enough or that I had peeled the wrong basket of carrots. With a large hand she grabbed the back of my shirt and lifted me off the ground. I was held as if I were a chicken about to have its neck wrung. I wriggled and kicked in panic. 'Stop it, you silly boy!' she barked. 'I want you to grab that pan.' Obediently I unhooked it from the wall, relieved when my feet touched the ground again. Then she placed her hand on my head and, in a moment of gratitude that probably took her as much by surprise as it did me, she patted me gently. From that moment, I was no longer the slave boy toiling away in the shadows, but a vital tool. She was pleased with her idea and used me all the time, more than she needed to. I, in turn, grew to enjoy those sudden lifts in the air and took pride in my new role. Yvette no longer hit me, even when I missed a bit on the floor, because I was now her special 'grabber'. I was sure I sometimes heard her chuckle as she held me, feet dangling, arms outstretched, managing to reach even the highest objects.

My favourite job was helping Lucie make up the rooms. It was a small hotel. There were only fifteen rooms and some of the guests, like the Pheasants, stayed for weeks on end. I didn't know how long Joy Springtoe was staying. I found out from my mother that she came every year to remember her fiancé, who had died in action after liberating the town at the end of the war. She thought it a dreadful shame that he should have died when it was all coming to an end, when the Germans were leaving.

Lucie wasn't pretty like Joy. She had dark brown hair which she plaited, and her round face was plain and colourless like an undecorated cake. She didn't speak much. As I didn't at all she probably assumed, like so many, that I was deaf too. I helped her make the beds and clean the bathrooms. She gave me the jobs she didn't like, but I didn't mind because, while I was in the Private Side, there was a chance I might bump into Joy Springtoe and, while I was with Lucie, I had a reason to be there.

Then one morning Monsieur Duval entered the room we were preparing. I shrank back into the bathroom, afraid that the sight of me might anger him. Through the crack in the door I saw the most extraordinary sight. Lucie stood in front of the bed. They didn't speak, not even a word. He pushed her back on to the mattress and launched himself on top of her. He fumbled with his trousers, his face buried in her neck. She turned her head and seemed to stare right at me. I withdrew for a moment, ashamed to be caught watching. But curiosity pulled me back again. When I peeped once more, she was still staring at the bathroom door, her eyes half-closed, her sallow cheeks suddenly flushed pink. This time she was smiling. Monsieur Duval was thrusting his hips like the dogs do before they are kicked into separating by Yvette. He groaned and growled, murmuring something unintelligible, while she lay with her legs spread, her hand caressing his wiry hair. She didn't care that I was in the bathroom, that I could see everything. After all, I had no voice, I couldn't tell. What she didn't realise was that I could write.

That evening I communicated the events of the day to my mother. When I wrote about Lucie she didn't seem in the least surprised. She raised her eyebrows and shook her head.

'There are some things that shouldn't be witnessed by a little boy like you,' she said, stroking my hair. 'That is not making love, my darling. That is nothing more than a dog peeing against a tree. Lucie was the nearest tree.' She took my hands in hers. Her face softened and her brown eyes filled with tears. 'When a man truly loves a woman, like I loved your father, they embrace and kiss and hold each other close in a tender way, never wanting to part, longing to remain like that for ever. Making love like that is special, when your heart is so full of love it fills the whole of your chest so you can barely breathe.' Then she laughed mischievously. 'Monsieur Duval is worse than a dog, he's a pig.' And she made a few grunting noises, screwing up her nose and tickling my stomach until I wriggled with pleasure.

'Does the boy have a father?' asked Debo. Her paintbrush had been poised over a clean sheet of paper for the last fifteen minutes. In her other hand she held a cigarette in its ivory holder, bringing it to her red lips every now and then to drag smoke into her lungs. 'I've seen his mother, she's a natural beauty.'

'He probably died in the war. So many did,' said Daphne who was well into her landscape, colouring in trees and fields of vines.

I lay on the ground flicking through the picture book she had brought me, beside her little dog, Rex. Having found me playing with Pistou on the bridge a few days before, they had gathered me up and taken me with them to lie in the sun and share their picnic. I liked them and I adored the picture book, which had page after page of photographs of England. I had a good view of Daphne's feet too, clad in rich green suede with little gold bells tied on the ends of the laces.

'A strange upbringing for a child,' commented Gertie, measuring distances with a paintbrush, squinting in the sunlight. She wore a straw hat and her hair, drawn into a chignon, had begun to escape in thin wisps that danced about her jaw on the breeze.

'The boy can't speak, one can hardly send him to school,' said Debo. 'And this isn't England, is it?'

'Are you suggesting that France is backward?' Daphne asked waspishly. 'I don't think a mute child would fare any better in Devon, do you?'

'Don't be ridiculous, you can't compare Maurilliac with Devon!' said Gertie.

'He's hardly going to grow up to be a lawyer. He'll probably work all his life in the vineyard. One hardly needs an education for that,' said Debo.

'And I suppose you know all about vineyards, Debo,' Daphne retorted with a sniff. 'It's not simply pressing grapes and bottling them up, you know.'

'Don't misunderstand me. I'm talking about picking grapes, not the science of turning them into wine.'

'This is a charming place for a child to grow up,' Daphne continued. 'Fields and fields of vines, a beautiful *château* with a stream, an enchanting little town. Then, of course, people like us, coming and going. I would say his life has more than enough colour to it.'

There was silence for a moment as they all concentrated on their paintings. Finally Daphne sat back in her chair and smiled at me from beneath her green sunhat. 'He's a dear little boy, though something worries me about his eyes.' Her voice trailed off and I looked away and stroked Rex. 'They're troubled.'

'Well, he was born in the war, poor darling,' said Debo. 'And France was occupied. Must have been horrid growing up with all those beastly Germans marching around all over the place shouting "Heil Hitler".'

'They took the best of everything,' continued Daphne, as

if she were talking to herself. 'The best wine, the best art, the best of everything. They drained France dry and then, on top of that, the poor young men had to fight for Germany. This little fellow's father was probably one of those poor sods.'

'Did you know the famous vineyards walled up their best wine?' said Gertie. 'I read about it somewhere. They collected spiders and placed them in the cellars so that they'd build their webs and give the impression that the walls were as old as the rest of the *château*. Very cunning.'

'Didn't stop Hitler running off with all those beautiful paintings,' added Debo. 'Shame they didn't wall those up too.'

'You know, when they reached Eagle's Nest they found half a million bottles of the best French wine and champagne and Hitler didn't even drink!' exclaimed Gertie. 'They were taken down the mountain on stretchers. Well, you know the French, wine is almost more important than people.'

They sat painting and arguing until teatime. Then they laid out a tartan rug and opened the picnic basket. There were biscuits and cakes and a flask of tea. I thought of the bakery in town, the one with the delicious display in the window, and eyed everything hungrily. Daphne, sensing my desire, lifted the plate. 'Help yourself, dear,' she said in French, and I reached out and chose a *brioche*. I could see the pleasure on Daphne's face as I chewed. She looked at me in the same way my mother did, her expression tender, her mouth a wistful smile. My cheeks full of *brioche*, I grinned back.

4

Joy Springtoe was my first love. I roamed the corridors of the *château* like a lost dog, hoping for another glimpse of her – hoping that she'd take me by the hand and invite me into her room again. My chance came one evening when my mother had gone into town and I had sneaked in from the gardens. I was only allowed in the Private Side when helping Lucie with the rooms. At all other times I was banned and the fear of being caught was ever-present. Hiding in my usual place behind the chair I watched the corridor, listening to voices and footsteps, my heart lifting every now and then when I thought it was her, only to sink when it wasn't.

When she finally did appear; with her friend, Diane, I crawled out and showed myself. 'Ah, my little friend!' she exclaimed happily and, to my joy, she handed her shopping bags to Diane and took me by the hand. 'Come, let me show you what I've bought. It'll be good to have a man's opinion.'

Once in her room, I felt safe. Madame Duval wouldn't find me there and, even if she did, I had been invited by a guest. Surely she wouldn't be able to punish me for that. The bed was made, Joy's nightdress folded neatly on the pillow by Lucie. I thought of Monsieur Duval and cringed, hoping that they hadn't used Joy Springtoe's bed as a tree. Diane placed the bags on the floor and sat down on a chair while I hovered by the bed. 'Sit down,' said Joy, patting the bed. 'I'll go and change into my new dress.' Diane smiled at me. I got the feeling that she assumed I couldn't hear. She looked uncomfortable, glancing at me awkwardly without speaking. I played with my rubber ball, turning it around and around in my hands.

Joy left the door to the bathroom ajar. I could hear her moving about in there, the shadow she made falling across the doorway as she walked around the room. I lowered my eyes. I did not want to intrude on her privacy. Finally the door swung open and she stood there, dressed in pink and blue chiffon, the prettiest dress I had ever seen. 'What do you think?' she said, smiling at me broadly. She knew she looked beautiful. The dress clung gently to her body as if it had been made especially to fit, like petals on a flower. It was low cut in a 'v', wrapping around her and tying in a bow at the side, falling just below the knees. The skin on her chest was smooth like cream, her breasts like peaches, her waist small, fanning out into wide hips. Her blonde hair fell over her shoulders in waves and her grey eyes shone down at me warmly. I blinked at her angelic form and felt myself blush. She laughed, bent down, took my face in her hands and planted a kiss on my cheek. It was then that I understood what my mother had talked about. My heart swelled with love to the extent that I could barely breathe. 'What do you think, Diane?' she asked, walking into the bedroom.

'I think it's swell. Real swell,' she said. 'You'll slay 'em dead! Every one of them.' Joy turned to me and placed her hands on her hips.

'I'm so pleased you like it,' she said. 'I needed the opinion of a man.' I blushed again and grinned. In my excitement I loosened my grip and the rubber ball fell to the floor, disappearing beneath the chest of drawers. I wanted to go after it but felt embarrassed to have dropped it. I would have to return with Lucie the following morning to retrieve it. My heart, however, was a different matter. Joy Spingtoe had it now and I didn't want it back. Not ever.

The next day, after a feverish night worrying about my ball, I followed Lucie along the corridor. Joy Springtoe's room was at the far end and, to my misfortune, we began our work at the beginning. I dreaded being called into the kitchen to grab things for Yvette before I was able to retrieve my ball. It was irreplaceable, you see. Lucie was particularly grumpy that morning, snapping at me and clicking her tongue in irritation. I was impatient to move on to the next room, while she seemed unhurried, happy to take her time. Finally we reached Joy Springtoe's room. I was on the point of diving to the floor when the door suddenly opened and Monsieur Duval entered. He smelled of stale tobacco and sweat.

When he saw me his face imploded into an expression of horror and disbelief. 'What is *he* doing in here?' he barked at Lucie, pointing at me. 'Get out! Go on! Get out!' He came at me with his hand raised. I ducked and ran as fast as I could out into the corridor, leaving my rubber ball lost under the chest of drawers. As I ran, their laughter rang in my ears. I hated them. I hated them both.

I reached the safety of the stable block and threw myself on to the bed, covering my head with a pillow so I could no longer hear their laughter. But it wasn't enough to cover my ears. Their taunts persisted in my head, in my memory, growing into the jeers of a multitude, until my head throbbed with the pressure of so many voices. My heart thumped in my chest and the love that had filled it was turned to fear. I rocked in an effort to shake them out, but still they mocked. When I thought I could bear it no longer the pillow was prised out of my hand and my mother's worried face gazed down upon me. She gathered me into her arms, stroking my hair and kissing me in desperation.

'It's all right, my love. *Maman*'s here. *Maman* won't ever leave you. Not ever. I'll never leave my little *chevalier*. I need you. There now, breathe, my love, breathe.' I felt myself grow hot in her embrace and her body stiffen against mine. This had occurred before. We both knew that a week of fever now stretched before us. 'What happened?' she asked in a low voice. 'What was it this time?' But I couldn't say. My eyes filled with tears at the frustration of it. I wanted so much to tell her.

The next week passed in a blur. I was hot, then cold, and sometimes, when I opened my eyes, the room seemed to have been stretched and the far corner was tiny and remote. I remember my mother at my side, always there, stroking my hair and telling me stories. I think I remember her crying softly into my neck: 'You're all I have in the world, Mischa. Don't ever leave me.' But perhaps it was a dream.

When, finally, the fever passed and I was able to sit up in bed and play, my mother came in, the grey pallor of her anxious face transformed to a radiant pink. 'I have someone special here who wants to see you,' she said. I looked behind her expectantly. She stepped aside and in walked Joy Springtoe in her pretty pink and blue dress, with a small bag in her hand. 'I hear that you have been ill,' she said, and sat down on the bed. I breathed in her perfume and smiled at her, my happiness complete. 'I have something you lost and something I would like you to have, from me.' She handed me the bag. I gazed at it, astonished. *A present, for me?* I looked inside. There, to my amazement, was the little rubber ball; my favourite toy. I lifted it out and held it tightly in my hand. No one but my mother knew why it was so precious. I squeezed it, sensing the pieces of my broken world coming together once again. Then I peered into the bag a second time. My mother was smiling at the door, her arms folded, pride and affection causing her skin to glow. I pulled out a model car, a little Citroen Deux Chevaux in the most delicious lemon yellow. The wheels turned and the bonnet lifted, revealing the little silver engine. I touched it with trembling fingers and was suddenly filled with longing – that the flag-stone floor in the hall hadn't been covered in carpet, so that I could push it along the stones and watch it go. Overwhelmed with gratitude and love, I threw my arms around Joy, resting my head on her shoulder. She held me very tightly for what seemed a long time. I did not want to pull away and, I think, neither did she. 'You're a very special little boy,' she said, running a finger down my cheek. Her eyes glistened with tears. 'I won't forget you, Mischa.'

That was the last time I saw Joy Springtoe.

5

Joy Springtoe had gone and the *château* echoed loudly with her absence. I felt heavy with sorrow. I roamed around the estate, throwing stones into the stream, not caring whether they bounced or sank. I spent countless hours staring at my yellow Citroen, lifting and shutting the bonnet, remembering Joy's face and her smell. Even Pistou was unable to raise my spirits. I was inconsolable. People think someone so young is incapable of such depth of feeling – after all I was only six and three quarters – but Joy Springtoe had taken my heart in her hands and treated it with kindness. She'd have it for ever.

Monsieur Duval banned me from helping Lucie. I no longer cared. There was no point hanging around the Private Side now that Joy wasn't there and, besides, Lucie had grown increasingly moody. I liked the Pheasants, but even the afternoons spent watching them paint had lost their attraction. I wandered about with my rubber ball in my hands; now it held even greater significance because Joy had given it back to me.

I hid in the *cave* beneath the *château* where it was damp and cold. Row upon row of bottles lay in crates like bodies in a catacomb. The walls were wet and mouldy, the air musty and stale. I ran up and down the aisles, my footsteps echoing off the walls, until I came across a little room. There was something eerie about that room that made me catch my breath. It was empty but for a single chair and yet I sensed a strange warmth, as if it had once been inhabited. I wandered in, my curiosity mounting, and sat down. I looked about, wondering what the room was for, when my eye caught sight of a group of names carved into the stone wall. I got up to take a closer look: Leon, Marthe, Felix, Benjamin, Oriane. I ran my fingers over them intrigued. They looked almost new. Perhaps they had been kept prisoners down there by the wicked Monsieur Duval, I thought, my misery lifting at the idea. I found a small stone and added my name, Mischa, in big letters. I was a prisoner too, of love and silence.

My fever had gone but I was still weak. My mother watched me anxiously and at night she held me tightly, pressed right up against her body, as if she were afraid that a demon would come in the dark and steal me away. I suffered my usual nightmares more often than before. Now my mother's face was transformed into Joy's and I'd wake up in a sweat, confused and tearful. Joy had left me but my mother was still there. The relief was overwhelming.

Then one night I awoke to the sound of the wind outside our window. It was a gale, tearing through the trees, bringing with it heavy, horizontal rain. It was extraordinary for summer. My mother woke too and we sat on the window seat watching the storm through the darkness.

'You know, Mischa, my mother, your grandmother, always said that a summer gale was a sign of change.' She rested her head on her arm and looked at me almost childishly. 'She was very superstitious. She was always right, of course. She was right about everything.' She sighed and her brown suede eyes grew dark with tears. 'What would she think of me now, I wonder? Do you think she can see me, up there in Heaven? She'll be folding her arms across her chest and clicking her tongue in disapproval, I should imagine. She'd have loved you, though, my little *chevalier*. Oh, yes, she'd be so proud of you.' She reached out and touched my arm. 'I know you loved Joy Springtoe, Mischa. I wish she hadn't left, too. She brought the sunshine into the house. I want you to know that I understand. Love hurts, my darling. It hurts when they're with you and it hurts when they leave and it hurts all the more when you know you'll never see them again. But it's worth every moment of suffering to have enjoyed those few moments of happiness. In time you'll remember her without it hurting, I promise. She may even come back next year. Her fiancé died liberating this town. He was a hero. She comes back to honour him. I think she'll be missing you too.' I managed a smile, then turned to watch the gale. Reading my thoughts, she spoke them out loud. 'I hope it brings change, for both of us.'

The following day was Saturday. My mother wasn't working so she suggested we walk into town. I immediately hunched my shoulders and pulled a face. I hated the town. It still reverberated with horror. But my mother wanted me to face my fears and to conquer them, for she said: 'It is only with practice that a *chevalier* learns to fight and win.'

Reluctantly I followed her down the wooden steps that led into the courtyard. Before the *château* became a hotel the stable block had been full of horses. Beautiful, shiny, muscular creatures. My father had allowed me as a very small boy to sit in the saddle. I remember the exhilaration of feeling the horse walking over those stones, clip clop, clip clop, while my father held the reins. Now there were only two horses and they were big, inelegant beasts used for work in the vineyard. Jacques Reynard had trained them to walk in a straight line through the vines and to pull with just the right amount of force so that the point of the plough drove deep enough into the soil to clear the weeds but not so strongly as to damage the main roots of the vines.

We walked down the path to the town, my stomach cramping with fear. I didn't feel like a little *chevalier* at all. I wanted to turn and flee, but always the thought of my mother on her own, among so many enemies, strengthened my resolve and I remained by her side. The storm from the night before had passed. The ground was wet and the leaves glistened on the trees, a little battered by the wind, but still clinging on. I had forgotten about my grandmother's prediction of change. I think my mother had forgotten about it too, for she didn't mention it.

We walked down the street, bracing ourselves for the stares, the hostility, the peering out from behind lace curtains. In the beginning there had been shouts: whore, Boche bastard, hun-head, traitor, little Nazi. Now their insults had boiled down to mutters and seething looks. I always noticed the children. Most of them copied their parents, singeing me with the hatred in their eyes. One or two frowned in confusion and to my surprise, that day, a pretty little girl smiled at me in sympathy. She had shiny brown hair and pink cheeks and her toothy smile was cautious but kind. I wanted to return it, but I couldn't because fear had frozen my own mouth into a grimace. My mother stopped outside the *boulangerie*. I hated the *boulangerie*. I wanted what it sold, those treats in the window, but I was afraid of the big fat man who owned it. I remembered his face in my nightmares.

My mother's grip on my hand tightened and I noticed her take a deep breath as if about to plunge into water. Then in we went. The little bell on the door alerted the owner to our presence. He walked out from behind a veil of beads, his white coat barely large enough to encompass his belly. When he saw us his face turned grey and a frown darkened his forehead. '*Bonjour, monsieur*,' said my mother politely. Monsieur Cezade grunted. 'What would you like, Mischa?' she asked breezily, as if we were just normal customers like everyone else. I felt his eyes upon me, his mouth twisted down at the corners as if the mere sight of me repulsed him.

I hesitated in fear and moved closer to my mother. At that moment the door opened, the little bell tinkling again, distracting Monsieur Cezade who withdrew his gaze, thus releasing me from its spell.

'*Bonjour, monsieur,*' he said boisterously to the new customer, emphasising by his enthusiasm his disdain for us.

'*Bonjour,*' replied the man and his accent was strong, like Joy Springtoe's. I looked up at him and my fear left me. He was the most dazzlingly handsome man I had ever seen.

'And hello there, Junior,' he said, smiling down at me. I liked him immediately. About him glowed an invisible aura that was warm and alluring. When he smiled, his bright blue eyes twinkled with mischief and his mouth turned right up at the corners, causing his cheeks to crease in a comical way, like an accordion. 'What are you going to choose?' he said, echoing my mother's words only a few moments before.

'He doesn't speak,' said Monsieur Cezade, clipping his words so they sounded hard and scornful. 'He's mute.' The American looked at my mother and smiled kindly.

'With a handsome face like that, he doesn't have to speak.' My mother's cheeks turned as red as a pepper and she lowered her eyes. I felt her palm grow hot and damp in mine. 'Coyote Magellan,' he said, extending his hand. She shook it. 'Now, perhaps you can help me,' he said to her. 'What's the most delicious cake in this store?' He spoke English. My mother's father was Irish so my mother spoke and understood English well. I hoped Monsieur Cezade couldn't understand.

'My son likes *chocolatine,*' she replied, pointing to the window display.

'And what good taste, so do I.' He looked pleased that my mother spoke his language.

'*J'en prendrai trois, s'il vous plaît,*' he said to Monsieur Cezade, who was looking on in bewilderment. With a heavy sigh he placed the pastries in a brown paper bag, guessing why the American had purchased three. Turning to my mother, Coyote said, 'I invite you both to join me in the café next door. I couldn't eat all of these on my own, even if I wanted to.' I'm sure if it hadn't been for Monsieur Cezade, my mother would have declined. However, it boosted her morale to be invited out by this handsome, charismatic stranger in front of the man who had humiliated her. It also appealed to her sense of defiance, for it was more than a little inappropriate to accept such an offer from a man she had only just met, of whom she knew nothing.

'We would love to,' she replied, lifting her chin. I felt my chest expand with pride. Coyote thanked Monsieur Cezade and we left, all three of us together. If I had had a sword at that moment, I would have shown my mother how I could use it.

My mother and I did not frequent the café. It came as a shock to those in the café when we entered. Silence fell upon the place. Even the waiters stopped to look, agape with astonishment. Everyone knew about my mother; she was notorious. There was nowhere for us to hide. Some people might have found it odd that we didn't leave the *château*, but my mother had married my father there and besides, it had always been home. Where else could we go? Would anybody want us?

Coyote acted as if he hadn't noticed the reaction to our arrival. He smiled at everyone in that disarming way of his and led us to a round table in the corner. My mother's jaw was stiff with resolve, determined not to show how much it hurt to be stared at. I was so in awe of this glamorous man, for the first time since it all happened, I didn't feel afraid.

'What will you have, Miss Anouk?' he asked, once we had sat down. 'I hope you don't mind me calling you Miss Anouk?' My mother was taken aback. She hadn't introduced herself.

He lowered his voice. 'I'm afraid I have to confess, I saw you and your boy in the street. You're a beautiful woman, I'm a man. I asked who you were.' He shrugged and delved into the pocket of his shirt for a cigarette. 'Will you have one?' My mother declined. She looked at him warily. 'I found that fat oaf in the bakery giving you a hard time. I hope you don't mind.' There was something so honest about his expression, my mother was unable to be angry. 'Besides, your son looks like he needs feeding up.' He winked at me.

'Mischa's been ill,' my mother replied. 'He'll have a lemonade and I'll have a cup of coffee.'

'How old is he?'

'Six.' *And three quarters*, I added silently.

'You're a fine looking boy,' he said, turning to me.

'He looks like his father.' She watched him steadily, testing him. I knew at that point I might never see my lemonade or taste the *chocolatine*. I slumped with disappointment.

'So, in the eyes of the French you're a traitor,' he said, shaking his head. 'Such is the tragedy of war.'

'Love knows no boundaries,' she replied, her face softening. My chances of a good meal just got better. He lit his cigarette, a Gauloise, and scanned the room through narrowed eyes.

'He's just a boy,' he said softly. 'So his father's a German. The war is over. It's time to forgive.'

'*Was* a German,' my mother added. 'My husband was killed.'

The waiter came with the tray of drinks and Coyote opened the brown paper bag. He handed me my *chocolatine*. 'We need to feed you up to be big and strong,' he said with a chuckle. 'Does he write?' he asked, turning to my mother.

'Yes, he does.' She smiled at me tenderly. She hated it when people talked around me as if I couldn't understand. 'He's lost his speech, not his mind,' she always said in rebuke.

Coyote asked the waiter for a pad of paper and a pencil, then took a bite of his *chocolatine*.

'This tastes as good as it looks, how's it for you?' I nodded emphatically, my mouth full of chocolate. 'Food tastes much better in France,' he said. My mother sipped her coffee.

'Where are you from?' she asked.

'Down south. Virginia. I'm staying at the *château*.'

My mother nodded. 'I work there,' she said.

'Beautiful place. Mind you, it's a shame it's been turned into a hotel. I bet it was quite something as a private house.'

'You cannot imagine. It was beautiful, elegant, and decorated in the best taste. They were a distinguished family. It was an honour to work for them.'

The waiter returned with the pencil and paper and Coyote placed them in front of me. 'Now, I hate to leave anybody out,' he said. 'Especially such a spirited young man as yourself. If you have anything to say, Junior, go ahead and write it down, 'cos I want to read it.' Excited by the challenge, I began to write. I wanted to show him that I could.

Thank you for my chocolatine, I wrote in French. He read it and smiled broadly.

'No, thank *you* for joining me. It's not much fun on your own.' He ruffled my hair.

I scribbled again. *We live in the stable block*.

'Are there horses?'

I put up two fingers and shrugged. *Workhorses*, I wrote. Then impulsively I added, *How long are you staying?*

'As long as it takes,' he replied. Then he sat back and grinned, looking steadily at my mother. 'I like it here. For the time being, Junior, I'm not going anywhere.'

6

We walked back to the *château* together. The sun was high in a cloudless sky, birds hopped about in the branches and crickets chirped in the undergrowth. The air smelled sweet with the scent of thyme. My spirits soared. I walked with a bounce in my step, feeling weightless, breaking into a run every now and then to chase butterflies, knowing he was watching me. I wanted to impress him. My mother ambled slowly beside him, as if, by taking her time, the moment would last. Her cheeks glowed, her eyes sparkled and she laughed softly, her voice low and languid. She played with a flower, twirling it around and around in her fingers. Then she began to break the petals off one by one, throwing them to the ground.

I had never seen my mother like that; at least, not that I could remember. Her hips swayed from side to side as she walked so that her dress danced about her body as if it had a life of its own. She looked beautiful. She looked happy. When we reached the stable block they lingered, talking on the cobbles. The horses were out with Jacques Reynard but the place smelt of their sweat, hay and manure, a smell that would cause my heart to stumble with nostalgia years later when I crossed the Atlantic to set my roots down in a foreign soil.

I climbed the fence and sat there watching them with the curiosity of a monkey in a cage staring at another species. I had observed people for as long as I could remember;

being unable to speak, I was rarely acknowledged. I had never encountered a man like Coyote. He had included me. He had regarded my condition as something colourful, something to make a feature of. He hadn't looked on me as a freak, as Madame Duval did, or as the devil's spawn, as the townspeople did. To him I was a boy who couldn't speak, as normal as a penguin – a bird that cannot fly. He had delighted in giving me the pencil and paper and seemed to have relished our 'conversation'. I was elated. I had only ever communicated like that with my mother. Coyote didn't know it, or perhaps he did, but he had made a lifelong friend in me.

He left and strode back towards the *château*. My mother watched him go, an incredulous smile on her face. She traced her fingers across her lips, for a moment lost in thought. Then she sighed and her shoulders dropped. 'Come on, Mischa,' she said. 'Let's go inside.' She looked at me. I was unable to restrain the smile that broke across my own face. 'Right now, Mischa, I'm very pleased you can't speak!' she teased, walking into the shadows. I skipped to her side and pulled her arm so that she looked at me again. My expression spoke the words I was unable to articulate. 'Yes, I like him. He's very charming,' she replied. 'He was kind to us, that's all.' But I knew it was more than kindness. He liked us. He liked us both.

That evening my mother sat at her dressing-table for a very long time, staring at her face in the mirror. Her hair fell about her shoulders and down her back in chocolate brown curls. She had pushed it off her face so that the widow's peak was clearly visible on her hair line. Her skin was bronzed by the sun, her cheeks pink like plums. I sat up in bed, watching her. To me she had always been my mother, neither young nor old. Now I looked on her as a woman. A young woman, for she was only thirty-one. I tried to see her as Coyote did.

Perhaps they'd marry and I'd have a father again. No one would disapprove of him; he was American.

'I'll never stop loving your father, Mischa,' she said, catching my eye in the mirror. Her expression was solemn, her eyes glittering in the dim light of the bulb that hung naked from the ceiling. 'Perhaps it was wrong to fall in love with the enemy, but he wasn't the enemy to me. He was kind. He was always a gentleman and I don't believe he ever hurt anyone. It doesn't matter where a person comes from. What colour he is, what uniform he wears, which side he fights on; he's just a human being and we're all the same. What makes a person different is what's on the inside. Your father was a good man, Mischa. Don't ever forget that. Don't let them tell you anything different. He was a man of honour. If they could see him as I did, as he was, they'd understand.'

She opened the dressing-table drawer and lifted out the frame that contained his photograph. 'He was handsome,' she said softly, running her fingers over the glass. I had seen it many times, taken it out myself, studied it carefully, trying to extract pictures from the inner core of my memory; a memory then too young to remember. I had only a few and they were precious – as precious as the rubber ball he had given me. 'You resemble him, Mischa,' she continued. 'Every time I look at you I think of him. The same light hair, the same blue eyes, the same sensitive mouth. He was so proud of you, his boy. My heart breaks when I think he will never see you grow up.' Her voice faltered, then hardened. 'You will grow up to be a fine, honourable man like him, Mischa. He is dead but he lives on in you.' She put the frame back in the drawer and began to brush her hair.

When she came to bed I was already half asleep. Her body was cold and I suspected that she had been sitting on the window seat with the shutters open, gazing up at the stars, hoping to find my father there. Or perhaps reflecting on the change the wind had brought. It had been a strong gale that had swept in Coyote Magellan. I hoped he'd stay. I feared he'd leave like Joy Springtoe. I feared I'd be left behind. Alone again, my mother and I. Always just the two of us.

That night I suffered my nightmare again. I am in the town square. My mother is carrying me in her arms. I'm clinging to her very tightly. I am frightened. There are shouts from the townspeople. Some are singing, their voices rising in celebration into the thick air, others are baying like dogs, their faces purple with anger, impatient for revenge. I see Monsieur Cezade, his fish eyes crazed and unfamiliar. I see Père Abel-Louis. His expression is impassive, the face of a stranger. He stands back and lets them take me. He does nothing to prevent the horror unfolding before him. His fingers fidget with the crucifix that hangs against his chest. But the man of God is unmoved.

They prise me from my mother like a limpet from its rock. I scream for her, my arms outstretched, my fingers spread in terror. A strong arm holds me across the stomach and although I kick and thump him with my fists, I am too small. I am two and a half years old. I don't understand what's happening or why it's happening. They shout 'traitor' and 'whore'. Fingers grab at my mother's clothes, tearing them from her body so that she stands naked and pale like a skinned rabbit. They force her to her knees and the women, there are three of them, begin to hack off her hair with knives. My mother does not cry. She is silent, defiant, watching me all the time, trying to reassure me with her eyes. But I feel her terror and my secure world spins rapidly away from me. '*Maman!*' I scream. My voice is lost in the cries of the people who want to punish her. I watch her hair fall like feathers to the ground, layer upon layer, until her scalp is tender and bleeding.

'Don't hurt my son,' she pleads over and over. Her voice is steady, determined, alien to me. The crowd is in a frenzy of hatred. They are capable of anything.

'Boche baby!' they shout and I am held in the air for all to see.

'He is only a child. Please don't hurt him.' Now her shoulders begin to shake and her eyes overflow with tears. 'Not my son. Please, not my son. Take me, but save my son.' The arms that held me now throw me to the ground. Dazed with fear, I begin to crawl to my mother. My life depends on reaching her. She seems so far away and the stones beneath me are hard on my bruised knees. At last I am safe. She scoops me up and I feel her body shaking with sobs, rocking me back and forth, kissing my temple, her breath loud and staggered in my ear. 'I'll never leave you,' she whispers. 'I'll never leave you, my little *chevalier*.'

Suddenly a man appears and the crowd disperses. He is wearing a uniform I have not seen before. It is green, like an olive. He takes off his shirt and places it around my mother's shoulders. 'You should be disgusted with yourselves. To turn against your own people!' he shouts, but they do not hear him. Then he places his hand on my head. 'You're gonna be all right, son.'

I try to reply. I open my mouth but nothing comes out. They have taken my voice.

I woke up to my mother stroking my hair and kissing my forehead. 'That dream again?' she murmured. I nodded and buried my face in her neck. 'No one can hurt you, my love. You're safe now.' I was just falling back to sleep when she said. 'We won't go to Mass tomorrow, Mischa. It's time we stood up to *le curéton*.' *Le curéton* was a childish word for priest. I barely believed my ears. Forgetting my nightmare I snuggled up against her, planting a kiss on her neck to show my gratitude. She pressed her lips to my forehead and whispered, 'He's a weak and frightened man, my love. A wolf without teeth. Trust me, I know.'

The following morning I awoke with a warm feeling of anticipation in my belly. Coyote Magellan was in the hotel and everything was going to change. I knew so because I believed in the wind. I think my mother knew too, because she hummed as she dressed. I don't think I had ever heard her hum. She played with her hair in front of the mirror and when she stood up, her body swayed from side to side in a distracted manner, as if her mind was somewhere else. She applied make-up and splashed her chest with cologne. Then she crouched down and kissed my nose. I was enveloped in a cloud of lemon. 'Be good today, Mischa. Don't rush around. You're still on the mend.' I ran my hand down her hair. *You look pretty*, I said with my eyes and she smiled at me, touched my nose with her finger and left.

I found Pistou in the courtyard. For the first time since Joy Springtoe had departed, I felt happy. With the rubber ball and yellow Citroen in my pocket we headed for the garden. There were loads of places to hide there: big balls of topiary, highly scented gardenia, viburnum in great heaps and thick sprays of yellow *genêts*. There were eucalyptus trees and weeping willow and terracotta pots of tall arum lilies. On the south side of the *château* there was a terrace where guests could sit in the sun and read, or drink coffee and chat at small round tables beneath a trellis of white roses. Pistou didn't need to hide, no one could see him but me. I, however, had to crouch on the dewy grass, and watch from the shadows. To my delight, Coyote was at one of the tables, reading a newspaper, a guitar leaning against a spare chair. He wore a short-sleeved linen shirt with pale trousers and brown leather loafers. He sat back with his ankle resting on his knee, his face partly obscured by a straw hat, a smoking Gauloise between his fingers. His face was in repose, but he still looked as if he was smiling, for his mouth curled in amusement, like a contented cat. Beside him sat the Pheasants, deep in discussion over cups of tea, Daphne's little dog Rex chewing on a biscuit at her feet. Pistou was in a playful mood and dropped another spoonful of sugar in Gertie's tea when she wasn't looking. We sat and giggled into our hands as she took a sip, swallowed with a gulp, then stared in bewilderment into her cup. She didn't comment, for what was there to say? She knew neither Daphne nor Debo were to blame for the extra sweet taste. Gertie hated sweet things.

After a while, Coyote got up, folded his paper and tipped his hat at the Pheasants. They were instantly charmed by him and they chuckled and nodded. They forgot their age and batted their eyelashes with the coyness of young girls. I noticed a sudden lightness to their movements as if Coyote's presence had filled them all with bubbles. They became animated, their laughter ringing out across the lawn like the tinkling of merry bells. The wind had brought change for them, too. The air felt different, charged with a kind of magic I didn't understand. The *château* was at once lifted out of a stolid gloom and seemed to glow from the inside like a hot-air balloon.

To my dismay, Coyote retreated indoors. The Pheasants watched him go, then broke into commentary. 'What a charming man,' said Gertie, forgetting all about her sweet tea and taking another gulp.

'If I were ten years younger,' said Daphne with a sigh.

'More like fifty, old girl,' retorted Gertie.

'I never imagined I was that old. I don't feel it, you know. I feel young inside.'

'*Vecchio pollo fa buon brodo,*' said Debo, placing her cigarette holder between her crimson lips and striking a match. 'Old chicken makes good broth,' she repeated in English. They all squawked with laughter.

I emerged from the shadows and approached their table. 'Mischa,' said Daphne, her laughter settling into a gentle chuckle. 'My dear boy, you look so pale!' I crouched down to stroke Rex. His little stump of a tail moved from side to side, so I could tell which end was his bottom. 'He's missed you. So have we. We haven't seen you for days.'

'Mrs Danvers has probably kept him locked away in the cellars,' said Debo. 'Hence the pallor.'

'He hasn't been well,' interrupted Gertie, pushing her half-finished tea into the centre of the table. 'I saw his mother and took the liberty of enquiring. She looked grey with worry, poor girl. So sad to have to raise a child alone. All the more so because he's deformed.'

'He's not deformed.' Daphne leapt to my defence. She was so angry, her mouth turned down. 'The child can't speak, you silly woman. That's not a deformity. He's not a hunchback, he hasn't got a club foot or one eye or . . . or . . . or a bent leg. There's nothing wrong with his form, therefore he can't be *de*-formed. Do you see? He's a very smart boy, I tell you. Shame on you for your ignorance.' Gertie remained silent for a long while, her jaw slack, her skin suddenly ashen. It was most unlike Daphne to get so excited. I stopped stroking Rex and sat up in amazement. Daphne looked down at me and patted my head. 'He's a dear little boy,' she said in a quiet voice. I noticed Debo shoot a look at Gertie then touch Daphne's hand. Daphne smiled at her with gratitude. Something passed between the two women that I didn't understand. I wondered then whether Daphne had children of her own, or grandchildren perhaps, or whether the tears that now welled in her eyes were an expression of some silent longing. A longing beyond the comprehension of a small boy.

Suddenly Coyote emerged through the French doors, followed closely by Madame Duval. Daphne forgot herself for a moment and pushed me under the table. I grabbed Rex and took him with me. Pistou was nowhere to be seen. I was obscured by the Pheasants and the pale blue tablecloth. From my hiding place I watched the pair set off up the lawn, pointing at plants, stopping every few paces to talk. He seemed very interested in the grounds, looking about in wonder, hands on hips. I had seen it all before. The *château* was indeed beautiful. Coyote, however, had endowed it with something else, something it hadn't had before. Even Madame Duval was filled with bubbles and walked with a bounce in her step.

The Pheasants began to discuss him again. The way he walked, with his shoulders straight, as if he had been in the military, the way he ran his hand through his thick, sandy coloured hair. But most of all they discussed his eyes: 'Forget-me-not blue,' said Daphne, and for once they all agreed.

I sat with Rex, peeping out from beneath the tablecloth. Daphne passed down a biscuit, which I shared with her dog. Then the most extraordinary thing happened. Pistou appeared in the middle of the lawn. He was kicking a white ball, grinning at me as he did so. He was foolhardy, because he knew he couldn't be seen. He ran after the ball, pinching Madame Duval's bottom as he hurried past. She flinched and placed her hand there, glancing at Coyote in surprise. She didn't know what to make of it. Her lips curled into a flirtatious smile – but to me she was still ugly.

My eyes shifted to Coyote, who, to my utter disbelief, was watching Pistou. Oh yes, he could definitely see him. Of that I had no doubt. His eyes followed the little boy as he skipped across the grass. Pistou suddenly stopped in his tracks, the ball disappearing altogether. He stood quite still, staring at Coyote. Coyote stared back, seemingly oblivious of Madame Duval who continued to talk regardless. He smiled and winked. Pistou was so alarmed, he didn't laugh as he would normally have done, but followed the ball to a place where even I couldn't find him. Coyote turned back to the garden as if Pistou had never been there and I was left wondering whether I had imagined the whole episode – or whether Coyote and I shared something special, an ability no one else could share.

7

Madame Duval and Coyote disappeared down the steps that led to the water garden and beyond to the fields of vines. I emerged from my hiding place with Rex. 'Monsieur Duval should keep an eye on his wife,' said Gertie, squinting into the sun as she watched them go.

'Good gracious, Gertie, the woman's old enough to be his mother,' Debo objected.

'What do you think he's here for?' said Daphne, picking up Rex and placing him on her knee. 'I mean, he's young, unmarried, as far as we know, and doesn't appear to be here on business. He's come all the way from America . . .'

'The man's enjoying a holiday,' Gertie interrupted. 'Does he need a mission to come here?'

'He's probably been lured by the wine. You know the ditty? How does it go?' Debo narrowed her eyes to remember. 'God made man – Frail as a bubble; God made love – Love made trouble, God made the vine – Was it a sin That man made wine To drown trouble in?' She gave a throaty laugh. 'I think he's come for the wine.'

'Well, of course he's come for the wine. Why would one come here if one wasn't interested in wine?' Gertie was indignant.

'It just seems odd to me, that's all.'

'There's nothing odd about it, Daphne,' said Gertie. 'You're far too romantic, that's the trouble. You read too many novels. Can't a man enjoy a holiday without you lumbering him with all sorts of intrigue?'

'Perhaps he's running away from someone.' Debo sipped her tea thoughtfully. Then her lips twitched at the corners and the beginnings of a smile tickled her face. 'Perhaps he's come here looking for someone,' she added darkly. 'A lost love.'

'Quite,' Daphne agreed, giving Rex another biscuit. 'What do you think, Mischa?' I shrugged. I had no idea why Coyote had come and I didn't care. I was only interested in how long he would stay.

'Let's invite him to join us for dinner,' suggested Debo. 'Then we can get to the bottom of it.'

'Marvellous idea, Debo,' said Daphne. 'I tell you, Gertie. There's more to all this than meets the eye. Holiday indeed! He doesn't look the type to take a holiday. He's far too . . . too . . .' She narrowed her eyes. 'Far too *busy*.'

Their conversation was diverted by the prospect of their painting expedition, so I left in search of Pistou. I found him by the river, sitting on the bank watching a butterfly that had landed on his hand. I sat down carefully so as not to frighten it and we watched it together for a while, until the colourful creature spread its wings and flew away, its movements jaunty as if it had sipped from the vine and grown drunk.

I remained there for most of the morning. We threw stones to frighten the fish, paddled our feet in the cold water, lay on our backs in the sun and I told him all about Coyote. 'He saw you all right,' I said gravely, the warm rays spreading across my face. 'Maybe I'll let him into our secret world. Maybe,' I added. 'I'll have to see.' But I longed for him to earn such an honour. Even my mother had never met Pistou.

I must have fallen asleep, for I awoke to the sound of a voice singing to the accompaniment of a guitar. I sat up and scratched my head. I felt groggy and hot. Pistou had gone, leaving me alone on the river-bank. I remained there for a while, listening to the song. I had never heard it before. It was sad, and the man's voice was deep and gentle, like a low hum. I stood up and followed the sound until I came to a clearing in a little copse. There, sitting in the shade of a plane tree, sat Coyote.

When he saw me, he didn't stop singing. His eyes invited me over and I was glad to sit opposite him, cross-legged on the grass, and watch his fingers play the strings. He was leaning against the tree, the guitar resting on his bent knee, his face dark beneath his straw hat. I noticed his long eyelashes and the bristly skin on his cheeks and chin. Two crooked teeth stuck out a little and reminded me of a wolf. Jacques Reynard said that before the war there had been wolves in Bordeaux, but no one believed him. Coyote sang to me, for his eyes never left me, not for a moment. I felt the warmth of his affection wash over me. I felt an expansion in my chest as if my ribcage were opening up to accommodate this sudden growing. I smiled at him. I knew then that even if I hadn't formally invited him into my secret world, he was already there. His song had penetrated deep and touched me right in my core, where it had been so frozen and still.

> Oh beat the drum slowly
> And play the pipes lowly
> Oh play the death march
> As they carry me along
> Carry me to the graveyard
> And throw the sod o'er me
> For I'm only a poor cowboy
> And I know I've done wrong

We stayed there, Coyote and me, for what seemed a very long while. He sang lots of songs, one after the other. I swayed to the beat, clapped my hands to the happy ones and listened to the sad ones without moving. I wanted to join in. Inside my head I did so and perhaps he could hear me. Inside my head, my voice was clear and bright like silver.

Finally, he rested his hands. 'I'm feeling hungry, what about you, Junior?' I nodded, but I wanted him to go on singing for the rest of the day. I didn't want to go home. There in the clearing reality was suspended. It was just the two of us in my secret world. 'Fancy coming with me for a bite?' I nodded again, but I hadn't anticipated him taking me into town.

I was scared. Even beside Coyote, I was scared. I wanted to take his hand, but I didn't want him to think me weak. I had only ever gone there with my mother, and she had always held my hand. As if sensing my discomfort Coyote patted my head. 'You okay, Junior?' I looked up at him and managed a smile. He smiled right back and the look of complete confidence on his face boosted my courage. We walked down the street. I glanced warily at the houses, their shutters closed to keep out the midday heat, and imagined hundreds of pairs of eyes watching me. I could feel the hatred seeping through the cracks like smoke.

Suddenly Coyote began to talk. He talked and talked and he didn't stop. He told me about Virginia. 'Now, it's south, but not deep south, you understand, Junior?' His descriptions took me somewhere else, far away, to an old stone wall that surrounded a cornfield. 'There was an old man who camped out there. I swear he talked to the animals for they ate from his hand as if he was an old friend. There were squirrels and hares and the odd prairie dog and of course birds, lots of birds. I was like you as a boy, I ran everywhere like a wild animal. I'd go up there to that stone wall and seek him out. We'd sit together and he'd tell me stories. He'd seen the world, you see. There wasn't a place he hadn't been. In fact, I bet you he'd been right here to this very *château*. Why, he'd probably drunk the wine they make for he wasn't one to miss out on a good thing.' While he talked, I listened. I listened so intently that when we arrived in the square it came as a total surprise for I had been unaware of the walk there.

He strode over to the bistro, I following in his shadow, hoping to blend in so no one could see me. 'Right, Junior, I think a table outside, don't you?' He called over a waiter. The man looked from Coyote to me, then back again. Coyote placed a protective hand on my shoulder. We were shown to a table in the shade of a blue parasol. The bistro was busy. Most of the tables were taken. I looked at the large stone containers of red geraniums placed in a square to contain the tables that spilled out on to the square. I had never noticed them before. We sat down and Coyote leaned his guitar against the spare chair. It wasn't long before the waiter returned with a pad of paper and a pencil. A couple of women waved at Coyote from another table. He raised his hat and smiled. They blushed and fell into animated conversation. When the waiter gave Coyote a menu, my new friend thanked him in French and asked for another – '*pour mon petit ami*,' he said, and I felt myself blush like the two women because he had called me 'friend'.

I felt very grown up with my menu. I read it carefully, understanding most of the important words, but not the numbers. 'Choose anything you want, Junior,' he said. 'We're going to enjoy a feast.' I pointed at the steak because my mother had gone into town when I was ill especially to buy me meat. She had said it would give me the strength to get better. Now I was tired of being 'on the mend' and having to refrain from 'rushing around'. I wanted as much strength as I could get.

While we were waiting for the food, I wrote on the pad. *Tell me more about the old man*, and Coyote was happy to oblige. He sipped his wine and I drank lemonade and he embroidered the richest story I had ever heard. He said that the old man had a coat so long it reached the ground. It was made out of patches and each patch came from a different country. There was a red one from China that depicted a golden dragon; his body had shining scales and out of his mouth he breathed fire. There was an orange one from Africa with a ferocious lion and happy children with black faces. There was a blue one from Argentina with men on swift horses, and a yellow one from Brazil with a picture of the sea. Each patch told a story and each story was more fascinating than the one before. The dishes came, we ate, and they were taken away. When I looked about me, the bistro was almost empty. It felt as though we had been there for hours.

After lunch we walked into the Place de l'Eglise to sit beside the fountain. I looked warily at the church, its doors shut in silent rebuke, the window opaque and hostile. I felt its cold presence as if Père Abel-Louis were bearing down upon me, questioning why we hadn't gone to Mass that morning. How dared we defy him? A group of children played *Colin Maillard*, among them the little girl with brown hair who had smiled at me the day before. Their voices rang out across the square as they weaved nimbly around the trees, bursting into laughter when one of them was caught.

Coyote sat on the edge of the fountain and began to play his guitar. '*When I walked out on the streets of Laredo*,' he sang and I soon forgot the church, Père Abel-Louis and the children from whom I was always excluded. My soul stirred inside me like the warm thawing of a winter bud. My chest expanded and I felt a boundless joy and a sense that I could achieve anything.

I suddenly noticed that the children had stopped their game and had come over to listen. They formed a circle around us, whispering to each other, watching Coyote intently, their eyes falling upon me like a herd of curious calves. I saw the little girl with the smile.

I hadn't imagined it the day before, because she now smiled again. Her expression was kind, inviting. Unable to communicate myself, I had learned to speak through expression and to read the expression of others. *I want to be your friend*, she said with her eyes. *You needn't be afraid of me.* And I smiled back shyly, incredulous at her generosity.

Coyote sang on and the children sat down. We huddled together as if we were all friends, the music uniting us. I felt my shoulder touch that of the boy near to me, but he didn't move away or even flinch, so I remained there, aware of our bodies, my shoulder on fire. Coyote sang a funny song, one which made us all laugh. He took off his straw hat and placed it on my head. I felt myself blush as the children's eyes settled on me once again. Then the boy, whose shoulder rested against mine, grabbed the hat and put it on his own head to cries of delight from his friends. Soon they were all trying on Coyote's hat. It was passed around and around as he sang on, his mouth a large grin, his focus always on me.

Then the little girl with brown hair stole the hat and wriggled past the others to place it back on my head. Before I could react she whipped it off and shouted 'Catch me!' I got up and ran into the square. Soon all the children were chasing her and I was among them, one of them, the sound of my feet echoing off the church walls with the rest of them. Coyote sang on, but I felt him watching me and I was glad. Surely he would be impressed by the number of friends I had.

I ran fast, as fast as I ran down the avenues of vines with Pistou. To my delight, I found that I ran faster than the other boys. I was smaller but lighter so I was able to dodge the trees with the ease of a monkey swinging from the branches. It wasn't long before I caught up with the little girl and grabbed the hat. 'Catch him!' shouted the others and they pursued me like a pack of dogs. For an instant my heart contracted with fear, remembering in a flash crawling across the stones to my mother as the crowd bayed for my blood. But when I glanced back their faces were full of delight, their mouths smiling widely, their voices friendly, teasing, as if I were one of them.

We played all afternoon while Coyote strummed his guitar. Sometimes he sang, other times he just played, but all the while we raced around the square the music he made reverberated off the walls of the church and surrounding buildings with the diminishing rays of sun.

Finally the shadows lengthened until the formidable shape of the church fell across the square, hungrily gobbling up the last shafts of light. The children stopped their game and began to disperse. One or two patted me on the back. 'Well run,' they said admiringly. I watched them go with growing disappointment. It had been an enchanted afternoon. Would they want me to play with them again? What if Coyote wasn't there to charm them with his music?

Coyote stopped playing and stood up. The little girl skipped over with his hat. 'Thank you, *monsieur*,' she said, then settled her smile on me. 'My name is Claudine Lamont. I know you're Mischa Fontaine and it doesn't matter that you can't talk. I don't mind.' I felt my chest expand again and a warm feeling grow beneath it. She looked bashful for a moment and cast her eyes down to her feet. 'You run fast,' she said, looking up from under long lashes. I saw that her eyes were green, like the vine in autumn. 'Thank you for the music, *monsieur*,' she added before skipping off and disappearing into the cluster of sandy brown buildings. 'Laurent!' she cried. 'Wait for me.'

'I think she likes you, Junior,' said Coyote, placing his hat back on his head. 'The language of love needs no words.' He chuckled to himself. 'Come, let's take you home to your mother. She must be wondering where you are.'

We walked back to the *château*. The evening sun cast the

fields in a warm amber light and birds chirped noisily in the trees, settling down for the night. The crickets rang out, hidden in the long grasses, and a lone hare hopped across our path. Coyote didn't speak. His silence didn't make me feel uncomfortable, I was used to it. I enjoyed silence. I liked to listen to nature and the irregular course of my own thoughts.

I was deeply happy. I had played with the children who had always frightened me, and Claudine wanted to be my friend. I looked up at Coyote. His face was pensive beneath his hat. My grandmother had been right; the wind had brought change. I couldn't wait to tell my mother. When we reached the stable block my mother appeared almost immediately. Coyote had been right, she had been worrying about me. 'Mischa, where have you been?' she cried, pulling me into her arms. 'You mustn't disappear like that. Not all day!'

'I'm sorry, ma'am. We had lunch in town and he spent the afternoon playing with the kids in the square.'

My mother looked incredulous. 'Playing with the other children?' she repeated, dusting down my shirt with her hands.

'They had a blast, didn't you, Junior?' She stared at me, first with fear, then her expression softened and she smiled.

'Did you?' I nodded. She embraced me and planted a kiss on my cheek. 'Oh, Mischa, I'm so pleased.'

She stood up and thanked Coyote. 'This is all your doing,' she said, curling her hair behind her ear. 'Thank you.'

They looked at each other for a long while until Coyote's gaze grew too heavy and she had to turn away. 'He's a brave *chevalier*,' he said finally, patting me on the head. My mother smiled with gratitude and watched him walk away.

8

The following morning my mother was humming again. Her hair was loose and her eyes shone and I noticed that her hips swayed as she walked, the way they had when we had walked home with Coyote on Saturday. I wasn't fooled. I knew they fancied each other. I had known from the start.

I was excited about going across to the *château* to grab for Yvette because there was a chance I might see Coyote. I would hide in the corridor and wait for him the same way I used to wait for Joy Springtoe. I dressed as quickly as I could and gobbled my breakfast while my mother drank her coffee and chattered away breathlessly. She was happy that I had made friends and had insisted I write down the events of the day before I went to bed. My writing was slow and laborious but she had waited patiently, prompting me for details, even though it took a while for me to relay them. 'He's a magician,' she had said. 'There's no other explanation.' Suddenly I wanted to confide in her about Pistou, how Coyote could see him too, but it frustrated me that I couldn't write fast enough, so I didn't bother.

We walked to the *château* together, across the cobbled courtyard to the back of the building where the kitchen was situated. It was early. The chimneys caught the first rays of sun as the *château* shook off the night-time shadows and stretched sleepily. My mother wore her working dress. It was black, imprinted with small yellow and white flowers. She looked pretty with her hair down. She smelt nice too, of lemons. I knew she was hoping to see Coyote just as I was.

As we entered the kitchen we were met by Yvette. We were surprised to see that not only was she smiling, a manic smile, like a woman possessed, but she was singing too. Her voice was terrible. It wobbled precariously like a bird too fat to fly. She didn't seem in the least bit ashamed of it; on the contrary, she sang with gusto, her large bosom rising and falling as she strained to reach the notes. '*Bonjour, Anouk, bonjour, Mischa,*' she sang, and we both stood in the doorway, blinking in astonishment. If she had grown a beard and moustache we would not have been more surprised. For a start, she never greeted anyone. Not my mother and certainly not me. She never called me by my name, either. I was simply 'Boy', even though, since I had become her 'grabber', she had said it with some affection. Now she swayed around the kitchen in her white apron, her wide hips narrowly missing the corner of the central table where the bloody flank of a cow was laid out in preparation for lunch.

My mother looked down at me and pulled a face. Yvette must have been drunk. Perhaps she had raided the *cave* where the wine was stored. There seemed no other explanation. We watched her weave her way to the larder, smiling at Pierre and Armande, who frowned at her with the same bewilderment as we did. In spite of the curious looks, she barely paused for breath. Pierre shook his dark head in a gesture of resignation, as one does when faced with an impossible riddle, and disappeared down the tiled corridor with a tray of silver coffee pots, the bald Armande following closely with the bread baskets.

The kitchen was warm and smelt of toast and hot milk. On the stove eggs boiled in a large saucepan. Fresh flowers had been placed in a vase on the table where I would sit to chop vegetables. I had never seen flowers there before. I knew it was because of the wind, because of Coyote: Yvette's singing, the flowers, the sudden change in the air that now vibrated with something pleasant and soft. When Yvette grabbed me, she swung me up with a loud trill, her voice wavering on the same note like an opera singer. I knew what she wanted and stretched out to reach it. When I landed she patted me on the head, singing in time to her hand.

My mother retreated to the pantry. She had her routine and she kept to it, staying out of everyone's way. The fact that she had worked at the *château* longer than anyone else, except Jacques Reynard, irritated the other staff, they couldn't bear her to be superior to them in any way. So she was given the most menial tasks. She washed the sheets and ironed, polished the silver and mended. My mother was a good dressmaker, but that skill was never put to use, out of spite, I think, which frustrated her as she loved to sew. The few dresses she wore she had made herself, out of old curtains and sheets – once, during the war, she had even made a shirt from a discarded parachute she had found in the fields beyond the town. My father had given her pretty dresses when such items were impossible to come by for the occupied French, but she didn't wear them now. That would have been too blatant a reminder of her collaboration, for which she was so cruelly punished. They remained hidden in a trunk in the stable block where no one could find them. She took them out occasionally, at night, when she thought I was asleep and unaware. She'd press them against her nose, hoping, I would imagine, to recall my father's scent. Or perhaps longing for those better times when things had been good for us, when the shoes that strode the corridors of the *château* had been shiny black boots.

Yvette sang all morning. Pierre and Armande washed and dried the breakfast plates, passing them to me to put away.

I scampered back and forth to the cupboard to stack them, but they barely noticed me; I was no more important to them than a dumb waiter. 'She's in love,' said Pierre with a snort. He obviously thought it inappropriate for a beast such as Yvette to love as others did. I doubted either Pierre or Armande had loved like my mother and father had loved. They were cold, passionless men who only ever saw the negative. They could find a flaw on the wing of the prettiest butterfly if they looked for it. And they did look for it, everywhere.

'I would say she's lost her mind,' Armande disagreed in his dull monotone. 'They will lock her away in the end, you will see.'

'Someone should tell her not to sing.'

'It is her swansong, Pierre. Indulge her.' Armande gave a throaty laugh and handed me another plate.

'I stand firm. She is in love. Look at the flowers on the table, for instance.'

'They are already wilting.'

'Look at the way she dances about the kitchen. Don't you think it's bizarre?'

'People paid good money to watch freaks in medieval times.' Armande paused his drying for a moment and narrowed his eyes. 'Besides, who do you think she's in love with? Jacques Reynard?'

'That American. He seems to have ensnared the heart of every woman in the *château*.' Pierre pursed his lips with ill-concealed jealousy. That a man had such effortless success with women was irritating enough. The fact that the man was an American infuriated him all the more.

'Monsieur Magellan,' said Armande with a nod of his small bald head. 'Everyone is talking about him.' Pierre took his arms out of the soapy water and dried them on a dish cloth.

'Everything has changed since he came. Look at Yvette

and Lucie; it was better when they were unhappy, at least one knew where one was.'

'Lucie smiles and Monsieur Duval struts about in a fury, like a bull denied his daily portion of oats. She's avoiding him and it's making him mad.' Armande shrugged. 'For that I thank Monsieur Magellan.'

'I would thank him to leave. I don't like change, especially in women. There is nothing more unsettling than a woman in love.'

Now Armande rubbed the frown on his forehead. 'It is a plague, Pierre. Madame Duval has painted her face like a doll. They think we do not notice, the fools. How ridiculous they all look, flirting with a man young enough to be their son.'

'He is not particularly handsome.'

'His French is appalling.'

'It is simply gratitude, Armande. If the Americans hadn't come into the war we would all be speaking German.' Their eyes settled on me. I shrank back into the shadows.

Armande's face stretched into a cruel smile. 'If the boy could talk, he'd speak German.' His eyes were cold with disdain.

'It is a blessing for him, then, that he cannot talk.'

'More like a gift,' Armande sneered. 'If he could talk I'd wash his mouth out with soap.' He moved his hand towards the soap with a vicious look of intent and I scurried away as fast as I could, their mocking laughter hounding me down the corridor.

My mother was not in the pantry, nor the laundry room. With my heart racing I searched for her everywhere I could think of. When I was afraid, she was my only refuge. On my search I had to hide twice. Once, when Madame Duval stalked down the tiled corridor towards the kitchen, her bony hand toying with the spectacles that hung against her chest, snapping instructions to Etiennette, her secretary. The other, when Yvette burst into the laundry room, probably looking for my mother. She paused for a moment, scanned the room with her small black eyes, then launched into another verse of song, before closing the door behind her. I dared not leave by the same way and scrambled out of the window instead.

I eventually found my mother in the kitchen garden. She was talking to Coyote. I crept through the gap in the gate, and crouched down against the wall. I was well hidden by the tall rows of beans, but I could see them clearly. My mother was on her knees, pulling carrots out of the earth, shaking their roots and brushing them down with her hands. I thought it a shame that she wore a headscarf, for her hair had looked so pretty falling over her shoulders and I wanted Coyote to see it. Her dress was covered by a dirty old apron, but she didn't seem to mind.

Coyote sat on the grass, smoking. He had taken off his hat and his sandy hair was thick and ruffled like a dog's. I could see his blue eyes from where I hid; they were so clear and bright, as if the sun were shining out from the inside. He was laughing, his mouth wide, causing his cheeks to crease and the crow's feet to deepen at the temples. I felt the warm thawing beneath my ribcage. It grew and it grew, filling the empty spaces in my heart until I found it difficult to breathe.

I crept closer so that I could hear what they were saying. I was used to hiding. It was something I was good at.

'I've worked here since I was twenty-one,' my mother said, pausing to wipe her forehead with the back of her hand. 'Though things were very different before the war.'

'What happened to the family?' Coyote asked, dragging on his cigarette. He didn't take his eyes off my mother, not for a moment.

'I don't know. The Germans came and they were forced to leave. They had talked about going to England. They had family there. But they put it off. The *château*, the vineyard, Maurilliac, it was their home. They couldn't bear to leave it. Besides, I don't think they ever imagined Marshal Pétain would sign an armistice with Germany. It was a terrible shock. They were fighters, not quitters. They were appalled. But they were left no choice. They asked us to remain to look after the place. I don't know whether they made it to England. I never heard from them again.'

'Perished, I should imagine.'

'How they would hate to see what the Duvals have done to their home.'

'But you remain?'

'In spite of everything, I remain.' She lowered her eyes and began digging again.

'It's home to Junior, right?'

'And it's home to me, too.' She placed the last bunch of carrots in the basket and stood up. 'Besides, I have nowhere else to go.'

I felt a sudden tickling in my nose. Before I could muffle the sound into my hands, I sneezed. My mother turned, startled. Coyote simply smiled. 'Hello, Junior,' he said laconically. 'We could have done with a spy like you in the war.'

'Mischa!' said my mother, a little crossly. 'You mustn't go sneaking around like that.' I withdrew from my hiding place behind the beans. Her face softened and she smiled too. 'Are you all right?' I nodded. 'Is Yvette still singing?' I nodded again. 'Good God,' she said, turning to Coyote. 'This place is turning upside down.'

'The hotel is full of eccentrics,' he said. 'Take those English women, for example. They're really something. They've asked me to join them for dinner tonight. There's one thing it won't be and that's dull.' He stubbed his cigarette into the ground, pushing it into the earth with his shoe. He strode over to me and ruffled my hair. 'What are you going to do, Junior?'

'He can come and help me with these,' said my mother, indicating the carrots with a nod of her head.

'I call that slave labour!' Coyote joked. 'Wouldn't you prefer to come exploring with me?'

'I really don't think . . .' My face obviously fell for my mother dropped her shoulders in defeat. She was rarely able to deny me anything. 'Well, perhaps this afternoon,' she conceded.

'I'll take my guitar and we'll sing some songs, right, Junior?' He turned to my mother and settled his eyes on her face. I noticed something tender in the way he looked at her, as if his restless eyes had found refuge there. 'Would you care to join us?' My mother's cheeks flushed. She tilted her head to one side, the way she did when she felt awkward.

'I don't know . . .'

'Come on. I'm a guest of the hotel. I'm asking for your company. Hell, I'm paying a fortune to stay here, surely they can do without you for a few hours.'

'Perhaps,' she replied, but I knew from the look on her face that she meant yes. She just didn't want to give in so easily. I think Coyote knew too, for he grinned boyishly.

'I'll meet you on the stone bridge.' He winked at me. 'That's our special place, right, Junior?'

In the kitchen I set about washing and peeling the carrots with renewed energy. All I could think about was Coyote and the fun we were going to have that afternoon. Yvette continued to sing around the kitchen, occasionally tapping pans with her wooden spoon. Pierre and Armande suffered her dissonant song by rolling their eyes and exchanging barbed comments out of earshot. Once or twice she looked over my shoulder, resting her doughy hand there, trilling her approval as if the uncharacteristic dedication with which I worked was inspired by the same magic that inspired her good humour.

Having only ever regarded my mother with contempt
Yvette now thanked her for picking the vegetables and asked
her, if she wouldn't mind, to be so kind as to pick some rasp-
berries for dessert. My mother didn't know how to react to
Yvette's strange behaviour. She didn't trust her, as if she
could change back into an ogre at any moment. She tried to
act normally, as if she didn't notice. If Yvette knew she was
causing a scandal she didn't show it. Though I suspect she
did know, for as she paused for breath between songs, her
mouth twitched mischievously at the corners.

I finished the carrots. Yvette had left the kitchen, taking
her song with her. Armande and Pierre had gone to serve
lunch in the dining-room and my mother was probably toiling
away in the laundry. I decided to sneak into the Private Side
to find Coyote. I relished the challenge. Coyote had given
me confidence. I really believed I would make a good spy. I
crept up the corridors with cat-like stealth, ducking behind
the furniture whenever anyone approached.

The dining-room reverberated with voices and the sharp
clatter of cutlery on fine china. The room was large with a
tall ceiling and big sash windows. It was a stunning room
with lots of light that spilled in from the garden, causing the
polish on the wooden floorboards to shine. My mother told
me that it had once been her mistress's sitting-room, leading
into a conservatory and out on to the lawn. When the
Germans came it was converted into a meeting room.

I crept outside and peered in through one of the windows.
I found Coyote immediately. He was sitting with a couple I
had not seen before. They were talking with animation and
laughing in unison. At the next table sat the Pheasants.
Daphne had Rex on her lap. He was chewing a piece of
bread. I had noticed recently that he had grown rather fat,
as had his mistress. She wore a deep purple dress with gold
braid lining the v-necked front. Her earlobes were heavy with

stones, matching the necklace that fell into the well between her breasts. On her feet she wore purple velvet shoes decorated with small pink feathers and shining pearls. I also noticed that they were far more interested in Coyote's conversation than their own.

My attention was suddenly diverted by Yvette who had walked into the room. She had taken off her apron to reveal a pretty pale blue dress imprinted with daisies. She smiled graciously as she wore her way through the tables, accepting compliments from guests, stopping every now and then to engage in conversation. Her behaviour was unbelievable not to mention audacious. For a woman who rarely smiled, who took pleasure from other people's misery, and exploded into fury at the smallest misdemeanour, this grace was most out of character. I wished my mother had been with me to witness it, and the bewildered expression on the bloodless face of Madame Duval.

When she finally reached Coyote's table she remained there for a long while, her hand on the back of his chair, her enormous bosom heaving with laughter. I thought Coyote would find her intrusive; after all, he had been deep in conversation with his new friends. But to my surprise he didn't make eyes or huff in annoyance as Armande or Pierre would have done. He smiled broadly, showing all his teeth – gleaming white, they were, with those sharp eye teeth that reminded me of a wolf. His eyes twinkled at her, holding hers for a long while before letting her go. He included his friends, gesticulating to them, then turning back to Yvotte, throwing his head back and laughing too. I tried to find insincerity in his expression, dishonesty behind his affectionate gaze – anything to prove that, underneath, he disliked her as much as I did. In spite of my scrutiny, I found nothing but honest charm.

I then recalled his politeness to Monsieur Cezade, the way he had waved at the other customers when he had invited me out for lunch, the gentle manner in which he spoke to everyone, even, I suspected, to people he didn't like. I wanted to know why. How was it possible to be nice to everyone?

9

My mother and I walked down the path that cut across the fields to the river. The hot afternoon air was filled with tiny flies and the musical ringing of crickets. She had taken off her headscarf and apron, and her thin summer dress flapped about her legs. She fanned herself with her sunhat and curled her hair behind her ear, which was quite useless, for a moment later a gust of wind blew it out, leaving it to bounce rebelliously about her jaw and neck. She walked with a dance in her step, swinging her hips, every now and then glancing down at me to read my thoughts.

I wanted to tell her that I knew she liked Coyote. I had known from that very first moment. I had watched her face flush and felt her hand grow hot in mine. I wanted to ask her about that morning, when I had found them talking together in the vegetable garden. But most of all I wanted to tell her about Yvette in the dining-room. The wind had brought great change. It had taken Joy Springtoe and given me Coyote in return. I didn't allow myself to think that Coyote would leave, as he surely would. My mother must have known, but perhaps, like me, she focused on the present, the future holding too much uncertainty and disappointment.

'What are you thinking about, Mischa?' she asked, smiling at me affectionately. I looked up at her and grinned. 'Ah, so you think you can read my thoughts, now that you're a spy?' She turned away and settled her eyes into the distance, but she was still smiling. 'He's a kind man. In fact, besides Jacques, he's the only man who has been kind to us in a very long time. Perhaps I'm a fool. I don't know. We have suffered so much. People have been cruel. Don't you think we deserve a little happiness? I mean, they are wrong about your father, he was a good man. But your father is no longer around to protect us. We have to look after ourselves, each other. I never thought I would love again. When your father died, my heart froze like a ball of snow. Only a part of it remained warm and that, my love, belongs to you.' She rested her hand on my shoulder and pulled me closer so that we walked side by side. 'I'm frightened, my little *chevalier*,' she said in a soft voice. 'I'm frightened to love again.'

We heard Coyote long before we saw him. His voice and the strumming of his guitar rose out of the wood and reached us on a pine-scented breeze. My mother put on her sunhat and I rushed forward like a dog in pursuit of a rabbit. I found him sitting in the same clearing as the day before, leaning against the tree trunk, his hat placed crookedly on his head. He smiled at me, a smile as crooked as his hat, but, as before, he didn't stop singing, not even for my mother.

'*As I walked out on the streets of Laredo . . .*' he sang and my mother sat down on the grass to listen. He had a deep, gentle voice, like fudge just before the sugar has totally melted – rich, brown and granular. He was completely at ease, as if singing in this way with his guitar was as natural for him as a bird singing from a treetop. He rested his eyes on my mother and they stared at each other. The look that passed between them was intimate, as if they had been lovers for years. Their silent communication was timeless, holding within it the past, present and future, unspoken but understood. I did not know it then, but my mother's very presence exposed her heart. She was in love. The swinging hips, the burning cheeks, the softening of her edges that tragedy had hardened, all indicated the way she felt, but nothing as much as this look. It said everything. It laid bare her heart.

I wondered how often they had seen each other over the last few days. When I had been grabbing for Yvette, or running through the vines with Pistou, had they been meeting in secret, like they had in the walled vegetable garden? This look indicated as much. I didn't feel left out, I felt glad. I wanted them to marry. I wanted to live happily ever after. Coyote was the prince of a fairy tale that I could believe in.

He continued to sing. My mother picked a small blue flower and began to twirl it around in her fingers. Coyote only took his eyes off her to look at me. The effect was as sun on a sunflower. My face aglow with pleasure, I smiled back at him, my trust naked for him to see. The warmth that spread through my body penetrated deep, to the cold nugget of my soul. My heart lurched with nostalgia for a man who had once gazed upon me with such affection and my eyes stung with tears. Ashamed, I lowered them. When I lifted them again, he was still singing to me.

My mother was so in his thrall that for once she didn't notice me. Her long wavy hair tumbled over her shoulders and down her back, the breeze picking it up and toying with it every now and then as she fidgeted with the flower. She looked less like my mother and more like a blushing young girl. Or perhaps, in that moment, I saw her through the eyes of Coyote: as tender and vulnerable as if he had peeled her skin off like a fruit.

When he stopped playing, my mother clapped. 'That was beautiful,' she exclaimed.

'There's nothing better to inspire a man to greatness than the presence of a lovely woman,' he replied and my mother laughed huskily. 'How about you learn to sing, Junior?' For a moment I thought he must have forgotten that I had no voice. 'Come and sit beside me and I'll teach you how.'

I did as he suggested. He placed the guitar on my lap.
Then with one arm around my back and the other placing
my left hand under the arm of the guitar, he showed me the
G major chord. My hands were small and the guitar almost
overwhelming, but Coyote placed each finger on the right
string and together we strummed. In that afternoon I learned
three chords: C, G and F. It's amazing how many songs one
can sing using only those three chords, and Coyote sang them
all.

I wanted so badly to sing. My voice rose up from my chest
like lava. It boiled and bubbled and grew so hot I felt the
sweat gather on my nose in small beads. I was ready to burst
with song. And yet the blockage at the top remained. I was
still a penguin: a bird that can't fly.

The sun grew mellow, falling just behind the tree line,
casting us in a deeper shadow. Coyote strummed while he
talked and I sat beside him, watching his fingers closely,
pointing excitedly whenever he played one of the chords I
had learned. He talked about his childhood in Virginia and
the old man he had befriended in the cornfield. 'He taught
me how to play the guitar,' he said, patting it. 'He told me
that music is a great healer. We'd sit up there on that hill, our
backs against the stone wall, watching the sun slip slowly
behind the horizon and he'd sing. He had this deep voice, like
a double bass. It was so sad. It had a break in it, you see. A
crack, as if his soul cried out from within. It moved me to
tears. All the while those black hands of his danced across the
strings with such joy, healing that crack little by little.'

My mother watched him as he spoke. I didn't see what
she saw: the neglected little boy who ran barefoot like a wild
dog, in search of love. That was the mother in her. She could
sense loneliness and longing as if they had a sound, like a
child's cry in the dark. There was a lot about Coyote that I
didn't understand then.

To me Coyote was a magician. He smiled at everyone and no one could resist him. He had rescued my mother and me from a dark place and lifted us up into the light. With his music and his voice he had enchanted Yvette and Madame Duval. Even the children in town had forgotten their contempt and included me. He had come so unexpectedly, with a heart full of compassion, and everyone seemed to have been charmed by it. I didn't question why he had come, I didn't need to. I had no doubt that the wind had brought him to us.

My mother and Coyote began to talk and my mind slowly drifted away to Pistou and the bridge over the river. I sensed he was there waiting for me, his hands full of stones. I was bored of sitting now, itching to run around and play with my ball. I glanced at my mother; she was very definitely spell-bound. Her skin was luminescent, lit up from within by an internal fire. The two of them had eyes only for each other. There were long moments of silence, during which Coyote aimlessly strummed his guitar, gazing upon her with lazy eyes. I found those moments awkward, not knowing what to do with my own eyes. I slipped away, knowing they'd be happy that I'd left them alone.

When I got to the bridge, I didn't find Pistou as expected, but Claudine. At first I was unsure whether to approach. She was leaning on the wall, staring down into the water, her long dark hair falling over her face like curtains, a straw hat on her head. But I recalled her friendly smile and was encouraged. When I stepped out of the trees, my foot trod on a twig and made a snapping sound that caused her to turn around suddenly, as if caught doing something she shouldn't have been doing. When she saw me her expression softened. Her shoulders relaxed and she smiled sweetly. 'Oh, it's you,' she said. I frowned and strode over to join her on the bridge. 'I shouldn't be here,' she replied to my silent question. Then her face flowered with admiration and she added, 'You weren't at Mass.' I leaned over the bridge and looked down. I saw Père Abel-Louis's face in the water and cringed with fear.

I didn't want to think of Père Abel-Louis and I didn't want to show my fear. I turned swiftly and whipped the hat off her head. She squealed in delight and took a swipe in an effort to retrieve it. I dodged her as she made another attempt and then went running off to the river-bank. She made chase, her objections half-hearted, her laughter effervescent. 'Mischa!' she cried in delight. 'Come back!'

Finally, I let her catch me. She placed the hat on her head and tied her hair back into a ponytail. Her cheeks were flushed, her eyes shining. I noticed that they sloped down at the corners, which made them look sad. Her smile, however, was large and toothy. 'You beast!' she exclaimed, but I knew she didn't mean it. I gesticulated to the river-bank where I usually sat with Pistou, throwing stones into the water. We sat down. The sun, now hanging low in the sky like a blood orange, was still warm. I took out my pad and scribbled.

The American is teaching me how to play the guitar. She was impressed. It felt good to be able to communicate with her.

'Everyone is talking about him,' she replied. I raised my eyebrows. 'He's always in town, in the café, reading the newspapers. He's handsome.'

He's a magician.

'He sings beautifully. The other day, in the square, even the boys stopped to listen. Perhaps he *is* a magician. No one seems to know anything about him. That makes him more exciting.'

All the girls are in love with him.

'Oh, yes. Madame Bonchance at the kiosk has started wearing lisptick. It's bright red and clashes with her hair! He's friendly with everyone, even Monsieur Cezade.'

I don't like Monsieur Cezade, I wrote.

She giggled. 'No one likes Monsieur Cezade. He's like a big fat red pig.'

How old are you?

'Seven. And you?'

Six and three quarters. I'm seven in October.

'You don't go to school,' she said. I had never spoken to anyone about the fact that I was an outcast. Claudine's compassionate eyes swept across my face and my stomach flipped over like a pancake. I felt I could tell her anything and she wouldn't despise me for it.

They don't want me, I wrote. *My father . . .* She placed her hand on mine to stop me writing.

'I know. He was German. It's okay. I don't mind who your father was and anyway, he was a good German, wasn't he? Otherwise your mother wouldn't have loved him.' I felt my eyes begin to sting and swallowed hard in an effort to suppress the tears. The way she put it was so simple. I stared down at my half-written sentence, her hand still on mine. 'Is that why you can't speak?' she asked. How could I explain that they had taken my voice? 'It'll come back one day,' she added confidently. Now, I had never thought of that. I had got so used to not speaking, to hearing my inner voice, I couldn't imagine what my speech might sound like. 'People can be so cruel. The way they treated you and your mother is unjust. *Le curéton* preaches forgiveness and yet he can't find it in his own heart to forgive. His words are empty and meaningless.' She sounded more like a grown-up than a seven-year-old child. She took her hand off mine.

Why are you different?

She laughed softly. 'Because I have a heart and I don't follow the crowd. I'm not afraid of *le curéton* like everyone else. I can tell you a secret because you can't sneak. *Le curéton* drinks. He drinks a lot and gets drunk. I've seen him weaving about in the chancel. I watched him through the window with Laurent. I told my mother, but she didn't believe me. I got into a lot of trouble for suggesting it. *Maman* shut me in my room until I apologised. Which, I didn't do, because I knew I was right. She had to let me out eventually, but she said that God would punish me.' She chuckled mischievously. 'I'm still waiting.'

You're brave.

'No, Mischa. *You're* brave. You and your mother go to Mass every Sunday, *le curéton* finds a different way to humiliate you. The people . . . well, you know. Yet, you remain in Maurilliac. That's brave.'

It's home, I wrote, having heard my mother say the same thing.

'You wouldn't be so handsome if your father wasn't German,' she said with a grin. I blinked at her in surprise. I had always been ashamed of the way I looked. The blue eyes and blond hair were a constant reminder of where I came from and why I was spurned. I had never considered myself handsome. Not for a moment. 'You're the only blond boy in Maurilliac, Mischa. It'll be an advantage one day.'

We sat for a while in silence. The sun had fallen well behind the horizon, the sky a pale grey, the first star twinkling through the evening mist. It felt warm there next to Claudine. In those couple of hours we had grown close. It was as if we had been friends for a very long time. She understood me in a way that no one else did. In spite of my German father, my mother's collaboration, the fact that we were outcasts, worse than rats, Claudine liked me. I felt my chest expand with happiness. And then, to complete my joy, the sound of Coyote's voice rose into the still, enchanted air. '*As I walked out on the street of Laredo.*'

My mother called my name. I didn't want to go. I didn't want to leave Claudine. 'I've had fun today,' she said, smiling at me.

Can I be your secret friend? I scribbled, my writing little more than a scrawl in my haste to seal our friendship.

She shook her head and frowned sternly. 'Secret?' she said emphatically. 'I'm not ashamed to be your friend.' I heard my mother's voice called my name again. 'You'd better go,' she said. She took my pad and pencil and drew a line through the word 'secret'. Then she added at the bottom, in large letters, the word YES.

I found my mother and Coyote still in the clearing. It was twilight. They assumed I had been playing on my own as I usually did. My mother was too busy smoothing down her skirt from where she had been sitting on the grass and running her hands through her hair to notice my own infatuation. Coyote stood with his guitar slung over his back, one hand in his trouser pocket, the other holding a smoking Gauloise.

'So, Junior, you had a good afternoon?' he asked. I nodded, hoping that he could see from my puffed out chest the bubbles Claudine had put there.

'You must be hungry, Mischa,' my mother said. 'Come, let's go home.'

'I'm having dinner with the English ladies,' said Coyote, chuckling in amusement as we made our way out of the wood.

'I call them *les Faisans*.'

'I would say Daphne Halifax is more of a colourful bird of paradise, wouldn't you? Have you noticed she wears a different pair of shoes every day, each pair more remarkable than the pair before? They have a life of their own, those shoes!'

I half-listened to their conversation as we walked up the

track, back to the *château*. They didn't expect me to contribute so my thoughts were at liberty to drift off. They settled on Claudine's gentle face and later, when I went to bed, they were still there.

10

My mother had changed. The constant humming, her voice rising and falling in a lazy rhythm like a swing. The way she moved, unhurried, her mind in another place. She looked younger. The hard edges to her face had been softened in the same way that Daphne smudged with her finger the charcoal lines of her sketches. Her cheeks were the colour of the apples now ripening in the orchard, her eyes dreamy, settling into the half-distance, mesmerised by something I couldn't see. Our world was shifting around us and yet she didn't seem to care. The wind had changed her too, but I don't think she was even aware of it.

It was the beginning of September. August had been long and hot. Now the heat had tempered, the light grown mellow, and the days began to recede like the tide, every day a little shorter. I left my mother to her daydreams and wandered over to the *château*. Pistou was waiting for me in the yard, kicking stones, hands in pockets, hair falling over his forehead like a frisky brown pony. We set off to the bridge, throwing my rubber ball between us. I thought of Joy Springtoe every time I took it out of my pocket. Sometimes when I sneaked into the Private Side I believed I could still smell her. That unmistakeable scent of gardenia that had lingered in the air in spite of the open windows and clung to my clothes after she had embraced me. I hadn't suffered my nightmare for a while. My dreams had been pleasant. I no longer clung to my mother when I slept, but awoke to find myself in my own space, only her arm draped over my waist.

Pistou and I mucked around on the river-bank. We built a camp in the wood, near the clearing where Coyote liked to sit and play his guitar. As we stacked the sticks and stuffed grass into the cracks I heard my voice inside my head singing *As I walked out on the streets of Lareda* . . . I remembered the words, every one, and my chest expanded with the desire to sing out into the air. Pistou, who heard my inner voice, was impressed. He said it sounded as clear as a flute. I told him I was learning to play the guitar. That impressed him too. I looked over to where the little clearing stood in a pool of sunlight, half-expecting to see Coyote there, his hat on his head, his mouth curled into a smile, his hands strumming the strings, and felt warm in the knowledge that he was nearby.

We played in the vines, running through them playing *cache-cache*. It wouldn't be long before harvest, when volunteers from the town would come by the dozen with large baskets in which to gather the grapes. I was never included. I would watch with Pistou and count how many times they put the grapes in their mouths instead of in the baskets.

Just before lunch we ran up to the old folly that stood neglected behind snakes of ivy and bindweed, crumbling like Hansel and Gretel's gingerbread house. We had played there often for it had been long abandoned. My mother told me that before the war it had been used for picnics. It was situated on the hill and had a lovely view of the vineyard right down to the river. Now it was forgotten and sad, filled with rusty machinery and sacks, overshadowed by walnut trees. I found it compelling, though. Behind the decay I could glimpse the odd twinkle of its former splendour like embers in an old fireplace that still glow when the wind blows. I imagined people sitting beneath the veranda, between the stone pillars that went all the way around, taking coffee in china cups with silver spoons, watching the sun slowly melt into the river, turning it red. Perhaps they had played music and danced in the lengthening shadows of those walnut trees. It fascinated me that people would build such a large, elaborate building for the simple pleasure of picnicking.

We reached the folly out of breath from running. We had played catch all the way up and hadn't once dropped the ball. As we approached, I sensed we were not alone. Pistou did too. He stopped laughing and put his hands in his pockets, sniffing the air like a dog. I put my rubber ball back into my pocket and hurried beneath the veranda to press myself up against the wall. I heard sounds coming from within. Low groans, a few grunts, then a sudden peal of laughter that tore the air. I recognised the laughter at once – that manic, high-pitched squeal that sounded more like an excited sow than a woman. I grinned at Pistou. He raised his eyebrows suggestively. We both peered in through the window.

Through the green mildew that stained the glass, I saw the most extraordinary sight. I immediately recalled the conversation I had heard between Pierre and Armande. 'Who do you think she's in love with? Jacques Reynard?' They had scoffed and sneered and yet, there was Yvette, her grey hair pulled out of its bun and falling over her face in disarray like a mop, her squat, fleshy body liberated from the buttons and clasps that incarcerated it within her dress and apron, sitting astride none other than Jacques Reynard. They were far too busy to notice us. Jacques' trousers were at his ankles, his boots covered in dust, his skinny legs hairy, twitching at the knees as Yvette rode him like one of his horses.

I pressed my face to the window to get a better look. I had seen the mating of animals. After all, I had grown up in the country and there were pigs, cows and goats on the estate. I knew what they were doing and anyway, they didn't look all that different. The same thrusting, the same primitive urgency that negates all around it, the same mindlessness; only the enjoyment set them apart from the animals: the inane smile breaking through the dough of Yvette's face and the distorted grimace on Jacques', more akin to pain than pleasure. They reminded me of Monsieur Duval and Lucie. They remained like that for a long while, stuck together like magnets: Yvette bouncing up and down, Jacques holding her bottom with his hands as if to guide her, an impossible task due to her bulk. Pistou and I giggled into our hands and winked at each other. When it all ended rather suddenly, Yvette deflated like one of her soufflés. She collapsed into his arms and he encircled her in a hug. It was a surprisingly tender moment, I thought, from a couple who, only moments before, had behaved like wild beasts.

Not wanting to be caught spying, I scampered off into the trees to wait for them to emerge. We lay on our stomachs like soldiers, excited by what we had just witnessed, the fact that we knew something no one else knew. After a long while I began to pick blades of grass, distracted by the tiny creatures I found there. I wondered whether they had fallen asleep and what Madame Duval would think if she were to stumble upon them. I had always hated Yvette, she had been so mean. However, since I had become her 'grabber' she had mellowed and I had feared her less. Then, all of a sudden, a smile had replaced the scowl. Now I knew the reason for her transformation I realised I did not hate her any longer. After all, there must have been something good about her for Jacques to love her. Just like Claudine had said about my father. Perhaps she had been unkind because of her own unhappiness. Jacques had made her happy. Was life really as simple as that? Unhappy people are nasty, happy people are nice?

Finally they emerged. Yvette had tied her hair back into the familiar bun, her dress was buttoned up at the front, and Jacques had pulled up and belted his trousers. They looked radiant, as if they had been for a swim in the cold river or for a brisk walk. They held hands and kissed. Jacques' red moustache must have tickled but Yvette didn't seem to mind. I liked his face; it was open and kind. He looked at her with tenderness, savouring her features. 'You're delicious,' he said, running his fingers down her cheek. 'Like a juicy grape.' When they parted, he back down the hill to the vineyard, she the other way to the *château*, I heard her voice break into song. It wobbled as before and grated all the more because I had heard Coyote sing so beautifully, but I minded less now that I knew the cause.

Later, in the afternoon, I found the Pheasants painting in one of the gardens of the *château*. Instructing them was the inimitable Monsieur Autruche. I knew that Monsieur and Madame Duval had gone to Paris for the day, leaving Etiennette to look after the guests, which is why Yvette had managed to sneak off to the folly. I knew that I would be safe in the garden with the Pheasants, as long as I didn't draw attention to myself.

Daphne was especially pleased to see me. 'My dear Mischa, we haven't seen you since Sunday. Where have you been?' I shrugged and grinned, having so much I could tell her. 'Rex has missed you, too,' she added, scooping him off her lap and into my arms. I sat down on the grass to pat him. 'We're very lucky to have found Monsieur Autruche. Apparently he's the best Paris has to offer and he's here, with us. What a privilege. Imagine!'

Monsieur Autruche (which means ostrich in French) was a very silly name for a man, I thought. He couldn't have looked less like an ostrich. He had shiny black hair, a brooding, handsome face, and dark brown eyes that gazed at me with such intensity I had to turn away. Having come from Paris, he didn't know my parentage. For all he knew I could have been Daphne's grandson. So, it wasn't with disgust that he stared at me, but with something else I couldn't fathom. His nose was aquiline, giving him a hawkish look, and his cheekbones stood out and caught the light. He wore pleated trousers high on his waist and a silk scarf around his neck, the yellow of which matched his yellow sleeveless v-necked sweater to perfection. I imagined he was very hot beneath all those clothes. '*Bonjour,*' he said, bowing to me slightly in an old-fashioned manner. He did not smile, though his expression was pompous rather than unkind.

'He's called Mischa,' said Daphne helpfully. 'He doesn't speak, but he's very intelligent.'

'Ah, Mischa,' he said and his voice was soft and nasal. 'Do you like to paint?' I shrugged. I couldn't remember ever having painted. '*Bon.* I have another pupil,' he said, looking pleased. He placed a sheet of paper and a small box of paints in front of me and handed me a brush. I pushed Rex off my knee. Monsieur Autruche sat beside me. I could smell his perfume. It was heavy and sweet, more like the perfume a woman might wear. I didn't think Coyote would wear such a scent. 'I want you to experiment with colour,' he said. 'Don't worry about what you draw or indeed what it looks like. Just use the colours as you desire.'

'Monsieur Autruche,' Debo called out. 'This damned sky, it's so dreadfully dull. I simply can't make it interesting. It looks like a boring lake in Switzerland. Blue.' Monsieur Autruche sighed impatiently. I imagine Debo and Gertie were rather demanding.

Debo sat behind her easel smoking into the breeze, a brightly coloured silk scarf wrapped around her head, falling over her left shoulder. She and Gertie both looked sulky and barely spoke, as if they were annoyed with each other. This didn't surprise me for they seemed to spend much of their time bickering. Monsieur Autruche wandered over to Debo.

He didn't walk, but glided, as if he had little wheels on the soles of his shoes.

'The problem is you drank too much last night,' said Gertie to Debo. 'If you didn't have such a headache you'd paint the sky with more sensitivity.'

'Utter tosh. I drank a couple of glasses, that's all. What should I do, Mr Ostrich?' Gertie pulled a horrified face and Debo muttered: 'Really, I can't call him Monsieur Autruche!'

Gertie clicked her tongue and shook her head in exasperation. Daphne continued as if she hadn't noticed their bickering.

'I thought Jack most charming. He's an old-fashioned gentleman. You can tell a lot about someone by the way they talk to the staff,' she said thoughtfully.

'He was certainly polite to the little people,' Debo agreed, watching as Monsieur Autruche repainted the sky for her.

'They're not dwarves,' snapped Gertie. Debo ignored her.

'You have to look at the colours within the colours,' Monsieur Autruche said, and Debo screwed up her nose. 'I see pink and yellow in the blue, don't you?'

'Absolutely,' Debo replied, though she clearly didn't. 'Did you notice, he told us precious little about himself?' she continued.

'You're right,' Daphne agreed. 'Every time one asked, he fired the question straight back.'

'What's he hiding?' Debo took a long drag of her cigarette and sat back in her chair.

Monsieur Autruche returned the paintbrush and glided away. No doubt he sensed her waning interest.

'For goodness sake, he's entitled to his privacy!' Gertie snapped.

'And we're entitled to pry into it!' retorted Debo with equal vigour.

'He's a fascinating man. He should join us, after all, he's quite an expert,' said Daphne.

'He's an expert on everything,' Gertie agreed.

'Or knew just a little more than we did,' said Debo. 'That's not too difficult. I wouldn't say my knowledge of Old Master paintings is very profound.'

'Well, I know very little about the Dead Sea Scrolls,' admitted Daphne.

'Or Peter the Great, Elgin, Chinese medicine or the fact that a ladybird starts off as a caterpillar,' Debo laughed. 'He seemed to know just enough about everything to impress us.'

Gertie was indignant. 'Oh, but what he doesn't know about antiques is nobody's business! His knowledge of that was very detailed,' she said.

'Well, it's his business. He *should* know about antiques,' said Debo matter-of-factly.

Gertie turned to her. 'Go on, admit it. You don't trust him, do you?'

She shrugged. 'He's too good to be true, only a character in a novel is that enchanting.'

'You're a terrible old cynic!' Gertie accused, clicking her tongue.

'Perhaps, but I have a good nose for people. I like him. Oh, yes, I like him enormously. He's funny, intelligent, shrewd and kind, he's just . . .' She hesitated, searching for the right word. 'He's just impenetrable. Like an actor in a play. I wonder who the real Jack Magellan is beneath the smile.'

'I think you'd be very disappointed, Debo,' said Daphne. Debo's crimson lips spread into a self-satisfied smile.

'Oh no, I think I'd be absolutely fascinated,' she said. 'I think the real Jack Magellan would be really something.'

I was enjoying brushing paint on to the paper. I dragged my brush left and right, using red and blue, yellow and green. I liked to draw at home, but we didn't have paint. When we had lived in the *château* I had enjoyed drawing with crayons. I used to beg my father to draw planes and tanks, which he did with endless patience. He even made German bombers out of paper and taught me to throw them across the room. I loved to watch them glide down, landing lightly on the rug in the sitting-room. My mother said that he had always carried one of my pictures around in his uniform. It can't have been good; I was only small. My mother told me that that wasn't the point; it was because I had done it that he liked it. I wondered what he'd think of my creation now?

Monsieur Autruche bent over my picture. It was of a boat in the sea. I had painted a large yellow ball for the sun and a few fish beneath the hull. I was quite proud of it. He sniffed his approval. 'For a little boy, you have a good sense of colour,' he said. I didn't want to continue with him looking over my shoulder but, as he didn't move, I had no choice.

'Wasn't it magical when he played his guitar?' Daphne continued. Rex had found his way back on to her lap and she stroked him while she painted.

'He sang beautifully,' Gertie added, perking up. 'It was very romantic to sing like that outside, beneath the stars.' For a moment she looked wistful, tilting her head on her long white neck.

'Don't talk of romance, dear,' said Daphne softly. 'We're all too old for that.'

'Nonsense,' Debo disagreed. 'You're only as old as you feel.'

'I feel old,' said Daphne.

'Or as old as the *man* you feel!' Debo added with a chuckle.

'Really, Debo, you're certainly too old for those sort of comments,' said Daphne, but she was smiling.

'Harold died so long ago, I've forgotten what a man feels like,' said Gertie, a little sadly. Debo nodded towards Monsieur Autruche and raised her eyebrows suggestively.

'Oh, do wake up, Debo!' Daphne hissed. 'I think his interests lie more in our little friend than in our younger sister!' Gertie put her hand to her mouth and Debo smirked and flicked ash on to the grass.

'Oh dear. Do keep an eye, Daphne. He's only little, and he is extremely pretty,' she said, sucking in her cheeks.

Monsieur Autruche now completely ignored the three women and concentrated on my burgeoning talent. His perfume was intoxicating, his presence beside me repellent. There was something in his eyes that caused me great unease. I didn't recognise it, having never seen such a look before, but I knew I didn't like it. After a while, I put down my paintbrush. 'Going so soon?' he said in surprise. I nodded, relieved for once that I didn't have a voice with which to explain.

11

I had loved Joy Springtoe with all my heart. It was a love
bright with awe and admiration, like one might feel towards
a rainbow or a golden sunset: a distant, unattainable, idealised
love. And I missed her terribly. But now I discovered another
kind of love to fill the hole that Joy had left. A love born out
of gratitude and an understanding beyond words: Claudine.
We were only children and yet I thought of her every hour
of the day as a man would. I lingered by the bridge in the
hope that she would seek me out, and she did seek me out,
as often as she could. When I wasn't with Coyote or my
mother, I was with her and, when I went to bed at night, it
was she who chased my nightmare away and filled my head
with her gurgling laughter and invincible spirit.

At first I couldn't believe that out of all the children in
Maurilliac she had chosen to befriend me. She was a popular
girl, as I had noticed watching her play catch with Coyote's
hat in the square. She was attractive too because, although
she wasn't pretty, she was fearless. While I fought my own
private demons every day, she seemed to have none at all.
In fact, she almost appeared to lament the absence of drama
in her life. Perhaps that is why she was drawn to me in the
first place, because she knew a friendship with the 'Boche
boy' was forbidden. Her mother had told her not to play with
me and I knew she enjoyed flouting her endless rules. '*Maman*
worries more about how things look than how they really
are,' she once said. 'We all have to smile in public with clean

hands and faces and no whispering. She hates whispering because it's beyond her control. Wouldn't she die if she knew we were friends.' But later, as our friendship deepened, I knew she liked me for me. I could see it in her eyes and read it in the subtext beneath her words.

Claudine did so much for me, more than she could ever know. We met in secret in the afternoons and played. Her father had given her an English games compendium for her birthday. It contained draughts, chess, Ludo, Snakes and Ladders, dominoes and cards, all in a beautiful hand-made box. We liked Snakes and Ladders best and got quite competitive over it. In her company my spirit soared. Her presence injected me with such energy and light that my whole body fizzed inside. Often we sat and talked, me with my pencil and paper, she chattering in her uniquely erratic way, changing subjects without warning and laughing at the silliest things. Other times we just sat. During those quiet moments we gazed over the river, at the little flies that hovered just above the water, and grinned at each other knowingly because she loved nature, too. Oh, we dug up worms and discovered the odd anthill, watched rabbits and tried to catch the crickets, but we liked best of all to observe it all in silence while it buzzed and hummed around us as if we weren't there.

I was grateful for her friendship. I never thought I'd be able to show her how much. But then one day I had my chance. I never thought I was brave. I never believed I could really draw my sword. But that day, when it really mattered, I did more than that. I know now that my small gesture made an imprint inside her that would never go away.

It all began with a game. We found some old fishing nets downstream in a disused shed, and set about trying to catch something. We were good at finding worms, but hopeless at ensnaring a fish. They scudded about so quickly, their shiny scales giving a flash of light before they darted into the shadow beneath the trees. We laughed at our own ineptitude and I teased her once by pretending to push her in, grabbing her just before she toppled into the water. She thought it hilarious. It could have been disastrous, neither of us being able to swim, but she just threw her head back and roared with laughter.

Suddenly, she stopped laughing and stared down at the water without moving. There, in her net, was a fish. It wasn't large, but it was alive and wriggling. I leaned across and we lifted it out together, settling the net on the ground where the fish continued to wriggle for some time. When it lay inert, its bulbous eyes wide open and glistening with slime, we ran our fingers over it to see what it felt like. Claudine put her fingers to her nose and sniffed them. 'Yuck, smells revolting!' she exclaimed. 'Perhaps I'll wear it as perfume to Mass. Give *Maman* something else to complain about!' I pulled out my pad and pencil and scribbled.

Madame Duval's knickers!

'Disgusting!' She clearly loved the idea for she giggled. Then her eyes lit up and she added gleefully. 'Let's plant it among Monsieur Cezade's croissants and cakes. In this heat the place will smell repellent in a matter of minutes!' I chuckled and nodded enthusiastically, but I never thought she'd really do it.

It wasn't long before we were walking into town with the fish hidden in my spare pocket. The other pocket contained my little rubber ball and I certainly wasn't going to contaminate that with fish slime. I had warned her that people would see us together and tell her mother, but she said she didn't mind. I think she wanted her mother to know. She relished the idea of being in trouble. 'I hate fat Cezade,' she complained. 'He's rude and unfriendly and drinks with *le curéton*. You know I told you I saw *le curéton* drunk in the chancel? Well, I've also seen him weaving his way down our street at dawn with fat Cezade hanging on to him for support. They're friends, and a nasty pair of sharks they make too! Now Cezade will smell like one!'

I followed her anxiously. I was afraid of Monsieur Cezade and wished Coyote were with us. I had seen that Monsieur Cezade was respectful of Coyote. Perhaps since he now knew that Coyote and my mother were friends he would show me some respect too. I knew the chance of that was slim. He'd just assume that he could kick me like a dog, while my mother's back was turned. They all assumed that because I had no voice, I couldn't tell. They assumed too much.

Our presence together aroused people's interest. Old men dozing on benches awoke, lace curtains twitched in the windows, and huddles of gossiping wives dropped their voices to whisper over baskets of food, all relieved no doubt that Claudine was not their daughter. My confidence shrank. Even there beside Claudine I felt isolated and alone. However strong their disapproval, she was one of them; I would always be an outcast.

On we marched. Claudine's head was held high, her chin jutting out in defiance, her eyes staring straight ahead, a wide smile slicing the pallor of her face. She took my hand and squeezed it hard. 'We're going to teach old Cezade a lesson, you and I,' she said. Then she added, 'Aren't they a stupid lot, gawping at us like that? Do you think if I shout "shoo" they'll all turn and gallop off in fright?' I smiled weakly. Inside I didn't share her relish at all.

We arrived at the *boulangerie patisserie*. I handed her the fish. She took it and slipped it up her sleeve. My stomach churned with nerves. I didn't know what frightened me more: the thought of stepping into that shop, or of not being able to. My fear must have been obvious for she touched my shoulder and smiled sympathetically. 'You stay here out of sight. If he sees you, he'll know we're up to something.' I was faint with gratitude. 'Keep watch.' For what, she didn't say. I wasn't sure what she wanted me to do if someone did come. I didn't have time to reach for my pad and pencil for she had already opened the door. I saw her thick brown hair bounce with her step and then the door closed behind her. There was silence except for the distant ringing of church bells.

I waited. She had said she was going to place the fish somewhere in the shop where he wouldn't find it: that way it would slowly rot until the smell would get so bad he would have to sell up and leave Maurilliac for ever. That sounded like a good plan to me. Perhaps then someone nice might set up shop and I could feast on as many *chocolatines* as I wanted.

Claudine was in shop for what seemed a very long time. I waited outside, toying with the little rubber ball in my pocket. The other pocket was all slimy. I wondered whether my mother would notice when she did the washing. Suddenly I saw a group of people wandering up the street and panicked. What was taking her so long? She hadn't told me what to do if people came. At that moment the door flew open and Claudine tumbled out shouting 'Run!' I pressed my back against the wall as Monsieur Cezade emerged in a fury, chasing her as fast as his big belly would allow. She didn't call out my name. She was too loyal to betray me. I watched, stunned, as they disappeared off down the street. What would he do once he caught her? I heard at the very back of my mind the cries of an angry mob and felt cold fear creep over my skin. Terrified that she was now in grave danger, I reacted contrary to my nature and ran after them.

I didn't act rationally but instinctively as the memory of that dreadful day returned to coagulate my blood. I was seized by the same horror, the same panic, and yet this time I felt strangely empowered because I was big enough to fight back. The air I sucked into my lungs was burning hot, but on I ran. It wasn't long before I had them both in my sights. He was gaining on her. This great big man bounding after such a small, skinny child. I saw her look over her shoulder and her eyes were crazed like those of a rabbit on the point of being eaten by a dog. I wanted to shout out to her so that she would know I was behind her, but all I could do was keep running.

Finally, as the distance between Cezade and myself grew shorter, he caught her in his large hands and she fell to the ground with a yelp. The still air was shattered with his abusive bellowing. I saw him raise his hand and then the townspeople gathered in a circle around them so that I could no longer see.

Maddened by fear and anger I hurled myself at them and fought my way to where Cezade was towering over Claudine. When she saw me, her eyes warned me to leave as quickly as I could but I threw myself between them so that he was forced to let go of her wrist. 'What are *you* doing here?' he growled.

'You shouldn't have come, Mischa!' Claudine hissed. I wanted to ask her if she was all right, but I could only gaze at her helplessly. I knew she was injured: her skin was white, her eyes shining. She lay panting on the ground but no one tried to help her: they simply stared, their mouths agape. My head was dizzy with the parallel. Surely he wouldn't hurt her?

Just then the crowd parted as Claudine's mother arrived and hurried to her side. 'What the devil is going on?' she demanded furiously, gathering her child into her arms. I noticed Claudine's knee was grazed. A trickle of blood was running down her leg. She began to cry.

'That little scoundrel tried to hide a dead fish in a pastry, but I caught her at it!' replied Cezade. His face was bloated and sweating. Claudine did not reply.

'Claudine?' Her mother's voice now had a sharp edge to it that I didn't like. I took out my pad and scribbled hurriedly. 'Tell me, Claudine. Did you do it?' Claudine was about to reply when I thrust the piece of paper at her mother. Madame Lamont looked at me in horror, as if I were worse than the dead fish. 'You!' she burst out, then hastily read the note which she knew would absolve her daughter. 'It was *your* idea?' When she raised her eyes they were filled with disgust. 'I might have guessed as much. Where would my Claudine get her hands on a dead fish?'

'It's not true!' Claudine replied. 'Mischa had nothing to do with it.' No one wanted to hear her. They had their criminal and they were all delighted.

'So, it was the little Boche bastard,' said Cezade, nodding his head thoughtfully. 'You're the thorn in the side of this town.' His eyes bore into me, but I stood defiant. 'Do you know how one treats a thorn?' I felt all eyes upon me and yet, for the first time in my life, I felt an inner strength. I had never stood up for myself and now, I was standing up for someone else and I felt proud. 'By pulling it out,' he continued and his spit splashed on my face. 'By pulling it out and getting rid of it!'

'How dare you try and corrupt my daughter!' exclaimed Madame Lamont, getting up and dragging Claudine to her feet.

'He didn't!' Claudine attempted to defend me, but it was useless. Her mother just shook her head, as if relieved to discover the root of her daughter's disobedience. 'Stay away from us,' she said to me. 'Come, Claudine.'

I watched the crowd part again and close behind them. As she was pulled away Claudine threw me a heavy look. It was a look that carried both gratitude and regret. She considered me brave and loyal. Perhaps I *was* that day. But deep down I knew that I had taken the blame because I was the natural scapegoat. I was, and always would be, an outcast, so what difference did it make? I would return to the *château* and yet she would always walk among them. Unlike me, she had to fit in. However, the game that had begun as wicked fun had cost us our friendship. I was heartbroken.

When Cezade shouted at me, I didn't hear, and when the back of his hand met the side of my head, I barely felt it. I walked away with dignity because I wouldn't let him see me cry.

Oh, what I would have done with a voice! How different it would have been.

12

I got up in the middle of the night and sat on the window seat where my mother so often sat, staring up at the stars. She always said that if I saw a shooting star I should make a wish. Well, I saw one that night. It was as fast as a rocket. It soared through the black sky in a large arc, one moment so clear, the next swallowed up into space. I closed my eyes tightly and made a wish from the bottom of my heart. There was no use asking for my father back, I was old enough to know that those kinds of wishes were not granted. I asked for my voice back instead.

Since Coyote had arrived, everything had changed. I was no longer satisfied with my pad and pencil, and the frustration of having to carry around a head full of thoughts was beginning to wear me out. At times my chest was so full I thought my heart might break through my ribcage like a jailbird. There was so much I wanted to say and yet I couldn't.

So, I stared up at the sky and prayed that I'd wake up in the morning and find my voice returned. I'd open my mouth and hear the sweet tone of communication. It would come back as quickly as it had gone, and soon I wouldn't even remember what it had been like to have lost it.

My mother slept, unaware of my midnight wish. She looked content as if pleasant dreams had wrapped their arms around her and carried her off to a better place. I cast my thoughts to Claudine, pictured her sad eyes and toothy smile, and felt my chest ache with longing. For the first time since I could remember, I had had a friend everyone else could see. Now I had lost her.

When I awoke in the morning, I was disappointed to find that my wish had not been granted. I opened my mouth to speak but all that came out was air. My mother hummed as usual, brushing her hair in the mirror, applying lipstick with care, smiling at her reflection, not noticing my despair.

To add to my misery, it was Sunday. We had missed Mass the week before; there was no possibility my mother would miss two in a row, wind or no wind. I locked myself in the bathroom, sat on the lavatory seat and put my head in my hands. A penguin that couldn't fly had a place in the world, I didn't. Coyote and Claudine had taken trouble to communicate, but they were unusual. Others wouldn't bother. I'd exist for ever behind a pane of glass, watching from my place of silence, always excluded.

Before the wind came I had been content playing among the vines with Pistou. I had accepted the fact that I couldn't speak without complaint. I had grown used to it. Besides, before, I had had no friends other than Pistou and my mother. Now, Coyote had opened my heart and Claudine had reached out to me. I wanted to break the pane of glass with song and touch them with words they could hear. I didn't want to be an outsider any more.

I felt hot tears sting my eyes and wiped them away in a fury. There was a knock on the door. 'Mischa? Are you all right?' The anger formed a ball in my throat so that I found it difficult to breathe. Unable to reply I picked up the soap dish and threw it into the bath. It landed with a satisfactory clatter. My mother's voice was now urgent. 'Mischa? What are you doing?' She rattled the door knob. 'Let me in, Mischa!' I stood up and kicked the tub with my foot, again and again. I began to sob. My mother must have heard my rasping

The Gypsy Madonna

103

breaths for she banged the door in an attempt to force the lock. I took anything I could find and threw it around the small room. I caught sight of a face in the mirror. I didn't recognise it as my own.

I was so busy raging about like a bull in a pen that I didn't notice my mother had gone, until the door suddenly flew open and Coyote fell in. Behind him my mother looked anxious, wringing her hands, tears streaming down her cheeks. Coyote didn't ask me what was wrong; he simply drew me into his arms and hugged me tightly. 'It's okay, Junior,' he said, his voice soothing. 'It's okay.' I felt his bristles against my face and the heat of his body penetrate mine and the anger drained away, like dirty water down a plughole.

I was sobbing like a baby, but I wasn't ashamed. Not in front of Coyote. It didn't matter. It felt good to be in the arms of a man. It felt familiar, like home.

We went into the kitchen and sat down at the table. My mother placed the pad and pencil in front of me. 'What is it Mischa?' she asked, her sad eyes beseeching.

I don't want to be different any more, I scribbled. I couldn't tell them about the wish I had made. It had been childish and silly. She caught eyes with Coyote. He held her gaze for a long while before looking down at me.

'We're all different, son,' he said gently. 'Every one of us is unique.' I tapped the words impatiently with the end of my pencil. That wasn't what I meant. I was more different than anyone else. I saw my mother struggling for words, her eyebrows knitted, her features contorted. She knew it was all her fault. The guilt gave her face a battle-weary look. She clasped my wrist with her hand.

'I'm so sorry,' she said.

Coyote smiled, but I could tell that he empathised because his eyes didn't smile; they were filled with sorrow. 'You're a *chevalier*, Junior. *Chevaliers* don't desert the battlefield. They fight on until they win.'

I want my voice back! I wrote. My writing was now almost illegible. He looked at it for a moment before replying.

'It will come back,' he reassured me. His certainty surprised me. Could I dare hope? 'One day it will come back. You just have to be patient.' A fat tear plopped on to the page, smudging my words. He didn't know that I had wished for it and that my wish hadn't been granted.

I don't want to go to Mass, I wrote instead.

'We'll go together,' he suggested with a grin. 'All three of us. Right, Anouk?' My mother stared at him for a while, her eyes heavy with implication beyond my comprehension. Then her face flowered into a beautiful smile that drew me out of myself.

'Yes, we'll all go together,' she replied. 'That'll surprise everyone, won't it?' I dropped my shoulders and put down my pencil. I no longer believed in wishes.

We walked down the dusty track towards the town. The sky was grey and heavy, a light drizzle floating on the breeze like sea spray. I walked ahead of them, isolated on my own silent island, my thoughts aimless and dark. I kicked a stone, my hands in my pockets, turning my father's ball around and around in my fingers. They talked quietly. When I wasn't tuned in, their English was as meaningless as Japanese. I concentrated on the stone, feeling sorry for myself. Then suddenly I caught a few words, like a dozing fisherman whose trap rattles with an unexpected catch. Perhaps it was the change in their tone that made my ears prick up. Their low voices were heavy with intimacy. They must have believed I couldn't hear them for they were careless, their voices just loud enough for me to pick them up. 'I'm going to take you both away from here,' said Coyote. A rush of excitement careered through my veins. My dark thoughts were flooded with light and my mood lifted out of the miserable quagmire that had been pulling me under. I pretended I hadn't heard and continued to kick the stone, my hands in my pockets, my face turned towards the town, now burning with hope.

We arrived in Maurilliac. I hung back to walk with my mother, the stone left in the middle of the track for the walk home. People were coming out of their houses dressed in their best, the women in dresses and hats, the men in suits and berets, the children scrubbed clean, their hair brushed until it shone. I noticed at once a change in the air; it no longer vibrated with disgust, but with curiosity. They shifted their eyes from my mother to Coyote. Coyote raised his hat, greeting everyone with a wave and a smile. His confidence was irresistible, his charm compelling. The women blushed and lowered their eyes, a small smile tickling their lips, the men returned his greeting, for it would have been rude not to. The children I had played with in the square waved at me cheerfully. I could tell from their keen expressions that they were impressed by Coyote. His presence there beside me gave me status. I pulled my shoulders back and changed my stiff walk to a casual saunter, like his. With my hands in my pockets I grinned back at them. They didn't know how much their gestures of friendship meant to me. There was only one person, however, whom I wanted to see. I wondered whether she'd come.

Coyote knew some of the townspeople by name. In his uncertain French he had a word to say to them all: a comment on a pretty dress, the week's business; enquiring after a sick nephew, an ageing mother. His limited knowledge of the language had in no way impeded his ability to befriend. He even commented on Monsieur Cezade's *chocolatines* and, to my surprise, Monsieur Cezade smiled. I noticed, however, that no one greeted my mother.

As we walked across the Place de l'Eglise I saw Claudine.

My heart stumbled with happiness. I quickened my step. I knew she wasn't allowed to see me, but her mother couldn't stop me coming to Mass. I noticed the plaster on Claudine's knee and her bandaged elbow. I was behind her, but she must have sensed me for she turned. A moment's hesitation passed across her face as she wrestled between her desire and the rule imposed upon her by her mother. What her mother couldn't have known, though, was that Claudine and I shared a bond. Often the deepest bonds of all are those forged in childhood. So it was with us. Claudine knew, too, because once again she defied her mother. She broke away from her family of brothers and sisters to run up to me. It was a very public display of friendship. No one had ever done that before, but Claudine was now more determined than ever to flaunt it. I caught my breath in surprise.

'Thank you, Mischa,' she said, her toothy smile affectionate. 'I won't ever forget what you did.' I could not reply. The frustration was enormous. '*Bonjour, madame*,' she said to my mother, her tone cheerful and innocent. My mother was as surprised as I for she forgot to smile back. Claudine's mother called to her, but she didn't listen. She winked at me as if to say, '*Remember what I promised*?' I wanted to tell her that I had kept the note where she had crossed out 'secret' and written 'yes' in bold letters.

'Claudine!' her mother called. 'Come here at once.' The woman's voice was furious. She looked around nervously, afraid of what the community would think of her daughter's friendship with the 'Boche bastard'.

'We will meet later,' Claudine hissed, before returning to her family. Her mother berated her in a low voice, but Claudine continued to smile regardless.

The church was abuzz with gossip. All eyes were fixed on my mother and Coyote, whispers passed along the pews behind hands and black veils. I didn't know it then, but their presence there at Mass that morning exposed their relationship for everyone to see. Coyote had decided to make it official. He was in love and he wanted everyone to love her as he did.

My chest was full enough to burst; with pride, with excitement, with love. I sat between my mother and Coyote. I could feel the tension between them as if it were a rubber band that was stretched to its limit. My mother was anxious but defiant. She sat with her chin up and her shoulders back and I noticed she didn't drop to her knees to pray. I imagined that Coyote gave her confidence, as he did me. We were a formidable trio. Coyote seemed not to notice the gossipmongers and returned their gazes with a gleaming white smile and a gentlemanly nod of the head. When Père Abel-Louis strode up the aisle, his robes swirling about him like demons in a fever of dance, I shrank back in fear, terrified of what he would make of my mother's friendship with Coyote.

Père Abel-Louis' impassive face would be forever etched on my memory. He had stood back and let the mob take me and abuse my mother when he could so easily have prevented it. He was a dark and frightening force, larger and more powerful than any other human being. When my mother had taught me about God and the Devil, Père Abel-Louis had automatically taken the part of the Devil so that now I believed it as fact. He had chased God out of His own home as he had set the mob against us. In my childish imagination I feared he would chase Him out of Heaven so that when I died I would have nowhere to go.

I tried to make myself as small as possible so that Père Abel-Louis would not see me. But his stone eyes alighted on us at once, probably because we hadn't shown up the week before. To my surprise, he didn't look angry, as I had expected, but disturbed. His thin white lips twitched nervously as his eyes swept over the three of us. They settled on

Coyote. There was a long moment of silence while the two men stared at each other. Père Abel-Louis was like a rat mesmerised by a snake. He looked petrified. I knew Coyote's expression without seeing it. He was expectant, devout, respectful, but totally self-assured. *Le curéton* was weakened and I didn't know why. I simply knew that we had won a small victory that day.

Père Abel-Louis shook himself out of his trance and welcomed the congregation to Mass. He did not look at us again, acting as if we weren't there. However, he appeared shrunken, as if Coyote knew him for what he really was: a usurper in God's house, and that knowledge robbed him of his power.

I knew then that Heaven would be safe. I knew that when I died I'd not only have somewhere to go, but that my father would be there waiting for me.

I thought of God that morning more than I had ever thought of Him. For the first time, I felt Him there in that church. His light was greater than the darkness Père Abel-Louis brought with him, and His love absorbed my fear until I had none left.

I thought of my father. I remembered his face, his cool blue eyes and his kind and gentle smile. I remembered the tender way he had danced with me in his arms, around and around the room, holding me tightly, my cheek pressed against his, the music of the gramophone ringing out and carrying us on the strings of an orchestra of violins. I could almost feel his laughter vibrating in his chest. I wanted to laugh, too, like I had then. Loudly and clearly with the abandon of a bell.

I watched Père Abel-Louis with the same inner strength I had found the day before in the face of Monsieur Cezade and the hostile crowd of onlookers. I didn't shrink into my seat any longer. With Coyote by my side I felt I could conquer anyone. I glanced to my right at Claudine. She was gazing at me, her eyes shining with pride. I knew she hated *le curéton* as much as I did. She must have seen him falter because she grinned at me, acknowledging our triumph with a wink. My chest expanded and grew warmer still, the *nugget* now opening at last, filling me up inside, making it hard to breathe.

The Lord's Prayer was said and then Père Abel-Louis sang the responses, his voice thin and wavering. '*Pax domini sit sempre voriscum.*' A strange tingling rippled over my body as if I were shedding a skin. I felt weightless, dizzy with happiness, although I didn't know why. The clouds must have cleared outside for the sun burst through the windows, filling the church with a glorious radiance. Then, in the midst of that celestial light I heard a voice. It was beautiful, as clear as a flute. The rest of the congregation heard it too. They stopped singing, trailing off one by one as the voice rose above theirs in glorious song. '*Et cum spiritu tuo.*'

It was a few moments before I realised that the angelic voice was my own.

13

The horrified expression on Père Abel-Louis' face made me catch my breath. I stopped singing. Suddenly there was silence. Not a single person stirred in the midst of what can only be described as a miracle. I felt a hundred pairs of eyes upon me and buckled beneath the weight. Even my mother and Coyote remained speechless.

Père Abel-Louis stood in the cascade of sunlight that poured in through the church windows. His skin had drained of blood like one of the slaughtered pigs that hung in the *boucherie* and his thin lips twitched in bewilderment. For a moment he floundered. God had spoken and His voice was infinitely more powerful than the priest's. There was no denying it. Anxious to claim the miracle as his own, Père Abel-Louis strode down the aisle towards me, his features strained. I was so shocked by the sound of my own voice that I didn't flinch, but remained standing, afraid to speak in case I no longer could. The priest towered over me. I could smell the stench that clung to his robes, a mixture of alcohol and body odour, and recoiled. He slowly reached out his hand. I hesitated, for my hatred of him was so deeply branded on my soul that I was frightened to touch him. However, his black eyes bore into me, finally overpowering me. To my shame, in the kernel of my soul a tiny, secret part yearned for his acceptance. I felt my hand tentatively stretch out to rest in his. I expected him to scorch me, but all I felt was the sweat on his spongy palm.

'God has blessed this house today with a miracle. The boy speaks. We must now find it in our hearts to follow the Lord's example and forgive.' His voice was loud and commanding as once again he took control of his church and its people. A smug smile played about his lips as if to say: 'I am the conduit between you simple people and the Lord – let no one believe he can reach God without me.' My cheeks throbbed and my heart pounded. I was reminded of the baying crowd and wanted to cry out in terror. But there was Claudine, her eyes wide with amazement, grinning at me in encouragement.

'Mischa!' My mother ignored the priest and sank to her seat, her voice a whisper. She held my upper arms and stared fiercely into my eyes. 'Mischa!' I could see doubt in her eyes and the fear behind them. She dared not believe the miracle in case it had been an illusion or a trick of sound. 'Is it true, Mischa? Can you speak?' I swallowed hard. My throat was tight with anxiety. The whole community now waited for confirmation. As surprised as they, I knew that if I failed now I would be further ostracised and accused of fraud. I thought of the shooting star, of my heartfelt wish and wondered whether it had indeed been granted, or whether, as I was more inclined to believe, it was Coyote's doing, brought about by the wind.

I took a deep breath. '*Maman*,' I croaked. She drooped in relief. I cleared my throat and tried again. 'Can we go home now?' She drew me into a strong embrace.

'My son, my son,' she breathed into my neck. I felt Coyote's hand ruffle my hair and with it a warm sensation creep over my body. 'Of course we can go home,' she said, rising to her feet.

'I invite you to partake in communion,' said the priest, reaching out to my mother. But she wasn't weak like me. There was no part of her that longed for acceptance. As far as she was concerned she had done nothing wrong. She would never find it in her heart to forgive or to forget.

Coyote led the way, my mother and I following closely. Such is the power of religion, the people of Maurilliac truly believed that God had spoken that morning. They stretched out their hands to touch me as I passed, hoping that God's grace, which now rested in me, would bring them luck. They smiled, crossed themselves, bent their heads, while Père Abel-Louis raised his hand in blessing, determined to be part of the miracle, in spite of my mother's rebuff. And Claudine just grinned at me in triumph – hadn't she said that my voice would come back one day?

Once we were in the square, the church bells began to peal in celebration. My mother wanted nothing to do with Père Abel-Louis and hurried me away. 'He wants to hijack us,' she muttered angrily. 'After all he has done. Well, I won't let him. As God is my witness, I won't let him.' Coyote strode along with us, his hands in his pockets, his hat placed at an angle on his head. While my mother fumed, we walked in silence. After years of not speaking, of carrying around a head heavy with thoughts, I was lost for words. Finally Coyote spoke.

'Now we can sing together,' he said. His casual tone confirmed to me his hand in the miracle. He was nonchalant, as if he had expected as much. While the rest of the community were left dazed with wonder, Coyote simply shrugged it off. 'I'm glad you haven't forgotten how to sing.' My spirits rose.

'I never stopped singing,' I replied. 'No one could hear me, that's all.' The vibration of my voice rising up from my chest felt alien to me. I was used to the sound of my thoughts. 'We surprised them all, didn't we?' I said with a laugh. 'Claudine said that I would get it back one day. She was right.'

'Claudine?' my mother repeated, her anger evaporating in the light of my recovered speech.

'She's my friend,' I told her proudly.

'The little girl with big teeth,' Coyote informed her. My mother smiled.

'What have you two been up to?'

'Me and Junior?' he joked. 'We have a whole secret life, don't we, Junior?'

'Will you teach me how to sing those cowboy songs?' I asked, finding the stone I had left in the track and kicking it hard. 'I want to learn how to play the guitar.'

'It would be my pleasure,' he said, watching me rush off in chase of my stone. 'The boy's a tough nut,' I heard him say to my mother. 'Tougher than you imagine.'

It wasn't long before everyone was talking of the miracle. The *château* buzzed with the news like a hive full of bees and the Queen Bee herself, having not gone to Mass that morning, was more intrigued than anyone. Lucie was waiting for us at the stable block when we returned. 'Madame Duval wants to see you both,' she informed us, her eyes not leaving me for a moment. 'Is it true, can you speak, Mischa?' She looked decidedly nervous, as well she might, considering the illicit goings-on between herself and Monsieur Duval that I had witnessed.

'It is true,' I replied, slowly becoming aware of the power my restored voice gave me. I lifted my chin and watched her steadily. She seemed to shrink, not that she was tall to begin with.

'She is in the library,' she added, before turning on her heel and hurrying back across the courtyard to the kitchen. I smiled to myself. I began to wonder how many other people might be afraid of me, now that I was supposedly touched by God.

'You had better go,' said Coyote, tenderly touching my

mother's arm. She didn't flinch but leaned towards him. Her mouth curled into a shy smile that held too many connotations for a boy of my age to understand. I had spent the last few years living within the subtext of life, unable to communicate. Yet, the messages Coyote and my mother passed between them in looks and smiles were beyond my powers of interpretation. 'Let's spend the afternoon at the beach,' he suggested.

'We'd love to,' my mother replied. 'You'd like that, my love, wouldn't you?' she said to me.

'You'll have to escape the pilgrims,' said Coyote with a smirk. 'They'll soon be coming from all over France to touch you. The sick, the dying, the lonely, the poor . . . God forbid.' He laughed cynically. 'We'd better smuggle you both out before they build a shrine in the stable block.' My mother laughed too, but only because she found him funny, not because she doubted the miracle. She didn't know it was Coyote who had given me back my voice. I think she really believed, like the rest of the community, that it had been a gift from God. Coyote and I knew different. I decided not to shatter her belief, but to keep the secret. I knew Coyote would want me to.

'I'll get Yvette to make baguettes,' Coyote continued. 'She can pack us a picnic.' He rested his laughing eyes on me and added, with a gentle pat on my shoulder, 'She'll make it extra special now you're a saint.'

My mother and I waited for Madame Duval in the library. I imagined she enjoyed making us wait. It emphasised her power over us. My mother didn't sit down and when I slumped in a chair she chastised me gently. I was rather keen to see what I could get away with. After all, I was a saint now; I could do what I liked. My mother looked so pained, however, that, reluctantly, I did as I was told.

Madame Duval entered with Etiennette in her slipstream.

'*Bonjour*,' she said curtly. 'Sit down,' she added to my mother. I didn't wait to be included in the invitation and sat on the sofa next to my mother. 'Is it true what I hear? That the boy can speak?' She did not smile, but looked at me down her nose as if the smell of me was bad.

'It is true,' I replied confidently. She stiffened and her jaw slackened, falling as if on a loose hinge.

'Good God,' she gasped, crossing herself. 'So it *is* a miracle.'

'God has been kind, *madame*,' said my mother. Her deferential tone irritated me so I decided to have some fun.

'I saw a light, Madame Duval,' I began. 'It was brighter than the sun. Le *curéton's* voice grew distant as if I was in another place, far away.' I felt my mother's gaze bear into me, willing me to behave, but I ignored her. In fact, her fear spurred me on. How could we have ever allowed this woman to frighten us?

'Go on,' she said, her voice low with curiosity. Etiennette sat in the armchair beside her, blinking at me as if I still blazed with heavenly light.

'I heard voices.'

'What voices?'

'They could only have been the voices of angels,' I said, making my face as pious as possible. 'They were beautiful. These voices surrounded me and then . . . then, I saw Him.'

'Him?'

'Jesus.' I whispered now, for effect. Madame Duval was perched on the edge of her seat, craning towards me, afraid of missing anything.

'Jesus?' she repeated, clearly in awe of me. 'You saw a vision?'

'He stood there, in this dazzling light, His arms outstretched, His face full of love.' I blinked out a few crocodile tears.

'What did He say?'

'He said . . .' I hesitated and took a deep breath.

'He said . . . *'Speak, my son, so that I can speak through you to the people of Maurilliac. Sing, so that through you they hear my voice for miles around. Spread the word of Christ and you shall sit on my right hand for eternity.'* So I opened my mouth and sang for Him.'

'My God,' she exclaimed. 'It is indeed a miracle.' Suddenly her eyes welled with tears. She took my hand and pressed it between her bony cold fingers. 'Forgive me, Mischa. I have been a fool. God forgive me. I only did what I thought was right. I should never . . .' Her voice trailed off. My mother intervened, embarrassed by my brilliant performance into comforting her.

'You have been good to us, *madame*. Please don't cry. You allowed us to continue living here when no one else would have opened a door for us. You employed me when no one else would. You have been good and kind. We have only thanks, *madame*.'

Madame Duval let go of my hand and pulled out a hanky. She sniffed and dabbed her eyes dry. Her mouth had twisted into an ugly grimace that ill became her.

'I will talk to Madame Balmain and ask her to take Mischa. He really should go to school now that he can speak.'

'Thank you, *madame*,' my mother gushed. I felt nothing but loathing for the woman who had always treated me with disdain.

'God has blessed you, Mischa,' she said. I noticed her hands were trembling, as well they might, for the only road ahead for her was the one to Hell. 'Now leave me, please. You too, Etiennette. I want to be alone.' She didn't look at me again. I knew she was afraid of me, I had seen it in her eyes. I sauntered out after my mother, feeling very pleased with myself.

As we walked down the corridor my mother bent down and hissed in my ear. 'Christ's right hand for eternity, for goodness sake! If you're not careful you'll be damned along with her!' I glanced up at her. She was unable to hide the pride that shone in her eyes or the little smile that danced upon her lips. 'It was better when you couldn't speak!'

We walked through the kitchen on our way out, passing Yvette, Armande and Pierre, who stopped gossiping and stared at us with ill-concealed fascination. My mother lifted her chin and greeted them politely. Intoxicated by my newfound power I sauntered up to Yvette. 'Is it true?' she asked. 'Can my little grabber speak?' Her hair had come away from her bun and her face burned scarlet. She had obviously been rolling in the folly with Jacques Reynard.

'It is true.' Then I couldn't resist. 'You look well, *madame*. Like a juicy grape.' The blood in her cheeks drained away and she stared at me in amazement. I blinked back innocently.

'I feel faint,' she stammered. 'Armande, get me a chair.' Armande hurriedly placed a chair beneath her bottom. She sank into it. Interpreting her sudden wilting as confirmation of the miracle Armande and Pierre gazed at me with fear in their eyes.

'As you can hear, I speak French,' I announced. 'If anyone needs their mouths washed out with soap, it's you.' Armande parted his lips to speak, but nothing came out but a hiss of air. 'My father was a good man. He sits on the right hand of God. I know because I saw him there, in my vision of light.' I knew I was going too far, but I was unable to stop. I enjoyed watching them squirm. Such was their devotion to God they didn't doubt me, not for a moment. Triumphant, I strode out into the sunshine where my mother was waiting for me.

Coyote's shiny convertible drew up outside the stable block. As he had promised she would, Yvette had prepared a picnic

of cold meat and cheese, baguettes and plums and a bottle
of white wine. He ruffled my hair and grinned at me knowingly, as if he was aware of my game and found it amusing.
We motored down the long driveway, beneath the avenue of
leafy plane trees, the wheels of the car gliding over the small
pools of sunlight that shimmered on the gravel. Then we were
out on the open road. With the wind in my hair, the scent
of pine and damp earth in my nostrils, I felt happier than I
had in a long time. I sat back and closed my eyes. The sun
was warm on my skin, although the wind was fringed with
an autumn chill. Already, I barely remembered what it was
like to be mute. My voice now sounded so natural. The wind
had brought me Coyote. How could I ever thank it?

When I opened my eyes I noticed Coyote's hand resting
on my mother's leg. She didn't push it away. To my surprise
she placed hers on top of his and curled her fingers around
it. They were talking but, because of the wind in my ears, I
couldn't hear what they were saying. Every now and then
my mother threw back her head and laughed, holding on to
her hat so that it didn't fly away. They looked like any couple
in love. I wondered whether my mother had sat like that
beside my father, his hand on hers, her laughter rising above
the wind like the ringing of bells. If he could see us now,
from Heaven, what would he think? Would he be sad that
she loved another, or would he be pleased for her happiness?
I knew she had struggled with it, for I had seen her late at
night when she thought I slept, staring into the immobile
features of my father. She had told me herself that she had
been afraid of loving again. Perhaps she meant she had been
afraid of betraying my father's memory. Well, I understood
there were many different ways of loving someone. I didn't
think it wrong that my mother should love more than one
man and I didn't think that my father would mind in the
least, after all, he wasn't here to look after her.

We set our picnic rug on the sand, sheltered from the wind by rocks. The Atlantic stretched before us, swallowed up into the large mouth of the horizon. It was choppy, the waves rising and falling like knives. The wind was colder here, racing up the beach, but we were warm in the sun. We ate our baguettes, hungry after the excitement of the morning. Coyote played his guitar and we sang his cowboy songs together. My voice was just like Pistou had said, as clear as a flute. My mother joined in, for we now knew the words by heart. Then he gave me the guitar, reminded me of the chords, and watched as I played, hesitantly at first and then with more confidence. 'We'll make a cowboy out of you yet, Junior,' he said with a chuckle, taking a sip of wine.

After lunch we lay on our backs, eyes closed, while he told us more stories of the old man of Virginia. I must have slept, for when I awoke my mother and Coyote were walking hand in hand up the beach, her dress swirling about her legs, her free hand holding on to her hat. For a while I watched them. Then, I grew bored and decided to wander up the beach in search of shells. I wondered where Pistou was. I hadn't seen him for a while. I wanted to tell him about my voice, about Madame Duval and Yvotte, but he was nowhere to be seen.

I took off my shoes and let the cold waves lap against my toes. I found loads of shells and a battlefield of dead jelly fish, their transparent bodies limp as the tide idly toyed with them. I didn't notice I had turned the corner, so busy was I searching for sea treasure. I began to sing. I liked the sound of my voice and the feel of the vibrations in my chest. I felt light-headed with happiness. I no longer felt afraid. The little *chevalier* had grown sure of his sword. Lost in my games, I didn't notice the sun sink low in the sky, turning the sea to molten copper.

When I eventually returned to our cove I was greeted by

a startling sight, and stopped behind the rocks to watch. Coyote was kissing my mother. They lay on the rug, their arms entwined, their faces nuzzling each other tenderly. It wasn't like Yvette and Jacques Reynard, there was nothing bestial about it, no humping and heaving. They were simply kissing, laughing, chatting, stroking each other.

My heart swelled with joy. Now they had kissed, surely they would marry. I recalled overhearing Coyote's remark about taking us away with him. Perhaps when the wind changed.

14

I'd always loved harvest time. Now I looked forward to it more than ever. I used to hide with Pistou and watch the pickers wander up and down between the neat avenues of vines, slowly filling the baskets with grapes. When the baskets were full they'd be taken to enormous sheds on carts drawn by oxen, to be sheltered there from the autumn winds and rain. We'd spy on the girls, their dresses lifted to their hips, pressing the grapes with their feet, their bare legs tanned and smooth. We loved watching the feasts in the barn – the pâtés, the vast tureens of soup and jugs of wine spread over red and white checked tablecloths. Monsieur and Madame Duval would preside over those meals like a king and queen. There was singing and dancing, chatter and laughter. Only Jacques Reynard looked sad, like a brown autumn leaf blown into a corner all on his own. His sorrow was mistaken for grumpiness. How they misunderstood him. He loved the fields and the vines. His roots tunnelled deep into that soil, having been set down there by his great-grandfather. He was as much part of the *château* as they were. When I asked my mother why he always looked so sad, she simply stroked my head and said tenderly, 'Some people will never get over the war, my love. You're too young to understand.'

Jacques Reynard had always been kind to my mother and me. We three had an unspoken bond. I had never heard my mother complain to him about Madame Duval's haughtiness or about the way they all treated me as vermin. They never spoke about the war, my father, the German occupation of the *château* or indeed the family who had once lived there. It was as if it was all too painful to remember. But the look in his eyes was tender and brimming with compassion. He never turned me away when I came asking to help, but set me tasks which I completed responsibly. Working with Jacques Reynard made me proud, whereas chores in the kitchen, watched over by Armande and Pierre, left me feeling worthless and hollow.

Since Coyote had arrived I had barely seen Jacques. We'd been too busy singing *Laredo* and he had been occupied with preparations for the harvest. I sought him out in the workshop. He was sitting on a log, mending a large wheel. His beret covered his balding head, leaving the hair on the sides and back, once red, now increasingly grey, to give the impression that he had a full head of hair. His moustache twitched as he ground his teeth, pounding the nails with a hammer. He wore the same pair of dark brown trousers, moleskin waistcoat and white shirt that he always wore, the sleeves rolled up to reveal strong brown arms and capable hands. When he saw me standing in the doorway, his gloomy face opened into a wide smile.

'*Bonjour*, Monsieur Reynard,' I said, beaming back.

'So it's true, is it?' he replied, resting his hammer on his knee. I nodded. His eyes twinkled with mischief. 'So you're a saint. Saint Mischa.' He shrugged. 'It has a nice ring to it.'

I wandered in, my hands in my pockets. I couldn't pretend to him. 'It's not a miracle, though,' I said sheepishly, letting my fringe fall over my eyes.

'If it's not a miracle, what is it?'

'Coyote.'

'Who?'

I looked at him in surprise. Surely he'd heard of Coyote. Everyone was talking about him. 'The American.'

'Is that what they call God these days?' He chuckled and picked up a nut and bolt. 'I suppose it's better than Abel-Louis.'

'Coyote's not God. But he is magic.'

'Is he now?'

'The wind brought him, you see. Ever since he arrived, everything has changed for the better.' I tried to explain, but I could see that he didn't believe me. Hadn't he noticed the change in Yvette?

'Good. Then we'll have an abundant harvest, for sure.'

'I told Madame Duval that I had seen Jesus.' Now he looked up at me in amusement, rolling the bolt between his oily fingers.

'And what did she say?'

'She burst into tears,' I replied, grinning proudly. 'She asked me to forgive her.'

'Forgiveness will not save her from damnation,' he mumbled. 'Sometimes forgiveness is not enough!'

'Père Abel-Louis invited *Maman* to take communion.'

He shook his head. 'Of course. I imagine your mother declined?'

'Yes, she did.'

'Why should she accept anything from that ungodly man? After all he has done, he should be ashamed of himself.' He wiped his forehead with the back of his hand, leaving a smear of grease on his skin. 'I bet he embraced you like the prodigal son. Yes, it would be just like him to use such a miracle to strengthen his hold over that bovine lot of ignoramuses. Your mother would be well advised not to go to Mass. I told her so years ago, after, after . . .' He drew in a deep breath and his face turned the colour of an old bruise. 'But she's stubborn, your mother. I think she goes just to torment him. Your mother isn't afraid of anyone.' He held my eyes for a long moment, then added in a gentle voice.

'Your father was a good man, Mischa. Don't let anyone tell you any different.'

Inside my trouser pocket I turned the little rubber ball round and round in my fingers.

'Do you think it's a miracle?' I asked.

'Perhaps.' He shrugged and twitched his moustache. 'Love is a miracle. The return of your voice is a miracle too, because it was brought about by your mother's love. You see, Mischa, you never really lost it; it just froze like a seed in winter. You give it enough sun and water and it grows.'

'They all want to touch me for luck.'

'They're a medieval lot. Primitive. I should milk it for all it's worth if I were you. You've deserved it. Shame on them all!'

'Have you ever been in love?' I asked suddenly, then blushed. I hadn't yet got used to restraining my voice. I was thinking about Yvette; Jacques Reynard clearly was not.

'I once loved a girl but she didn't love me back. I thought it didn't matter, because I had enough love for both of us. I thought she would grow to love me. I suppose she did in her way, but it wasn't enough.'

'What happened?'

'She fell in love with someone else. The thing about love is that you can't turn it off like a tap.' His eyes took on a haunted look and he added in a quiet voice, 'I'll always love her. In spite of everything, I'll never stop. Because I can't.' He shrugged helplessly, as if aware of his own foolishness.

'Where is she now?'

'It was a long time ago,' he said with a sigh. 'She is a memory now. Besides, there are many different ways of loving; I have learned that over time.' I wanted to ask him about Yvette, but felt that would be one step too far.

He stood up, holding the wheel with his hand. 'Don't just stand there, lazybones, help me put this wheel on the cart, otherwise we'll have to carry the barrels to the sheds ourselves.'

I helped Jacques Reynard for the rest of the morning. I enjoyed being in his company. He was cosy and familiar. With him I didn't feel the need to speak, even though I could.

After a picnic lunch with my mother and Coyote by the river, I left them alone and sought the company of the Pheasants. I found Daphne sitting alone on the terrace with Rex. She looked sad.

'Hello, Mrs Halifax,' I said, approaching her across the lawn. Her face opened, like a sunflower turned towards the sun.

'My dear boy, it really is true what they're all saying. You're a walking miracle. God be praised.'

'Why are you on your own?'

'Goodness me, you speak English and we believed you never understood us. What have we been saying?' She blushed but continued to smile. 'Come and sit with me and Rex. Now we can have a proper chat. However do you speak English, young man?'

'My grandfather was Irish. My parents spoke English together.' I shrugged. 'I suppose I just picked it up.'

'You clever boy. I always knew you were clever. Didn't I say so? You're not hiding any more I see?'

'Madame Duval thinks I've been touched by God. She's afraid of me now.'

Daphne chuckled. 'I never liked her,' she hissed. 'Cold woman. Not kind. Not kind at all.'

'Why aren't you painting?'

'I don't feel like it today.' She sighed heavily.

'Are you sad?'

'A little. Can you tell?'

'You don't look sad now.'

'I'm not. I've got you to talk to, Mischa. I've always liked you. But you know that, don't you?'

I nodded. 'I've always liked you too, and Rex. I like looking at your shoes.' She stuck out one foot and wiggled it around.

'I'm particularly fond of these.' They were crimson velvet with a large pink rose on the toe. 'I like red and pink together. Most unusual.'

'You can't be sad with shoes like that.'

'You wouldn't have thought so, would you? However . . .' She looked wistful again. 'We're leaving tomorrow,' she continued in a quiet voice, staring out over the lawn, her gaze lost among the vines. 'I don't want to go.'

I suddenly felt bereft. 'I don't want you to go,' I exclaimed truthfully. 'Do you have to?'

'I'm afraid we can't stay here for ever, my dear. We've been here for weeks. Besides, it's expensive. England's very drab. There are still rations, London's very grey, and part of it's barely standing. I don't live in the city, of course, but still, it breaks my heart. So many lost, so much mourning. While here, it's green, sunny, fragrant – one could forget it all in this enchanting place.'

'Do you have children?' I don't know why I asked, it just popped out.

She turned to me. That simple question had aged her by years. Her face had fallen so that her cheeks looked heavy and sallow and the pouches beneath her eyes sagged. 'I had a little boy like you, Mischa,' she replied.

'What happened to him?' My voice was a whisper for I sensed tragedy before she answered.

'He had polio, the poor little devil. He was very lame. I only had him for a short time. Then he died. You see, he was so special God wanted him back. I begged for a little more time, but it was not granted. I carry him here.' She pressed her old hand to her breast and forced a smile. Her eyes, however, remained dull with sorrow. 'He's always here.'

I reached out and touched her hand. It was trembling. She squeezed mine back. 'You're a very special little boy, Mischa. You're not like others. You're old beyond your years. To think you're only six. Like you, George was an only child. Bill and I tried to have more, but it wasn't to be. One imagines time will heal. I'm old, it all happened a long time ago. I have no children or grandchildren but I am still a mother. Never a day goes by when I don't think of him.'

'What was he like?' I still held her hand and she didn't slip hers from my grasp.

'He was blond, like you, and handsome.' Her skin regained its elasticity and she looked happy again. 'He had brown eyes the colour of sherry. Gold they were, almost. He was a cheeky little thing. He loved kicking a ball about. Bill and George spent a lot of time in our garden playing football. They got on like a house on fire. Of course, he was lame, so he wasn't able to play with the other children, but Bill played with him. Bill was his true friend. Once, when I asked him if he minded that he didn't have any friends, he smiled at me brightly and replied that he did. "Daddy's my friend" he said. That was very touching.'

'Is Bill waiting for you in England? Is that why you have to go home?' I so wanted her to stay.

'No, my dear, Bill died a few years ago. He's with George now. That brings me a great deal of comfort. They're playing football together and George is fit and well.' She took her hand out of mine and ran it down my face. 'I have Rex and my friends. I'm not alone, God forbid. I'll miss you, though, Mischa. I'll miss you very much.'

'I'll miss you too, Mrs Halifax.'

'Good God, child, call me Daphne. Mrs Halifax makes me feel dreadfully old!'

15

The following morning I went to school. I walked with my mother, bursting with pride in my new blue smock. I didn't hold her hand but strode beside her with my hands by my side, my fingers toying with the little rubber ball that I always kept on me for comfort. My heart raced like it did every Sunday when we went to Mass. Now we were more of a curiosity than ever. I was a miracle. To many I was living proof that God existed. The eyes that watched me from behind lace curtains were full of gratitude not malice. Jesus had taught them forgiveness more directly than any sermon from Père Abel-Louis could. An old man sitting on a bench in the pale liquid light of morning, puffing on a pipe, nodded at me as I passed, and a couple of old women shrouded in black crossed themselves before hobbling back into the shadows like crows, more certain than ever before that Death, when it came, would carry them off to a better place. However, school children were a different matter altogether.

Young children don't think about death. They don't need miracles to convince them of a higher power; instinctively, they know it to be true. They don't follow the example set by the priest and often they ignore that of their parents. They follow each other, and the strongest of the group sets the trend. They think nothing of brutality, that's instinctive too; the law of the jungle rules. Weakness is abhorred; the strongest survive and those, like me, who are different, are outcast and vilified. I remembered playing with them in the square and hoped that my association with Coyote would protect me from their cruelty.

My mother was anxious, I could tell. She had worn a constant frown on her forehead all morning. The skin between her eyebrows was pinched, making her look cross. I knew she wasn't cross. Ever since my voice had returned she had been in a state of confusion. She was religious. To her, as to the rest of the congregation, it had been a miracle from God. She had no problem with that. I had seen her on her knees beside the bed, thanking God over and over again in barely audible mumbles and silent tears. What she found hard to deal with was the change in people's treatment of us. She was happier before, when she knew what to expect. She was indignant. According to her, they shouldn't have mistreated us in the first place. She would never forget what happened in that summer of 1944 and she certainly wouldn't forgive.

We stopped at the school gate and she crouched down to smooth the creases in my smock. 'You'll be fine,' she reassured me, kissing my cheek. 'You'll learn so much and you already have a huge advantage over them because you speak English.'

'Don't worry about me, *Maman*. I can look after myself.'

'I know you can,' she replied, a proud smile breaking the solemn mask of her face. 'You're my *chevalier*.' I noticed she had missed out the word 'little'.

I braced myself and walked in with the other children. No one spoke to me but they all stared at me in the shameless way children do. I felt conspicuous, like a fish that finds itself beyond the safety of the coral reef, in the wide open sea with nowhere to hide. Suddenly a teacher pointed at me and hurried over.

'Mischa,' she said kindly. 'Come with me.' She had straight brown hair and rich golden eyes and her smile was wide and sincere. 'This is your first day, dear. You must be very nervous.

You don't need to be. My name is Mademoiselle Rosnay and I'm your teacher.' She put her hand on my back and guided me through the noisy swarm of children into a classroom. There were rows of wooden desks, a blackboard, pictures the pupils had painted pinned to the walls, and the strong smell of disinfectant. A group of boys lingered around a desk playing with a yoyo. When I entered they stopped their game and turned to me. A hush fell over the room.

'Mischa!' I recognised her voice immediately and felt a surge of relief.

'Claudine!'

'Ah, you have a friend. That's good,' said Mademoiselle Rosnay

'You're in my class!' she exclaimed happily. 'I'll look after him, Mademoiselle Rosnay. Can I?'

'Well, of course you may,' replied Mademoiselle Rosnay, showing me to my desk. 'This is yours,' she said. It was scuffed and covered in ink stains and carvings scratched into the wood by previous generations of children, but it was mine. I felt a wave of pride. This was my very own desk. My place in the school, just like everyone else. I put the pencil case my mother had given me neatly inside and closed the lid.

'I'm so pleased you got your voice back,' Claudine said, touching my arm. 'I knew you would.'

'It feels a bit strange,' I replied, which wasn't true, but the whole situation was overwhelming. I didn't know quite what to say.

'I bet it does. *Le curéton* was shocked. He went white, then blue, then grey and finally pink. That horrid sweaty pink that smells of alcohol. Everyone's talking about it. You're a saint, Mischa. You know, my mother says that if I touch you, you'll bring me good luck – turncoat.'

'You mean, she doesn't mind us being friends?'

'Not at all. In fact, she's encouraging me. I'm to touch you as often as possible and wonderful things will happen.'

I looked at her conspiratorially. 'I don't think they will,' I whispered. 'I'm not really a saint.'

'That's okay,' she said with a grin. 'I prefer you as you are. Saints are dull.'

'Let me introduce you to the others,' she suggested, waving at the group of boys. Warily they sidled over, watching me from behind long fringes, hands in pockets.

'So you're a miracle?' said one.

'God gave him back his voice,' said Claudine. 'He saw a vision, didn't you, Mischa?'

'A vision?' repeated another.

'Really?' they exclaimed.

'What did you see?'

They took their hands out of their pockets, pushed their hair off their faces, and blinked at me with admiration. I sat on the desk with my feet on a chair and told them what I had told Madame Duval. I exaggerated a little more for effect, encouraged by their wide eyes and dropped jaws. Claudine went along with my lie like a good accomplice, prompting me with suggestions. We were a double act, and a good one at that. I savoured the sense of friendship and the warm swell of my heart that went with it.

A few girls hurried over, keen not to miss the inside story. Their families had been talking of nothing else since Mass the previous morning and they were eager to hear it from the horse's mouth. I repeated the story for the second time. By now, I almost believed it myself. They badgered me with questions: What did Jesus look like? Had I seen God? Was my father in uniform? What did Heaven look like? I did my best to answer them, relying heavily on what my mother had told me and the religious pictures I had seen in church. My answers must have satisfied them for, when

Mademoiselle Rosnay clapped her hands, signalling everyone to return to their desks, they all patted me on the back.

'*Bonjour, tout le monde,*' she said, standing in front of her desk.

'*Bonjour, Mademoiselle Rosnay,*' we all chanted in unison. I followed the other children and sat down. Claudine, who sat at the desk beside me, smiled at me toothily. I noticed the desk on her other side was empty.

'I would like to welcome the newest member of our class, Mischa Fontaine. I ask you all to be as helpful as you can so that he settles in as quickly as possible.' I felt deliriously happy. Claudine was proud to be my friend and I had already won over the rest of the class. This sainthood business had done me a huge favour. I didn't feel in the least bit guilty lying about my vision; after all, who was to say that God hadn't had a hand in the miracle? Perhaps God was responsible for the wind and hence for Coyote. Besides, I was doing Him a favour, strengthening the people's faith and that, surely, was a good thing.

I was keen to learn, too. My mother had taught me as well as she could, but there was no substitute for real schooling, and the excitement of having proper books and a teacher scribbling on a blackboard was intoxicating. I was just getting into the lesson when the door opened. A scruffy looking boy with dark hair and heavy eyes sauntered into the room. Mademoiselle Rosnay wasn't pleased. She placed her hands on her hips and pursed her lips. 'Laurent, I have had enough of you turning up late in the morning. Either you are here on time for my class, or you will be punished.'

'I'm sorry,' he said with a shrug. 'Trouble at home.'

Mademoiselle shook her head and sighed. 'That's no excuse and you know it. Now settle down as quickly as possible.'

As he walked past my desk he did a double take. I recognised him from the time we had all played in the square. He had patted me on the back and said, 'Well run.' He sat down and whispered to Claudine. After that, I noticed him out of the corner of my eye. I could feel his attention. But, unlike the rest of the class, it wasn't sympathetic.

In the break, the class dispersed into the playground. Claudine was by my side, my loyal conspirator, whispering more suggestions into my ear to embellish my story. I noticed Laurent linger. He watched us go outside, his brow low and brooding. I soon forgot about him though, for I was at once surrounded by those who had not heard my story and those who wanted to hear it again. I found myself holding forth with the ease of an actor confident of his role. I knew the script by heart and had now learned when to pause for optimal effect.

Claudine became my manager, sensing when the interview was beginning to tire me out and demanding a break. We ran off to some steps that led up to a classroom and sat huddled together, laughing at our success. 'You're brilliant!' she enthused. 'They're eating out of your hand.'

'It's not *all* untrue,' I said, not wanting her to think me a total liar.

'I know it isn't. There's no harm in colouring it a little for entertainment. Never let the truth interfere with a good story, I always say.'

'I did *feel* something,' I said, turning serious. 'I didn't see God or Jesus, but I felt them, and I felt my father too. The church was flooded with light and I got a tingling all over my body. That's the truth. I haven't told anyone but you.'

She smiled tenderly. 'I believe you, Mischa. We can laugh as much as we like, but the fact is, you got your voice back. That kind of miracle only comes from God, vision or no vision. It doesn't matter. You can speak.' She shrugged. 'It doesn't matter how.'

'I don't think Laurent likes me,' I said, thinking of him smouldering in the classroom.

'He's only jealous. We've always done everything together, Laurent and me. He's cross. His parents fight all the time because his father has affairs.'

'Affairs?' She knew an awful lot for a seven year old.

'He's in love with Madame Bonchance, you know, the lady at the kiosk.'

'The one with red hair?'

She giggled. 'Ever since she's been screwing Laurent's dad she's taken trouble with herself. She wears bright red lipstick, her hair all curled, green shadow above her eyes. What a sight! It obviously pleases Laurent's dad, though.' I thought of Yvette and Jacques Reynard, another unlikely pairing.

When we returned to the classroom, Laurent's face had darkened, as if he had spent the whole break brooding on Claudine's new friendship. I ignored him and answered more questions about Heaven and God. Suddenly, he squared up in front of me. 'You might have been touched by God,' he sneered. 'But your father's still a Nazi pig.'

The room fell silent. Claudine made to intervene. It was her white face that gave me the confidence to draw my sword. I squared my shoulders too, and stood tall, though not as tall as Laurent.

'You know why my father wasn't a real Nazi? Because Nazi is a state of mind not a nationality,' I replied with as much arrogance as I could muster. 'You, Laurent, might be French, but you're more of a Nazi than he was.'

I felt my cheeks flush with the brilliance of my retort. I didn't know from where those words had come, or what they really meant, but they sounded good. From his reaction he thought so too. He backed off, his eyes black with rage. Claudine turned on him.

'How dare you speak to Mischa like that, Laurent! I thought you were a decent person, but you're just as prejudiced as your parents!' When Mademoiselle Rosnay came in we all returned to our desks, I flushed with victory, Laurent, his head bowed in shame.

That afternoon the wind picked up. The leaves were torn from the branches, tossed about in the air and thrown to the ground where they swirled about helplessly. I did not speak to Laurent again and Claudine ignored him, which cost her, for she grew quiet and sad. I returned home at the end of the day, the taste of victory now bitter on my tongue. I told my mother about Mademoiselle Rosnay and Claudine, but not of my boasting nor of my fight with Laurent.

By evening the wind had turned into a storm. Rain fell in a torrent, splashing on the ground, forming large puddles in the mud. My mother thought of Jacques Reynard and the harvest that was only a week away. I thought of Coyote. Wasn't it a storm like this that had brought him to Château Lecrusse? If my grandmother was right, surely the wind would take him away? I was uneasy, not wanting to believe the folklore but too afraid not to. I lay awake in bed, my mother's breathing regular and gentle against the rattling windows and clattering glass. The wind howled like one of Jacques Reynard's wolves. I snuggled further beneath the blanket, drawing it over my head. I fell into a restless sleep. Images of Laurent rose in my thoughts, clashing with Claudine, Madame Duval and Yvette. Then those images cleared and I was living my nightmare again, so familiar to me now that I knew, in my dreamy state, that it was not real. However, it was none the less frightening. The same faces, the same hatred, the same fear, except this time it ended differently . . .

Suddenly a man appears and the crowd disperses. He is wearing a uniform I have not seen before. It is green, like an olive. He takes off his shirt and places it around my mother's shoulders. 'You should be disgusted with yourselves. To turn against your own people!' he shouts, but they do not hear him. Then he places

*his hand on my head. 'You're gonna be all right, son.' I look up
into his face. He smiles kindly, his eyes turquoise against the dark
tan of his skin, and he ruffles my hair. 'It's okay, Junior,' he repeats.
'You're going to be okay.'*

I opened my eyes with a gasp. My mother was still asleep
beside me, her face flushed, a small smile betraying the nature
of her dreams. I slid out of bed and searched for my clothes.
The light was on in the hall, but I couldn't find anything.
When I opened a drawer I was baffled to find it empty. I
scratched my head and tried to think. I didn't believe I was
still dreaming. I was confused. Finally, I was left no option
but to put on my coat and boots over my pyjamas. Still dazed
and disoriented, drunk on sleep, I staggered down the steps
and made my way through the storm to the *château*. I didn't
know how I was going to find him. But I had to tell him not
to leave without us. I drew my coat about my shoulders and
buried my chin into my chest. The rain drenched my head
in a second and began to drip down my back like the tracing
of cold fingers. I shivered, blinked the drops off my eyelashes
and hurried on. My thoughts were erratic, my feelings numb.
What had become of my clothes? I still wasn't sure whether
or not I was dreaming.

I reached the stone walls of the *château* and cowered for
a while against them, my back turned towards the wind. Had
Coyote been there in 1944 when the Americans liberated
Maurilliac? Had *he* rescued us from the mob? Was *he* responsible for our salvation? Is that why my mother and he shared
a bond? Is that why he could see Pistou when no one else
could – because he really *was* magic? I shuddered as another
drip careered down my spine. I had to get into the hotel. I
had to find him. He must not leave without us.

The front doors were locked and the shutters all closed.
It was very dark. Occasionally the clouds separated to give
a glimpse of the full moon, far above the storm, way beyond

the influence of the wind. I knew that if there was a way to get into the *château* it would be through the conservatory. When the clouds parted I dashed around to the back, through the box garden that Joy Springtoe's room had overlooked. By the time I reached the conservatory I was soaked to the skin and cold to my bones. Frozen to sobriety, I crouched against the glass, my head in my hands, wondering what to do when I heard the sound of a shovel being forced repeatedly into the ground. At first I thought it was the wind rattling a loose shutter, but the more I listened the more I realised that it was someone digging in the garden. I stared out into the blackness but saw only the darkest night and driving rain. I held my breath and listened again. My heart beat so loudly it was hard to hear above it. The sound reached me, hard and violent. Then the clouds divided and, for an instant, the moon shone a spotlight on the far border at the end of the garden, against the wall, where a man was on his knees, digging up the earth. I caught my breath in horror, imagining nothing less than the disposing of a body after a murder. The moment the clouds came together again I hurried away as fast as my shaking legs could carry me. I was terrified. Thoughts of Coyote stealing away in the middle of the night disintegrated in the furnace of my fear. I no longer cared for anything other than being as far away from the *château* as possible in case the murderer saw me spying and had to kill me too.

I reached the safety of the stable block. It was warm in there and smelt of my mother's lemon cologne mingled with the scent of pine. I undressed and hung my pyjamas in the bathroom to dry. Then I wriggled down the bed naked, as close to my mother as I could get without touching her. It was warm beside her and it wasn't long before I drifted off, too tired even to worry about the murderer in the garden.

It was still dark, but it had stopped raining when my mother woke me. 'Shhh,' she instructed. She was already dressed, her hair pinned back, her eyes sparkling with intent. If she had noticed my pyjamas in the bathroom she didn't let on. 'Your clothes are on the chair. Hurry.'

'Where are we going?' I asked.

'To America,' she replied with a smile.

'America?' I repeated in disbelief. The night couldn't get any weirder.

'Coyote is waiting in the car. Let's not talk now, my darling. We haven't got time.' In her hand she held a brown envelope. I saw the name Jacques Reynard written on it in her looped handwriting before she slipped it into her coat pocket.

I did as I was told. I now realised why the drawers were empty. I looked around: the room was bare, as if we had never been there. I suddenly felt an overwhelming sense of sorrow. Maurilliac was all I had ever known. My father's spirit walked the corridors of the Château Lecrusse. I sometimes heard his boots on the wooden floorboards, the sound of orchestral music from the gramophone, my mother's rippling laughter as he danced with her around the room. My heart lurched at the thought of leaving everything I loved about my home: the green rows of vines, harvest time, the sunset that turned the river golden, the view from the folly, Daphne Halifax, Jacques Reynard . . . Claudine. A large tear welled in my eye and rolled down my cheek. 'It's all right to be sad, my love,' said my mother, her own eyes glittering with tears. 'We're embarking on an adventure,' she reassured me. 'We're going to another country. We have an opportunity to start again.'

'But what about Papa?' I croaked. I didn't need to explain. She took me in her arms and held me tightly.

'Papa isn't here, Mischa. He's in Heaven.' She held me in front of her so that I could see her face. 'We carry him around here, in our hearts. He'll always be with us, you see. I haven't stopped loving him. I love Coyote in a different way. There are many ways of loving, Mischa. Our hearts have an enormous capacity for love. We'll come back one day. But we'll never be free of the past if we remain here.' She laughed sadly. 'You're a saint now, Mischa. That's a very hard thing to live up to. I don't think it's fair to burden you with that as well. Come, we must hurry. Trust me, this is for the best. The *chevalier* has fought and won. There's nothing left for us here.'

PART TWO

My friends and relations
They live in the nation
They know not where
Their boy has gone
First came to Texas
And hired to a ranchman
I'm only a poor cowboy
And I know I've done wrong

Someone write me a letter
To my grey-headed mother
Then to my sister
My sister so dear
But there's another
far dearer than mother
who'd bitterly weep
If she knew I was here.

16

I stood in the snow feeling helpless, as if I were a little boy again. I scratched my chin, bristly from neglect, and stared bleakly at the grey coats that hurried along the sidewalks. I felt I had lost Coyote all over again and my stomach lurched with regret. What had he come back for? Where had he been for the last thirty years? I was angry with myself for letting him walk away without giving him the chance to explain. I seemed to be angry all the time these days; even Stanley was wary of me, I could tell. Esther, on the other hand, was afraid of no one. I shook my head, feeling despair wind itself around me like a boa constrictor until I found it hard to breathe. I shoved my hands in my pockets and strode back to the office, stifling sobs that were long overdue.

The city had woken up. Yellow and black taxis rattled down the streets, tooting their horns, splashing slush on to people in hats and boots hurrying off to work. Vagabonds in cardboard boxes slept on, hungry and cold, avoiding as much of life as possible. I wondered whether Coyote was reduced to that indignity. How had he managed to sink so low? How I had longed to hold on to the past and yet, time had carried me on like a river and I had been forced to let go. My childhood in Bordeaux was lost to me, a place upstream I could never go back to. The Coyote I had loved was lost to me, too.

When I reached the shop I was grumpy, all six foot four of me. I must have been a horrifying sight: unruly hair covered in snow, blue eyes navy with fury, my mouth a grim line on a grey, unshaven face, my posture hunched and ungainly. Stanley had opened the shop. The little bell tinkled when I entered. He looked up from the desk when he saw me and I noticed him recoil. 'Morning,' he said. I grunted, strode past him and mounted the stairs to my office. I hated myself for letting my anger get the better of me, but I was unable to control it.

I sat at my desk for a long time just staring ahead bitterly into the space that Coyote had occupied only an hour before. I could still smell the sweet scent of his Gauloise and the recollections it aroused; the room might just as well have been filled with pine trees and eucalyptus and that damp earthy smell of the ground after rain.

I hadn't wanted to go through my mother's things. I had been afraid of what I would find, of what memories would be stirred. Her apartment was still as she had left it. Nothing had been moved, nothing at all. Now Coyote had returned and ripped off the dressing that had covered the wound to my heart. It hadn't healed as it should have, but was as raw and smarting as the day it was dealt. I decided to take the day off and go through her belongings. There was no better time than the present and, the longer I left it, the longer the memories would fester and the harder it would be for me to get over her death.

Coyote's sudden appearance had sparked my curiosity. My mother had rarely spoken about him, save to say time and again that he would come back one day. 'And when he does, my love, I'll be waiting.' I had believed her at first, and then, as the years passed, I had given up and my hurt had turned to anger. She had insisted on always laying a place for him at the table, like an errant Elijah, right up until the very end when she had sat alone. You see, she had felt death approaching, like the wind sucked into a tunnel as the train comes. She had heard the whistle in the distance, ready to carry her off to the Heaven in which she so strongly believed. She ate alone, the tumour growing inside her, draining her life away with her hope.

I grabbed my coat and went downstairs. Stanley was with a customer, talking in a low voice over an English seventeenth-century walnut bureau. He looked at me over his glasses, his expression guarded. Esther was at the desk, the telephone receiver swallowed by her mass of curly grey hair, surrounded by untidy piles of papers and books. When she saw me she hung up and greeted me with the same warmth as she did every morning.

'What a stunning day!' she enthused, oblivious of my ill humour. 'I love the snow. Ever since I was a child, I've loved the snow.' She had a strong New Jersey accent, reminding me of the small town of Jupiter where my mother and I had settled with Coyote after our flight from France. 'Would you like a coffee, Mischa? You look tired. I imagine you're not sleeping. I didn't sleep for a month after my mother passed. I put gin in my coffee just to keep going.'

'I'm taking the day off,' I said, shrugging on my coat.

'Good idea. Go for a walk, enjoy the snow, watch the world, deep breaths, call a friend, you'll feel better.'

'Thanks.'

'Don't thank me, it's my pleasure. Nothing like a brisk walk to raise the spirits.'

'You know me so well,' I said, humouring her, and feeling guilty for imposing my bad mood on so sunny a human being.

'Yes, I do,' she replied with a small shake of her head. 'My father was a right *schliemiel*. Never smiled, walked around as if he carried all the worries of the world on his shoulders, face grey with gloom, eyes like a sad dog, grumpy as hell, lashing out at anyone who tried to cheer him up. I'm used to your sort.'

'Thank you, Esther. That's made me feel a whole lot better.'

'Good, I'm glad. That's how I can get up every morning, because I know I make the world a better place.' I smiled, but she had said it without irony.

The little bell tinkled as I opened the door and strode out into the snow. Was I really as bad as Esther's father? Out of the corner of my eye I saw Zebedee, the clock-maker, chatting to the mailman on the sidewalk. He raised his hand to greet me. Determined not to be a curmudgeon I acknowledged him with a wave. 'Lovely day! Shame about the snow!' he said with a chuckle, his pale eyes glancing up over the small spectacles perched on the end of his nose. When he chuckled he looked like a garden gnome. His hair was grey and woolly around the back and sides of his head, leaving the top bald and his large, fleshy ears exposed. I watched the snowflakes land on his naked pate like feathers, melting on the warmth of his skin. 'Unlikely visitor you had this morning.'

'Did you see him?'

'Oh yes, I did. There are too many tramps in this neck of the woods. Somebody really ought to do something about it, especially in this weather. The poor creatures will freeze to death.'

'Had you seen him before?'

'They all look the same to me.' He thanked the mailman, who strode off to continue his route.

'Did you see him enter?'

'I assumed he had a key. He let himself in. I thought perhaps he was an English aristocrat. They all look like tramps, so I'm told.'

'He broke in, Zeb, although there's nothing to prove it.'

'Well, I'll be damned . . . Did he take anything?' I shook

my head. 'Well, that's a miracle.' It had been many years since I had heard anyone say that.

My mother's apartment was on the Upper West Side. When I entered, Marcello, the porter, leaped out from behind his desk to embrace me. 'I'm so sorry,' he exclaimed into my chest, for he was much smaller than I. 'Your mother was a good woman, Mr Fontaine.'

'Thank you, Marcelo,' I replied, feeling my throat constrict again. My mother had grown into a formidable woman but, she had always smiled for Marcello. Perhaps he reminded her of Jacques Reynard; he had the same reddish hair and kindly face.

'I have collected her mail for you,' he said, pulling away and walking back to his desk. 'It's been piling up. Some of it is for you, I think. Letters of condolence, I should imagine. Today was the first day she received nothing. Word gets around, doesn't it?'

'Thank you,' I said again, taking the pile and making my way to the elevator.

I couldn't face looking through her mail. Not yet, anyway. So I put it on the table in the hall. The apartment still smelt of her and of the scented candles she had always burned. The curtains were all drawn, making the place dark and gloomy. It felt still and empty and reminded me of a crypt. There was no music, no movement, no life at all, not even flowers. I imagined she had been relieved to go. I didn't get the feeling that she was lingering, holding on. She had gone and I was alone. I was a man in my forties and I missed my mother. It had always been the two of us. *Maman* and her little *chevalier*. Now it was just me.

I wandered the rooms in a daze, the sense of loss heavy on my shoulders, making me stoop all the more. She had always had plain tastes. She hadn't liked fuss and frills. She remained very French, her tastes elegant and understated.

The wooden floorboards were dark and polished, the furniture mostly antiques from France and England, the upholstery pale, neutral colours. A baby grand piano stood in the corner of the living-room beneath neat piles of heavy, glossy books on art and decoration. She had played, although I didn't know at what stage of her life she had taken lessons. When the curtains weren't drawn the apartment was light and airy. When she had lived, lilies in tall vases and gardenia in pots had been her garden. Now the place was dark and there was no garden, just the scent of her flowers that still hung in the still, stagnant air.

I remembered her in every inch of the apartment. Her absence made the place seem much bigger and strangely unfamiliar. I noticed things I had never noticed before, the odd ornament or picture, as well as the things I remembered from our life in France, like the tapestry footstool my grandmother had made for her when she was a girl. We had left with little, or so I thought until I came across a trunk on top of the chest of drawers in her bedroom.

It wasn't a large trunk, although it had seemed large to me as a child. Back then it had been filled with the dresses, hats and stockings my father had bought her in the war. She had kept it in the stable block and only worn the clothes in private. Later, when we moved to America, she had kept them there because by then they had become sacred relics. She could have worn them, but she never did. They were part of the chapter that belonged to my father. A chapter she visited only in her dreams because she had given her life to Coyote and started anew. That chapter was closed and I was afraid to open it.

I placed the trunk on the floor. I didn't open it immediately but went to help myself to a drink. Mother had a little drinks cabinet behind the living-room. The crystal bottles were still on the shelves as she had left them, the liquids shining silver and gold like the contents of an alchemist's laboratory. I poured myself a glass of gin and took a handful of peanuts from the olive-green bucket that depicted greyhounds racing across the English countryside. Then, fortified by the alcohol, I sat on the carpet in her bedroom and lifted the lid of the trunk.

What first struck me was the smell. Lemon, mingled with her own unique scent. My chest swelled with sorrow as I was transported back to my childhood. That smell had meant refuge, security and home. Enfolded in her arms I had breathed it in and everything had been all right. I lifted out a pale green chiffon dress and pressed it to my nose. In my mind's eye she was a young woman, her hair cascading in waves over her shoulders and down her back, her skin soft and smooth like a petal, her dress dancing about her legs as she walked with a swing in her hips, back up the dusty track to the *château*. She had been in her sixties when she died. Her illness had eaten away at her flesh so that her bones had stuck out and her cheeks had sunk in, making her look much older than she was. Her eyes, though hollow, had remained the same. Those of a girl trapped inside a decaying body.

I put the dress on the floor. There were five more and they were all beautifully preserved. I pulled out a couple of hats I had never seen, along with gloves and stockings, each item carefully wrapped in tissue paper. Beneath the clothes there were some old books: *The Count of Monte Cristo* by Alexandre Dumas, *Nana* by Zola, a couple of English children's books and an encyclopaedia. They were all beautifully bound. I wondered whether they were from her childhood, or gifts from my father. Only the children's books were inscribed: *To darling Anouk, of fairies and other magic, Daddy*. I added them to the pile on the floor and delved inside again.

Fascination overcame my grief when I found a black photo album. It was bound in thin leather, the pages inside of black paper. The photographs were small, black and white, carefully slotted into little white corners pasted on with glue. My mother had written in white ink beneath each one, her writing looped and girlish, but most of the names meant nothing to me. However, the pictures of my grandparents held my attention for a long while as I tried to find traces of my own features and those of my mother in their faces. My mother had told me so little about her childhood. I knew that she had grown up just outside Bordeaux. That her French mother had met her Irish father there when, as a young man, he had travelled to the city to learn about wine. More than that I didn't know – oh, except for my grandmother's superstitious belief in the power of the wind.

As I turned the pages the name Michel began to appear more regularly. He was in all the family groups, usually beside my mother, and the more I looked the more I noticed how much he resembled her. My mother had never mentioned that she had a brother. The name Michel had never been uttered. But then, she had rarely talked about her parents. She had told me her mother had died. What of her father? If she had had a brother, what had become of him? Had he died in the war – or, perhaps more likely, had her family disowned her following her marriage to my father? What struck me in the photographs was their obvious closeness and warmth. There was no doubt that they had once been a very united and loving family. Considering the album, it was strange that they had played no part in my growing up. Considering my German father, perhaps it wasn't so strange after all.

I put the album down on the floor on the other side of the trunk so that I would remember to take it home with me to study further, then delved inside again. I pulled out a small box. Inside were a couple of letters in envelopes, a jewellery box containing a suite of diamonds I had never seen before, old medals and another black and white photograph of my father, unframed. This one was very different from the one she had kept in her dressing-table drawer in the stable block, more casual, more joyous. He was wearing a dark grey polo-necked sweater and slacks, his hands thrust into his pockets. His head was inclined, his handsome face smiling broadly, his short blond hair ruffled in the wind. My stomach lurched, it could have been me. I held it for a long while, mesmerised by what could have been my own reflection. Though I hadn't laughed with his abandon for some time. Then my eye was drawn to the bottom of the trunk, for there, lost to me for decades, was my little rubber ball.

I took a large swig of gin. It left a burning trail from my gullet to my stomach, but the sensation was pleasant. I held the little rubber ball in my hands and toyed with it pensively. In my mind's eye I saw Pistou, the bridge over the stream, the regimental rows of vines, Jacques Reynard, Daphne Halifax, Claudine, and Joy Springtoe. The sandstone walls of the *château* loomed into view, its pale blue shutters open to let in the sun, the white linen curtains billowing in the breeze, the birdsong, the clamour of crickets, the tall plane trees, those black iron gates, the watchful lions and that long, sweeping driveway that carved its way up the hill. I couldn't remember at which point in my life I had lost the ball, but now I had found it again I recalled how important it had once been to me. It was not just my security, but the only link I had had to my father. How and when had I allowed that link to be broken? I didn't know.

So, the medals must have belonged to my father, the suite of diamonds a gift from him to my mother. I had never seen her wear them. I presumed it had taken on a sanctity like the clothes, shut away in the trunk with the chapter of her life she had closed. The two letters I presumed were love letters. I couldn't bear to read them. Not yet. I put them with the photo album and ball to take home with me. Then I lifted out a shoebox tied up with string. My mother had written 'Jupiter' on the lid in black pen. I put it on my knee, untied the string and lifted the lid. Inside were mementoes: from the passage to New York from Bordeaux aboard the *Phoenix*, menus, soap still wrapped in paper, bus tickets, and pressed flowers. I had never imagined my mother would keep so many things. She had been so practical, running the business once Coyote had gone. I hadn't thought there was much room for sentimentality. Her hoard of treasures surprised me.

I went through them, one by one. Each item reminded me of a moment. Each moment was more wonderful than the last. How much of those times I had forgotten. They had been good, possibly the happiest in my life. However, it was a single green feather that drew the curtain aside to reveal the stage in all its colour and splendour. I twirled it between my forefinger and thumb and I felt myself smile: I could see the sign now, as clear as if I were a child again: *Captain Crumble's Curiosity Store*.

17

'So who is your young friend?' asked Matias, his doughy fingers toying with a long green feather.

Coyote ruffled my hair. 'The *Chevalier* or, by his more popular name, Saint Mischa,' he replied with a smile.

Matias laughed, a great big belly laugh that echoed round his large ribcage as if it were inside a barrel. 'I've seen saints and he doesn't look like a saint to me! *Dios mio*, when did he fall from grace?'

'We escaped before he fell, Matias,' Coyote replied, pretending to be solemn. 'In Maurilliac they are building him a shrine. Pilgrims will come from all over Europe with their sick and their dying. We know better, though, don't we, Junior?' I recalled with a twinge of guilt my shameless exaggerations in the school playground and smiled up at him sheepishly.

'So, Saint Mischa, how do you like our store?' Matias asked, placing the feather behind my ear.

I liked Matias instantly and I adored the store. Matias was a giant of a man. His hair was a wild froth of black curls, his face soft and fleshy, his eyes as bright as candy. He spoke with a strong accent that I later learned was Chilean. He showed me where he came from on a map of the world pinned to the wall in the office out back. 'This little slice of a country,' he said, 'is so long and thin it contains the best of the continent – mountains, canyons, lakes, sea, desert and plains – the Atacama desert is the driest place on earth and only blossoms into flower once every ten years. Chile is where my heart is and one day, when I am old and no longer beautiful, I will return to Valparaiso and breed birds.' He had a way of saying things that rendered them funny, even when they weren't meant to be. It was hard to take him seriously. Once he told me that people expected him to be funny on account of the circumference of his belly. 'Fat people are here to amuse. If I became thin, no one would find me funny any more.' Coyote and Matias loved each other, that was plain to see. They patted each other on the back constantly, shared jokes I didn't understand, and plotted like a couple of thieves, sharing the spoils when they made money. They celebrated their successes over a bottle of champagne and commiserated in the same way, the only difference being the price of the champagne.

Captain Crumble's Curiosity Store was a warehouse on the outskirts of Jupiter, New Jersey. On the outside it was nothing spectacular, just a white, clapboard building sheltered by towering trees, with nothing to distinguish it except for the sign over the door. However, inside it was like Aladdin's cave. Every inch of the building contained something extraordinary that Coyote and Matias had managed to acquire, from furniture to trinkets. There were wooden cages containing stuffed birds, drum-bashing toy monkeys, antique desks from England exquisitely inlaid in walnut with secret drawers and cupboards. Ornate gilt mirrors from Italy, stuffed leather pigs from Germany, rich tapestries from France, vibrant silk lanterns from China, rugs from Turkey, gigantic carved doors from Morocco, glass from Prague, wooden toys from Bulgaria, leather and suede from Argentina, lapis lazuli from Chile, and silver from Peru. Daylight flooded in through windows high up on the walls, making everything glitter like gems. It was a wonderland for a young boy. I had never seen anything like it in Maurilliac. I stood transfixed, my eyes as wide as moons. Then, when I grew used to the dazzling sight, I spent hours clambering over tables and chests, chairs and dressers, to play with the cymbal-bashing mice, to open the secret drawers, to search behind things where there was always more treasure, hidden out of sight, often forgotten.

Everyone knew about Captain Crumble's Curiosity Store and they flocked to it from far and wide. Jupiter, being a seaside resort, was full of people in the summertime, but quiet during the winter months. However, Coyote's shop was always busy. Some days there weren't enough staff to look after all the visitors, so, when I wasn't at school, I was down at the warehouse, helping Coyote and Matias, proud of my growing sense of belonging. It wasn't long before I learned the trade and I discovered, to my surprise, that I was a natural salesman.

We lived like any normal family, Coyote, my mother and I. We arrived like a pair of new butterflies, the emotional baggage we had carried about Maurilliac left on the quay-side in Bordeaux like chrysalises. Our presence in Jupiter was celebrated. No one knew that my father had been German. They were interested not in my parentage, but in my pretty face and impish antics and they encouraged me to show off. I was only too happy to oblige, having tasted admiration that day at school. I soaked up their appreciation like Matias's Atacama desert, unused as I was to friendly people. The hostility of Maurilliac withdrew into the recesses of my mind and only resurfaced with humour when I told stories of Pierre and Armande, Yvette and Madame Duval and our dear old friend, Jacques Reynard.

Coyote returned from France like a conquering *chevalier*. There were small parties for him everywhere. The people of Jupiter all wanted to meet us and hear over and over again how Coyote won my mother's heart with his voice and his guitar. We enjoyed late autumn barbecues on the beach, the sun still hot, the wind turned cold, the leaves a spectacular palate of reds and golds, yellows and browns. We had tea in their gardens among apple trees laden with fruit, where dogs were treated like people and we were treated like royalty and every time we walked down Main Street the townspeople smiled and waved as if proud to know us. In time I thought less of Jacques Reynard and Daphne Halifax. I wrote once to Claudine – my mother posted the letter for me – but soon even she retreated to the recesses of my mind to reappear later in times of unhappiness. I dwelt little on the *château* and Maurilliac and I fell in love all over again; with America. America, land of milk and honey and Joy Springtoe.

I grew up in those early Jupiter days. I no longer shared my mother's bed. In our small white house on Beachcomber Drive I had my own room. In France I hadn't had much to call my very own, just my rubber ball and the Citroen Joy Springtoe had given me, along with a few wooden toys I had had as a small child. My mother hadn't had much money and what she did have was mostly spent on food and clothes. I wasn't used to excess. When we arrived in America, however, I was astounded by the quantity of luxurious things. They hadn't suffered from the war like we had. There were no rations. Butter and eggs and sugar were in huge supply. The shop windows on Main Street were bursting with goodies: toys, clothes, items for the home. It was a feast for the eyes, that short walk. Coyote wasted no time in spending on my behalf. My room was soon filled with toy cars, a train set, a smart red and blue quilt, a writing desk full of paper and pens and my very own box of paints. At night I didn't miss my mother's presence beside me, I relished my newfound independence. I had left my nightmare behind on the quayside with my old skin. I had left Pistou there too, and I hadn't even said goodbye.

Coyote indulged my mother with the extravagance of a very wealthy man. I knew we weren't rich. I had heard them discussing our flight from the *château* on the *Phoenix* bound for America, laughing because Coyote hadn't settled his hotel bill. They imagined Madame Duval's fury and roared with laughter. My mother felt sorry for the others, who would suffer horribly because of us, but Coyote just blew smoke rings into the air and chuckled. On the liner we hadn't enjoyed the luxury of first class. – that was a level of the ship I could only gaze up at – and our house on Beachcomber Drive was very modest. But Coyote showed no restraint in buying my mother dresses, hats and gloves, new shoes and silk stockings. He said, 'I want my girl to be the best-dressed girl in Jupiter.' And she was, there was no doubt about it.

In France my mother had done her own hair, rubbing it furiously with a towel to dry it. Now, she had her hair done once a week at Priscilla's Salon. Priscilla Rubie was a small red-haired woman who existed in a pink cloud of perfume and dreams and barely drew breath, so that one had to choose one's moment to speak with great precision, like crossing a busy road. Sometimes Margaret, the young beautician, painted my mother's nails while she sat with her head in a dryer, her hair curled up into rollers. She swung her hips more than ever when she walked down Main Street, glancing appreciatively at herself in shop windows, smiling softly, her cheeks enflamed with love and gratitude.

I had never seen my mother so happy and her happiness was infectious. I might have regained my voice but I was still a spy – and a good spy at that. It was a habit I hadn't managed to shake off. I was curious about people, what they were like when I was present, and what they became when they thought I was gone. My mother and Coyote were a perfect example of the differences. In my company they touched only occasionally. They sang together to his guitar, laughed at each other's jokes and kissed very rarely. When I lingered behind doors, peeped between cracks, listened through the walls, they were altogether more tactile. I watched them slow dancing to the gramophone in the parlour, kissing in the corridor. I even saw Coyote slide his hand up under my mother's blouse – at which point I returned to my room like a scalded cat. In those moments, my mother became less of a woman and more of a girl. She giggled and tossed her hair, looked up coyly from beneath her eyelashes, teased him by chewing on his ear lobe. They were playful, laughing about the silliest things, and they even had their own special language that I did not understand.

I was only just seven, but I wanted to be in love too. I went to school now as other children and no one knew my past. I could invent anything I wanted to. I was like a blank sheet of paper just waiting to be painted. So I told my fellow pupils that we had lived in the *château*, which was almost true. I described the fields of vines, the harvest, the river and the old stone bridge. I pretended I had walked tall in Maurilliac, sat eating *brioches* in cafés, chatting to the locals who were all my friends. Daphne Halifax was my grandmother, Jacques Reynard my grandfather – and my father? I told them he had been killed in the war. They didn't need to know any more than that.

I made friends quickly. There was no Laurent with his dark eyes and black hair to intimidate me, but there was no Claudine either. The girls were pretty and smiley. They seemed more outgoing than French girls, more confident and grown-up. But I missed Claudine with her toothy smile and mischievous twinkle. I wished I had been able to say goodbye. I wished I had had time to explain why I was leaving. Sometimes I caught myself wondering whether I would ever see her again.

In Bordeaux I had been stigmatised from birth. In Jupiter people took me as I was. I wasn't a sinner's spawn and I wasn't a saint either. I wasn't deformed and I wasn't a walking miracle. I was simply Mischa. For the first time in my life people reacted to my face and my spirit. I was instantly popular. The cool boy in the school. I was exotic, coming from France and speaking English with a foreign accent, but I was handsome, too. I realised, very quickly, what an advantage that was.

The first Sunday, we went to church. Jupiter Church wasn't Catholic, but it didn't matter: Coyote said it was the same God, just a different house. The night before, my stomach was scrambled with apprehension. I remembered all too well the walks to Mass on a Sunday morning, anticipating the hatred, cowering against my mother's legs, my hand trembling in hers. Père Abel-Louis' face rose up in my mind like a hideous gargoyle, questioning our sudden disappearance and my shameful lies. 'I'll find you wherever you are,' he was saying, his voice hard as granite. I drew the sheet up to my neck and remained awake for as long as possible with my eyes open, afraid to close them in case I dreamed my nightmare again. I didn't dream at all that night, but awoke with my belly turned to liquid.

Coyote looked raffishly handsome in a suit and hat, and my mother had on a new pale blue dress imprinted with small flowers. Her hair was shiny and curled over at the ends like a movie star, her face dolled up with make-up. She wore a tidy hat and gloves that almost reached her elbows. When she saw my face her expression darkened with that old, stomach-clawing anxiety that would never quite leave her. 'Darling, are you all right?' It hadn't occurred to her that I might be nervous.

'I don't want to go to Mass,' I said.

'It isn't Mass, my love,' she said, sinking to her knees and taking my arms in her soft gloved hands. 'It's different here.' When I didn't look convinced she continued. 'The pastor is a very kind man, Mischa. He's not at all like Père Abel-Louis, I promise.'

'He can't find us here, can he?' I asked. My mother's face relaxed into a smile.

'No, he can't. You'll never see him, ever again.'

'I didn't really see Heaven, or Papa, or Jesus or an angel. I didn't have a vision. God had nothing to do with my voice coming back, it was Coyote,' I blurted, unburdening myself of a terrible secret.

My mother frowned. 'Coyote?' She looked up at him. He looked as surprised as she did. 'How did he do that?'

'Because he's magic. He saw Pistou . . .'

'Is that why you don't want to go to church?' she said, ignoring what must have sounded to her like a childish rant. 'Because you're afraid God will punish you for lying?'

'Yes.' It was a relief to share my worry.

'Well, it's not a good thing to lie on the whole. But in this case, I don't think God will mind. After all, He gave you back your voice, whether it was with Coyote's help or not. That kind of miracle is God-sent, whichever way you look at it.'

'So, it'll be all right?'

'Everything's different now.' She touched my nose with her finger like she used to do when I was very small. 'You're my *chevalier*, aren't you? *Chevaliers* aren't afraid of anything.'

I had expected the church to be a dark and imposing stone building with a spire rising up into the cloud. But it was a white clapboard building like our house and situated on the sea front, beside the little cafés and boarding houses that swarmed with people during the summer months. Now it was quiet, the vacation over, the holidaymakers gone back to their homes and their lives. The locals all knew each other. They wore large smiles and their Sunday best and the Vicar,

Reverend Cole, stood at the door in his black and white robes, greeting them all warmly, shaking their hands, sharing the odd joke.

Priscilla Rubie bustled over to comment on my mother's new dress and hat, her husband looking apologetic as she chattered on like one of Coyote's clockwork mice. 'It really is a lovely dress. How clever of you to have chosen it. The colour goes so well with your skin. You have that gorgeous olive-brown skin we Americans envy the French for. Why, I feel all pasty and grey beside you and it wasn't so long ago that we were sitting in our garden, bathing in the sun, isn't that right, Paul?' Paul took her by the arm and ushered her into the church before she began her next sentence.

Reverend Cole raised his eyebrows when he saw us approach and smiled, revealing a perfect set of ivory teeth. 'Welcome to Jupiter,' he said to my mother, taking her hand and squeezing it between his. He had a large face with small blue eyes rather too close together and a big, aquiline nose. His hair was grey and shiny like feathers. I imagined it repelled the rain like a duck's back.

'Thank you,' my mother replied graciously. 'We're very happy to have settled here.'

'Coyote has made a good marriage,' he continued. My mother lost her tongue. She was mute with shock. 'I hear you tied the knot in Paris.' He turned to Coyote. 'Very romantic.'

'Well, I don't like to do things by halves,' Coyote replied smoothly. 'Junior, this is Reverend Cole.'

'My son, Mischa,' my mother croaked and I extended my hand. I knew Coyote was lying. I wasn't shocked; after all, I had a made a friend of lying back in Bordeaux and we had become the very best of buddies. I was thrilled to enter into the spirit of it all with Coyote. I knew he'd be pleased if I did.

'I loved Paris,' I said enthusiastically. 'It was a big wedding with lots of friends. They would have got married in Maurilliac if it hadn't been for Père Abel-Louis. He's really the Devil, you see. *Maman* wanted God at her wedding. God isn't in Maurilliac.' Reverend Cole frowned down at me as if I were a curiosity in Coyote's store.

Coyote chuckled and ruffled my hair. 'Kids,' he said, shaking his head. As we moved off, he leaned down to me and said, 'You talk chicken shit, Junior, but you're my ally.' I walked ahead with my chin high. I could hear my mother hissing angrily at him behind me, her voice rising until it was in danger of becoming a squawk.

I enjoyed Reverend Cole's service. For a start there were songs. A round-faced, bespectacled woman played the piano with aplomb and everyone sang heartily. My mother didn't sing and she ignored Coyote. He sang regardless, his voice deep and gravelly, but even that failed to soften the hard expression on my mother's face.

Afterwards there were drinks and biscuits at Mrs Slade's house. As we had accepted her invitation we couldn't back out now, even though my mother made it quite clear that she wanted to go home. 'She's feeling a little tired,' said Coyote when we arrived.

'You do look pale, dear,' said Mrs Slade, hurrying over to get her a cup of coffee. 'This will put the colour back into your cheeks.' She laughed then, to my amusement, made a little snorting noise like a pig. I ignored my mother's ill humour, and tried to make Mrs Slade laugh again.

'I prefer wine,' I announced.

'Aren't you a little young for alcohol,' she exclaimed.

'I was raised on it,' I said, then listened.

'Oh, you little devil . . . *oink*!' I laughed with her, glancing up at Coyote. But Coyote wasn't laughing, he was watching my mother apprehensively.

'Let's raise our coffee cups to you both,' continued Mrs Slade. 'Newly weds.' She squeezed my mother's arm. 'You're quite the blushing bride.'

'I hardly think so,' replied my mother coolly. 'It's not the first time.'

'No, of course not,' said Mrs Slade, grinning down at me.

'After all, Mischa wasn't conceived by immaculate conception.' My mother's tone was dry, but Mrs Slade took it as a joke.

'Immaculate conception. How very funny . . . *oink*! How are you settling in, dear?' she asked my mother.

'Very well, thank you.'

'I imagine it's a little overwhelming. So many people to meet. Everyone wanting a piece of you. Only today I was at Priscilla's and I heard Gray Thistlewaite talk of getting you both on to the radio. Coyote probably hasn't told you that Gray runs the local radio from her sitting-room on Main Street. She has an hour devoted to people's stories. Nothing exotic, of course. Nothing much happens around here at this time of year. Your story would be wonderful to listen to. I butted in and told her it was a splendid idea. The whole of Jupiter is talking about you. You see,' she leaned in closer, 'we haven't seen anyone as pretty as you except at the movies.' My mother was flattered. She smiled although I could tell she was reluctant to do so. 'Now, you go along in and get to know everyone. Don't be shy, we're all friends here.'

On the way home in the car my mother and Coyote had their first argument. 'Why have you told everyone we're married?' she exclaimed furiously. 'Everyone's asking about our wedding in Paris. What wedding in Paris?'

'Calm down, sweetheart,' he began.

'I'm not going to calm down. How dare you not consult me? I feel degraded.' Her French accent cut into the words with fury. 'Do you have so little respect for me? Do you?'

'I have enormous respect for you, Anouk. I love you,' he said. I sat in the back trying to be invisible.

'Do you love me?'

'Yes, I do.'

Her voice shrank and she sounded like a little girl. 'Then why not marry me for real?'

18

My mother stayed in their bedroom for three days, refusing to let Coyote in. When he tried, she shouted at him in French, throwing things at the door so that they smashed loudly against the wood. I knew she'd let me in, but I didn't want to see her. I feared she'd decide to move back to Maurilliac and I was just beginning to settle into Jupiter. So I pretended everything was okay. Coyote and I had breakfast together. I got myself ready for school and took the big yellow bus with the other kids. After school I hung out with my friends a little before walking home beneath the coppery trees. Coyote and I didn't discuss my mother's self-imposed siege. We sang songs to the guitar and played cards. But I could tell that Coyote was anxious. His face looked drawn and tired, his eyes hollow, his mouth fighting the impulse to turn downwards like an unhappy clown.

I didn't understand their fight. It didn't bother me that they weren't married. No one knew the truth. Besides, surely it was romantic to have got married in Paris. I had never been to Paris, but I had seen pictures and knew the history. It was the cultural centre of Europe and the most beautiful city in the world. Why on earth would my mother mind so much that people thought she had married there?

On the morning of the third day she emerged. She looked thin and pale. Her eyes were dull with resignation. Coyote leaped up from the table, but she raised her hand to keep him at a distance. 'I will go along with the charade, God help me,' she said in a quiet voice. 'I am a fool, but what can I do?' She bent down and planted a kiss on my temple. 'I have one condition.'

'Anything,' Coyote said, the colour burning his cheeks.

'I want a ring.'

'You can have any ring you want.'

'It's a question of morality, Coyote. Not for me, but for my son. You understand?'

'I understand.'

'Now, let's not talk about it any more. I want to go back to how we were before.' Coyote pulled out a chair and she sat down. She took my hand in hers.

'How are you, my love?'

'Fine,' I replied, chewing on a piece of toast.

'Have you had fun at school?'

'Yes.'

'Good.'

Coyote poured her a cup of coffee, which she drank, savouring the taste by closing her eyes and sighing contentedly.

I was delighted that they had made up, not least because Coyote looked happy again. I was relieved I didn't have to go back to Madame Duval and Père Abel-Louis. I walked to the bus stop with a spring in my step, humming Coyote's songs, the sun streaming through the drying leaves in shafts. I felt the whole world opening up for me, presenting endless possibilities and opportunities. I loved Jupiter, my new friends at school, the small seaside community, but mostly I loved who I was. For the first time I was happy in my own skin.

After school my mother drove me out to Captain Crumble's Curiosity Store. On the third finger of her left hand sparkled a small diamond ring against a plain gold marriage band. She looked different about the eyes. There was something hard in them that hadn't been there before. In spite of all that she had been through in the aftermath of the war, she had retained her innocence. That had now gone. In its place was an unfamiliar look of worldliness.

'Your ring looks pretty,' I said. We had now begun to speak English, even when we were alone together. Only when my mother was angry, hurt or overwhelmed with excitement, did she revert to speaking French.

'It does, doesn't it,' she replied, turning her hand and glancing at it with a sigh.

'Is everything going to be all right now?'

'Everything is going to be just fine, Mischa.'

'I like it here.'

'I know you do.'

'I like the Curiosity Store.'

'So do I.'

'I'm going to help out after school. Can I?'

'Of course you can. I'm going to help out too.'

'You are?' It shouldn't have seemed odd that my mother wanted to work. After all, she had worked at the *château*. But it did seem odd somehow – in her new dresses she no longer looked the working type. Perhaps it was the determined look on her face that had replaced the look of resignation that had mollified her features in France, as if she knew in her heart that although Coyote had rescued us from Madame Duval we were still on our own: *maman* and her little *chevalier*. Just the two of us. Always just the two of us.

At the warehouse Matias greeted us in his deep, resonant voice. 'Extra hands! Coyote, the relief force has arrived!' I pulled the green feather he had given me out of my pocket and stuck it behind my ear. He smiled down at me, his large face aglow with enthusiasm. 'Now you look like you were raised here with the Indians,' he said, laughing heartily.

'Where's Coyote?' my mother asked, striding past him.

'Out back, in the office, working on some papers for a change.'

Coyote hated paperwork. It was a struggle for him to sit still at his desk. He was a free spirit, happier when his wings were spread. Paperwork was like a lead weight hanging from his big toe. But my mother was going to relieve him of this burden. She wanted a job in the store. She wanted to take part in his operation. She needed to know how things were done.

While my mother went to talk to Coyote, I followed Matias around the warehouse like an adoring puppy. He told me how they acquired the goods. 'From all over the world, Mischa. From Chile to Russia, and all the countries in between.'

'You must travel a lot,' I said, picking up a large ivory tusk.

'I don't travel as much as I used to.' He placed his hands on his stomach. 'It's not so easy getting around these days. I was thin as a child. You might find it hard to believe, but I was nicknamed *flaco* – skinny. Coyote is the one who travels the world. He returns with the goods.'

'Are they valuable?'

'Some are, some aren't.' He bent down and whispered in my ear. 'But I can assure you that to the customer *everything* is precious, hard to come by, rare. You understand?' I nodded. 'The first thing you need to learn in order to work in the store is that *everything* is priceless. The customer is exchanging money for something that is unique. This elephant foot, for example. A one-off. Mrs Slate won't find it in Mrs Gardner's parlour, or in any parlour in New Jersey. There is only one.'

'Is there a three-legged elephant hobbling about some-where?'

He chuckled. 'I don't think so. The elephant would have been dead first.'

'What's it for?'

He shrugged his big shoulders. 'A dustbin, perhaps. An umbrella stand.'

'And this?' I picked up the ivory tusk.

He took it from me and held it up. 'This once belonged to a rhino. Sharp, isn't it? An ornament. As I said, no one else will have one. It's an exhibit.'

'How does Coyote find them?' I imagined him with a gun, shooting animals in Africa, and felt my admiration for him swell.

'He has his ways and means. The thing is not to ask too many questions. Coyote is an enigma. He's very secretive. He doesn't like people to know too much about him.' He lowered his voice. 'He's a shadow, Mischa. I don't think anyone knows the real Coyote.' *Except me*, I thought proudly. *I know him better than anyone else, even my mother.*

Matias took me around the warehouse, telling me about the origins of some of the items. I was curious about each one. There was a 'magic carpet' from Turkey that Matias said had once possessed the power to fly; a set of miniature chairs from England, supposedly the ones at the Mad Hatter's Tea Party; and a whole suit of armour almost as small as me. 'In medieval times, Mischa, men were as small as you. Look, here's the shield and sword. For a "*chevalier*" you don't look too familiar with them!' He laughed, patting me on the back, nearly sending me flying into the heap of wares. There was a beautiful tapestry of Bacchus, the god of wine, surrounded by wood nymphs and a unicorn in a lustrous green forest. The colours were rich, though faded. Matias unfolded it proudly. 'This,' he said, 'was found in France at the beginning of the war.'

'It's beautiful,' I said truthfully. There was a similar one at the *château*, hanging in the hall.

He rolled it up again. 'Do you know what this is?' He held

up a long, patchwork quilt. My eyes opened wide with disbelief.

'The old man of Virginia's patchwork coat!' I said breathlessly.

Matias frowned. 'It's the coat of many colours and older than America!'

Matias was distracted by a woman and her son. 'Can I help?' he said, opening his arms like a father welcoming his family home.

'Yes, you can,' she replied. 'I'm looking for a present for my daughter-in-law.' She didn't seem very happy about it.

'What is she like?' asked Matias.

'Ask him, he married her,' she replied with a shrug. The young man sighed. He was tall, like Matias, but willowy, dwarfing his mother like a tree. 'They're coming for Thanksgiving and we're celebrating her birthday,' she continued. Her face was large, with big spongy features that sagged down into her neck. 'Go on, Antonio, tell him what she's like.'

'She's very feminine,' he began. His mother snorted. He pushed on. 'She likes pretty things. For the house?'

'I have just the thing,' said Matias, setting off towards the back of the warehouse. Mother and son didn't notice me loitering behind the elephant foot.

She turned to him and started to hiss. 'You don't call, you don't write, you barely come around. Anyone would think you lived in a different country. You're in the same State, for God's sake. What would your grandmother say if she were alive? I brought you up to put your family first.' Antonio tried to appease her but she shrugged him off. 'That's okay. I'll die alone. I'll be fine.'

'But . . .'

'Your father? He's never home. Don't even ask about your father, Antonio. He says it's work but it's probably another woman. I can take it. What else can I do?' She lifted her chin and breathed deeply through her nose.

Matias returned with an antique box of beautifully cut, glass dressing-table bottles with round silver lids. 'She'd love that,' said Antonio, eyes brightening.

'That's too good for her!' said his mother.

'Mamma . . .'

'What's she going to do with them? Hasn't she enough lotions already?'

Matias turned to me. 'Mischa, come and have a look at this.' I emerged from behind the elephant foot, my hands in my pockets, pretending I had been busy.

'What is it?' I asked, peering into the case.

'This used to belong to a Victorian lady. You see the initial W? That stands for Wellington. It used to belong to the Duchess of Wellington. This, my good lady, is a genuine antique of great value all the way from England.'

'It's lovely,' said Antonio. 'How much is it?'

'It'll be too expensive, Antonio. It belonged to a duchess,' his mother argued.

'You can have it for twelve dollars, if you give me a smile.' Matias grinned down at the ill-humoured woman.

'What is there to smile about?' she asked gloomily. 'I never see my son any more. If I had known I would die alone I would never have gone through those twenty-four hours of labour.'

'Mamma . . .'

'Do you love your mother?' she asked me.

'Yes,' I replied.

'Don't forget her like Antonio when you fall in love, will you? Don't forget your old mother. She's given her life for you.' Antonio gave me an apologetic smile. 'You'll give that to me for twelve bucks?' She turned to Matias.

'Twelve bucks for you,' he said.

'Twelve bucks it is, then,' she said, her face lifting into a smile. 'That's as close to a duchess as I'll get.' She laughed with pleasure. 'You can tell her it belonged to royalty, Antonio. She'd like that, for sure.'

'And she'll like you for giving it,' said Matias.

'If she comes in here, small woman with a sharp, pointed face and blonde hair, tell her I'd like the boy.'

Matias laughed heartily. I was shocked. 'If she gives me a good price he might be for sale.' He patted my back.

'You're too good for me,' she said, pinching my cheek until it hurt. 'And too expensive. You're worth your weight in gold. Handsome too. Antonio was never blessed with good looks. What can you do but survive with what God gave you?' She let go of my cheek. An hour after she had gone it was still tender.

'Your first customers,' said Matias with a chuckle. 'We get a lot of those in here.'

'Her son hardly said anything.'

'They never do. They're dominated by their mothers, *pobrecitos*! Those Italian matriarchs see their daughters-in-law as competition. I'd like to be a fly on the wall for their Thanksgiving dinner.'

'Did that case of bottles really belong to a duchess in England?'

'Of course,' Matias responded, but he had a twinkle in his eye.

'Why was it not more expensive?'

'Everything is relative. What is expensive for one person is a bargain for another.'

'She smiled though, when you told her the price.'

'*Si, señor*, she did. She's probably got a whole lot of cash hidden under the mattress in her bedroom. I know the type.'

'Do you think her daughter-in-law will come in?' Matias laughed at my anxious face.

'You have to learn to take a joke, *Miguelito*,' he said. But he couldn't have known that those kinds of threats were never jokes at the *château*.

I left Matias to go and find my mother and Coyote. I walked through the warehouse like a panther, my feet silent on the wooden floor. I reached the office but, instead of going straight in, I stood on tiptoe and peered through the window. My mother was sitting on Coyote's knee and they were kissing. I remained there for some time, just staring. I had a strong sense of *déjà vu*, recalling the time Pistou and I had spied on Jacques Reynard and Yvette in the folly. Coyote's hand was on my mother's leg, having slipped up her skirt, and they were laughing between kisses. They had obviously made up. My mother's ring glittered on her finger, catching the light in the dim room. Her small hat was still on her head, her green cardigan buttoned up, her pearls hanging down her front. Coyote's hand toyed with the fastening on her stocking. She looked small on his knee, like a little girl, though there was nothing innocent about their kissing. I stayed a long while, fascinated by these secrets of the adult world, then, for fear of being caught spying by Matias – or worse, my mother – I retreated into the warehouse to help with the sudden arrival of a large group of customers.

My life in Jupiter flourished. I grew into my skin and for the first time it fitted to perfection. I was happy to be me. We celebrated Thanksgiving with Matias and his wife, Maria Elena, with a great big turkey Coyote claimed he had killed himself. I sat at the table, my plate piled high with food, and delighted in the feeling of being part of a family, a proper family.

'You want to know about Thanksgiving, Junior?' said Coyote, taking a swig of warm red wine. I nodded, eager to learn as much as I could about this bright new country I now claimed as my own. 'North-east America was home to the native peoples, who made their living for thousands of years by farming and fishing. Then the settlers came out from Europe in the sixteenth century and killed most of them off, poor sods. If they weren't killed in warfare they died of disease. Many of the first settlers were Puritan pilgrims, some of whom sailed to Cape Cod on board the famous *Mayflower*. They were English, mostly persecuted for their religion, determined to found a brave new world in America. They called the newly discovered territory, New England. Thanksgiving is celebrated by all Americans and commemorates the end of the *Mayflower* pilgrims' first year and their successful harvest.' He paused a moment and settled his eyes on my mother. They were heavy with drink and affection. 'I raise my glass to the most recent arrivals to this brave new world. I celebrate their flight from France and their safe crossing and wish them a future that is both healthy and happy, but also full of opportunity. Because that is what America is to me: the land of endless possibility.'

19

There was no avoiding Gray Thistlewaite's 'Another True Story' hour on local radio. My mother refused to do it. She felt it was beneath her dignity to speak about her life to a whole community of strangers. She relished her privacy, the fact that people knew hardly anything about her. She was loving her anonymity, having been unable to enjoy such a luxury in Maurilliac. But Gray Thistlewaite was not the sort of woman to whom one said no. At first sight she appeared a mild-natured grandmother. She was small and slight with neat grey hair tied into a soft bun at the back of her head. Her face was wide and pretty with bright blue eyes, the colour of the clear autumn sky above Jupiter. Her lips were full and pink, her skin pale and powdered, her scent lily of the valley. What gave away the rod of steel hidden down her back was her determined jaw. It jutted forward a little too much, the bone too brittle for such a gentle face. It didn't do any good to offend her. That jaw would jut out even further and she would stiffen, reducing you to pulp with those blue eyes turned to winter. Once she got an idea into her head, there was no avoiding it. It was early December, we had been in Jupiter almost three months and were very much in her sights. We couldn't decline her request without being rude.

Coyote understood my mother's position and was wise enough not to push her. He had witnessed her temper and wasn't keen to repeat the experience. He had managed, so far, to avoid going on the show himself, so there was only one other option: me. I was delighted. Yvette had always listened to the wireless in France. I was thrilled that I was going to be on it and overwhelmed by the thought that hundreds of people would hear me. 'She only wants to know how you enjoy Jupiter, Mischa. You can tell them about the *château*, the harvest, the wine. You can tell them about Jacques Reynard and Joy Springtoe if you like,' said my mother, smoothing the creases out of my shirt.

'Don't you think you should tell him what not to say?' Coyote asked.

'No,' my mother replied. 'He knows, don't you, Mischa?'

She was right. I did know. There were things we never talked about, not even on our own. Things we both wanted to forget. Things I would never tell a soul. We had a silent pact, my mother and I.

'Are you sure you don't mind?' she asked with a frown, perhaps feeling guilty that I was being sent on her behalf.

'I don't mind,' I replied, shuffling my feet with excitement. She had no idea what this meant to me. 'I *want* to go,' I said with emphasis.

'Then you shall go,' said Coyote. 'But remember, you must always have your sword drawn, ready, just in case.'

Gray Thistlewaite's house was small and tidy, just like you would expect a grandmother's home to be. It was warm, with a fire burning in the grate, trinkets on tables and photographs in ornate silver frames of sons in uniform and smiling children. There were pictures on the walls of boats, and hounds racing across the English countryside in pursuit of a fox. There was not a surface that didn't have something on it, something of sentimental value, like a little enamel box or a posy of dried flowers, a porcelain doll or glass figurines. The place smelt of wood-smoke and her perfume. There was a set of shelves against one wall, stuffed full of books. On a round table in the corner, next to two windows veiled with lace curtains, were the black box and microphones of her home-grown radio station.

It had been arranged that Maria Elena, Matias's wife, should take me, in order to avoid Gray Thistlewaite persuading Coyote or my mother to participate in the show. Maria Elena accepted a cup of tea in a pretty china cup and saucer and sat on the blue floral sofa, while I followed Gray to the table.

'Come and sit down,' she said, pulling out a chair. 'This is my modest little radio station. It doesn't look like much, but it communicates with the good people of Jupiter and gives enormous pleasure to the old folks who can't get out.' She obviously didn't consider herself old. I watched her take her seat, smooth her tweed skirt and white cotton blouse. She put on a pair of small silver spectacles, which hung on a chain around her neck, gave a self-important sniff and tapped the microphone. 'Before we start, Mischa, I want to tell you one thing: just be yourself. Don't be nervous, they're all friends out there. They just want to hear your story and so do I. Shame they can't see how handsome you are. Never mind, I'll be sure to tell them. Now, put these on.' She gave me a pair of large black headphones, which I placed on my ears, and pushed a microphone on a stand towards me so that it stood right in front of my lips. 'Can you hear me, Mischa?' she asked. I nodded. 'No, dear, speak into it.'

'I can hear you,' I replied obediently.

'Good.' She looked at the large clock on the table. 'I'll begin in a few minutes. I have a few notices to share before I begin the interview, so bear with me.' My heart began to race and I felt my body tremble Maria Elena smiled at me with encouragement, willing me to do well. We sat in silence and watched the clock. The second hand seemed to move so slowly. When, finally, it reached eleven o'clock, Gray pressed a button on the mysterious black box and began to speak in a low, whispering voice.

'Hello out there, you good folks of Jupiter. Welcome to my show. For those who don't know, it's Another True Story hour and I'm Gray Thistlewaite, in your living-rooms, in your kitchens and in your lives, making them better and brighter in my own small way. Today, I have a very interesting guest. He's as charming as he is handsome, but before I introduce him there are a few notices I would like to share: Hilary Winer is throwing a little pre-Christmas party at her store, Toad Hall, on Main Street on Thursday night at six; you're all welcome to stop by. Santa Claus will be there to entertain the children, so look out for that man in red and put in your requests for Christmas Eve. Deborah and John Trichett have had a baby boy called Huckleberry. Please don't send flowers. Deborah is allergic and we can't have her sneezing over the new arrival, can we? Clothes and toys are most welcome and Hilary Winer says she has a new range of delightful baby blankets, hats and mittens in baby-boy blue. Margaret Gilligan's bitch, Hazel, is in heat so please keep all dogs away. She doesn't want another litter of mongrels. Stanford Johnson's Christmas trees are now on sale at Maple Farm. First come first served, so get on down there before he runs out. It's not healthy to be disappointed at this time of joy and celebration. It wouldn't do to forget Captain Crumble's Curiosity Store which has something for everyone this Christmas. Which brings me on to Coyote's new stepson, Mischa Fontaine. He's right here with me now and ready to talk to you good people of Jupiter. Hello, Mischa.'

'Hello, *madame*,' I replied, not knowing how to address her.

'Call me Gray, they all do,' she said with a smile. 'How are you liking your new town?'

'I love it,' I said enthusiastically.

'I'm so pleased. We love it too. Now, tell all those listening out there how old you are.'

'I'm just seven.'

'Seven. You're getting on a bit. Your English is mighty good for a French boy.'

'My grandfather was Irish.'

'My great ancestor was English. He was one of the very first to settle here. He was a Lord.'

'Did he come out on the *Mayflower*?' I asked. She raised her eyebrows, impressed with my knowledge.

'Why, he did indeed, Mischa. We might even be related.' She laughed lightly and her eyes twinkled at me behind her glasses. I warmed to her, settled into my chair and no longer felt nervous. 'Tell everyone what life was like for you in France?'

'We lived in a *château* in the small town of Maurilliac.'

'Now, just to inform our listeners, a *château* is a castle, right?'

'A big house,' I corrected.

'How wonderfully grand. I'm sure we're all proud to have a genuine French aristocrat in our midst. Tell us a little about the *château*, Mischa.'

'It has a vineyard and we made wine.'

'I bet it tasted good,' she said.

'I was raised on it,' I replied, recalling the laughter that comment had provoked from Mrs Slade. Gray Thistlewaite laughed and shook her head. I felt my confidence grow.

'Do you miss France?'

'I don't think of it much, now I'm here. When I think about it, I miss the vineyard and the river and my friend Claudine. There's a folly which looks down the valley. It's very pretty, especially at sunset. I once saw Jacques Reynard and Yvette kissing in there.'

'Who are Jacques Reynard and Yvette?'

'Jacques runs the vineyard and Yvette is the cook. They are in love.'

'Love is bountiful in France. Tell me, how did your mother meet Coyote?'

'He came to Maurilliac with his guitar and his magic and she fell in love with him.' I blushed, hoping my mother wouldn't mind.

'Is he magic?'

'Oh, yes, he's magic.'

'How so?'

'I just know,' I said, not wanting to betray him.

'Oh, you must tell. He's one of the most beloved characters in Jupiter. But I never knew he was magic.'

'He has a special gift.'

'Really, what sort of gift?'

'Well . . .' I hesitated.

'Well?' Her jaw stiffened and stuck out. 'We're all longing to know.'

'He gave me back my voice.'

'Had you lost it?' She looked at me incredulously.

'I didn't have one.'

Her forehead creased into a frown. 'You were mute?'

'Yes. Coyote came and my voice returned.'

'How incredible! How did he do it?'

'He told me it would come back and it did.' She didn't know whether or not to believe me.

'Just like that?'

'Just like that. He's magic.' I was tempted to tell her about Pistou, but decided not to. If she didn't believe Coyote was magic, she wouldn't believe in Pistou. She wouldn't believe in the wind either, even though she was a grandmother. 'Everyone in Maurilliac thought it was a miracle. Perhaps it was, but I'm not a saint. *Maman* says God gave my voice back to me, but really it was Coyote. With his magic.'

'Tell us about the wedding,' she said, changing the subject.

'It was in Paris,' I said, knowing I was now on shaky ground. I remembered my sword and drew it a little out of its holder, just in case.

'How romantic. I bet you were best man,' she said, smiling across at me with affection.

'I don't know,' I replied. I didn't know what 'best man' was and I had never been to a wedding. 'I think I was second best. Coyote was the best, that day.' Again she laughed. I laughed too, at the pleasure of entertaining her.

'Tell me, what happened to your father?'

'He died in the war,' I replied.

'I'm so sorry.' She reached out and touched my hand.

'Me too. He would have liked Coyote,' I said in all innocence.

'I'll bet he would, too,' she said with a chuckle. 'I don't know whether you've been playing with me, Mischa, but you've been most entertaining. Will you come on the show again?'

'Yes please,' I replied, truthfully.

'To all you folks out there, I say, we're none of us too old or cynical to believe in magic. It's healthy to have a fertile imagination, and entertaining too. I'll put Mischa back on his magic carpet now and watch him fly off to Captain Crumble's Curiosity Store to his magic stepfather, Coyote. If any of you out there would like a little magic in your own homes, you know where to find it. You heard it here first. Gray Thistlewaite, in your living-rooms, in your kitchens and in your lives, making them better and brighter in my own small way. Thank you for listening.'

Maria Elena took me for an ice-cream. I liked Maria Elena, she was warm and gentle and spoke with an accent that held within it the resonance of exotic places. 'You did well,' she said and I recognised pride in her eyes and something else, almost motherly. 'Gray doesn't believe in magic, but I do. Though I believe the magic is within you. More than you know.'

'Coyote really is magic,' I insisted.

'All children are magic and he's just a big boy.'

'He saw Pistou, but he won't admit it.' I had never confided that before.

'Who is Pistou?'

I felt foolish for having mentioned him, but now that I had, I couldn't turn back. 'My friend. No one else can see him but me. He lives at the *château*. I left without saying goodbye.' I pulled a sad face.

'And Coyote saw him?' She didn't dismiss me with an amused look, but stared at me, her expression serious.

'Yes, Coyote saw him. I know he did.'

'I'm sure you're right. Don't worry that you didn't say goodbye, he'll understand.'

'Do you think?'

'I know.' She ran her knuckles softly down my cheek. 'Spirits have a greater understanding of the world than we do.' I didn't really know what she meant. Pistou wasn't a spirit, he was a magic boy.

'I'll return and see him one day, won't I?'

'Of course you will, Mischa. France is just a plane ride away, like Chile. I miss my home country, like you miss France. But it won't go away. It will always be there to go back to and so will Pistou. Trust me on that.'

After my interview on the radio, everyone wanted to know more about the miracle of my restored voice. Coyote shrugged it off when he was asked about his magic, putting it down to 'a young boy's imagination', but I knew the truth. He was magic, however much he denied it. He knew too, because when he smiled at me his eyes communicated his collusion in a twinkle. My mother said I had done all right, though she sat me down and told me what a best man was. She was anxious that I was being encouraged to lie. 'I don't think you should talk about our "marriage", if it means lying,' she said. After a while it no longer mattered because no one asked. As far as they were concerned, my mother and Coyote had married in Paris. No one doubted it. They were far more interested in me, anyhow. I hadn't intended to bring my own lies over from France. I had wanted to start afresh, with a clean slate. But it was now unavoidable. Unlike the people of Maurilliac, they did not consider me a saint in Jupiter. They smiled at me indulgently, shook their heads and showed only delight in what they believed to be the fancies of a little boy who had lost his father in the war, been uprooted from his home and been taken overseas to a strange place. They were kind, but they didn't believe me. 'He's such a handsome boy,' they said, as if that excused everything. The children believed me, though, and I found myself holding forth in the playground about my vision.

My first year in Jupiter was the happiest of my life. Or certainly, the one I remember the best. Coyote, my mother and I went to the pictures when the store made money. As well as celebrating with imported champagne we watched a movie, had dinner in a restaurant or spent the day on the beach. One moment Coyote was rich, the next he had nothing. 'I live by the seat of my pants,' he had once said, ruffling my hair. 'You'll understand one day when you're older.' He travelled a lot. Much of the time he wasn't around. I missed him, but our home was so cosy and happy that it made missing him easier to cope with. I spent a lot of time at Matias and Maria Elena's house. They became second parents to me, spoiling me with toys and games and laughter. I felt cherished by them and understood. Maria Elena read me poetry and stories of magic and mystery which I adored. I'd snuggle up beside her, breathe in the warm, spicy smell of her skin, and bask in another woman's affection.

I played the guitar well and had begun to compose songs of my own. I hung out with boys from school and we made music together. Joe Lampton played the saxophone, Frank Mullet the drums and Solly Halpstein the piano. We'd gather at Joe's house – his mother had a piano in her sitting-room – and we'd play things together. Not that we sounded very good. In fact, we sounded awful, but we didn't care. We felt we were making music and it was better than loitering outside in the cold.

My mother kept the accounts for the store and Maria Elena became her closest friend. She and Matias joined us for dinner and we went over to them. Sometimes, I'd go to sleep in their house and Coyote would lift me into the car afterwards and drive home, carrying me up to bed while I still slept. The four of them did everything together and I tagged along. Matias and Maria Elena had no children. I wondered whether they had suffered a disappointment like Daphne Halifax, but I knew it would be impolite to ask.

In summer the tourists came. The small cafés and boarding houses vibrated with noise, the beach teemed with sunbathers, the shops burst at the seams with customers. Couples wandered up and down the boardwalk, children played in the sand, dogs rushed in and out of the water, everyone was happy. Coyote came and went, filling us with love and merriment, returning with more extraordinary things he had found on his travels. He always had stories to tell of the people he had met and the places he had been to. But I loved the Old Man of Virginia best of all and made him tell me those tales over and over again. Sometimes he returned with a beard, other times clean shaven, looking dapper in shiny shoes and a newly pressed suit. Sometimes he hadn't shaved for days and thick stubble covered his face like the cornfields after harvest time; other times he was as polished as the saddle of a prince. He brought me gifts whichever way he returned, rich or poor. He never arrived empty handed. Sometimes there was fabric for my mother, who had started making her own clothes again, and toys for me; other times shoes, or jewellery, a little box or a book – always something and she was always pleased.

I noticed the affection growing between them, like the roots of a tree that burrow down deep into the soil as the tree spreads its branches to the sky. It was in the way they looked at each other, the little smiles they exchanged, the manner in which they brushed against each other or tenderly glided a hand over an arm or shoulder. Coyote's face changed completely when my mother came into the room. It lit up with joy like one of his red silk lanterns from China. His eyes followed her, their expression loving, his lips suddenly swollen with sensuality. My mother flirted with him, striking poses when she stood as if aware all the time of him watching her.

When he went off on his travels she took to laying the table for him from the day he left to the day he returned. He never gave us warning of his homecoming. She worked hard in the store in order to prevent herself pining, but in the evenings she'd sit by the window and stare up at the stars, as she had done in the stable block, as if they had the power to carry him home. She talked about him all the time, her face rosy with the glow of love. When he finally walked through the door she'd fall on him, smothering his face with kisses, her arms around his neck, forgetting that I was there, watching. Then he'd stride over and pull me into his arms. 'So, how're you doing, Junior?' he'd ask, burying his face in my neck. 'Did you miss me?' They'd go to bed early and I'd hear them laughing through the wall. Oh, they fought too. Coyote could make my mother mad. She'd scream and shout at him, her hair wild about her head like a fiend. They always made up, though. Coyote was anxious never to let her withdraw from him again, as she had done about their 'wedding'. They were very happy and so was I. Until something unexpected drove a dagger into the heart of our small family.

20

It all began in the autumn of 1951. I guess it was symbolic that that decisive moment was on the evening of my tenth birthday – in effect, the end of my childhood. Looking back I can pinpoint that evening and say: That night changed me for the rest of my life. The events of 1944 had had a monumental effect on my psyche, but I had managed to overcome it. With the help of Coyote I had broken the mould that could have constrained me. However, this time, when I needed him most, Coyote wasn't there.

My mother was excited. Maria Elena had invited us for supper at her house and had insisted on baking the cake. My mother had been active in the store and hadn't had time to think about a party. The summer had been busy. The boardwalk had been crowded with holiday-makers, the beach awash with bodies soaking up the sun, and they had all wanted to shop in the afternoon. I had been on vacation from school and had helped out in the store. But now it was quieter. The vacation was over, the beaches empty; there were just the locals and the old folks who didn't have jobs to rush back to. By now I knew all the goods in the warehouse and had become a competent salesman. I enjoyed it. I exchanged banter with Matias and we laughed behind the customers' backs. I felt like a member of the team, not like a little boy loitering on the border of the adult world, and they treated me as such. In the evenings, when we closed, Coyote picked up his guitar and we sat outside on the grass, in the shade of a maple tree, and sang old cowboy songs. Sometimes, if we'd done well, he'd open a bottle of wine and I'd be given a small glass. If I was lucky he'd tell me more stories of the Old Man of Virginia.

I had always loved my birthday. It was my special day. If I think hard enough, squint my eyes, rummage through my oldest memories, I can remember my third birthday at the *château*. My father wasn't there. I don't remember minding. I don't recall my mother being unhappy. I was too small to notice anything except the cake my mother had managed to bake for me, in the shape of an aeroplane, and the expectant faces as I blew out the three candles. However, I do remember the sense of importance the festivity gave me and the smell of comfort in the vanilla.

The stone walls of the *château* were the walls of my security, my mother's embrace the inner sanctum where I fled when the outer walls were penetrated by the enemy. But on my third birthday, as on my tenth, I had no sense of the enemy lurking in the shadows.

Matias loved to barbecue. He said it was called an *asado* in Chile and claimed that the meat was much better there. So, for my birthday, he invited friends from the neighbourhood and we all sat in the garden, savouring the charcoal smell from the grill and the sweet scent of autumn. Matias had tied Maria Elena's apron around his enormous waist, which looked ridiculous as it barely met at the back, and wiggled his big bottom to the rhythm of Coyote's guitar. Maria Elena approached him from behind and wrapped her arms around him as best she could, moving with him in a lazy dance. Coyote sat with his hat askew, leaning against a tree as he had done in the little clearing by the river in France. My mother was cross-legged in a pair of white trousers, a scarf holding her hair off her face, exposing the widow's peak in her hair line. She was smiling at Coyote. The sun had brought out the freckles on her nose and her complexion was as brown as toffee.

They had invited some of my buddies from school: Joe, Frank and Solly, and some girls brought by their parents who were friends of Maria Elena and Matias. It was only in the company of Maria Elena and Matias and their large throng of friends that I realised my mother and Coyote didn't have friends of their own. Coyote was loved by everyone, but he was an enigma, like a beam of light that is alluring but intangible. Everyone knew him. He was constantly called upon in the store, especially by women, all dolled up with black eyelashes and lipstick, but he never let anyone get too close. Only my mother and I were allowed beneath his skin. But whereas I never saw beyond his smile, my mother saw so much more. She heard the silent cry that echoed from his childhood, clawing at the mother in her, demanding to be understood. She did her best, I know she did. But it wasn't enough. There was always a part of Coyote that was impenetrable. I suppose my mother was too busy trying to understand him to have the time for friends besides Maria Elena.

I hung around the garden with my pals, showing off to the girls who giggled into their hands and whispered to each other. I no longer had the sense of being an outsider. Those days of longing to join in with the children in the square were distant, as was the memory of Claudine. I had other friends now. I possessed the power not only of my good looks but also of knowledge. My mother, herself well educated, had taught me things that now served me well. I was good at history and geography and world affairs. I knew more than my contemporaries. What's more, I was interested in the world beyond Jupiter. I envied Coyote travelling overseas. I yearned to go with him to all the countries depicted on the Old Man of Virginia's patchwork coat. He told me that one day, when I was older, he'd take me with him so that I'd know how to run the business once he had gone. But I never got the chance; he was gone before I grew up.

We kids ate on our knees. There were tables, neatly laid with gingham cloths and matching napkins. The grown-ups sat there, with their wine and their manners, and discussed grown-up things while we sat on the grass with Matias's two bull terriers, eating hot dogs and beef burgers. However, when the cake was brought in, by my mother and Maria Elena, the garden fell silent and they all sang 'Happy birthday' to me. I was told by Matias to sit at the foot of the table, the place vacated by his wife who now put the cake with ten candles in front of my glowing face. 'Go on! Blow them out!' they all cried and I took a deep breath and blew as hard as I could.

'There will only be one woman for you!' said Coyote, referring to the single blow it had taken to snuff out the flames.

'I should hope so too,' Maria Elena replied, clapping her hands.

'One woman!' Matias gasped, his booming voice rising about the noise. 'Don't sentence the poor boy to a life of purgatory!'

'Oh, behave, *mi amor*,' said Maria Elena, laughing. 'He's only ten.'

'And there are many years ahead of him.' He raised his glass. 'Let the future hold an abundance of wine, women and chocolate cake!' They all raised their glasses cheerfully and my mother winked at me. She was proud, I could tell.

In the lengthening shadows of the dying day we played games on the grass. Coyote sat smoking, listening to the conversations around him, his eyes sometimes distant as if caught by a wistful dream. My mother rested her head on his shoulder. I noticed him kiss her hair, now and then nuzzling his face against her. In the midst of all that animation they appeared alone and still in their own world. An island. Always an island: my mother, Coyote and me.

When it was time to go the sun had sunk well below the horizon. There remained only a few hours before my birthday was officially over. I had received presents from all the guests. I hadn't opened them all, some were still neatly wrapped in paper, tied with ribbon. My mother and Maria Elena packed them into a shopping bag emblazoned with the words 'Toad Hall', Hilary Winer's store on Main Street. The sight of all my new toys sent a shiver of delight down my body and I hopped excitedly from foot to foot. 'Oh dear,' said my mother, 'I don't think Mischa is going to sleep at all tonight.'

'I wouldn't worry. It's once a year.'

'I'm happy that he is happy,' she said suddenly with a deep sigh, as if I wasn't there listening. 'After all he has been through, you and Matias have made us both feel right at home and given him such a strong sense of security. It's all I ever wanted for him: to feel he has a place in the world. You give a person confidence and he can just about do anything.' For some reason my mother's French accent was more pronounced than usual.

Maria Elena touched her arm affectionately. 'You're a wonderful mother, Anouk.'

'I do the best I can.'

'I'm glad Coyote brought you both here. You've enriched our lives more than you can know and been a wonderful friend to me.' Now it was her turn to sigh and get emotional. 'Matias and I cannot have children, as you know, so having Mischa so close is a blessing we count every day.'

'You can borrow him whenever you like.' They both laughed and looked down at me. My mother's eyes were glassy and wet. 'Come on Mischa, we'd better get you home to bed.' I thought if anyone needed putting to bed it was her.

We drove home in Coyote's car. The night was clear and bright, the moon large and round like a buoy in a sea of stars. Coyote held my mother's hand, only letting go to change gears. 'What a lovely evening that was,' she said. 'So kind of Maria Elena to bake the cake and everything.'

'Junior enjoyed it, didn't you, son?'

'I've got so many presents,' I replied, setting the toy cars in a line on the seat. They'd go nicely with Joy Springtoe's yellow Citroen. I often thought of Joy; after all, we were in America, surely we would bump into her.

'You can unwrap the rest tomorrow at breakfast, Mischa,' my mother said. 'It's already way past your bedtime.'

'It's way past ours too,' said Coyote, giving my mother's hand a squeeze.

But when we got home, none of us went to bed.

As he drove into the driveway, Coyote sensed there was something wrong. He lifted his nose in the air like a dog and sniffed. 'Stay in the car,' he instructed. 'Don't make a sound.' He crept out, leaving the door on the latch so as not to make a noise, and walked silently up to the door. He pushed it gently and it opened on its own.

'*Mon Dieu!*' my mother exclaimed under her breath.

'What's happened?' I asked, my heart pounding against my ribcage.

'Someone's broken into the house, I think,' she replied in French. She only spoke French to me if she was agitated. 'I hope they're not still there.'

I could see the anxiety in her profile, the way her eyebrows dipped low over her eyes, and her mouth grew thin and taut. We both sat there waiting, hoping. The air in the car was suddenly charged with suspense as if electric fibres floated on it like particles of dust. We waited and waited, wondering what he could possibly be doing in there, until finally, he came out.

His face was serious. More serious than I had ever seen it. He climbed into the car. 'What's happened?' my mother asked, her face eerily pale in the moonlight.

'Someone's turned the place upside down,' he replied. His voice sounded unfamiliar.

'What have they taken?'

'Nothing, as far as I can tell.'

'Well, that's good,' she said, her voice brightening a little. 'What is broken, we can mend.'

He started the engine. 'I want to go and check out the warehouse.'

'You think they've gone there too?'

'I don't know. It's just a hunch.'

'Did they go into my room?' I asked, worrying about my toys.

'They went everywhere, Junior. There's not a drawer they haven't rummaged through.'

Once at the warehouse Coyote pulled out a gun. My mother gasped. 'Don't worry, angel, I'll only use it if I have to.'

'Why don't we call the police?'

'I'm not calling the police. I'm not calling anyone, do you understand? This is no one else's business but ours. We have our own ways of dealing with this sort of thing, without the intervention of the law.' There was a steely edge to his voice.

'Don't do anything stupid, Coyote. For Mischa's sake, please.' My mother was afraid.

He kissed her. 'If he's in there, he's going to be sorry.' With that he climbed out of the car. He locked us in, instructing us to lie down so as not to be seen. 'Are you all right, Mischa?' my mother asked once he was gone.

'I'm fine,' I replied, rather enjoying the drama.

'You're not afraid?'

'No.' She no longer called me her little *chevalier*, I was too big now for childish talk, but I felt like one that night – my hand on my sword ready to draw it against the enemy.

Coyote took a long time. We lay in the shadows listening

to the sound of our own breathing. 'I hope he doesn't have to use that gun,' said my mother.

'Did you know he had one?'

'No.'

'Do you think he's ever killed anyone?'

'Don't be silly, Mischa. Of course, he hasn't.'

'But you don't know for sure.'

'No, I don't. But I know the man.'

'He must have killed people in the war.'

'That's different.'

'What are they looking for?'

'Valuables, I imagine. They didn't take anything because we don't have anything worth taking.'

'We do here,' I said.

'Not much, Mischa. It's a load of junk in there.'

'Really? There's nothing precious there at all?'

'Oh, there are original things, some are worth a bit. But nothing's worth a great deal. If it was we'd be rich.'

'Matias says they're worth a fortune. Coyote collects them from all over the world.'

She laughed cynically. 'But they're not the crown jewels of England, Mischa. They're things he finds in markets and souks. What makes them interesting is that you can't get them here, like that silly elephant foot.'

'And the tapestry?'

'I don't know where that is from,' she said quickly. 'What he gets up to when he goes abroad is none of my business.'

The sound of the key in the lock alerted us to Coyote's return. 'You can come out,' he said. He sounded himself again.

'Is everything all right?' my mother asked.

'They've done the place over, but taken nothing important.'

'Thank God!'

'What did they want?' I asked, clambering out of the car.

'I don't know, Junior, but whatever it was, they didn't find it. They've left the place in a real mess.'

We walked inside. I was horrified to see it in such disarray. They had been over everything like an army of ants. There was shattered glass all over the floor among splinters of wood and broken furniture. They must have climbed all over it, throwing things to the ground as they worked their way through the heaps of merchandise. 'It's going to take weeks to get this place sorted out,' said my mother in despair. 'They've ruined us.' Suddenly the store wasn't full of junk after all, but their livelihood. I was going to point that out, but felt it probably wasn't the moment.

'Don't worry, angel, they haven't ruined us,' said Coyote, rubbing his chin thoughtfully. 'There's nothing here that we can't fix.'

'But they've broken so much . . .'

'Come on. Let's go home. We'll sort it out in the morning.'

'I really think we should telephone the police,' my mother insisted.

'No.' Coyote's voice was firm. 'No police and not a word of this to anyone, do you understand.' My mother nodded slowly, a frown darkening her brow. 'And you, Junior. Not a word.'

'Not a word,' I said, feeling like a spy again. 'Do you know who did it, Coyote?' I sensed he did, even though he denied it.

'No, I don't.'

'Will they come back?' my mother asked.

'Not if I can help it.'

We arrived home to the same chaos. All the rooms had been turned over thoroughly, even some of the floorboards had been ripped up. My mother covered her face with her hands and began to cry. 'Our beautiful home,' she sobbed.

'They've destroyed our beautiful home.' I was speechless with shock. For the first time that night I felt afraid. Images of Père Abel-Louis resurfaced and suddenly I felt insecure again. If they could rattle Coyote and ransack his house, they must be very powerful indeed. They had shaken the very foundations of my security.

We slept at Matias's house that night. I lay awake in bed, surrounded by my new toys that had now lost their brilliance, and listened to them talking downstairs. I couldn't make out the words, just the low hum of conversation. My imagination whirled. Perhaps it was Père Abel-Louis looking for me. If they were thieves and didn't find what they wanted, would they be back? What if they were after Coyote? Would they come back for him? I wanted answers but got none.

The following day Maria Elena and my mother began the hefty task of putting our house back together again. Matias and Coyote returned to the warehouse. 'I don't know why he just doesn't call the police,' said my mother in exasperation.

'That's Coyote. He believes he can fix it all himself,' replied her friend.

'Well, he might think he can, but he clearly can't.'

'Don't worry. He knows what he's doing.' Suddenly my mother stopped tidying and sat up on her knees.

'You don't think he knows who did it, do you?'

'What makes you say that?' Maria Elena asked. She, too, stopped working. I pretended I wasn't listening and continued putting things back in the drawers as I had been told to.

'I don't know. Just a feeling.'

'A hunch.'

'Yes, a hunch. I think he knows what they wanted.'

'What?'

'I don't know. He didn't say. He just seemed rather pleased last night when he came out of the warehouse. The whole place had been turned over, our home ruined and yet he was smiling.'

'Matias has worked with him for years. He'd know if there was anything valuable in the place.'

'Perhaps it's not valuable.' She shook her head. 'I don't know. I'm being silly. I just don't know why he doesn't call the police, that's all.'

'Matias wouldn't call the police either,' Maria Elena said, back on her hands and knees again. 'Men! They hate to think themselves incapable. It makes them feel unmanly if they can't sort these things out by themselves. In Chile we call it *machismo*.'

'Only we weak and feeble women would turn to the law.'

'Right!' They both laughed. But to me, what my mother had said made perfect sense. Perhaps the warehouse wasn't full of junk after all.

A week later Coyote announced that he was going away again. He explained that so much had been ruined in the break-in that he was left no choice but to go off and find replacements. He kissed my mother, lingering for a long while, pressing his lips to hers with anguish. Then he embraced me. 'Look after your mother for me, won't you, Junior?' he said cheerfully, ruffling my hair. He smiled, the corners of his mouth turning upwards into his cheeks, but my mother must have seen the grim resolve behind it for she said, 'Be careful, my darling. Don't do anything stupid.'

We watched him climb into the car, his case and his guitar piled on the back seat. My mother's face was solemn and she was biting the skin around her nail. Coyote waved and we waved back as we always did, but we both felt that this time was different, although we didn't know why.

Once again we were alone. Just the two of us. My mother and me.

21

That was the last I ever saw of Coyote – until he turned up in my office three decades later, a dirty, malodorous vagabond. I twirled the green feather between my fingers and stared down at it while the old feelings of resentment and hurt resurfaced to cut me with their spikes and make me bleed all over again. It wasn't his leaving that did it – he had left countless times – but his failure to come home.

At first we continued as before, my mother and I. She laid the table every evening, setting a place for him, just in case. I remember the white tablecloth with red cherries on it and the matching napkins. Coyote's was clean and ironed, ours crumpled and used. It sat there, that napkin, in its silver holder, day in day out, until his place became like a shrine. I remember my mother's lemony perfume, the sight of her shining hair and expectant face, the joy in her walk, the song on her lips, the light in her eyes, because Coyote loved her and she never doubted he'd come back. After all, he always had.

But Coyote didn't come back. It was months before we had news of him. I rummaged around in the trunk until I found his postcards. It didn't surprise me that my mother had kept them; they had brought rainbows into our home, rainbows that lasted only moments before disappearing into nothing, because I now realised that she kept everything. They were gathered in a slim bundle, tied up with string. I counted them. There were eight. They kept us going for the first couple of years and then, when they dried up, hope and faith filled the void and let us glimpse those elusive rainbows from time to time, until I descended into a world where there was no sun, no light and no rainbows. I hated the world. I hated my mother. But, most of all, I hated Coyote for what he had done to me.

I did not like to dwell on those years. They were painful. I looked back instead to that summer at the *château*, when Coyote had come to us with his mystery and his magic and transformed our lives. He had given love and healed the past. He had taught me how to trust and I had given him my heart, my soul, my faith; my all. The first three years in Jupiter was a time of light. For once the great sun had shone on my face and I had felt special, beloved, cherished, valued. Then Coyote had left and I was no longer good enough or worth enough for him to bother coming home. I took my mother's love for granted, but I measured myself against his. He had rejected me and what followed were years of darkness, rebellion and self-hatred. The *chevalier* faced the biggest battles of his life against the most deadly enemy of all: himself.

My voice should have been my means of communication. After all, I had longed for it as a small boy, believing it to be the key to solving everything. I had assumed that, with its return, the world around me would shift into place again and I would no longer be at odds with it. At first, that had been the case. I had been proclaimed a saint in Maurilliac, and in Jupiter I had been everyone's darling. But then Coyote abandoned me and the rot set in, eating away at my spirit little by little until I could barely look at myself in the mirror without an overwhelming sense of self-loathing. You see, the war had taken my father away; Coyote had left on his own accord. My father hadn't abandoned me; he had been killed. Yet Coyote had chosen to go because he no longer loved me.

I meant nothing to him. He moved on, leaving me behind like unwanted baggage.

My voice was useless because I didn't know how to express my anguish. I didn't know the vocabulary. In fact, I now realise that there simply aren't words to describe that sort of pain. So, as I couldn't speak, I used violence instead. The first time I smashed a window the feeling of release was so intoxicating, I was temporarily cured. I strutted off home, dizzy with pleasure, empowered by the sense of control it gave me. The blood that gushed from my broken skin seemed to carry with it all the poison that had accumulated inside. My mother took me to hospital in a frenzy of worry, while I just lay, as pale as death, smiling serenely into nowhere. When I caught her eye I saw something unfamiliar there, as if I were a stranger to be feared.

For the first couple of years it was just petty violence, nothing more. I hooked up with a few other lost children and went out after school in search of trouble. We vandalised walls with paint, scratched cars, shoplifted. But mostly we just talked about it. Plotted and planned, smoked what cigarettes we could scrounge and shared stolen bottles of spirits. We giggled over girlie pictures and talked about sex, which none of us had yet experienced. Having been the darling of Jupiter I now grew into a menace whom people crossed the street to avoid. My blond hair and pretty blue eyes could no longer hide the criminal I had become, and what did I care? I hated myself, why on earth shouldn't they? It wasn't until High School that I began to fall into more serious trouble: sex, drugs and violence. At fifteen I looked much older. I had been such a small boy, but now, perhaps due to the abundant American food, I was tall beyond my years. Strong broad-shouldered, and my inner fury made me brave. I joined a gang of older boys who met in a disused apartment after school to smoke marijuana. They called themselves the Black

Hawks. They were feared in the school playground because they preyed on the younger, weaker children from whom they stole pocket money in order to pay the peddlers who lurked outside the schoolyard. I didn't care much for that; I had been the weaker child in Maurilliac and I knew what it felt like. I was more interested in sex and violence, because those were ways to lose myself.

The street fights we got ourselves into gave me status and a sense of importance; I was bigger and stronger than anyone else. I could beat the shit out of a giant. I'd see the red mist and that was it; I was all over the place, punching, kicking, snarling. The sense of release was exhilarating, like slicing open an abscess on my soul and feeling the venom trickling out. I enjoyed seeing fear in the boys' eyes because I had always been the child afraid of everyone else. Often I super-imposed Monsieur Cezade's face on to that of my opponent, before ramming my fist into his jaw. Violence gave vent to my anger and blotted out the pain; sex enabled me to forget the little lost boy I really was. If I was a man I could shove my troubled boyhood into the past and close the door.

The first time I fucked a girl I was thirteen. She was called May and had slept with just about every male in Jupiter. She was pretty enough, with tousled brown hair, hazelnut eyes and skin that had soaked up too much smoke and alcohol to be considered rosy. She was soft and curvaceous and heavily perfumed. I don't know how old she was and I didn't care; I just wanted to lose my virginity as quickly as possible and be a man. Besides, she was cheap. I could afford her with a few weeks' pocket money plus a little saved from helping out in the store. She gave me a discount, she said, because I was so young and handsome.

I wasn't the blushing first-timer she had expected. I explored her body without embarrassment, running my hands enthusiastically over the white plains of her thighs, delving my fingers into the folds between her legs, taking her nipples in my mouth until she wriggled away, protesting that she'd throw me out unless I let her show me how it was done. 'You're like a dirty dog,' she complained, taking my hand and trailing my fingers over her flesh. 'Touch me slowly and gently. I'm not a bone!' I was a willing student and a quick learner. While I feasted on her body I could ignore the nagging ache of rejection within me and, for an hour or so, bathe in the sensation of being adored.

Once the mystery was gone, I wanted sex all the time. After I joined the Black Hawks sex was easy. I could have anyone I wanted, except the posh girls who crossed their legs for marriage; no one could have them. I was good-looking and a member of the Black Hawks, which was a big deal. There were plenty of girls wanting a piece of me.

Girls who were game fell into two categories: those who fucked without strings and those who needed the security of a relationship in order to fuck. Obviously the first category suited me better but, to me, women were like countries to be conquered and explored: once I had satisfied my curiosity with one, I looked to the next. I didn't want to go back over old ground unless there was no other option available. So, I had to hop from relationship to relationship, which was hard work, but also a challenge. I soon gained a reputation, but this seemed to do little to dampen my allure. I was angry and aloof. There was no shortage of girls wanting to tame me and, besides, girls are always drawn to the dark side.

If my mother knew of my after-school activities she didn't let it show. I suppose she was too busy running Captain Crumble's Curiosity Store to bother with my low grades and truancy. She was barely at home, anyway. I didn't notice our drifting away from each other, the increasing expanse of waves that flowed between our boats as we sailed in opposite directions without so much as a backward glance. We were both in pain, but I thought only of my own and the temporary refuges I found in the arms of pretty girls and in the bosom of the Black Hawks. My Saturdays helping out in the store dwindled, and I began to spend less time at home and more time getting into fights. The one place I always felt comfortable, however, was at Maria Elena's and it was probably due to her that I never killed anyone for, while she was there, the lines of communication remained open and I always had one foot in a sane and stable place.

'You should really talk to your mother,' she said one day. 'She's very worried about you.'

'I don't think she cares,' I replied with a shrug.

'You don't know what you're saying. She cares very much.'

'What's there to talk about?' I grunted, turning away from her.

She sat down on the sofa beside me and took the bottle of soda out of my hand. 'You're in trouble, Mischa, and we only want to help.' Her voice was serious. 'Look at me.' Reluctantly, I turned to face her. 'Don't think we don't know about your after-school activities. We weren't born yesterday. Besides, that bruise under your eye didn't appear in the night.' Her face softened and she looked at me sadly. 'You were such a sweet little boy. Where's he gone to?' I was stunned into silence by the love on her face. I felt my throat constrict and fought back tears. 'Your mother misses Coyote as much as you do.' The mention of his name caused my shoulders to hunch defensively.

'I don't miss him,' I replied sharply. She smiled at so blatant a lie.

'We all miss him. What do you think he'd make of your behaviour?'

'I don't care.'

'We care.' She gripped my hand tightly. 'We care about you. To Matias and me you're like family. We don't want to see you descend into drugs and crime. You go there, Mischa, and you'll never come out. There are gangs out there far worse than yours and they think nothing of killing people. You're too good for that. You should be concentrating on your studies so you can make something of your life. It's not going to happen on its own. We all have our sorrows and disappointments, but we all have to work through them. We can't choose what happens to us in our lives, but we can choose how to react. Coyote has gone. You can either let yourself go and end up in a ditch one day or move on.'

I sat reflecting on her words. She had touched a nerve and it hurt. I had to bite the inside of my cheek to restrain myself from losing control and throwing everything in her tidy sitting-room out of the window.

'Your mother is all alone. She has not only lost her husband but she's losing her son. Look beyond yourself for a moment and think of her. It's not her fault that Coyote left. He abandoned you both.'

I saw my mother in my mind's eye, naked and shaved, trembling on the cobbled stones in the Place de l'Eglise, and my heart softened. It had always been just the two of us: *Maman* and her little *chevalier*. My eyes stung with tears.

'I have to go out,' she said, getting up. I heard the door close and the echo of silence that followed. I leaned forward, placed my head in my hands and cried. I had never felt so alone.

That night I got into terrible trouble. We had arranged a midnight fight with a rival gang in a parking lot outside Jupiter. It was an industrial park out in the middle of nowhere, the perfect place for a fight. The night was unusually dark, the place badly lit, the wind that whistled around the buildings icy cold and sharp. I was like a bull in a pen, snorting and stamping, eager to vent my fury with my fists. I never expected them to be carrying knives. It all happened very quickly. I suppose they wanted to teach me a lesson. I was arrogant, cocksure: the Black Hawks' deadly weapon. Within a minute I had about three on me at once. I jabbed one on the nose, and heard the breaking of cartilage beneath my fingers, and kicked another, right in the crotch. He doubled up, gagging in agony. But then a sharp pain seared through the side of my body and my legs gave way beneath me. I looked down to see the silver glint of a switchblade catch the light as it withdrew from my coat. I placed my hand there and saw blood turn my skin red. Letting out a deep groan I fell to the ground. The patter of running feet grew distant until they disappeared altogether into the night.

'Man, that's bad.' I felt a hand prise my own from the wound before quickly replacing it. 'Blood. Shit, he's a goner. What the fuck do we do now?'

They didn't have to do anything. A night watchman had witnessed the whole episode and telephoned the police. As their car headlights illuminated the parking lot, the Black Hawks deserted me. Every one of them. Suddenly I was alone on the wet tarmac. I thought of my mother. She wouldn't have deserted me. Not ever. As I lay dying, alone in the drizzle, my thoughts turned to my mother. I had to live to say I was sorry.

When I came to, I was in hospital, my mother at my side. She was holding my hand, looking at me with that worried expression creasing the skin between her eyes. When she saw me open my eyes, she smiled. 'You silly boy!' she said. 'A *chevalier* only fights for good, how could you have forgotten?'

'I'm sorry,' I replied in a whisper.

'It's going to be okay.' Her face glowed with resolve. 'We're going to move to New York. I've had enough of Jupiter. We need a change, don't you think?' I felt a sudden panic fall heavily on my chest.

'How will he find us there?' I asked hoarsely. Now her eyes

glittered and the corners of her mouth twitched in an effort to hold on to her smile.

'If he wants to find us, he will.'

'Do you think he'll come back?'

'I know he will. One day.' She was so sure. I wanted to be as sure as her.

'How do you know?'

'Because I just do. Call it a hunch. The wind brought him once, it'll bring him again, I promise.'

'I didn't think you believed in magic.'

She reached out and stroked my forehead. 'You should be ashamed of yourself, Mischa Fontaine. I taught you all the magic you know.'

So we packed up our things and moved to the Big Apple.

22

I liked Manhattan immediately. With the share of the money my mother got from selling the warehouse and all the crazy things inside it, she bought a small apartment above a shop in downtown New York, next to Mr Halpstein, the eccentric clock-maker. It was simple but it didn't matter. We both felt a sense of liberation, like shedding our skins and emerging clean and new.

I liked the anonymity of the big city. I could put the Black Hawks and the violence behind me. I could choose to walk away from it all, into a place where no one knew me or my history. I could wander down the sidewalks without sending people flocking to the other side of the street as if I were a wolf among pigeons.

My mother set about building up a business. She called it Fontaine's and began buying and selling real antiques, not the junk Coyote had collected at Captain Crumble's Curiosity Store. She went to auctions and house sales and, little by little, she created a fine industry. My mother had beautiful taste. After all, she was French and had spent a great deal of her life at the *château* when the owners had been people of culture and refinement. She was an intelligent woman. It didn't take her long to grasp the trade. When she wanted to charm, few were able to resist her and it wasn't long before she gained a reputation for having a good eye and sound sense. I think it gave her enormous satisfaction to use her mind. She had been wasted in the laundry room at the *château* and helping Coyote with the accounts at the warehouse. Now she ran her own show and she relied on her own instincts. She made contacts, but I don't think she made friends.

I missed the only friends we had had: Maria Elena and Matias. They visited us a few times in those early days, but I never went back to Jupiter. I had made the decision to change. I did not want to be reminded of what I had become. But even they gave up in the end. My mother had changed towards Maria Elena. She was no longer warm and confiding. They didn't laugh the way they used to. Something had gone and I sensed it was irretrievable. I had believed my mother and I had drifted away from each other, but I realised then that it had been my mother who had been slowly drifting away from us. Maria Elena and Matias returned to Chile. Their leaving wasn't a rejection, but I felt once more isolated and alone.

My mother had taught me nearly everything I knew. Now she included me in the business and we grew close once more. 'One day it will all be yours,' she said, as I endeavoured to recognise a Louis XV from a Louis XVI. But I never thought it would be. My mother had always been there, I couldn't imagine life without her.

At Fontaine's, the interest I had had as a boy in Coyote's magnificent warehouse was reignited and I grew to love those old chairs and tables to the exclusion of people. Why would I want to trust human beings, when those I had known had never stuck around for me? Every time I loved, I lost. And every time I lost I grew a little more cynical. People had blown in and out of my life like seeds in springtime. Not one had settled and taken root even though the ground had been ripe and hungry. My mother was all that was left, and the furniture in which we invested our hearts.

Although I was no longer a member of the Black Hawks, I was still angry and aggressive. Above all, I was desperately lonely. There were plenty of gangs in New York, from the social gangs to the 'bopping' and 'jitterbugging' fighting gangs, and yet I didn't yearn to be among them. That knife wound had taught me two important things: one, that there's no loyalty among gang members and two, that I was better off living than dead. So, I turned my back on the violence and concentrated on my work. It was all I had left.

The years passed. I grew less aggressive. I hid my anger and I gathered acquaintances along the way. My good looks drew people to me. Outwardly I was funny. Humour was my way of hiding my unhappiness. I made a joke out of life and I made fun of myself. My dry, cynical wit made people laugh, and laughter is a surer bond than any other. Like my mother, I could be charming when I wanted to be yet, beneath the charm, I ached so badly I felt as scared as a child.

There was a club around the corner from our apartment called Fat Sam's. I'd go there in the evenings and meet girls. I slept with countless women, searching for something I couldn't put my finger on. Each one provided a temporary refuge. Yet, every morning the gnawing would begin again. Something gave me pain, but I couldn't locate the spot and I didn't know how to relieve it.

Then, one afternoon I was walking through Central Park. It was summer, particularly hot, I remember. Children were playing, dogs chasing balls, families lying on the grass, their carefree laughter ringing out into the sticky air. I walked with my hands in my pockets watching them enviously, looking at them in the sunshine, from my dark place in the shadows. I was now in my late twenties and what had I achieved for myself? I had no deep relationships of any kind, except with my mother; only a thriving business that I shared with her, buying and selling beautiful things that couldn't reciprocate my affection. I watched those people who all had someone and felt a deep longing to love again. I remembered Joy

Springtoe, Jacques Reynard and Claudine – I didn't allow myself to recall Coyote because of the pain his memory induced. Suddenly I noticed a distraught young woman striding towards me. Her face was flushed, her brown hair tied in a ponytail, her big eyes shining and anxious.

'I'm sorry to trouble you, but have you seen a little white dog?' I noticed at once that she spoke with a strong French accent.

'I'm afraid I haven't,' I replied in French. She looked startled for a second and then continued in her own tongue.

'I have looked for him everywhere. I am so worried. He's only small.' I don't know whether it was the language or the vulnerable look in her eyes that stirred the *chevalier* within me, but I offered to help her look for him. 'I'm so grateful to you,' she said, forcing a smile. We marched on, calling for him. 'My name is Isabel.'

I introduced myself. 'I'm Mischa. Where are you from?'

'Paris,' she said. 'I came here a few years ago. I'm a photographer. Bandit! I hope he hasn't been stolen. He's such a beautiful dog.'

'We'll find him. Just keep shouting and walking and he'll come back.'

'I hope you're right.' She looked up at me, desperation etched around her eyes where the skin was taut. I noticed how lovely she was, her skin smooth and brown, her eyes like toffee. She was petite, like so many French women, perfectly formed, with a small waist and full breasts neatly concealed by a crisp white shirt.

'I know I'm right,' I added confidently. She seemed to relax a little. I sensed I gave her reassurance. She was no longer on her own.

We shouted for Bandit all over the park. I knew we'd find him. I felt it in that old sixth-sense way I used to feel things in France. I knew we'd be lovers, too. I could taste her skin already, as if I had been there before. She was as familiar to me as those fields of vines I used to run up and down with Pistou. My coolness calmed her down, so that we were able to walk and chat at the same time. 'How long have you had Bandit!' I asked, knowing that she only really wanted to talk about her dog.

'He's three. I had him as a puppy. He's everything in the world to me.'

'Has he run off before?'

'Never. I don't know what's come over him. Bandit!'

'Is he a randy dog?'

She glanced up at me and caught my grin. 'Aren't all dogs randy?' she said with a smile.

'Perhaps there's a bitch on heat in the park. You know what they're like. They get the scent and can't let it go.' *A bit like men*, I thought to myself. I liked her scent a lot.

'What should I do? They don't run brothels for dogs, do they? Bandit!'

'Everyone needs someone, even dogs.' The words came out of my mouth without thought. My whole body tingled with excitement. I needed someone to love, it was as simple as that. Everybody needs someone. Finally, I had recognised where the ache came from – where else but in my heart? That mere acknowledgment of the problem made it go away. I blinked in the dazzling light of the summer's afternoon and felt my spirits soar.

It didn't surprise me one little bit when Bandit eventually scuttled over, covered in dust, wagging his tail with happiness. Isabel fell to her knees and gathered him into her arms, kissing him all over his face. 'You naughty boy!' she cried, but clearly she didn't mean it. Bandit obviously hadn't a clue of the worry he had put her through, for he looked so pleased with himself, like he deserved an award.

'How can I ever thank you for helping me find him?' she

said to me, standing up. She still had the dog in her arms. Her face was no longer drawn, but glowing pink, and her eyes were bright, but not with tears. I knew exactly what she could do to thank me, but decided to be a little more delicate about asking for it.

'Let me take you out for tea,' I suggested. 'I don't know about you, but I'm starving.'

'I know just the place. A little French café on West Fifty-fifth street where they make fresh croissants and *chocolatines*.'

'*Chocolatines*?' My head was spinning with the memory of the *patisserie* in Maurilliac.

'My favourite.'

'Mine too,' I said. 'I could kill for a *chocolatine*!'

The taste of pastry and chocolate, the smell of cigarettes and coffee, transported me back to my childhood in France. I could almost feel the eucalyptus-scented breeze against my face and hear the crickets in the undergrowth. We spoke French together, making a small island of the round table where we leaned across to talk like old friends. I felt I knew her already. I had smelt her before, heard her voice, run my hands through her thick brown hair. She had come from somewhere long ago and I welcomed her like a man lost at sea.

She had a dusting of light freckles on her cheeks and nose and when she smiled, her whole face opened up and radiated sunshine. She made me feel light-headed, as if I had drunk the wine of France and grown drowsy with nostalgia. We laughed until our bellies ached, about nothing at all, but everything I said was brilliantly witty and hilariously funny. Bandit sat on her knee, eating biscuits out of her hand like Rex had done on Daphne Halifax's lap, and she stroked his head and kissed him, as she might a child.

She invited me back to her apartment and we made love all afternoon. In that bold French way, she considered love-making a pleasure to be taken when desired. She wasn't saving herself for marriage like so many American girls I met. She had enjoyed lovers before. Besides, she was made for it. Both brazen and nonchalant, there was little she hadn't tried and the more I caressed her the more she wanted.

Beneath her clothes she wore pretty silk panties trimmed with lace and a matching brassiere. Her skin was smooth and smelt of tuberose. We fell on to the sofa and I traced my hands all over her body, savouring the slight dampness against my fingers, like the morning dew in the gardens of the *château*. I licked her all over, tasting the salt of the sea on my tongue. I celebrated the end of my search. I took Isabel in my arms and reclaimed the country I had lost. In the brown undulations of her flesh I found France.

That night I dreamed of Claudine. We were on the bridge. It was a hot, summer's day. Not a cloud in the sky. Small flies hovered over the water and birds whistled gaily in the trees. I felt serene by her side. We didn't need to speak for we understood each other perfectly. We stood there watching the flies and the little ripples of water where the fish swam. I thought of Monsieur Cezade and the dead fish and she looked at me as if she was remembering too. She smiled that familiar toothy smile and her face was warm and gentle. Then she took my hand and her eyes spoke to me. 'I'm here, Mischa. I'll always be here.' I squeezed it and felt my eyes fill with tears. When I awoke I pulled Isabel into my arms and kissed her. In her kiss I tasted France.

My mother should have been pleased that I had found love. She should have enjoyed my happiness. But perhaps my bursting heart emphasised the gaping hole in her own heart. The Coyote-shaped hole into which no one else could fit. I thought she would love Isabel as I did. Not just for me, but because she was French. She was a part of the country we had both loved and left behind. France was in our veins and no amount of America could supplant it. But she didn't. She closed up like a flower in frost, shutting her petals and withdrawing. She wasn't intentionally rude, but her unwillingness to welcome Isabel caused offence. She never mentioned her name. It was as if she didn't exist. I wanted to share my happiness but I sensed it was making her bitter.

I encouraged her to go out with the men who tried to court her. She was a beautiful woman. But she insisted Coyote would come back one day. She kept that shrine of a place laid for him at the table with grim determination, as if the place itself would draw him back, and I know she prayed. In their bedroom she knelt beside the bed and put her face in her hands as she had done in the church in Maurilliac. Perhaps she believed the power of prayer would lead him back to us. Sometimes she sat at the window as if she hoped the wind that had brought him to us in the first place would blow him home. She waited for him and saved herself for him, but Coyote never returned.

My mother had loved twice. First, my father and then Coyote, and both men had left her. Was it madness that sent her dancing to the gramophone, alone in her bedroom in the middle of the night? Had my father and Coyote merged into one? Was it that confusion that provoked the tumour that eventually killed her? My mother needed me, and while I cared for her I took my eye off Isabel. I thought I loved her, but perhaps I just loved France. Maybe I wasn't ready to trust again. I grew possessive, suspicious, and the initial excitement dulled into squabbles and accusations. 'I can't get close to you, Mischa,' she said, over and over until I wanted to break the record. 'You won't let me in.' So, I didn't confide in her. I didn't share the past. I thought I could share, but I was unable to. I kept it all to myself and once more I was alone. Once again it was just us: *Maman* and her *chevalier*.

23

But that was all in the past now. I pushed myself up and stretched, heavy with sorrow. I walked stiffly over to the window and leaned on the sill. Outside, the snow on the ground was still crisp and white, except on the street where the traffic had already turned it grey and slushy. The patches of sky above New York were pale and wintry, the trees bare, crippled with cold. If I closed my eyes I could smell the heat of France.

I was jolted from my trance by the telephone, its ring was loud and intrusive. I jumped, as if afraid it would wake Death who slept there in that silent apartment.

'Hello?'

'Stan told me you were there.' It was Linda, the girl with whom I had shared my life for nine years.

'Now's as good a time as any to go through her things.'

'I see.' Her voice was tight. 'Do you want any help?'

'Thanks, but I'm better on my own.' There followed a pause that weighed heavily with disappointment. I felt bad. I had been rotten company lately. I'd barely spoken to her, so added reluctantly, 'Well, if you've got nothing better to do.'

'I'll be right over,' she replied brightly. I hung up and sighed. I didn't want to share this with her. I didn't want to share it with anyone. My mother had closed chapters and so had I. I found a bag and put the photo album and letters inside to take home with me. The little rubber ball I put in my pocket.

I was in the hall when Linda arrived. She had walked. Her face was scarlet and her blue eyes glittered from the cold. She took off her woolly gloves and hat and shook out her blonde mane. 'It's freezing out there!' she exclaimed with a sniff.

'You want a drink?' I asked.

'Yeah, what have you got?' She followed me through the sitting-room to the drinks cabinet. 'It's ghostly in here. Why don't you open the curtains, let some light in?' I shrugged. 'You'll get even more depressed in the dark.' The reference to my supposed "depression" irritated me. Of course I was depressed. My mother had just died. I poured her a glass of bitter lemon. 'It's really bizarre,' she continued. 'Nothing's changed in here, I mean, everything's in the same place and yet it feels so different, like the breath has gone out of it.'

'It has,' I replied, helping myself to another glass of gin.

'I see she's still getting mail. Do you want me to go through it for you?'

'No, I'll get around to it.'

'Mischa, I want to help.' Her voice was beseeching. I braced myself for what was to come. 'Don't hunch your shoulders like that,' she said. 'It's rude. Like I'm the enemy.' She stifled a sob and opened the curtains with vigour, pulling the rings across the pole. The light tumbled in, exposing the dust on the furniture. I recoiled like a vampire. 'That's so much better, don't you think?' she said, breathing deeply.

I watched her stride across the room, her leather boots clicking on the wooden floorboards. 'We need to organise this with military precision. I'll get a couple of refuse sacks.' I heard her rummaging around in the kitchen, cupboard doors opening and closing, and felt my irritation mount. She appeared in the doorway with her sleeves rolled up. 'I'll go through the kitchen. I don't imagine there's much that's senti-mental in there. You start in her bedroom.'

I was unable to control my temper. 'Just stop, Linda. I don't want you to do the kitchen. I don't want you to do anything. I should never have let you come.' She didn't look hurt, as she usually did when I shouted at her, but angry. She exploded like a pressure cooker.

'No, Mischa, *you* stop. I can't take any more of this. You're like an ostrich. If I don't help you, all this stuff will just sit here for months. You've got to get a grip. Sort it all out. Keep what you want, dump what you don't want, sell the place. Get rid of it. Move on.' I was astonished by her sudden outburst. It was so out of character. 'You're bad-tempered and rude. I'm tired of riding your moods like I'm at the rodeo, playing the glad game to humour you, mothering you like a slave. You're the most selfish human being I've ever come across. All you think about is yourself. You know what? You're wallowing in self-pity. You're in so deep you can't even see the way out. But I have needs too, Mischa. I need someone to take care of me as well.' I stared at her as she threw her complaints at me, layer by layer, like the leaves of an arti-choke, until, finally, she reached the very heart of the matter. 'I can't reach you, Mischa. I've tried, I really have, but I can't get close to you.'

I sat down, elbows on my knees, and rubbed my temples with my fingers. I didn't need this right now. She sank on to the sofa and began to cry. 'I don't know what you want from me,' I said, but of course I knew. She wanted me to tell her I loved her. How could I? I wasn't capable of loving. She wanted commitment. Didn't they all? She wanted communi-cation, but I didn't want to let her in. I couldn't give her what she wanted and, what was worse, I hadn't even the desire to try.

'I want you to let me love you. That's all,' she said in a

small voice, pulling her knees up to her chest. She wiped her face with the back of her hand.

'If I'm such a miserable bastard, why would you want to?'

'When we met nine years ago, I saw this giant, angry man with smouldering blue eyes and enough charisma to set the city alight. You were funny too, when you weren't angry. Then, when I got to know you a little better I saw how vulnerable you really were underneath. The angry person was just masking the pain. It sounds silly now, but I believed I could save you. I was young, barely twenty-eight, and all I wanted was to make you happy. I thought in time you'd let me in.' She shook her head and her forehead creased into a frown. 'But you never did.'

'I'm sorry . . .'

'Sometimes love isn't enough. A person can give and give and give, but if she doesn't get any back she runs out. I've run out, Mischa. I haven't got any left.'

'You're too good for me, Linda.'

'Oh, don't throw that at me like it's a criticism. It's not true. I'm not too good for you. I've just lost patience and my reserves have dried up. You know, I thought when your mother died things would change for us. She never liked me. She wanted you all to herself. But they haven't changed. Even in death she won't let you go and I don't think you want her to. You're still holding on to her, aren't you? I can't believe we've been together for nine years and I barely know you any better now than when we met.'

'I'm not very good at talking about the past. I don't even want to think about it myself.'

Her voice hardened. 'Well, you're not going to be able to move on until you confront it. Share it, then let it go. If you can't talk to me, get a shrink.' When she saw that I had nothing to say on the matter she launched her final attack. She stood up and placed her hands on her hips. 'While you wallow in the stagnant pond that is your life, I am going to move on. I want to get married, have children, make a home. I want to grow old surrounded by grandchildren. I've given you the best years of my life, Mischa. But I'm not going to give you any more, that would be suicide. I'm still young and there's somebody out there deserving of my love.' And with those words she left the apartment and my life. I wasn't even sorry to see her go.

I drained my glass and pondered my life. She was right, of course. It was stagnant, going nowhere. I wanted to move on but I didn't know how to. It wasn't a question of settling down with a woman, breeding a family, building a home, because the stagnation was *within* me. It was a state of mind. A state of emotion – or in my case, a lack of emotion. I had settled back into the way I was when I was six, before Coyote had sauntered into our world and thawed it with love. I trusted no one. I had made myself a little island, except now it wasn't *Maman* and her little *chevalier*, but me, alone, for ever alone.

When I got home Linda had packed her things and left. Nine years of her life gone. She had walked out on me once before but, this time, I knew she wasn't coming back. I was overwhelmed by a sudden feeling of loneliness. I went from room to room like an abandoned dog, regretting my outburst, wishing she would come back. The place seemed empty, like my mother's apartment. It was tidy and soulless. I soon realised that although the walls echoed with memories of our togetherness, the years all merged into a sludgy washed-out colour, making them barely distinguishable. I had invested my time but not my heart. She had come into my life but made no impression, like rainfall on the back of a duck; because I hadn't let her.

I put the album and letters on my desk. I had brought my mother's mail home too, but didn't feel ready to read it. The telephone rang. It was Harvey Wyatt, my lawyer.

'How are you feeling, Mischa?'

'Fine. What's up?'

'I've finally had an answer from the Metropolitan.'

'And?'

'They can't accept the Titian as a gift, because they don't know where it comes from,' he said.

'I can't help them there.'

'Your mother never said anything?'

'She never mentioned it.'

'Family!' he sighed.

'I didn't even know she had it, for Christ's sake.'

'She didn't steal it, did she?'

'Don't be ridiculous, Harvey, my mother couldn't even lie, let alone steal!'

'Just kidding.'

'Where the hell would she have stolen it from?'

'Your guess is as good as mine.'

'So, what are they going to do with it?'

'They'll accept it 'on loan', in case the real owners come back for it.'

'Didn't they find out anything? It can't have come from nowhere. Someone must have a record of it, surely?'

'Robert Champion, the head curator, says that he suspects your mother's *Gypsy Madonna* was an earlier version that was either lost or stolen. It's not uncommon for an artist to do a repeat. The later version, the one we all know, which was painted in 1511, hangs in the Kunsthistorisches Museum in Vienna. They're not identical, but they're very similar. The point is, there's no record of your mother's version anywhere, which suggests it's been in the hands of private collectors for hundreds of years. With all the publicity, whoever it belongs to might come out of the woodwork and want it back. You don't know how long your mother had it by any chance?'

'I've already told you, I never even knew she had it. Christ!'

'Calm down, Mischa.' I took a deep breath. 'You have to understand that this is a big deal. A painting by a world-famous painter suddenly comes to light after almost five hundred years. The art world is going berserk.'

'It's not a fake?'

'No. It's genuine.'

'What the fuck was she doing hiding it away? Why didn't she sell it?' I laughed bitterly. 'We'd both have been rich!'

'Mighty hard selling a painting like that – it's priceless.'

'It's a mystery. Now she's dead, I'll never know.' But then I had a thought. There was possibly one man who might know. I was astounded that I hadn't thought of him before. 'Listen, I've got to go. Call me if anything comes up.' I hung up, then searched for a number I wasn't even sure I had kept. Matias had retired to Chile with his wife in 1960 I didn't even know whether he was still alive.

That night I went out alone. I often frequented a small bar called Jimmy's round the corner from my apartment but they all knew me in there and they all knew Linda. So, I wandered somewhere else, I didn't notice the name. I sat on a stool and stared into my drink. I didn't smoke, but I could have done with a drag or two that night. The scent of Coyote's Gauloise still clung to my nostrils, setting me off-balance, dragging me back into the past. There were so many un-answered questions. I wasn't ready to go through them, because I wasn't ready to solve them. I was happier with my head in the sand, as Linda had said. I didn't really want to know why Coyote hadn't come back. The little boy in me still hurt from his rejection.

After a while the alcohol melted the tension in my neck and shoulders and my breathing grew deep and regular. I looked around. A man played the guitar while a pretty woman sang sad songs. The mood was mellow, the light dim, the air thick with the scent of smoke and perfume. I felt I was lost in there and began to feel better. Perhaps it was a blessing that Linda had gone. I'd have to do my own washing, so what? I considered my newfound singledom and realised that it felt good. What I needed was to get away. I needed to get out of New York, go abroad. I hadn't travelled in years. I'd slipped into the routine of work like a blinkered horse pulling a cart. I'd find Matias and take a vacation at the same time. My spirits rose. I asked for another shot.

'Hi.'

I turned to see a woman sitting on the stool beside me.

'Hi,' I replied.

'You on your own?'

I nodded. I found myself appraising her, my eyes tracing her thick red hair that fell over smooth creamy shoulders, full breasts barely restrained by the body of her black dress, and a soft, fleshy face.

'You on your own too?' I asked, finding something almost beautiful in her hazel eyes.

'No, they're all my friends in here.' I raised my eyebrows. She laughed and placed a hand on my arm. 'I own the place. My name is Lulu.' She must have registered my blank expression for she said, 'You haven't been here before, have you?'

'No, I haven't,' I replied.

'No, I would have noticed *you*.' She caressed my face with her eyes. 'Do you have a name, or shall I call you Handsome?' When I laughed at that lame joke I knew the alcohol had really got to me.

'My name's Mischa, Mischa Fontaine.' I extended my hand. She shook it. Her skin was soft and moist.

'Well, Mischa, I'd like to welcome you to my bar. You're tall, aren't you? I like tall men. You're not from here. You're foreign. You have an unusual accent.'

I shook my head. 'You're wrong, I'm afraid. I am from around here.' There was something about her expression that made me laugh. It was as if even she wasn't taking herself very seriously. As if flirting was a game she enjoyed playing.

'Oh, you might be *now*, but you didn't grow up here.'

'What makes you think that?'

'It's in the eyes. There's another world in there. That's what I like about you. You have that look of another world.'

I chuckled and raised my glass. 'It must be the drink.'

'Oh, the drink does other things to a man.' She placed her hand on my crotch. 'We wouldn't want you to have too much of it, would we? No, you're a river that runs deep. Very deep. If I cast my rod, I might find that world down there.' She moved closer and whispered into my ear. 'Why don't you let me take you back to my apartment?' She placed a long red nail through the gap between the buttons of my shirt. 'I'd like to fuck you, Mischa. You're in my bar, you're my guest, it's only right that I show you *all* I have to offer.'

I let her take me home. Her apartment was small but tidy, the air light with the scent of flowers and cheap perfume. I wasted no time, lifted her off her feet and carried her into the bedroom, although I tried the cupboard first, causing her to scream with laughter. She was delicious in bed: large, soft and juicy. She had an enormous capacity for pleasure, spreading her legs without shame so that I could touch her there. She writhed beneath my hand like a cat, moaning and mewing, gyrating her hips until I buried my face in her folds and used my tongue. I hadn't enjoyed sex so much in years. She was a woman of experience, and one who took pleasure as if devouring a hearty meal. When we lay in each other's arms, our hearts still racing with adrenaline, she murmured softly into my chest. 'I knew you'd be a good lover.'

'How did you know?'

'The French always make good lovers.'

'How do you know I'm French?'

'Your accent. There's a trace of France in it.'

'I was French, long ago,' I said, sensing a sudden longing in my heart for those fields of vines and that warm, pine-scented air of the *château*.

'Just like I said. There's another world in those eyes of yours.'

'You have no idea,' I replied. 'But it's a lost world.'

'Nothing is ever lost, Mischa,' she said wisely. 'You can get it back if you want it.'

'I don't believe you can.'

'That, my handsome stranger, is the very thing barring your way.'

24

The following morning I went into work with a spring in my step. Stanley looked at me with amazement, as if I had grown a second head or something. 'Hey, you all right?' he asked. Esther bustled out from behind the desk.

'I hear Linda's walked out,' she said, folding her arms and shaking her head. 'It's too bad.' Stanley shot her a look.

I smiled at them both. 'I'm taking a vacation,' I declared.

Stanley took off his glasses. 'A vacation?'

'You know, the thing people do when they need a break,' I replied sarcastically.

'But you never go on vacation.'

'Of course you are,' interrupted Esther, her face crumpling with sympathy. 'Your mother's died, your girlfriend's walked out, it's cold, snowy, grey, gloomy. Where you going?'

'Somewhere hot.' I shrugged. 'Chile.'

'Is that a country?' Esther joked. 'It doesn't sound hot at all.'

'I'm leaving tomorrow and I want you two to hold the fort while I'm gone.'

'You look better than you did yesterday. Your face is glowing.' Esther grinned. 'You're in love or you got laid. Whichever, I wish you did it more often!'

I shook my head. 'I've just realised I need to get away for a while.'

'If you see anything interesting while you're there, be sure to pick it up,' said Stanley, cleaning his glasses with his tie.

'Why don't you go to Europe? You'll be pushed to find anything worth buying in Chile.'

'Europe!' said Esther. 'Ooh, I'd love to go to Europe. Sure you don't want to take me with you? I'm a great travelling companion. I might talk a lot but I'm never dull.'

'Oh, let me think about that and get back to you.' I pretended to ponder. 'No, thanks for the offer, but I'm going alone.' I smiled broadly at her.

Esther laughed. 'You're *meshuggah* – nuts! I'm glad to see the old Mischa is back. I almost lost patience with the grumpy old *schliemiel* who took his place. I hope you have a good rest. It'll take the years off you and boy, do you need it! No one would ever believe you're only in your forties!'

I spent the day sorting out my desk so that Esther and Stanley could run the business in my absence. It was doing well. My mother had sold off the rubbish Coyote had accumulated and begun collecting antiques in earnest. She had taught herself, listened to experts, taken advice, charmed her way into the market and carved out a niche. When I was a boy she had taught me to read and write; when I was a young man she had taught me about the business so that later, when she fell ill, I was able to take over. She had patience, my mother, and her dedication to my tuition reminded me of those quiet evenings in the stable block in France when I had laboriously learned my letters and she had prompted me gently, her eyes brimming with love. As a troubled young man I worked with her because I didn't know what else to do and because it suited my nature. I was a loner. I always had been. And I was lost. Her store was a place of refuge where I could hide among inanimate things that didn't judge me, or love me, or let me down. Later, when my rebel days were no more than painful memories, I grew to love those things like I had loved the bric-à-brac in Captain Crumble's Curiosity Store; they didn't disappoint like people did.

I looked out of the window into the snowy street below. I saw Zebedee on the sidewalk, chatting to a young woman with two small children, one in a stroller, the other holding her hand. They had pink cheeks and shiny eyes and their breath rose on the cold air in small clouds of steam. I thought of Linda. She would make a good wife and mother. I wondered whether I had been a fool to let her go. Had I let a perfectly acceptable future slip through my fingers, like the string of a bright yellow balloon? Would the chance ever come around again? Zebedee was waving his arms around and making the children giggle. The mother looked on indulgently, pleased that her babies were happy. It looked so simple, love.

I tracked Matias down. It wasn't as hard as I had expected. The number I had for him was out of date, which wasn't a surprise as it was more than twenty years old, but I remembered he had said he was going to retire and breed birds, so when I mentioned that to the woman who answered the telephone, she suggested I call the aviary in Valparaiso. The man from the aviary chuckled when I mentioned his name. '*El gordo loco*?' he said the mad fat man – but he gave me his number and address without hesitation. Matias was unforgettable; I smiled when I thought of him. Larger than life in Jupiter, unforgettable in Chile; he'd be easy to track down anywhere in the world.

When Matias answered the telephone, he sounded exactly the same as he always had. '*Hola*?' he said in his deep, resonant voice and I felt an overpowering sense of 'home'.

'Matias, it's me, Mischa.' There was no pause while he searched through his mental files. He simply greeted me with the same enthusiasm as if he had spoken to me only the day before.

'Mischa, you must be a man now!'

I laughed. 'An old man, Matias.'

'If you're an old man, I should be in the grave! How's your mother?'

'She passed away,' I said after a small pause, wishing I had called him earlier.

'I'm sorry, Mischa.'

I felt my throat constrict with the effort to contain my grief. My mother and I had always been a small boat adrift in a hazardous sea. Coyote had been the rock against which we had set our anchor for a while; Matias the cove that sheltered us when that rock had slipped away. I wanted to harbour in his big arms again, as I had done as a boy, when I had gone adrift, and sob my heart out for my dead mother and my deadened heart. I didn't want to be alone any more. 'I want to come and see you,' I croaked.

'You're always welcome, Mischa. You're the son I never had, you know that.' He must have sensed my sorrow for his voice became low and tender. 'Come tomorrow. I'll pick you up from Santiago myself.'

I wasted no time. I packed little and with haste. I suddenly felt the need to leave the city as soon as possible, as if the very air was choking me. I left my mother's apartment as it was, her mail on my desk unopened, her bag of memories on my bed. Only my little rubber ball came with me, in my pocket, as it always had done.

The moment I was on the plane I was able to breathe again. The ostrich hadn't simply put his head under the carpet but let it spirit him off to another life far away. As I escaped, I didn't realise that I was embarking on a journey that would force me to confront my demons.

I watched the lights of New York City diminish as the plane climbed into the night, and relished a growing sense of optimism. Perhaps Matias would shed light on Coyote's disappearance; we had never discussed it and, if he had talked it over with my mother, she had never said. Anyhow, I had been a boy and then, when I had become a teenager, I hadn't wanted to know. It had been a form of self-defence, I know, but it had overridden my desire to know what had become of him. If I didn't confront it, it wouldn't hurt me, so I had thought. The problem was, the wound cut deep. Even though my skin grew over it, the flesh was as raw and bleeding as ever. I went with the intention of finding Coyote but, really, I just wanted to go home.

The flight was long, but I didn't mind. I used the time to reflect. I felt I was in limbo, suspended between two worlds: the present, which I had left behind in New York, and the future, that was really a return to my past. I perked up when the plane flew low over the brown suede Andes mountains. The sky was cerulean, the sun dazzling white as it rose with the morning. The heat shimmered off the arid sierra, and my spirits soared. Only when we began to descend into Santiago did I notice the famous smog that sat in the valley between the mountains, like a bowl of steaming soup, waiting for the wind to blow it away. I forgot about Linda, my cold office in downtown New York and my mother's silent apartment. It wasn't until I saw Matias, standing in Arrivals, that I realised how lost I had been.

The years had left little impression on his skin. Only his curly black hair had turned grey. When he saw me his cheeks glowed pink and his jovial face lit up into a wide smile. We fell into an embrace and, although I was now taller than he was, he still felt like home. '*Dios*, you've grown like a beanstalk!' he exclaimed with a hearty chuckle, patting my back so hard, I winced. 'What have you been eating?'

'You don't know how good it is to see you,' I said, holding his thick shoulders, sinking into the familiar glaze of his toffee-brown eyes.

'Of course I know, because it feels good for me too.' He shook his head and shrugged. 'We shouldn't have let time

get the better of us. I'll blame it on Maria Elena. It's easier
to blame a woman!' He lifted my case, surprised by its lightness, and led me out into the car park.

I savoured my surroundings. Coming from snow and ice
I was uplifted to feel the hot sun on my skin and breathe in
the floral scent of midsummer. It was early, but the humidity
had already turned the air to syrup. Birds squawked in the
rubbery palm trees and the borders hummed with bees. He
stopped at a dirty white truck. In the back were empty wooden
bird cages all piled on top of each other, sacks bursting with
seeds, and other paraphernalia. He threw my case in with the
cages. The truck smelt of hot leather and dust. There was a
hole in the passenger seat and the broken gear stick was
mended with a red sock. He put on a pair of sunglasses and
climbed in.

'What are all those cages for?' I asked, shuffling my long
legs to get comfortable.

'I buy birds from the aviary in Valparaiso and set them
free in my garden,' he said with a shrug.

'Do they fly away?'

'Some do, some don't. I lay a feast before them, most are
as greedy as I am, so they eat and stay.'

'I got your number from the aviary.'

'I thought Maria Elena had sent your mother our new
address. We moved fifteen years ago.'

'You always said you'd retire and breed birds.'

'How clever of you to remember.' He patted my knee and
I noticed that although his face looked young his hands were
covered with brown age spots. 'I'm glad you took the trouble
to find me, *hijo*.' Matias always peppered his sentences with
Spanish. I don't remember exactly when he started, but at
some stage after Coyote had left he began calling me *hijo* –
son.

'You haven't changed at all,' I said, watching the white

buildings of Santiago scatter until we were cutting through the desert towards the coast. It was very hot, even with the windows open. The warm air blew in, through my hair and over my skin, and I felt renewed.

'Perhaps a little fatter,' he shrugged again. 'Otherwise, I'm still me, which is a good thing. I would hate to be anyone else.' He laughed that familiar bellow, lifting his chin and puffing out his barrelled chest. 'Whereas you, *hijo*, look like a man.' He slapped my leg. 'A man. The beautiful little boy finally grew up!'

After about an hour Matias pulled up in front of a little shack. A group of small, grubby-faced children played in the dust beneath the umbrella of a large tree where a donkey slept on his feet, tethered by a rope. Bright flowers waved their petals in the soft breeze and an old woman in black sat, fanning herself with a magazine. 'Let's have a juice,' he said, climbing out of the truck. He raised his hand to the old woman who nodded back. The children stopped their game and stood staring at me. I imagine I was a strange sight with my pale hair and skin. A little boy kicked an empty Coca Cola can. It rattled across the earth and stopped in front of my feet. The children waited to see what I would do. When I kicked it back, they erupted into squeals. Matias responded in Spanish then roared with laughter. 'They think you're a giant,' he said, wandering into the shack. 'They're worried you might eat them.'

'What did you say?' I asked, for they were in a frenzy of excitement.

'I told them that you only eat dogs. That where you come from there are none left. That's why you're here!' I rolled my eyes and followed him inside.

It was cool in the shade and took a while for my eyes to adjust. There was a counter behind which a young man was sitting, listening to the radio. There was a fridge of cold drinks and a large display of sandwiches that made my mouth water. 'I recommend the avocado ones,' said Matias. 'And their fresh juices are the best in Chile.' A young woman emerged from behind a curtain of ribbons. She was brown skinned and pretty, her long black hair tied into a plait that almost reached her bottom. She looked at me and I noticed her flush. She smiled shyly. Matias greeted her in Spanish and they engaged in conversation for a while. Although she spoke to Matias her big eyes kept glancing at me as if she was unable to draw them away. I was flattered and surprised – I must look a sight, having come straight from the airport and in need of a shower and a shave.

Matias bought a couple of raspberry juices and *palta* sandwiches and we moved outside to sit at one of the wooden tables to enjoy them. 'Still a hit with the ladies,' he said, nudging me playfully. 'You had them wrapped around your little finger as a pretty little boy. Now you're an unwashed, stubbly man who looks like he's been through a mangle and yet, they still sniff something alluring in you.'

'I don't deserve such high praise,' I said with a smile.

'You got a girl back home?'

'Not any more.'

'*Qué pena*. A handsome man like you. Still, I can't say I'm surprised.'

'This place is a gem,' he said, as we sat down. 'I stop off every time I drive to Santiago. They're a sweet couple. That old woman there is Jose's mother.'

'She must be hot dressed like that,' I said.

'She's in mourning,' Matias stated, biting into his sandwich.

'When did her husband die?'

'About forty years ago.' When he saw the surprise on my face, he shook with laughter. 'Don't ask me how he died because I don't know. She'll wear black until she joins him.

I shouldn't think it'll be long.' He suddenly turned serious and put down his sandwich. 'I haven't had the courage to ask, but now I feel the time is right. Tell me, Mischa, how did your mother die?'

'She had cancer.'

He shook his head and heaved a sigh. 'It's always the good who die young.'

'She knew she was going to go. By the time she passed away, she had handed the business over to me and settled all her affairs. There's one thing, though, that took me by surprise. I thought you might know something about it.'

'Go on.'

'She had a Titian.'

'A Titian?'

'Yes, *The Gypsy Madonna.*'

'A real Titian?'

'Yes, it's real. She gave it to the Metropolitan.'

'Your mother must have been a shrewd businesswoman to invest in works of art.'

'That's just it, Matias. I never knew she had it. She certainly couldn't have afforded to buy it.'

He sat up and frowned at me. 'Then do you have any idea how she acquired it?'

'No. I know nothing at all.'

'Didn't you ask her?'

'She didn't want to talk about it. She simply said that she had to give it back. She said it with such force, such determination. Christ, Matias, at the end she was so sad. So, so sad. As if by giving it away she was giving away her very soul. It sounds strange, but she could barely bring herself to do it. I told her she should hold on to it, but she just simply shook her head in that resigned way of hers and said that she had to give it back, that she couldn't explain why.'

'Did someone give it to her? Did she have a man in her life? Lovers?'

I shook my head, disappointed. I had thought he might know something. 'No one. I was going to ask you if maybe it had something to do with Jupiter.'

He bit into his sandwich again. 'There was nothing like that knocking about in Jupiter. *Dios mio*, if I had had that kind of merchandise in the warehouse I would have bought a palace, not a humble bungalow by the sea. I'm sorry, *hijo*, I can't help you. But the mystery does intrigue me. Perhaps Maria Elena knows something about it. They were once as thick as thieves those two. Although, I'd be surprised if she kept something as important as that from me. Maria Elena is good at most things, but she can't keep a secret, not on a grand scale like that anyway.'

We drove on through the desert. The road was long and straight. Sometimes we passed horse-drawn carts, small settlements made up of shacks with corrugated iron roofs and children playing among the trees. Skinny dogs trotted aimlessly about in search of scraps, their noses skimming the dry ground with little success. Large billboards advertised nappies and washing-up liquid, while the desert behind was barren and unforgiving. Finally, from high up in the mountains, we could see the Pacific Ocean below, dark blue and glittering in the sun. The road wound its way down into Valparaíso, a large port town of tall office blocks and lush green parks from which palm trees soared to the sky. Traffic-congested scruffy streets passed crumbling walls and once glorious houses with elegant driveways and doors framed by grand porticoes. To me there was immense charm in the decadent disintegration of the place. The cracked sidewalks, the uneven streets, the crumbling plaster; the violent scars of Chile's regular earthquakes were everywhere.

We drove along the winding road that followed the coast.

There were seals on the rocks, basking in the sunshine, and women and children playing on the sand in small coves that punctuated the black rock. It was cooler by the ocean. Finally, after climbing a steep hill, the truck turned into a driveway bursting with large green bushes of gardenia. Matias tooted the horn. 'Welcome to my home,' he said. 'Your visit is long overdue!'

When Maria Elena emerged in a pale blue dress, her grey hair tied into a loose plait, the joy that overcame me was fringed with sorrow. I climbed out of the truck and hurried to embrace her. She felt small and frail in my arms, in spite of the fact that she was a large-boned woman. She buried her head in my chest and held on so tightly that her knuckles turned white. She was too overcome to speak. Her breath hissed up from a constricted windpipe. When she pulled away my shirt was stained with her tears. I turned to Matias, but he now looked as desperate as she did. He strode up with my case and patted me on the back, once again nearly winding me with the force. 'We're pleased you've come,' he said, and Maria Elena nodded, smiling shakily.

'Finally,' she whispered. 'I've waited twenty-five years for this moment. Twenty-five years. You don't understand. How could you?' Then she reached up and placed her hands on my face, pulling me down so that she could kiss me. I felt her wet lips on my skin. She was right, I didn't understand, but I didn't care.

25

We sat on the terraced veranda, overlooking the garden and the sea below. The air was sweet with the scent of gardenia mingling with the slightly marshy smell of the ocean. Birds of every colour and size played about the trees, their squawks loud as if crying for attention along with the children who played in the street behind the house. A green parrot perched on the back of Matias's chair. When he sat down the bird stepped across to his shoulder, stretching its legs with the agility of a dancer. As Matias talked he fed the bird nuts, which it took in its beak, turning them around and around with its claw, shiny black eyes watching us with interest.

Their house was white with a red-tiled roof and green shutters. It needed a new coat of paint and a thick crack shot up one side in a jagged line, but the flowers that clung to the plaster were bright and so abundant that the eye was drawn away from the flaws. I liked the feel of it the moment I arrived. Surrounded by dark green bushes of gardenia and leafy palm trees, it gave one an immediate sense of refuge.

A small, elderly maid in a pale blue uniform walked out with a tray of drinks. 'You have to try Pisco Sour,' said Maria Elena. 'It's a traditional Chilean cocktail made with lemon. I think you'll like it.' The maid left the jug and glasses on the table and disappeared back into the shadows. 'I'm so pleased you're here,' she said as she poured a glass and handed it to me.

'Christ, this is good!' I exclaimed as the sour liquid burned its way down my gullet.

'You were still a boy when you left,' she continued. 'Tall and gangly with incredibly long legs and arms. You've grown into yourself.'

'Neither of you have changed,' I said, taking another sip. 'You're both the same as I remember you.'

'A lot older, I'm afraid,' she said with a sigh.

'Time does that,' growled Matias, passing the parrot another nut.

'What's he called?' I asked.

'Alfredo. I rescued him from the pet store.'

'They must enjoy a nice life here.'

Matias chuckled. 'They're fat and happy like their master.'

'The mess is quite something,' said Maria Elena, looking exasperated. 'But what can I do?'

'Quiet, woman, I know you like them because I watch you feeding them and your face is alight with the glow of love.'

She laughed and shook her head. 'You silly old man!'

We talked and drank and the heat made my tongue loose and my heart swell. I was happy to be there, far from New York and the snow, far from Linda and my mother's empty apartment. After a while, I asked Maria Elena about the painting.

'A Titian?' she exclaimed in surprise. 'A genuine Titian?'

'Yes.' I shrugged helplessly. 'She never mentioned it to me until the end, when she was dying. She said she had to give it to City.'

'The City?' she repeated with a frown.

'Well, she didn't exactly say it like that. She said she had to "give it back". She gave it to the Metropolitan.'

Maria Elena thought for a moment. 'Back? To whom?'

'I don't know, because I don't know who gave it to her. I'd hoped you and Matias might have known something about it.'

'If that painting had belonged to an individual, or a family, she would have given it back to them. If it was stolen, well, that's another matter.'

'You don't think my mother stole it, do you?'

'No. Your mother was an honest woman and anyway, how would she go about something like that? It's inconceivable. Besides, what's the point of stealing a painting of such fame? Who'd buy it?' She looked at Matias in a shifty manner that caught my attention. 'I'm sorry she suffered,' she added, lowering her eyes. 'Although we drifted apart, I was always very fond of her.' I wondered what it was that they weren't telling me.

'I saw Coyote,' I said, putting down my empty glass. They both stared at me in astonishment. 'He appeared in my office a few days ago.'

'How is he?' Maria Elena asked.

'Almost unrecognisable,' I replied. 'He looked more like a tramp than the dashing man I used to know.'

'*Dios mio!*' Matias gasped. Alfredo climbed on to his chest and began picking at one of the buttons with his beak. Matias ignored him. 'What happened to him?'

'I don't know. He didn't say.'

'You didn't ask?'

'I was angry.'

'Of course you were,' said Maria Elena sympathetically. She filled my glass. 'Besides, it's been, what? More than thirty years?'

'It was only after he'd gone that I wished I'd asked him. I ran out into the street, but he disappeared. I lost him again, I suppose.'

'Why do you think he came back?' she asked.

'He had read about the Titian. He didn't know my mother had died. He was shocked. Well, the painting was all over the papers, you can imagine. An uncatalogued work by such a famous artist – everyone wants to know where it came from, even him.'

'Your mother gave no clue?'

'Nothing.'

'But Coyote wriggled out of the woodwork,' said Matias, nodding his head with disdain. 'We can cancel him out from our enquiry. If it had had anything to do with him he would have come back earlier. Though, I wouldn't put it past *him* to steal a Titian!'

'He wasn't that good,' Maria Elena scoffed.

'Where did he go?' I asked and my anguish must have shown all over my face, for they exchanged looks again. 'You know something, don't you? You can tell me now; I've painted the town red already and washed it clean.'

Matias picked up Alfredo and placed him gently on the floor. With a big, sausage finger, he stroked the bird's feathery head. Then he sat up and poured himself another drink. We were all feeling light-headed. The heat, combined with the drinks, loosened us all up like oil poured on to stiff hinges. There were to be no more secrets. 'Coyote was already married,' he stated simply. I was shocked. In a flash I remembered the time my mother locked herself in her bedroom. Now I understood what that was all about.

'Christ, I didn't understand it then. I wondered why she was so furious that he was pretending to everyone that they had married in Paris. I thought Paris was a very romantic place to get married! Now I know he couldn't marry her.'

'He had a family in Virginia, just outside Richmond.'

I shook my head in amazement. 'My mother was devastated. She shut herself in her bedroom for three days and refused to come out. But she did in the end and declared that she didn't want to talk about it any more. I remember she made him buy her a ring. She claimed it was for my sake.'

'She didn't want people to think their relationship was improper. People can be very unforgiving.'

'Don't I know it,' I replied. But I doubted they knew what had gone on in France. My mother had always been very guarded. 'So every time he went away on business, he was with them, in Richmond.'

'I imagine so,' said Matias gravely. 'Although, I can say with complete confidence that he loved your mother in a way that he had never loved anyone else.'

I looked about the small paradise that surrounded me and wondered whether anyone really knew what Coyote's heart contained. 'If he had loved her so much, why did he leave her?'

'Coyote was a mystery, even to those like me who knew him best. I don't know much about his life in Virginia growing up. I can tell you, though, he had a tough start. His father drank and beat him, his mother was out holding down two jobs. He was left to run about the place like a wild dog. I don't know if he had any siblings. He received little education. He lived . . . how do you say?'

'By the seat of his pants.' I could hear Coyote's voice in my head. That gravelly tone seasoned with irony.

'By the seat of his pants.' Matias chuckled. He must have heard it too.

'He married young, but couldn't cope with being tied down. He was a free spirit. He travelled about the country with his guitar and this incredible magnetism. I met him in Mexico. He was Jack Magellan, just plain Jack Magellan. But they all fell in love with him, even then. We were young, barely twenty. We got on and set up our business in New Jersey and he changed his name to Coyote, because that was what this old black fugitive called him when he was a child, running wild.'

'The Old Man of Virginia,' I said, hearing the satisfactory

clink of another piece of puzzle. 'The one who taught him to play the guitar. Why New Jersey?'

Matias's eyes misted a moment with nostalgia. 'Coyote didn't do anything in the conventional way. He took a map of America and closed his eyes. I turned him about a few times. He put his finger down on New Jersey and that was that.'

'But he fought in the war, didn't he?' I asked, recalling the face in my dream.

'Yes, when America entered the war, Coyote wanted to be part of it. He loved adventure.'

'What about his family?'

'God knows whether his wife put up with it or not. He never talked about her and I didn't ask.'

'Coyote was always running away, Mischa,' said Maria Elena kindly. 'He ran from his wife and children. He ran off to war. When he returned he was rarely around. He travelled for business, picking things up all over the world. I think he was running from himself.'

'He was a different person in each county, *hijo*. I bet his name wasn't even Jack Magellan. Coyote was a nickname that suited him. He was a wild dog!'

'I don't think he really knew who he was,' Maria Elena added.

'So he ran away again?' I stated simply. 'From us.'

'That is the part that baffles me, *hijo*,' said Matias, shaking his curly head. 'Business was doing well. We were making money. He was happy with your mother and he loved you.'

'Oh, he was passionate about you, Mischa, and so proud,' said Maria Elena.

'Then why didn't he come back?'

'I assumed he was dead,' said Matias gravely.

'At least then it would all make sense,' agreed Maria Elena. 'Now we know he's not dead, the mystery only thickens.'

'It doesn't add up. You don't think his disappearance had anything to do with the break-ins?' I suggested.

'Perhaps,' said Matias. 'Coyote was a secretive man, while giving you the impression that you knew him. No, he was like an onion with many layers, no one knew what was at the core. I imagine there's a story there that would blow our socks off if we ever found out. Coyote never did anything in the conventional way.'

'Or in an honest way,' Maria Elena chipped in. 'He was a shadow one could never pin down. I might add that much of the stuff he sold at the store was either fake or stolen.'

'But no Titian,' I said.

'No Titian. Believe me, if he'd had a Titian stashed away in the warehouse he would never have left.'

That evening we dined at a fish restaurant in Viña del Mar, looking out over the sea. I noticed the women were very beautiful, with golden skin and long black hair, their eyes shining dark and mysterious in the flickering candlelight. I appraised them shamelessly, tracing their features appreciatively with lazy eyes. They caught my gaze and lowered their eyes hastily, with a coyness one wouldn't find in America, like timid birds. Linda was now a distant memory, aided by the thousands of miles that separated us. 'I'm glad you've found your feet and made a success of your business,' said Maria Elena, looking at me with motherly affection.

'It was my mother who made it a success. It wasn't hard for me to keep it going.'

'You must have an eye, though?'

'I love old things. I like to feel the pasts that lie within them. They all echo with the vibrations of the people who owned them and the places they've sat in. I love to imagine the English castles and French *châteaux*, the Italian *palazzi* and those great German *Schlösse*. The grand families who've lived in them and collected treasures from all over the world for hundreds of years. Those great tours they did, returning with their pieces of history. I love to run my hand over the wood and feel the heartbeat, because they do beat, you know, if you listen.' I was aware that I was opening up in a way that I had never opened up to anyone. I had never been able to talk about love, on any level.

'As a boy you loved a certain bureau made from walnut,' said Matias.

'I remember,' I said with childish enthusiasm. 'It had secret drawers and beneath the floor of the desk there was a hidden level. It was glorious!'

'You always asked about the origins of all the goods. You were fascinated by a tapestry,' he added, gulping down a mouthful of wine.

'I remember. Bacchus and his drunken nymphs. I loved it because it reminded me of the *château* where I grew up.'

'Your mother never spoke of France,' said Maria Elena softly.

'That's because we didn't live in the *château*. It belonged to a family before the war and my mother worked there. Then, when the Germans came, they occupied it and my mother fell in love with one of the officers.'

'She never told us that,' said Maria Elena, frowning. 'I assumed he was French.'

'No, my father was a German and my mother was severely punished for her betrayal at the end of the war. I lost my voice because of her humiliation and because they nearly killed me.'

'Oh, Mischa, I never knew!' Maria Elena's eyes filled with tears and she placed her hand on my arm. Without thinking, I placed mine on top of hers and left it there.

'You know, I've never spoken about this to anyone, not even Linda, my girlfriend for nine years.'

'You bottled it up all that time?'

'I never needed to communicate. My mother understood and she was my best friend.'

'I know. She loved you with every fibre of her body.'

'You said Coyote gave you back your voice,' said Matias. 'I remember hearing you on the radio!'

'Gray Thistlewaite,' I chuckled. '*In your living-rooms, in your kitchens and in your lives, making them better and brighter in my own small way.*' I imitated her voice to perfection and Matias roared with laughter like an old lion. 'I meant it when I said that Coyote was magic. You see, he arrived and everything changed. I can't describe to you how people treated us before. We were outcasts. I was worse than the rats they set traps for in the cellars. Coyote played his guitar, sang old cowboy songs and defrosted people's hearts. First the children included me in their games, then the grown-ups began to forgive. He enchanted them all, or put them all to shame. I have a distant memory. I don't know whether it's true. That it was Coyote who rescued us from the crowd at the end of the war. My mother was naked and shaven, her face as hollow and pale as a ghost. They held me up to the crowd and all I heard were their cries and their hatred. Then I was in her arms and an American put his shirt around us. I swear it was Coyote.'

'It might well have been. Perhaps that is why he returned, because it was the town he helped to liberate,' said Maria Elena.

'It makes sense,' I said with a shrug. 'I was only three.'

'Go on with your story,' she insisted. 'I want to know everything.'

'So, one Sunday he came with us to Mass,' I continued. 'I hated going because it was like running the gauntlet every week. Staring at me were the very people who had bayed for my blood. They had come with their pitchforks and hammers intending to beat us to death. Even the priest had stood by and let it happen. Yet, every Sunday my mother insisted on going to Mass, to sit in their midst and pray. I don't know why she did it – defiance, probably. She wasn't one to let people believe they had beaten her. But I was so afraid. When Coyote came with us, it was different. I saw admiration in their eyes, not hatred. Then, in the middle of the service, I thought I heard the voice of an angel. But it wasn't an angel. It was my own voice, audible at last.'

Maria Elena wiped her eyes with trembling fingers. 'Mischa, *mi amor*, you suffered so much and we never knew.'

'But Coyote put it all right, you see. If it hadn't been for him we would have always lived in the shadows and I would have continued to live behind a screen, unable to reach anyone.'

'Then he left,' said Matias.

'And I lost my way.'

'It's understandable.'

'But you owe yourself better,' said Maria Elena. 'Coyote might have opened your heart, but you did all the rest on your own.'

That night I walked up the beach with Maria Elena, just the two of us. The sky was crisp and clear, the stars little eyes into another world beyond our senses where my mother existed with my father, in peace, I hoped, still holding on to her secrets that I was now unravelling one by one. 'Now I understand why your mother was so protective of you,' Maria Elena said, taking my hand.

'We were always alone. It was always just the two of us.'

'Because there was no room for anyone else.' I frowned. She looked up at me, the lines on her face illuminated by the moon like rivers on a map. 'You know I'm right. Don't you think Linda might have felt like an outsider?'

'Perhaps, I never gave her a chance.'

'You were like the son we never had, Mischa, and your mother knew that. Why do you think you left New Jersey?'

'Because Coyote had gone, there was nothing left for my mother there.'

'No, because she couldn't bear you to be close to anyone else but her.'

'That's not true!' I exclaimed, but my voice was weaker than I intended.

'Yes, it is. She held on to you jealously. When you moved to New York I tried to see her numerous times because I wanted to see you. But she was always busy with this or that. You slipped away.'

'I was going through my difficult stage,' I said with a bitter chuckle.

'And I wanted to be there for you. You'd had such little stability. After Coyote left, you went into a terrible decline. I wanted to help you through it, but your mother didn't like it. I regret that I didn't try harder. You left for the city and we were bereft. In the end the only way to move on was to start a new life in Chile.'

'I remember sitting in your garden playing with your dogs,' I said, suddenly feeling weighed down with sorrow.

'Gringo and Billy.'

'Gringo and Billy. Whatever happened to them?'

'They went the way of all creatures,' she said, raising her eyes to the sky. 'Your mother was a good woman. Now I know more about your past, I understand why she held on to you. You were all she had.'

'And she was all I had, too,' I said.

Then something broke inside me. I heard the snap but I was too late to stop the flood. We sat down on the sand and Maria Elena wrapped her arms around me, a giant of a man in her frail embrace. I sobbed like a child and all the grief I had retained over the years was expelled so that the healing could begin at last.

26

I stayed with Matias and Maria Elena for a fortnight. During those long summer days we spent time just getting to know each other again. We drank far too much Pisco Sour, laughed until our jaws ached, and reminisced. With them I had nothing to hide. I opened up like a clam, whose shell, once prised apart, remains agape without any effort. We wandered up and down the beach, our feet in the sea, the warm amber light of sunset bathing us in an almost heavenly glow while the tides took my grief and washed it away. I watched Matias with his birds, the way he caressed them and fed them, nursed them and played among them, and realised that they, not me, were the children he never had. We had reunited but I couldn't stay, as much as I wanted to. I had to return to Maurilliac and dig up the skeletons of the past. Matias and Maria Elena had given me the courage to do so.

I hated saying goodbye. I hated to see the pain in their eyes. Matias slapped me too hard on the back, then embraced me with such fervour I nearly suffocated. Maria Elena planted a kiss on my cheek. It remained on my skin the entire journey to France, like a whisper. They said they'd always be there for me. But that wasn't true. Nothing in life is permanent. Time would carry us on, but it would run out eventually. One day they wouldn't be there any more and I'd be alone again. Always alone; a solitary *chevalier*.

I was anxious about returning to France. Logic told me that the old demons would have all died off, like Monsieur

Cezade and Père Abel-Louis, or be so decrepit they'd no longer pose a threat. I was in my forties and yet, inside I was still the little boy who used to hide behind the chair in the corridor of the *château* in the hope of spying Joy Springtoe or Daphne Halifax.

I remembered everything and was afraid of change. I wanted the fields of vines to be the same as they were when I had run up and down the narrow aisles with Pistou. I wanted Jacques Reynard to be in his workshop with his cap askew and his eyes twinkling with mischief, but if Monsieur Cezade and Père Abel-Louis were old and senile, then Jacques would be too. I wondered whether, as a man, I would see them all through different eyes, like the old teacher from New Jersey I had since bumped into in New York and shared a coffee with. I had never much liked him as a school boy, but I found, to my surprise, that we had more in common than I would ever have imagined. Would I then share a joke with Monsieur Cezade? Would I empathise with Père Abel-Louis?

Logic told me that I'd probably recognise no one. I was six years old when I had left. Faces from my past had faded with the years like photographs left in the sun. The few that featured in my nightmares I remembered too vividly, but the others were gone. Another generation would have grown up in the time that I had been away. New shops would have set down their roots in the Place de l'Eglise, children I did not recognise would play *cache-cache* among the trees until the shadow of the church would fall over them and they would scatter home like pigeons. Perhaps I'd recognise Claudine in the face of a little girl, or Laurent in the features of a dark-haired, black-eyed, boy. If I had stayed, perhaps my children would play among them. And what of the people of Maurilliac? Would time have blunted their knives and dulled their memories? The war had finished forty years ago, but was forty years enough to wash away hatred such as theirs?

It didn't surprise me at all that Coyote hadn't paid his hotel bill. He had looked like a man of means, but that was his genius; he could assume the identity of anyone he wanted, like a good actor. In spite of all that Matias and Maria Elena had told me, I believed the Coyote I had loved was the real man and not a creation. I didn't believe that love could be feigned. I remembered it in his eyes, I remembered the feel of it, like warm treacle in my heart. No, the Coyote I knew had loved me.

I hoped to see Claudine. I hoped she hadn't moved away from the village. So many French people did these days. I wondered whether I'd recognise her. I closed my eyes in the plane and remembered her. That toothy smile, her long brown hair and green eyes. She had enjoyed breaking the rules and defying her mother. She had possessed great courage befriending me. I remembered playing with her on the stone bridge, throwing pebbles into the river, stealing her hat and running off with it, panting with laughter. I remembered her encouragement in the school playground and the dead fish plot that went so badly wrong. I remembered, too, my confrontation with Laurent. I wanted to see her again, to thank her. She was my only childhood friend, except for Pistou. And what of Pistou?

With his dark hair and impish face and those deep-set brown eyes that were full of understanding, he had appeared in the night to comfort me when I suffered those terrible nightmares. I recalled him with clarity, as if he had been real and not imaginary. I realised now, of course, that he had been a figment of my imagination. I didn't believe in spirits. Alone so much of the time, I had fabricated a little friend for company. Surrounded by so many enemies, I had created an ally in Pistou. Where I was so misunderstood, he had understood me completely. With him I hadn't needed to speak, for he could hear my inner voice. It wasn't surprising that out of loneliness and fear I had invented a little boy like me who could do all the things that I couldn't. Like pinch Madame Duval's bottom and hide her glasses, and steal Monsieur Duval's cigars. I had believed Coyote could see him, because I had *wanted* him to share something with me that no one else shared. In my memory, though, he had been real. I remembered his touch, his smell, his voice, his laughter. But my grown-up mind told me that it simply wasn't possible. If I hoped to see Pistou on my return, I would be disappointed.

The journey was long, the plane hopping from country to country like a grasshopper until finally I took a flight from Paris to Bordeaux. The moment I stepped out of the plane the scent of France caused my stomach to flip over. It wasn't hot, for it was February. The sky was grey and a light drizzle fell from heavy clouds, but there was something in the air that reminded me of home. I stood on the tarmac bewildered and becalmed, the years unravelling around me like a ball of string. I must have turned pale for a kindly air hostess approached me. 'Are you all right, *monsieur*?' she asked.

'I'm fine,' I replied in French. 'I think I need to sit down.' She escorted me into the baggage reclaim where I sank on to a chair.

'Can I get you a glass of water?'

'Thank you,' I replied, my mouth suddenly dry and sticky. While she disappeared in search of water, I watched the people around me. Everyone had someone: mothers with children, husbands with wives, grandparents with grandchildren. There were a few men on business, in suits with briefcases, but even they wore the contented faces of men who surrounded themselves with friends. I was not like them. I was alone. I had built a wall like a fortress around myself; I hadn't let anyone else in. Not even Linda, who had tried. No one had been able to penetrate those walls and I hadn't left their security. While they had kept everyone else out, they had kept me in, a prisoner.

The air hostess returned with a glass of water, which I drank thirstily. 'Where are you staying?' she asked.

'I'm going to hire a car and drive to Maurilliac,' I replied, handing her back the plastic cup.

'It's a very pretty place. I've been there. I have an uncle who lives there, although he's a horrid man so I see him as little as possible. There's a beautiful *château* and vineyard.'

'I thought I'd stay in the *château*. It's a hotel, isn't it?'

'Do you have a reservation? It's very popular.'

'No. I thought I'd just turn up.'

She shook her head. 'I'll telephone for you. It's always best to book, just in case.' She looked at me quizzically. 'You're not from here, are you?'

'I was born here, but I've lived most of my life in America.'

'Ah, that's why you have an unusual accent. My name's Caroline Merchant. I live in Bordeaux.'

'Mischa Fontaine,' I said, extending my hand.

'I tell you what, why don't you come home with me while I telephone and make the reservation for you.'

I was surprised by her forwardness. 'Sure,' I replied, standing up.

She looked pleased. '*Bon*! My car's in the car park.'

Caroline had a lime green Citroen Deux Cheveux that reminded me of the little car Joy Springtoe had given me. She lifted the boot and I placed my suitcase beside hers. There were no holes in the leather of her car, no dust and no bird cages. She placed a pair of glasses on her nose and settled into the seat. 'I have to wear these to drive,' she said with an embarrassed chuckle. 'I don't like them.'

'I think they suit you,' I said truthfully. With her hair tied back into a severe bun, she reminded me of a young school teacher. I wanted to pull her hair out of the band and watch it fall over her shoulders. She was aware of me watching her and blushed.

'Where have you come from?' she asked.

'Chile,' I replied.

'I noticed you on the plane.'

'Do you always pick up stray Americans?' I asked with a smile. She blushed again.

'No, you just looked more lost than the rest.'

'You're right. I am lost. I haven't been here for over thirty years.'

'Did you fight in the war?' she asked and it was then that I realised what a sight I must look. I threw back my head and laughed, recalling Esther's brutal comment: 'No one would ever believe you're only in your forties!'

The entrance to Caroline's apartment was hidden at the back of an inner courtyard. She opened the iron gate with a key and we walked up an old stone staircase to the second floor. We had stopped on the way to buy milk and *croissants* from a small shop on the corner of her street. While she was inside I cast my eyes over the eighteenth-century cobbled streets and sandstone buildings. The drizzle cast the scene in a soft, melancholy light and I found myself feeling sad, for I didn't remember it at all although my heart yearned to recapture it.

She made coffee in her kitchen and we sat at the table by the window chewing on warm *croissants* with butter and jam. 'Are you married?' she asked.

'No,' I replied, savouring the sweet taste of France.

'Neither am I. I don't think I want to, either. Both my parents have married again. They didn't set a very good example.' I thought of my mother and Coyote's relationship and knew why marriage didn't appeal to me either.

'You'll want to one day,' I said cynically. 'Women always do.'

'Well, if I do it won't be for a long time. I'm only twenty-six.' *Christ!* I thought, *I'm old enough to be her father*. She lifted her chin and smiled at me, the smile of a woman in command of her actions. 'In the meantime I shall take lovers until I am ready to settle down. If I find the right man I might marry and have children. But right now, I feel like a shower.' She walked out of the room. A moment later I heard the sound of music resounding through the apartment. Then she was standing in the doorway, her hair down and falling over her shoulders. She looked beautiful and sensual and French.

We tore off our clothes until we stood naked on the wooden floorboards of the bedroom – she pale and smooth except for the triangle of black hair below her belly button, my own skin darkened by the Chilean sun. I towered over her but she wasn't intimidated.

She ran her eyes up and down my body and smiled appreciatively. 'You have a nice body for an old man,' she said with a smirk. 'How did you get this?' She ran her fingers over the knife scar on my side.

'An accident,' I replied automatically because that was what I told all the girls or, in fact, anyone who saw me without my shirt on. I had never confided this part of my past to anyone.

'I bet it hurt.'

'It did.'

'It's manly. I like it.'

'That's lucky. It doesn't come off in the wash.'

She laughed and I followed her into the bathroom. The white tiles were cold against my feet. I noticed the goose bumps on her flesh and a faded brown birthmark on one buttock. She leaned forward and turned on the shower. We climbed into the small space and I lifted her up to kiss her. The water was warm and I turned around so that it fell over her hair and face and down between our bodies in streams like heavy summer rain. She brought her legs up and wrapped them around my waist. She was nice to kiss. Her mouth was soft, her tongue gently probing. As we kissed she made mewing noises, like a contented cat.

'You have a nice cock,' she said as she covered me in soap. She might have seemed the epitome of French sophistication but her comments exposed her youth. Girls used to say that when I was in my teens, thinking the compliment would increase my ardour. It was better when they didn't speak at all. I took her hand and led her out of the shower. She giggled as I wrapped her in a towel. 'Take me to bed, my handsome American,' she said. But I didn't want to talk, I just wanted to make love.

While crass talk decreased my ardour, sexual confidence aroused it. Caroline didn't only mew like a cat, she responded like one too, stretching out, purring, moving her hips in a slow, rhythmic dance, spreading herself wide until the rhythm of her gyrations became disjointed and her breathing shallow. When she stopped talking, Caroline was a feast to be devoured and enjoyed. Her body was fulsome, her skin velvety, the secrets beneath the soft triangle of black hair pink with youth and glistening with pleasure.

Later we lay in each other's arms as lovers do. She laid her head on my chest and ran her fingers up and down my stomach. 'You're delicious,' she said with a sigh. 'I wish you didn't have to go to Maurilliac. Don't you want to stay here with me? I don't fly out until the day after tomorrow.'

'I'm afraid I have to go,' I replied.

'I'm back again in three weeks.'

'That's a tempting thought.' But I knew I'd never see her again.

'Have you ever been in love?' she asked, running a long nail over my skin.

'No, and I don't think I ever will.'

'You're not too old for love,' she said. 'I can tell.'

'Age has nothing to do with it. I'm not the type.'

'You can't go through life alone, surely?'

'I'm not alone,' I lied. 'I shared nine years of my life with a woman. I just didn't want to marry her.'

'Don't you dream that the right woman will come along?'

'I'm not a romantic.'

'You don't have to be a romantic. You're handsome and sexy and tremendously good in bed.' She giggled into my chest. 'I don't think I've ever had that many orgasms in one session, which is amazing as I'm very orgasmic.'

'I don't rate romantic love very highly. Perhaps I have a cold heart, I don't know.' I ran a hand down her hair. She was so young. Life's disappointments awaited her and she didn't even know it.

'I don't think you have a cold heart. It just hasn't been warmed by the right woman yet. She'll come into your life one day and set that heart of yours on fire. It's not about sex, it's about caring about someone more than you care about yourself.'

'I'd like that,' I said. 'I'd like not to grow old alone.' It was true, I would have liked to love with the intensity with which my mother loved Coyote, but I doubted it would happen. How would I know if the right woman came along? How would I know to let down the drawbridge and let her in?

'Well, if in three weeks' time you haven't found her, give me a call and we can enjoy each other again. I like you, Mischa. It's a skin thing. You can press your skin against mine whenever you like.'

She telephoned the *château* and made the reservation as she had promised. Then she wrote down her telephone number and drove me to the car rental in her tidy Deux Cheveux. We kissed goodbye like lovers, but we parted as friends. 'Do come and see me before you go back to America.' But I knew I never would.

PART THREE

Oh once in the saddle
I used to go dashing
Once in that saddle
I used to ride gay
But I first took to drinking
And then the card playing
Got shot by a gambler
I'm dying today.

Someone bring me
A glass of cold water
A glass of cold water
The poor cowboy said
But ere we could get it
His soul had departed
His soul had departed
The cowboy was dead.

27

I saw the towers of the *château* long before I reached Maurilliac. The dark grey spires rose above the trees in fine triangles just as I had remembered them, tantalisingly close. A noise disturbed a flock of pigeons and they scattered into the watery sky like a spray of bullets. My heart began to race and it grew hot in the small car. I opened a window and took a gulp of air. I was coming home, at last.

I stopped the car at the bottom of the hill. The driveway swept up in a graceful curve, the grass on either side glittering in the pale, liquid light. I imagined the times I had been driven up and down as a small boy, like another life now, and yet I remembered them as if they had taken place only yesterday. I might have grown into a man but the heart that beat inside me belonged to a little boy.

It was winter. The earth was barren. The wind that blew into the car was laced with frost. But my memories were of the summer when Coyote had driven us to the beach in his open top car. I recalled the sensation of the wind raking through my hair, the sense of freedom, the feeling of optimism and endless possibility, my heart swelling with love and pride. I remembered Coyote's hand on my mother's knee. She hadn't pushed it away, but rested her hand on top of his with a gentle squeeze. I had seen everything, heard everything, but I couldn't remember what it had been like not to speak. I could smell the heat, although the air froze in my nostrils, the scent of pine and sweet grass, the balsam poplar and jasmine. I could hear the crickets, the clamour of birds, the low hum of bees, and feel the brush of a butterfly's wings on my skin, although only a couple of crows alighted upon the ground in search of worms. I could have been young again but the hands that gripped the steering wheel were those of a man well into middle age. I yearned for the past to come alive but it was as dead as winter.

I started the car and the sound of the engine disturbed my thoughts like a stone thrown on to the mirrored surface of a lake. I drove up the drive and towards the place that had always held my love in spite of the hatred of the people who had lived there. I wondered whether Yvette was still alive and what had become of Monsieur and Madame Duval. If they were still there would they recognise me or had I changed beyond recognition? I caught myself in the mirror and realised that they probably wouldn't know me; it had been so long ago. Only someone who had loved me would recognise the lonely little boy behind the eyes of a man, old beyond his years.

The *château* was exactly as I had remembered it. Nothing had changed. I drove up to the front of the building with its pale stone walls and tall sash windows, the light blue shutters open to let in the sun, the grey-tiled roof, interrupted only by pretty dormer windows and slender chimneys, and the two graceful towers. I had never appreciated its beauty, only what it had stood for. Now it represented a bygone era but its beauty remained. I pulled up and climbed out. A young man in a black and grey uniform emerged from the hall and offered to carry my suitcase. I followed him inside and was struck immediately by the limestone floor. They had removed the blue and gold carpet.

I was met by a handsome man in his thirties. He stood tall with his shoulders back and his chin high, his sleek black hair combed off his face. He introduced himself as Jean-Luc

Lavalle. Assuming I was not French he spoke in English. 'Welcome to Château Lecrusse. Have you come far?' His saccharine smile and air of self-importance irritated me already. He couldn't have imagined that my father's black boots had strode across the stones of that floor and that I had raced my little cars here, that this grand hotel had once been my home.

'From America,' I replied, not wishing to engage in conversation.

'We have lots of guests from America,' he said proudly. 'It's because of the history. The *château* is sixteenth century. You don't have much history in America.'

'Then you know little about the world, *monsieur*.' My reply did not deter him.

'Americans love the culture of Europe.'

'I suppose they have no culture of their own,' I replied. He did not detect the sarcasm in my voice.

'*Exactement.* You will find Maurilliac is bursting with culture.'

'I'm sure I will. Right now, I would like to go to my room.'

'Certainly, *monsieur*. If you please, I have a form for you to fill in. Your case has already been taken upstairs.'

'Tell me something,' I said, taking the seat he offered me. 'Who owns the hotel?'

'It used to be owned by a couple called Duval. They sold it about a decade ago to a company called Stellar Châteaux who own a number of *châteaux* in France.'

'And you are . . . ?'

'The manager. If you have a problem or any questions I am the man at your service.'

'That is very comforting to know,' I replied. 'Who runs the vineyard?' He looked uncomfortable at my questioning.

'Alexandre Dambrine.'

'What of the church? Who is the priest?'

'Père Robert Denous.'

'Ah, Père Abel-Louis has gone?'

'He has retired. He lives in the town, on the Place de l'Eglise.' He watched me fill out the form. 'Excuse me for asking, *monsieur*, have you been here before?'

I raised my eyes to his face and stated simply, 'I used to live here.' Then added with some amusement, 'Before you were born.'

Jean-Luc's eyes lit up. I could see there were dozens of questions he wanted to ask, but he sensed my boundaries like an insurmountable wall around me, and withdrew. I finished filling out the form and he showed me to my room. As we walked down the corridor, I noticed the upholstered chair behind which I had often hidden as a boy. It was in the same place, even the silk was the same, though faded from the sunlight that fell in through the window adjacent. It looked so small now I couldn't imagine ever being tiny enough to hide behind it. As Jean-Luc put the key in the lock I cast my eyes further down the corridor to the room where Joy Springtoe had stayed. I remembered it well. I thrust my hand into my pocket and pulled out the little rubber ball I had nearly lost for ever beneath her chest of drawers, and recalled with nostalgia the moment she had given it back to me. I could still taste the scent of her skin as she had embraced me for the last time, and felt a slight pull at my heart as I recalled the painful days that followed her departure. Few people gave me love as a little boy; I would never forget them.

'This room has a charming view over the vineyard,' said Jean-Luc. 'It is far more beautiful in summer, but you must know that, of course.'

'Thank you,' I said dismissively. His questions were on the brink of bursting forth and I wanted to be alone.

'Very well, if you require anything, dial zero for room service. Otherwise, I shall leave you to rest.' He closed the door with some reluctance.

I walked to the window and gazed out over the fields that had been my playground.

I unpacked my clothes, which didn't take long as I had brought little, then decided to take a walk around the estate. I was anxious to see the stable block and the rest of the *château*. I was disappointed that the Duvals had gone. I would like to have tormented them a little as they wouldn't have known who I was. I had planned on being the most tiresome of guests, just to make their life hard and to watch them squirm. It was satisfactory to be on the other side of the fence. I recalled the time Madame Duval had caught me watching the guests alight on the gravel and had dragged me into the kitchen by the ear where she had beaten me in front of Yvette and her gruesome band of staff. Now I was a guest myself and the moment for revenge had passed. I hoped for divine justice. I hoped their pitiless hearts had turned them into unhappy creatures doomed to grow old in darkness.

I strode downstairs and wandered about the rooms. Everything looked so much smaller. I dwarfed my little hiding places, and the dining-room that had seemed so vast and noisy was really a cosy room with bad acoustics. The smell of the place was the same, transporting me back into the past: a mixture of polish, old wood smoke from the fire in the hall, and four hundred years of life. It entered through my nose and penetrated the marrow of my bones so that I felt I had slipped back in time. I grew dizzy with bittersweet nostalgia. From the conservatory I looked outside. The terrace was wet and mossy. Brown leaves had blown on to the stones where the Pheasants had sat in the shade talking about Coyote, where I had hidden beneath the table with Rex. There were no tables now, as it was the middle of winter, and the garden that stretched out to the fields had taken a battering from the wind, strewn with the debris of autumn. I remembered crouching in the bushes with Pistou to watch the guests

taking tea. I didn't scan the landscapes for a glimpse of him.
I knew he wasn't there. I could feel the hollowness of his
absence. I was no longer able to conjure him up as I had
done then. I had grown up and left him behind.

I wandered into the kitchen. A chef in a white hat and
apron was leaning over a large copper pot of soup with a
ladle while a member of his team stood waiting for his
comments. He spoke in a low voice, the opposite of Yvette's
bellowing shriek. When he saw me, he raised his eyes and
nodded before returning to his work. The atmosphere was
industrious and efficient, but most notably happy. I glanced
up to the pots stacked on top of the cupboards, to the rack
where utensils hung along with pots and pans from the ceiling
and knew that I could reach them all simply by lifting my
hand. Yet, back then I had been Yvette's 'grabber' and my life
at the *château* had changed dramatically from being useless
to suddenly being of importance. I smiled to myself, then left
the room.

One thing that had changed was the stable block.
Machinery had taken over from horses and ploughs. The
apartment at the top of the stairs was now used as offices,
the stables for tractors and other equipment. Jacques
Reynard's workshop was still there, but his spirit had gone.
I felt a wave of sadness. I realised that in all the years since
Coyote's disappearance I hadn't let anyone into those places
in my heart that Jacques Reynard, Daphne Halifax and Joy
Springtoe had made their own. I left the stable block with a
sense of loss.

I ambled about the *château*, soaking up the memories,
touching things, listening to the echo of voices that resonated
across the years. But I yearned to talk to someone who had
shared it all with me. My mother had gone, Pistou had existed
only in my imagination. The Duvals and Yvette had left and
anyway, I had no desire to see them, now. Yet, part of me

craved revenge. I wanted to slay my demons. The *chevalier* yearned to draw his sword on all those who had tormented him, to derive pleasure from their pain as if, in some perverse way, their pain would negate his own. So, I set off to town in the hope of finding Père Abel-Louis.

The sun was now high in the sky. I was hungry, although I had eaten with Caroline, *croissants* and a cup of coffee. It was cold, the heat from the sun weak and ineffective, but I insisted on walking. I put on a coat and hat, thrust my hands into my pockets and walked down the road, the path that cut through the fields being too wet and muddy and I didn't have boots. I savoured the surroundings, listened to the odd bird that braved the chill, and remembered. It was somehow more pleasant out in the open. The memories were less claustrophobic. The cold was bracing. The views of the fields, the wide horizon, the sense of space, invigorated me. I felt ready to confront my biggest enemy.

The town had changed little in forty years. There were a few new houses on the outskirts, there were cars where there had mostly been horses and carts, and I didn't recognise anyone. No one at all. I wandered down the road, peered into shop windows and small cafés. I didn't relish being anonymous, I had got used to that long ago and besides, I was a different person now, at least on the outside. I was an adult walking through my childhood and everything that had once seemed so large now appeared very small and unimportant.

When I reached the Place de l'Eglise I sat down on the edge of the fountain. There was no water springing out of the mouth of the fish that stood at the foot of the saint, it was frozen like the trees. The square was busy with children, mothers standing chatting in the sunshine, pigeons picking up scraps on the ground. It was hard to imagine that there, in the shadow of the church that still dominated the square,

my mother had been stripped, shaved and humiliated in front
of a baying crowd. That I had been held up for all to see like
a sacrificial lamb. Of course, we weren't alone, my mother
and I. There had been others, punished in the same way,
paraded naked like animals, but I didn't know them; I only
remembered my own horror. But now the place vibrated with
life and cheerfulness. Maurilliac had moved on. There was
no statue of little Mischa Fontaine, the boy who saw a vision
and received a miracle. There were no pilgrims who came in
search of a similar experience. It hadn't been turned into a
shrine. No one remembered. Or so I thought.

28

The church of St Vincent de Paul did not frighten me any more. Having cast a sinister shadow over my childhood, it now radiated serenity, not menace. The statues of the saints did not bear down on me from their pedestals with condemnation but with contemplation; after all, they were made of stone, not flesh. The sun cast beams of light over the chairs, illuminating the places my mother and I had occupied every Sunday. I sat down, alone in the silent building. I expected to feel God's presence there, now that Père Abel-Louis had gone, but I did not. If I felt Him at all, it was in the fields, out in the open air, beneath the sky. When I stretched my eyes as far as I could see, I believed I could sense infinity, perceive a higher power, out there in the mists. But not here. Not within these cold walls of stone.

I remained there for a while. I forgot my rumbling stomach. Lost myself in the still quiet of my solitude. But my legs were too long and it wasn't long before I grew stiff. The seat was uncomfortable, the wood hard, the air stale with the smell of age, like a musty old man. I knew there were bones beneath my feet and was sure that I could smell them The flowers that adorned the altar were pretty enough but there had been too much unhappiness there. Beneath the serenity vibrated an undertone of all that had passed. History could not be erased. I stood up and walked back down the aisle. Père Abel-Louis had chased God out of His own house and God had never returned.

I ate at a restaurant that gave on to the square. The locals were used to tourists and although they looked me over with the wary eyes of people who had never ventured further than their own town, they left me alone to eat in peace. The food was good. I had eaten in this spot with Coyote but that old bistro had long gone; in its place this fancy restaurant serving foie gras and champagne. I was just tucking into dessert when my attention was diverted to the door where a couple were leaving. I only saw her profile. One moment she was there at the entrance, the next she was out in the square; but she was unmistakeable: Claudine. I froze and stared out of the window, hoping she'd turn around so that I could see her better. So that I could be sure. Her hair was shorter, shoulder length, and she hunched a little in her heavy coat. But I recognised the nose, the short upper lip, the mouth. She was no longer toothy but I knew it was her. There was nothing I could do; by the time I had got to the door, she had gone.

I drank my coffee with renewed energy. The blood shot through my veins and my heart quickened. I suddenly felt hot. I took off my sweater and loosened the collar of my shirt. Claudine was still in Maurilliac. I knew I could track her down. It wasn't hard. Maurilliac was a small place. I'd wait until Sunday and find her at Mass. She had never missed Mass as a child. Like me she had been dragged there every Sunday morning. We had shared a hatred of *le curéton*. We had laughed about him on the bridge. I longed to discuss the past with her. She was one of the few people who had understood me. She had taken the time, like Coyote and Jacques Reynard.

As I paid the bill I asked for Père Abel-Louis' address. The waiter was suspicious and asked why I should want it. 'I'm an old friend,' I replied. He hesitated a moment before giving it to me.

'I should warn you, he's very ill,' he said. He narrowed his eyes. 'He doesn't like visitors.'

'Oh, I think he'll like me,' I said with a smile. The waiter shrugged and reluctantly gave me the details. I tipped him a little extra and walked out into the square.

Père Abel-Louis' front door was unremarkable, as if the plainness was designed to assure he receded into obscurity. It wasn't the showy residence of a former priest, the most important man in town. I stood there a moment, collecting myself. I did not know what I was going to say to him. I just knew that I wanted to see him, the more old and decrepit the better. I lifted my hand and knocked. When no one answered, I knocked again. I heard a rustle from within, then the metal clink of keys and bolts. It sounded like a jail. I wondered why he locked his doors like that. I wondered from whom he was hiding.

A withered old man looked at me suspiciously. I recognised him immediately. His hair was thinner, whiter, his scalp crimson beneath it. His face was grey and gaunt, his cheeks sunken, his lips little more than a thin scowl. But his eyes were the same unfeeling balls of glass that had once burned holes in my resistance. He ran a dry tongue over his lips and stared up at me blankly. It was clear that he did not recognise me. 'Père Abel-Louis,' I said, and he grunted.

'Who are you?'

'Mischa Fontaine,' I replied. His tongue darted back into his mouth and he blinked.

'I know no one of that name,' he said quickly, attempting to close the door. I stuck my foot inside.

'I think you do.'

'I am ill.'

'And I have come to visit you,' I said, pushing open the door. He was frail; I didn't even have to draw my sword.

'I don't wish to see anyone. Who gave you my address? Why didn't you telephone first? Have you no manners?'

I forced my way inside and closed the door behind me.

He hobbled up the corridor, leaning heavily on a stick. He had been so tall, but now I towered above him. I noticed he was trembling. Didn't he know that little boys grow up to be men?

He sank into an armchair. The room was dim, the shutters closed to allow only a little light to penetrate. The air was stale. It stank of incontinence and death. I pulled the cord so that the shutters opened further. He winced as the sun tumbled into the room, placing a hand in front of his face with a yelp.

'What do you want?'

'I wanted to see you, Père Abel-Louis. I wanted revenge for making my life miserable. But I see that you are dying.'

'I am old and weak. Leave me to die in peace.' I could almost hear the rattling of his bones, but I felt no compassion, just hatred.

'But you are a man of God, are you not?' His lips trembled and he turned his face away. 'How do you think God will judge you?'

'God performed a miracle in my church.'

'That had nothing to do with you, Père Abel-Louis, and you know it. But you made it your own, didn't you?'

'I forgave you, what more do you want?'

'Forgiveness?' I scoffed. '*You* forgave *me*?' My laughter terrified him. His eyes flickered like those of an animal caught in a trap and his mouth twitched. A light, white foam began to collect at the corners of his lips and his breathing grew laboured. 'You let them punish my mother and you let them torture me. As a man of God, how do you explain that?'

When he looked at me his eyes were no longer glassy, but bloodshot and frenzied. 'You prey on a weak and feeble man who cannot defend himself?'

'You preyed on a little boy too small to defend himself.'

'It is all in the past.'

'You think it remains there for me?'

'I only did what I thought was right!'

'How many innocent people died because you turned a blind eye? Tell me that, Père Abel-Louis. How many retributions took place in the shadow of your church?'

'I don't know what you're talking about.' I realised that I had touched a nerve, although I didn't know why.

He sat there, a trembling skeleton of a man. 'May the Devil take your soul,' I said quietly. 'Because you promised it to him, didn't you, Père Abel-Louis?'

'May God forgive me,' he said suddenly, the terror burning in his eyes, turning his face red. 'Forgive me, Mischa.' He closed his eyes and grew very still. The room suddenly grew hot. The air was sucked out of it, as if the walls were closing in around me. I took off my coat and sat down on the sofa. The house hadn't been cleaned, he was living in squalor. 'I regret the past,' he said, his voice a whisper. 'I have hidden from it for most of my life. Bolted the door, barely ventured out. I welcome death because I cannot live with myself and the things I have done.'

'There is still time to wipe the slate clean. Doesn't Jesus welcome the sinner who repents?'

His eyes welled with tears. 'But I've done unspeakable things, Mischa. In pursuit of worldly goods. Now I face death I realise they mean nothing. I will meet God naked and alone. I have nothing. Nothing. You cannot understand. You were only a boy.'

'I am a man now and I do understand.'

'No, you don't. But let me tell you. Then I want you to leave and I don't want to see you again. I knew one day it would all catch up with me. Now it has, I do not fear it.'

'I promise,' I said. My heart began to pound and my hands grew sweaty. Unlike Père Abel-Louis, I was afraid of the past, afraid of what he was about to tell me.

'When the Germans came I was left no choice but to welcome them. We didn't know how long they would stay, whether the Allies would defeat them. I believed the Germans were here for good, I backed the wrong horse. They were pleasant enough. They treated us with respect. No one was hurt. They simply marched in and took over the *château*. Your mother was working there for the Rosenfelds. When they left, she stayed on with Jacques Reynard to look after the place. She thought the family would return at the end of the war. The Germans were a shrewd lot. They knew the key to peace rested with me. I was the keeper of the flock. If they had me on their side, the rest of the community would follow. So, they invited me for dinner. They attended Mass. They were generous. Times were hard for the French but they made sure that my life was easy. Your mother fell in love the moment she saw your father. It was plain to see. But they kept it secret. Only I knew because I saw it with my own eyes. Then you were conceived and your father asked me to marry them. They didn't want you to be illegitimate. I conducted the service in the little chapel at the *château*. There you lived like any normal family and no one argued. Your father was powerful man. I was fond of your mother. She had great charm and wit and, of course, a rare beauty.' He paused a moment while he cleared the phlegm in his throat. He requested a glass of water. I found the kitchen at the back and filled a glass from the tap.

'You see, Anouk and I were friends. It is impossible for you to imagine.'

'What went wrong?' I asked.

'The Allies came and the Germans left. Your mother knew too much.'

'So you punished her?'

'I betrayed her. I told the people that she had married

Dieter Schulz and that her child was a Boche baby, the devil's spawn.'

I felt a sharp pain at the sound of my father's name.

'And you let them do that to her?'

'I stood by and let them punish her.'

'And me? I was three years old.'

'You were a baby.' He heaved a long drawn out sigh. The air rattled down his windpipe. He coughed again to clear it. 'I did it to save myself. I hoped she'd leave. But she stayed to torment me. She knew the deals I had done with the Germans, she knew the people I had betrayed. She knew my hands were tainted with the blood of the innocent, but she didn't speak out.'

'Why not?'

'Because no one would believe her. I was a man of God. Who would believe a fallen woman over a man of God?'

I leaned forward with my elbows on my knees and rubbed my forehead. So Père Abel-Louis had sacrificed me and my mother in order to save his own skin. Now I knew why my mother had insisted on going to Mass every Sunday: her presence reminded him of his sins and she knew those sins would torment him. She refused to leave; she wouldn't let him beat her. I was surprised she had never told me. Not even when she was older, when the past was just a memory. But she never spoke about the war, my father, Père Abel-Louis. Perhaps that was the poison that fed the cancer that finally killed her. If only she had shared it all with me she might have saved herself.

'I lost my voice, Père Abel-Louis. We were outcasts.'

'I had no choice,' he hissed, averting his eyes so he didn't have to look into mine.

'You could have talked to my mother. Surely, if you had been such friends, you could have kept the secrets together.'

'Anouk wasn't that sort of woman. She was defiant, wilful . . .'

'But she loved the Germans.'

'No!' His voice was now a growl. 'She loved *a* German, your father. She loved France and its people. The moment the Allies arrived she celebrated with the rest of them. I knew it was only a matter of time before she betrayed me. I had to look after myself. Maurilliac needed a Father, I couldn't let them down.'

'You were not worthy to serve them.'

'They needed direction.'

'You showed them the way of hatred and vengeance.'

'I was confused. I was afraid. You cannot understand.' I knew instinctively there was something he wasn't telling me. His eyes swam around the room, anywhere but into mine. His evasiveness was chilling.

'Then help me to understand so that I can forgive you.' Once more he closed his eyes. His face blanched and seemed to shrink into itself. His white hands lay in his lap. They did not move. He sat hunched and defenceless as if death had already come and was slowly swallowing him up. I knew that he was not going to tell me any more.

I left as I had promised. I had no intention of returning to that airless room. It wouldn't be long before he joined those he had betrayed and faced *their* judgement. I wanted so much to believe in Heaven and God, just so that justice would be done. I leaned against the wall and gulped in lungfuls of fresh, cold air. It burned my windpipe but it felt good.

As I walked back up the road, I longed to share my experiences with someone. I wanted to find Jacques Reynard but feared he was dead. I couldn't take such news today, after confronting Père Abel-Louis. As long as I didn't know, there was hope that he still lived and that I would find him in Maurilliac. I couldn't bear that the evil priest was all that remained of my past. I now doubted my own eyes. I resigned myself to the fact that the woman I had believed to have been Claudine was probably someone who just looked like her. It was wishful thinking, nothing more. I hunched my shoulders and slipped my hand through my coat, into my trouser pocket. I pulled out the little rubber ball my father had given me and rolled it around in my palm. Perhaps it had been a mistake to come. I was only digging up painful memories. Père Abel-Louis had cleared his conscience, but what about me? His revelations hadn't changed anything, only the way I saw my mother. But what was the use? She was dead.

Suddenly I heard a familiar voice. It rang out from long ago, when I had been wretched and alone. The years dissolved like mist and I was a little boy again, my heart aflutter with the excitement of first love. I turned around slowly, not knowing whether her cry was simply an echo of my own longing. 'Mischa?' she exclaimed.

'Claudine, it *is* you.' She stood in front of the post office, her eyes glittering in the cold, her expression incredulous.

'What are you doing here?'

I shrugged. 'I had to come back,' I said, gazing into her face, stunned by the woman who stared back at me.

'You grew up,' she said, then smiled. Her front teeth still stuck out a little, reminding me of the little girl I had befriended on the bridge.

'So did you.'

'You're still Mischa.'

'You're still Claudine.'

She shook her head and a frown wobbled between her eyebrows. 'No, I'm not.' She sighed and averted her eyes. 'I'm not her any more. I wish I was.'

At that moment a man stepped out of the post office. He was dark-haired and olive-skinned, tall with broad shoulders and an unshaven chin. There was something unkind about the twist of his mouth. '*Bonjour,*' he said. His arrogance already grated. He didn't recognise me but I recognised him. He was the same, just older.

'You remember Laurent, don't you Mischa?' she said. 'Laurent is my husband.'

29

I watched them walk away. Side by side, husband and wife, leaving me alone and bewildered on the pavement. Her parting glance was not enough to assuage my anger, in spite of its tenderness that caused my stomach to flip over. I had no justification for being furious. We had been children, after all. But she had been my special friend: Laurent, my enemy. It amazed me how time did so little to erase old grievances, even those of a small child. I was now certain that, before that moment, I had never been in love. I had never suffered the dizziness in the head, the rush of blood to the heart, the spinning sensation in the stomach, the sense of grappling against gravity to hold on to someone and the terror of losing them. I felt that now. She had never belonged to me, but I was overcome with a need to hold her.

I hunched my shoulders against the cold and thrust my hands into my pockets. With a pang of regret, I watched them disappear around the corner. She didn't look back. I was an old acquaintance, nothing more. Perhaps we'd meet again in the square, but then I'd return to my life in America and she'd remain here, among the memories I so cherished. Events that we had shared but which she had undoubtedly forgotten. I turned and walked back up the road towards the *château*, my heart heavy with sorrow.

When I reached the hotel, I ignored the cheery greetings from the staff. Jean-Luc wasn't there, which was a blessing. I wasn't in the mood to talk or listen to his ignorant chatter.

I hid myself in my room, leaving a grey cloud in my wake, warning anyone off coming near. I sat on the bed with my head in my hands. I forgot my meeting with Père Abel-Louis. He paled in the brilliance of my chance encounter with Claudine. I replayed it over and over in my head. I had turned and there she stood, the toothy child grown into an attractive woman. She had smiled, brushed her hair off her face with a gloved hand, and gazed at me in a timid way, her soft green eyes full of disbelief and joy. I had felt it then, like the dawn after a long dark night; the sudden realisation that there was only one woman in the world for me and that there she stood, gazing at me as if she knew it too. And then the horror of seeing Laurent. The sensation of falling and desperately struggling for balance. I had shaken his hand, but I had not smiled. I couldn't pretend that I was pleased to see him. I couldn't hide my jealousy that he had the woman I wanted. My manners deserted me, as did my ability to dissemble. Claudine had shaken me up and nothing was in the right place any more.

I had to see her. But, how could I with Laurent by her side? He wasn't stupid. He'd know my motives. I could hang about the Place de l'Eglise in the hope of catching her on her own. I could follow her home and wait for Laurent to leave. I could be devious; after all, I had once been an accomplished spy. But what would come of it? She was married. She had a life. I would return to mine, as empty as it was, and I would have to forget her.

It was now dark. The wind was up. I stood staring out over the lawn, the vineyard beyond engulfed in darkness. I remembered my grandmother's belief in the wind. Well, it was blowing one hell of a gale tonight. I felt disgruntled and unhappy, beginning to wish I had not come. The only thing I had achieved was tormenting Père Abel-Louis. A hollow victory. It didn't make me feel any better. I was haunted by the past even more than before. The demons were still there; I hadn't slain any. I had just fallen in love with someone I could not have.

I bathed and dressed for dinner. Once again I would eat alone. I was tired of my own company and, yet, I was determined not to allow my solitude to evoke pity in others, for pity brought invitations. I resolved to look as grumpy as possible. I walked down the stairs and across the hall towards the library, where I intended to have a drink before eating. As I made my way across the floor where I had pushed toy cars as a child, I was detained by a receptionist. 'Excuse me, *monsieur*.' I turned and settled my eyes on him. He seemed to wilt beneath my gaze. With a shaking hand, he held out an envelope. I took it and frowned. The writing was neat and looped, as all French writing seems to be. Only when I reached the library did I realise that I hadn't even bothered to thank him.

There was a boisterous fire in the grate. I ordered a Martini and sank into a leather armchair. A few people sat reading the papers. No one spoke. The room was pleasantly quiet. I tore open the envelope and read the note: *Mischa, please meet me tomorrow morning on the bridge at nine-thirty. Your old friend, Claudine*. I stared at it in disbelief. Had she, too, felt the sense of destiny? I read it again, taking pleasure from her handwriting, as if her very essence was captured in the ink. The waiter brought my Martini and I sat back in the chair, staring into the fire, suddenly feeling a whole lot lighter.

'*Bonsoir, monsieur*.' I looked up to see Jean-Luc, the manager. Had it not been for Claudine's note I would have grunted and opened a newspaper to avoid him. But I felt euphoric with excitement and, to my own surprise, offered him the chair opposite. 'I trust that everything is to your liking,' he said, settling into the chair.

'Yes,' I replied, folding the letter and slipping it into my breast pocket. 'Everything is just perfect.'

'I have been wanting to ask you about your childhood here at the *château*.'

'I was born here,' I said, taking a sip of Martini.

'Then perhaps you might be interested in old photographs of the place before it became a hotel. When it was a family home.'

'I would be very interested,' I replied, unable to think of anything but Claudine.

'The Duvals kept everything, which is very lucky, because the archives are full of documents, albums of photographs, visitor books, game books, inventories, even shopping lists. I thought, seeing as you lived here then, you might find some photographs of old relatives.' His reference to my great age did not offend me. I was amused.

'I was born in 1941, Jean-Luc. I am not a fossil. Nor was I here before the war. My mother worked here, that's all. I don't remember much about the *château* before it became a hotel.' I didn't wish to inform him about my father and the other Germans who had resided here during the Occupation.

'I beg your pardon.'

'I'm glad you got rid of that horrid carpet in the hall.'

'The beauty of these old *châteaux* is in their original forms. The less one changes the better, don't you agree?'

'When I was a boy, Jacques Reynard ran the vineyard. Is he . . .' I shuddered. The drink and Claudine's note had made me reckless.

Jean-Luc smiled. 'He lives just outside Maurilliac. About forty minutes from here.'

I was stunned. 'He's alive?'

'Of course. He bought a small farm. Now he has retired, but he still runs his farm.'

'Why did he leave?'

He shrugged. 'I don't know. He was old.'

'But he loved it here. I would have thought he might have

moved into one of the cottages on the estate, or into Maurilliac at least.'

'You'll have to ask him.'

'I shall. Is he married?'

'His wife died about eight years ago.'

'Do you remember her name?'

'Yvette, she used to . . .'

'Cook. Yes, I knew her. Well, I'll be damned.' I pictured them in the old folly. What a sight they had been for a young boy. He had had a funny name for her, I tried to remember, but could not.

'I met her once or twice, a charming woman,' Jean-Luc continued. I didn't answer because in spite of elevating me to 'grabber,' I had always feared and hated her.

That night I was unable to sleep. I lay awake, staring up at the ceiling, my childhood replaying before my eyes like an imaginary reel of film that I could rewind and fast-forward at will. I was amazed that although it all seemed like another life it was, at the same time, strangely tangible. I had recognised the familiar brightness in Claudine's eyes, but also noticed a warm maturity and, if I was not mistaken, a shadow of pain. She was the same person beneath the layers of experience accumulated over the years, just older and wiser and more than a little frayed around the edges. I longed for dawn to break. I was desperate to see her. I didn't know what would come of it, if anything. But that night, while my heart thumped against my ribcage and I lay willing the hours to pass, all I wanted was to talk to her. I must have slept for I awoke at eight. It was already light. I pulled back the curtains to find the ground was covered by a thin layer of frost. The air was full of mist, casting the lawn and fields beyond in a magical glow. The day held such promise. I dressed and shaved, tried to make some sense of my hair that was long and unruly, greying at the temples, the colour of wet sand.

There was no avoiding it; the glossy blond boy of my youth had not fulfilled his early promise. I had breakfast in the dining-room, reading the papers, although only my eyes took in the words; my mind was already at the bridge.

I put on my coat and hat and strode out of the conservatory on to the lawn. The ground was so hard it didn't matter that the shoes I wore were inappropriate for cross-country excursions. My breath rose on the icy air and my cheeks stung. I thrust my hands into my pockets and made my way to the track that led down to the river. How often I had taken it with Pistou. We had chased rabbits and birds, played catch with my ball or simply ambled along, kicking stones. The landscape hadn't changed in the years I had been away. The hill retained its gentle curvature, the forest still smelt of pine. The river still wound its way down the valley, the bridge, when I reached it, was as it had always been. Only our lives were transient like the leaves that came and went, blown about on the wind of Fate, battered by the rain, warmed in the sun. Standing on that stone link between one land and another I sensed more than ever before my own mortality. If my past was a blink, then so was my future. One day I'd be gone but all this would remain. It would continue without me. Where would I be? In an eternal sleep or in some spirit world with those who had gone before me? I had wasted so much time already. Years I had chosen to fill with anger and bitterness. It now appalled me. I was determined not to waste any more time.

I looked at my watch. It was past nine-thirty. I strained my eyes to see if she was coming. The mist hung low like a shroud, making it difficult to see beyond fifty yards. I imagined her running through it, shouting for her hat. Once or twice I thought I heard her footsteps, but it must have been an animal stepping on a twig, a deer or a hare. A spray of birds flew into the air, disturbed by the crackling sounds on the ground, but it was not Claudine. I wondered suddenly whether I had got the wrong time and burrowed about in my pockets for her note, before I remembered that I had worn a dinner jacket the night before and had placed it in the breast pocket, where it remained. Perhaps she had said pm and not am. Or perhaps she had got cold feet. Maybe Laurent had stopped her coming. I started pacing the bridge, up and down, up and down, stamping my feet to keep warm. The minutes dragged, but as they moved on, so diminished the likelihood of Claudine turning up.

At ten the mist began to lift and the sun to shine through. I was affronted by the beauty of the morning. The dew sparkled on the leaves, the particles of mist that remained glittered and twinkled in the air, and the frost that clung to the grass sparkled like little jewels. My disappointment would have been easier to cope with had the day not been so magical. It was hard to feel miserable in the midst of such beauty. I knew there was no point in waiting around in the cold. My dreams dissolved with the fog and I was faced once again with the possibility of leaving Maurilliac without seeing Claudine again. I wished I hadn't seen her; then, at least, I wouldn't have had to suffer such disillusionment. That fleeting meeting the day before had held within it the promise of something tremendous. My life now seemed more dull and monotonous than it had before and certainly a great deal lonelier. I turned and walked away.

30

'Mischa!' I heard her voice and turned around. She was running up the path beside the river. 'Mischa! Wait!' I hurried back down the track towards her. My elation was so great that any formality that might have dictated our encounter was banished and I swept her into my arms so that her feet dangled above the ground.

'Claudine!' I breathed into her neck. 'I'm so happy to see you.'

'I'm sorry I was late. I couldn't get away sooner.'

'It's okay. You're here and you don't know how happy that makes me.'

She laughed and my stomach lurched with nostalgia. Her laughter had bubbled and gurgled like that of a child. I found myself laughing too. I put her down but we continued to hold each other. For a long moment we simply stared at one another, taking in the faces moulded by time and adulthood, finding that we hadn't changed that much after all.

'You're still Mischa,' she said at last, smiling incredulously.

'You're less toothy,' I replied and she laughed again.

'Thank Heaven for that. I looked like a donkey.'

'No, you didn't. I liked your teeth.'

'They're still crooked, but they seem to have sorted themselves out as I've got older, or perhaps I'm just used to them now. Why am I talking about my teeth?' She shook her head and smiled. 'God, Mischa, it's been nearly forty years. Where have you been? What have you done?' She stared at me for a long moment, her gaze a caress that turned my blood to honey. I realised then that I hadn't lost the gift of clairsentience that I had relied on as a child, I just hadn't needed it. As a mute child I had dwelt in the subtext of life; a part of me was still there, reading in the eyes the words that remained unexpressed.

We started to walk along the river-bank towards an old iron bench that I had once made into a pirate ship with Pistou. 'Well, it's a long story.' I took the hand that she had linked through my arm. 'We lived in New Jersey for about seven years and then my mother and I moved to New York.'

'How is your mother?'

'She died of cancer.'

'I'm sorry. That must have been a terrible blow for you. It was only when I grew up that I realised the truth about your past. Oh, I knew who your father was and why they treated your mother as an outcast, but I never really understood what it all meant. You and your mother must have shared an incredible bond, to have gone through all that together. I'm sorry she's gone. Are you married?' I noticed the change in tone, as if she were trying to sound jolly but in reality, feared my answer.

'I've never married,' I replied.

'A handsome man like you?' she laughed, the brightness in her voice restored.

'I'm a bit of a sight actually.'

'You're still Mischa. It could have been yesterday, couldn't it?' She sighed and fell on to the bench.

'We were children and yet with you, I don't feel I have changed all that much,' she continued. I sat down beside her. 'I mean, when I saw you yesterday, it was as if we had always remained in contact. You weren't a stranger. You were my old friend.' She turned to me and smiled bashfully. 'You still are my old friend, Mischa. You know, I loved you over and above everyone else.'

'Why? I've always wanted to ask you. Why did you bother with me? After all, I couldn't speak.'

'I don't know. I suppose I looked at you as another human being, not as a freak. Everyone talked about your mother and how you had the devil's blood in you. But I knew that wasn't true: your blood was the same as mine. I thought the grown-ups were stupid and superstitious and the children lame sheep without minds of their own. I resented them. I wanted to show them, by example, how silly they all were. At first my smile was a small show of rebellion, but then, when you looked at me, your eyes were so full of fear, like a wild animal, my heart bled for you. It didn't matter that you couldn't speak. It made me like you all the more. I felt sorry for you and yet, at the same time, I admired you for being different. You had incredible charisma and you were also handsome, with those light blue eyes and pale hair. People talked about you in whispers. You were like a forbidden fruit. I've always been attracted to things I shouldn't have.'

'Like Laurent?' I couldn't help the jealousy that stuck in my throat. I wished I hadn't sounded so bitter.

She shook her head. 'I was very young when I married Laurent. We had been friends for years; it was the logical thing to do.'

'Do you have children?'

'Two. My son, Joel, is now twenty-five. He works in London for Moët & Chandon. My daughter, Delphine, is twenty-three and works in Paris for a magazine. They have both grown up.' She sighed and lowered her eyes.

'And what about you?'

'Oh, I do nothing much. I look after Laurent.'

'Does he need much looking after?'

'He's more demanding than both my children put together.

We all have to run around Laurent.' I noticed that shadow around her eyes once again and heard myself ask:

'Are you happy, Claudine?'

She turned to me, her face pink with embarrassment. 'You're not supposed to ask that question.' She was indignant. 'You can't ask me, Mischa! It's rude!'

'Why not? Because I'm not happy. I thought I was fine until yesterday, when I saw you. I realise now that I've been miserable for years, I just hadn't noticed. Unhappiness was so much a part of my life I was no longer aware of it. But you, Claudine, you've changed everything. I'll never be the same again.'

'What are you saying, Mischa? You don't even know me.'

'You know that's not true.' Once again she turned away. 'Would you have sent me that letter if you weren't unhappy? If you hadn't felt something too?'

'I wanted to see you, that's all.' She shrugged helplessly. 'Laurent doesn't like me to have male friends. He says it's inappropriate. I feared you might leave without having spoken to me.'

'No, you sent me the note because you felt it too.' When she turned back her eyes were glittering. 'Tell me you felt it too.' She inhaled the icy air. Her lips were pale and trembling, her cheeks white but for two spots of red, like bee stings. The moment felt surreal, like I was floating in cloud. 'I know it's silly,' I persisted. 'I haven't seen you for decades. But it doesn't feel that way. I feel I've known you all my life. Tell me, Claudine, that you felt it too.'

'You're right.' Her voice was barely a whisper. 'I felt it too.'

I drew her into my arms and kissed her warm mouth. Her face was cold, her nose red, but her lips were soft and tender, parted a little, inviting. She didn't resist but yielded as if she had anticipated this moment, too. As if, like mine, her whole life had been leading up to this crossroads. She had on a heavy coat and boots, polo neck and scarf, gloves and hat. I was only able to reach her face. In an attempt to get closer, I pulled off her hat and scrunched her hair in my fingers. It was thick and hot and a little sweaty around her forehead. We didn't speak, or even try to. We simply clung to one another. I savoured the sensation of her skin beneath my lips. I breathed in her scent, and tasted the salt of her tears. I realised that I had been looking for her all my life.

'Is this possible?' she asked after a while, drawing away. Her eyes searched my features, incredulous of what they saw.

'If I had been asked that a week ago, I would have said no. It's not possible to fall in love instantly. I believed that kind of love to be the stuff of bad fiction and film. I would never have imagined it would happen to me.'

'I feel I've known you for ever. That you're meant for me. I often thought about you, you know. I missed you. Especially when you left without a word. My world felt suddenly empty. I felt bereft. Everywhere reminded me of you. Everyone talked about you. You dominated the town and yet you left without saying goodbye.'

'I was spirited away in the middle of the night. I had no time. I cried all the way to America.'

'And I cried too. You were my friend. I knew you were special to me then, but more so after you had gone, because it hurt for a long time after and I never forgot you.'

'I thought about you, too. At first America was so colourful and bright, I left Maurilliac behind. But later, in the years after Coyote left, when I hated myself and everyone around me, I searched for you without even realising it. I was subconsciously drawn to French women only to be disappointed. I never lost my heart to anyone. I didn't let it go. I just knew it didn't feel right. Oh, Claudine, where have the years gone? They suddenly appear to have been but a blink. It's like we've never been apart. Yet, look at us, we're middle aged.'

'Nothing matters. You're here, in Maurilliac, and it feels right. You should have stayed. You weren't meant to leave me.'

'I know. I wish I'd had the courage to come back. I've been treading water until now. I feel I've been waiting for you. Now I've found you.' Neither of us dared ask the inevitable question: Where do we go from here?

'Why did you return to Maurilliac?' she asked instead.

'It's a long story.'

'I've got all day. Laurent works in Bordeaux, he's a solicitor. He won't be back until evening.'

'Then I will hold you until sundown.'

'Why did you leave it so long?'

'I was afraid to come back.'

'Afraid? But you were a miracle. You had the town at your feet.'

'I was a freak. I was different from everyone else. I was the Boche baby whose mother had collaborated with the enemy. No miracle could wash away that stain, however much Père Abel-Louis appeared to sanction it. You know, I still dreamed of this place. Sometimes I awoke with the smell of summer in my room.' I didn't really know the answer myself. 'Oh, it was a combination of things, I suppose. My mother died, taking with her the only link to my past. There are so many questions I need to find answers for. So many shadows I need to shed light on. I realised the past would torment me for ever unless I confronted it.'

'Have you seen *le curéton*?'

'He was my greatest enemy. Now he's a sad, decrepit old man teetering on the edge of his grave. I wonder why I feared him like I did.'

'You spoke to him?' She stared at me incredulously.

'I paid him a visit.'

'What did he say? Did he recognise you? Was he surprised to see you?'

'No, he didn't recognise me until I said my name and then he pretended he had never known me. He was terrified.'

'How I hated him. He was an evil man.'

'More evil than you could possibly imagine. He collaborated with the Germans. He married my parents in secret, then, when the Allies liberated Maurilliac, he turned against my mother because she knew too much.'

'He stood back and let them torture you both to save himself?'

I nodded gravely. 'He knew that once she was ostracised as a collaborator no one would believe any story she told about him. He has blood on his hands, I tell you. Although I think there's more. He wouldn't tell me the rest and I don't care to know. He's buried as far as I'm concerned. He no longer exists.'

'I bet he betrayed Resistance fighters in exchange for comforts. Everyone trusted him. They confessed their innermost thoughts to him. He knew everyone's secrets. He's disgusting. I hope he rots in Hell.'

'Don't worry, Claudine. He's already there,' I said, remembering the locks and bolts on his door and the rancid stench of fear. 'He's been there for years.'

'I'm ashamed to be part of this town. Ashamed for my own family's part in its history. I understand why you didn't have the courage to return and I admire your courage now.'

'There's something else,' I said, unburdening my thoughts.

'Yes?'

'My mother gave away a very valuable painting just before she died. She gave it to the Metropolitan as a gift.'

'How very generous of her.'

'I never knew she had such a painting. It's a Titian. *The Gypsy Madonna*. It's supposedly an original of the one that hangs in Vienna. Apparently Titian's first was stolen, so he painted another. It's very valuable.'

'Where did she get it from?'

'That's what I want to know.'

'Do you think she found it here?'

I shrugged, but Claudine had a point. 'I don't think she stole it.' But I wasn't sure. I felt a moment of dizziness as the idea of theft grew ever more plausible.

'Then who gave it to her?'

I shrugged. 'I don't know.'

'Did she hang out with people in the art world?'

'Yes, she did. In her business she met all sorts.'

'What did she do?'

'Antiques.'

'Did she sell paintings?'

'No.'

'Then she must have been keeping it for someone else. Why would she give a *stolen* painting to the Metropolitan? That would just heap a whole load of trouble on to your shoulders and she wouldn't have wanted that, would she?' She rubbed her chin thoughtfully. 'Whatever happened to Coyote?' Coyote – the mere mention of his name had the power to sting me, like lemon juice on a wound.

'The elusive Coyote!' I shook my head and chuckled bitterly. 'Coyote disappeared when I was ten years old. Just like that. One day he was there, the next he was gone and he never came back. I now know that he had a double life. A wife and children living in Virginia. He wasn't all that he seemed. However, if the painting had been his, he wouldn't have left without taking it with him, or he would have certainly come back to retrieve it.'

'Do you hope to find the answers here?'

'My gut tells me there's something here. I have vague memories, like dislocated images that come and go. If I could see the whole picture I'm sure I'd discover something important.'

'I can't believe your mother never told you. Even when she was dying.'

'She wouldn't discuss it.' I looked at her anxiously. 'That suggests guilt, doesn't it?'

She took my hand and squeezed it. 'If she had got it by legal means, surely she would have shared it with you? A painting of such value is something to celebrate and show off. Not to hide away. Perhaps she was given it for safe-keeping and then the owner died. Who knows what went on in the war? Maybe she found it without realising its value. There are lots of possibilities, but you shouldn't beat yourself up about it. It's not your problem. If she had wanted you to know, she would have told you.'

'Well, there's another twist in the story.'

'Go on.'

'Coyote appeared in my office a few weeks ago. He suddenly turned up after more than thirty years.'

'Did he say where he'd been?'

'No. But he looked like a tramp. He hadn't washed for weeks and his clothes were rags.'

'I remember him with his hat and his guitar. He was a hugely glamorous figure back then. Like a film star. He set the town ablaze. No one talked of anything else for years after he left. Especially as they said he hadn't paid his bill at the *château*. He had appeared a rich man.'

'He wasn't. He just charmed his way through life.'

'And charmed your mother.'

'I believe he loved my mother and I believe he loved me.'

'He gave you back your voice.'

'You remember. It wasn't a miracle after all.'

She smiled and my heart stumbled. 'I remember everything about you, Mischa.' She blushed. I took her hand and rested my gaze on her face. 'What did he want?'

'He asked after my mother. He didn't know she had died.

He didn't know that she had loved him until the end. I didn't tell him either. What was the point? You see, he didn't come back for her, but for the painting. There had been a bit of press interest, as you can imagine, and he had read about it. That was why he had come.'

'But he didn't say it belonged to him?'

'No. He thought we were rich. He had flown in like a vulture.'

'Surely he gave you an explanation?'

'He said he didn't want anything from me. He said that he was "chasing rainbows".'

'What did he mean?'

'I don't know.' I shook my head and kissed her forehead. 'But I now know why *I* came back. The Fates brought me back for you, Claudine. And you are the reason for me staying.'

We wandered up the hill to the old folly, our hands entwined like young lovers on a carefree walk, not like a couple of old friends on the brink of adultery. We reminisced about the old days. She told me a little of her life, of which every detail fascinated me. I wanted to know more about Laurent, but she didn't want to talk about him. I wanted to know if she loved him, if he treated her well. I knew she wasn't happy, but was her unhappiness something that she could live with, or was it enough to drive her away? I wanted her to come with me to America, but I didn't dare ask. It was too soon and, besides, I couldn't bear the answer to be no.

We reached the little round folly where I had spied on Jacques Reynard and Yvette. It stood on the top of the hill like a small winter palace, proud and discreet but abandoned to the depredation of time. The pale stone blended in with the frosty trees and grass, shrouded in a veil of mist that caught the light and glittered magically. The wood had encroached further so that snakes of ivy wound their way up the pillars, and blackberry bushes had been allowed to overgrow. If it hadn't been for the frost the little folly would have been a sorrowful sight. However, it possessed a mysterious beauty, enhanced by the transience of the morning. The sun would melt the frost, the ice would turn to water, and the magic would eventually disappear with the mist.

'Its loveliness makes me feel melancholy,' said Claudine. 'We're getting old and what have I done with my life?'

'You've brought up two children. That's a triumph in itself,' I replied, swinging her around to face me. I cupped her face in my hands and rubbed my thumbs over her red cheeks. For a moment she was too shy to look into my eyes.

'I shouldn't be doing this,' she mumbled. 'I'm married.'

'Look at me, Claudine.' She turned her head and blinked up at me helplessly. 'If I didn't feel so strongly, I'd never compromise you in this way. Look, I've wandered this earth with a great big hole in my heart. I've tried to fill it with all sorts of people of different shapes and sizes but no one's been the right shape. You know why? Because you made that hole in the first place and you're the only person who fits. I knew you were special when I was a boy. You had courage. You weren't afraid to defy authority, to be unpopular, to be ridiculed and you took me for your friend when no one else would. You still fit, Claudine, because the hole has grown with you. It only got bigger. I can't help myself. I love you.'

She took my wrists in her hands and smiled anxiously. 'I don't regret it, Mischa. I don't regret coming to meet you and I don't regret kissing you. I regret Fate that took you to America. I married the wrong man.'

'You don't have to stay married to him.'

'I've only just met you.'

'Trust me.'

'I'm frightened to. If Laurent finds out he'll be furious.

I'm scared, Mischa.' I kissed her pale lips, hoping to persuade her that I wouldn't change my mind. How could I explain that, until our meeting the previous day, I had never lost my heart? As a little boy I had loved those who had loved me: Joy Springtoe, Jacques Reynard, Daphne Halifax and, of course, my mother. I had never loved a woman as a man should. Isabel gave me a taste of France but that was all. Linda was unable to reach me. She had given me the best years of her life and in the end, she never really knew me any better than the day we met. One glimpse of Claudine had been all it had taken to shatter the protective shield I had built around myself. One glimpse, and she had penetrated deeper than any woman ever had. I had let her in. If she had known me better she would have understood that now I would never let her out.

'Don't leave me,' I said, my voice a whisper. 'I need you, Claudine.' She didn't reply. She just wrapped her arms around my neck and held me close.

My trip to Chile had re-established my bond with Matias and Maria Elena. My arrival at the *château* had shown me that the past can never be recaptured, however many stars are wished upon. Claudine was the love I wanted to take back with me. Claudine was the home I had been searching for.

31

The next couple of days we spent as much time as we could together. At night I longed to feel her beside me and my longing caused my whole body to ache. I wanted to hold her, to kiss her all over, to possess her completely. I wanted her to be mine. When I couldn't sleep I paced the room like an animal, imagining her sharing a bed with Laurent. I tormented myself wondering whether they made love. Whether they lay apart or entwined, whether Laurent forced himself upon her. And if he demanded his marital rights, did she resist him or was she too afraid? Afraid of hurting him? Or of *him* hurting *her*? I had to know.

If he so much as laid a finger on her I vowed to draw my sword. I imagined sending my fist through his face, shattering his arrogance with a single blow. I was bigger than he was, taller and broader, and I had more experience in that department than he could possibly imagine. Laurent had no hope against me. I visualised sweeping Claudine into my arms and stepping over his battered body. I'd rescue her from her unhappiness and we'd start a new life together in America.

Desperate to know my enemy and frustrated that I couldn't realise my daydreams, I went to Mass. I was not a religious man and I had always feared the Church. It held a dark allure that both fascinated and frightened me. I believed the institution of organised religion to be full of self-serving masters who only wanted total domination of weak people. I did not want to be one of their flock. However, my desire to see

Claudine and to know more of Laurent superseded my anxiety and I attended the service. I sat in my coat and hat at the back of the church, watching the people traipse in. I recognised some of the faces, but most were strangers. I heard the echo of their voices, '*Hun-head, Nazi boy, Boche bastard,*' but no one cast me more than a glance, not even the people I recognised. They were old now and their sight bad. Like Père Abel-Louis, they focused on the life to come, not the past. They didn't even toss me a second glance. The boy who had once been different from everyone else now blended in.

I waited for Claudine and Laurent. I knew they'd come. During our short time together we had laughed about Père Abel-Louis and she had told me that the current priest was as he should be: a respectable servant of God. She trusted him as a priest and liked him as a man. In spite of a rebellious start, she was a good Catholic. I wondered what she said in confession and how much influence Père Robert had over her.

Finally they walked in, behind a mother with five young children. I was so busy watching the children, regretting for a moment that I had none of my own, that I almost missed them. Laurent strode in with his shoulders back, his chin high. Claudine walked beside him, hunched a little, her eyes on the group in front. Her face was in repose, her expression solemn. Her hands were in her pockets, his hanging by his side. They didn't touch. They found places on the opposite side of the aisle, about eight rows in front of me. I had no fear of being seen. And anyway, why shouldn't I be at Mass? I considered stopping them on the way out and engaging in conversation, but then the spy in me took over. I'd follow them home and watch. I wanted to see how he treated her. I wanted to know my enemy so that I could work out a strategy. I didn't want to leave without her. I didn't think I could.

Père Robert Denous was young and vibrant. His presence there injected the place with vitality, like spring after a barren winter. Gone was the ominous grey aura that had surrounded Père Abel-Louis. Père Robert was gently spoken with deep-set, kind eyes. He conducted most of the service in French, not Latin, and his sermon was encouraging and positive. I found myself drawn into it, having initially focused all my attention on Claudine and Laurent. I understood why these people flocked there every Sunday. If Père Robert was the gateway to Heaven, he was a welcoming one; a gate that embraced everyone no matter what. I couldn't help but wonder how different things might have been had Père Abel-Louis been more like him.

At the end of the service, I left the church with the first few congregants, shook the priest's hand, then lingered on one side where Laurent and Claudine wouldn't see me. It didn't take them long to come out. They, too, shook the priest's hand. Laurent didn't smile, his mouth curled into a mean grimace, but Claudine did. She said a few words, sand-wiching Père Robert's hand between hers, gazing up at him with reverence. The priest smiled at her warmly and I got the impression that she knew him far better than her husband did. Perhaps she had sought solace from the Church to help her live through her unhappy marriage. They shared a joke, but Laurent didn't smile. He remained a little apart, as if, like me, he thought little of the institution that meant so much to his wife. He took her arm and they moved on, into the square.

I followed them as they walked home, keeping my distance. Laurent had dropped his hand and they walked a little apart. They didn't talk much. Claudine was the one to initiate a conversation. He answered monosyllabically then withdrew again, until, undefeated, she ignited another. I trailed them through the town, down the back streets, wondering where their friendship had gone, for the silences between them were not the warm silences of old friends, but the awkward pauses of a marriage turned cold.

They stopped at last outside a pretty house built in the same pale stone as the rest of the town, with a red-tiled roof and white shutters. However, it didn't vibrate with cosiness, but looked as empty as the window-boxes that hung on the black iron balconies on the first floor. I hid around the corner, beside a bleak-looking hair salon, and watched Laurent unlock the door and stride inside. Claudine glanced up and down the street, a frown wrinkling her forehead, before she followed him indoors. I wondered whether she felt me watching her.

It was a dull, grey morning so when they turned on the lights, I was able to see clearly into the sitting-room. They both disappeared for a while. I waited like a lion stalking a pair of wildebeest, with a wary patience. Finally, they returned. Laurent lit the fire and Claudine stood in front of the window, staring out, her arms folded in front of her chest, biting her nails. I knew she was thinking about me. She had that faraway look on her face, a melancholy expression of longing I recognised, because I had seen it on myself.

Laurent came up behind her like a shadow. He stood over her and placed his hand on her shoulder. She shrugged it off. This angered him. He raised his hands to the ceiling and let out a stream of words that I could not hear. Claudine shook her head and moved away. A few minutes later the light went on in the upstairs window. Again she looked out into the street before closing the curtains. Laurent remained at the downstairs window, hands on hips, before disappearing. I don't know what went on after that. I remained as long as I could stand. Then, when it grew too cold and my stomach began to twist with hunger, I reluctantly left and walked back up to the *château*.

I ate alone. Claudine dominated my thoughts and stole my appetite. I ate because I knew I should and because I couldn't bear the long, empty hours of waiting before I could see her again. I tried to think of a way of smuggling her into the hotel, but it was too risky; someone would recognise her and our secret would be out. I wondered whether there was somewhere else we could go. Somewhere we could lie naked together. I felt that if we made love that would somehow seal our affair. That it would make it impossible for her to stay. I wanted so much to take her away with me to America.

After lunch I sat in the library leafing through books I had no desire to read. I was consumed with anxiety and jealousy. Laurent grew into a powerful demon in my mind, the kind of demon Père Abel-Louis had been in my childhood. I let myself spiral into decline.

Suddenly Jean-Luc appeared before me, his face wide and smiling. In his hands he carried a faded green book. 'Excuse me, *monsieur*. I thought you might be interested in looking at the old family photographs of the Rosenfelds.' I was grateful to be drawn out of myself and offered him the armchair opposite. He gave me the book and I placed it on my lap.

'Whatever happened to the Rosenfelds?' I asked, not really caring.

'They all died in the war,' he replied.

My interest was aroused. 'Of course, they were Jewish.' I had never cast more than a passing thought to the Rosenfelds and my mother had never spoken of them.

'They must have died in the camps.' With a pulsating heart, I opened the book and looked through a window into a secret world; my mother's secret world.

There were photographs of the family at Longchamp in Paris, the women in fashionable dresses and wide-brimmed hats, the men in pale suits. Photographs of grand banquets and balls, garden parties and charity dinners. There were pictures of trips to London where they went to the races and the Chelsea Flower Show, sightseeing in Vienna, New York and India. Safaris in Africa and an annual visit to Jerusalem. They had chauffeurs who drove shiny cars, their white-gloved hands on leather steering-wheels, their faces solemn beneath the peaks of their black caps. They seemed to me gracious people with large, generous hearts. They were always smiling and laughing, but what struck me most about the family scenes was the obvious affection they felt for their children. It appeared to me out of step with the norms of society at that time. They were always embracing, kissing, holding hands, and cuddling the little ones. There were playful scenes of their five children rolling around on the lawn with their father, or teasing their mother, and tender moments of tranquillity when they seemed not to know they were being photographed. This was a sheltered world, ignorant of the régime that was quietly gathering power over the border, preparing to stamp it out for ever. The knowledge of what was to come made their gaiety unbearable. My heart buckled at the thought of those beautiful, innocent children suffering at the hands of the Nazis. Of their blithe, carefree faces turned grey with fear. Of their glossy, vibrant bodies reduced to ash.

My mother had known these people. She had held the children in her arms, been privy to their intimate life. I knew now why she had never spoken of them. It must have been too painful. But to have remained in the *château* after their rarefied world had been shattered? That I didn't understand.

It was strange to see the *château* as it was when it was a home. The furniture had changed but the rooms were the same. The mouldings and plasterwork on the ceilings had not been touched and the grand fireplace in the hall roared with the blaze of a similar fire. The limestone floors were partly covered with rugs where black dogs lay sleeping after running around the vineyard, before the Germans came and removed them. I believed in my father's innocence although my rational mind told me otherwise. I didn't want to believe that he had been part of the régime that tortured and destroyed millions of innocent people.

I was about to close the book, because the window into their world had now misted with sorrow, when I was struck a terrible blow. There on the wall, behind a formal portrait of the family, hung *The Gypsy Madonna*. I was frozen with horror. I felt my face throb. Jean-Luc leaned forward in alarm. 'Are you all right, *monsieur*?' he asked. I nodded, unable to speak. 'Let me get you a glass of water.' I barely noticed him get up and stride across the floor. I was swallowed into the photograph, all sorts of scenarios rising in my mind like lava from a once-dormant volcano. Had my mother stolen it? Had she kept it safe from the Nazis, believing the family would return at the end of the war? Had my father purloined it and given it to her as a gift? One thing was for certain; it had originally belonged to a Jewish family. It was a valuable piece of stolen Jewish art and therefore its possession was a war crime. I was both sickened and saddened. No wonder my mother had never told me about it; she must have been too ashamed.

Jean-Luc returned with the glass of water, which I drank in one gulp. 'I imagine it's hard for you to look back into your past. So much here has changed.'

'Actually, you'd be surprised at how little has changed. Just the people,' I replied, closing the book.

'I'm sorry. Perhaps I should not have shown it to you.'

'I'm glad you did, Jean-Luc. I think I need something stronger than a glass of water, though.'

'*Absolument*!' He took the book and leaped to his feet.

I stared into the fire, reflecting on all that the Rosenfelds had lost during the war. I realised that I knew very little about them. My mother hadn't spoken of them; like so many who had suffered, she hadn't been able, or perhaps was unwilling, to share her experiences. Yet, the *château* had been the foundation stone upon which I had built my life. My parents had met here, married here and I had been born here. My earliest memories were of the hall where my father's presence still cast a ghostly shadow. I deserved to know what had gone on within these walls, however horrific, however great my disillusionment.

I drank the whisky, which burned down my gullet into my stomach, and immediately felt better. 'You said Jacques Reynard lives nearby,' I said. 'Would you be able to give me directions?'

'Of course. I'd be happy to,' he said. I was suddenly gripped with the desire to find out more about my mother's past. Jacques was the only person who would know. Jean-Luc went off to write down the address and the route. I returned to my room to retrieve my wallet and car keys. I glanced out of the window, to the fields of vines that stretched out beneath the grey wintry sky, and thought of Jacques. How he must miss them. I realised that I hadn't thought of Claudine for a few moments and that my jealousy of Laurent had subsided. At least she was alive. At least I had found her. I was lucky.

The cold hit me hard. I breathed in the icy air and let it invigorate me. I felt a surge of energy in the face of the mystery unravelling before me. Never had I been so inspired to find out about the past. It no longer frightened me; it intrigued me.

The drive across the countryside was uplifting in spite of the dreary monotone of the landscape. I reflected on the photo album and the shock of discovering the rightful place of *The Gypsy Madonna*. I now believed my mother gave it to the Metropolitan because she knew the Rosenfelds were all dead. That is why she said she had to 'give it back'. Perhaps she had held on to it all those years hoping they might miraculously appear to reclaim it, or perhaps she only revealed that she had it when she was on the point of dying and beyond the reach of the law. I would telephone my lawyer and explain it to him on my return.

Finally, I drove the car into a rustic farm entrance. There were barns on either side, their walls pale beneath red tiles like the houses in Maurilliac. I noticed a red tractor and smiled; in the days when I had lived at the *château*, Jacques had used horses. I drew up outside the house. It was pretty with tall slim chimneys and windows framed by white shutters. Ivy grew up the walls like the beard of an old man. I stopped the car and stepped out. Standing a moment on the gravel I looked about me and soaked in the warmth of Jacques' home. I knew he was there because I could feel him. A moment later, when he stood in the doorway, his wizened face broke into a tearful smile and he opened his arms to welcome me home. As I said, those who had loved me recognised me instantly.

32

Jacques took off his beret and embraced me like a son. I towered over him, but still he held me against him, his tears soaking into my coat. Neither of us spoke but we both thought the same thing: why did it take me so long to come back?

Age had withered him like a gnarled tree. He must have been in his mid-eighties at least. But when he withdrew and I looked into his face I noticed that the light that radiated from within was as brilliant as ever. 'It's good to see you,' I said. He laughed at my understatement and shook his head.

'I should reprimand you for not even writing.'

'I'm ashamed of myself,' I said truthfully.

'Disappearing like that in the middle of the night!'

'I was a boy.'

'That's why I forgive you.' He sighed and turned serious. 'But I don't forgive your mother.'

'Let's go inside. I'm freezing,' I said, rubbing my cold hands together.

He showed me through the hall into the sitting-room where a fire burned in the grate. By contrast to the grandeur of the *château*, Jacques' house was cosy, threadbare, and filled with objects and books that held sentimental value. Like the barns outside, his home was orderly. I sank into an armchair and warmed my hands against the orange flames. Jacques poured me a drink and came over to stoke the fire. He knelt down stiffly and poked the logs with an iron rod. 'That's better,' he said. 'It's been a harsh winter.'

'You left Maurilliac?' I said. He nodded.

'Nothing left for me there. Besides, I was too old to continue working.'

'So you bought this farm and settled down with Yvette.'

'Yvette,' he chuckled and looked at me with a twinkle in his eye. 'Yvette was a good wife. I ate well and grew the belly of a satisfied man. She was an earthy woman, nice to lie on, too!'

'I spied on you, you know.' He got up and sat opposite me, sighing with pleasure as he fell into the chair.

'You did?'

'Yes, I saw you making love in the folly.'

'You devil!' he growled, clearly enjoying the memory.

'I remember now. You said she was as juicy as a grape!'

'I was very fond of Yvette.' I didn't tell him how much I had hated her. He obviously saw a side of her that I never did. But then he said something that surprised me. 'She was very fond of you.'

'She hated me,' I replied.

'She might have hated what you represented, Mischa. But I put that right.'

'She treated me better when I became her grabber.'

'Her grabber?'

'She lifted me up to grab things from the tops of cupboards and from those racks hanging from the ceiling. She hated heights.'

'She found it hard to resent you. I know she wanted to. You have to understand that this was a country ashamed of what had happened in the war. You were an innocent reminder of a national disgrace: the defeat and rape of France. But you were a very dear little boy and of course, I loved you like my own. You might find it hard to believe, but she cried bitterly when you left.' He sipped his coffee thoughtfully. '*I* cried bitterly when you left.'

'You and Daphne Halifax were the only people who were kind to me,' I said. 'And another woman from America called Joy Springtoe. You see,' I added, looking at him steadily, 'I don't forget them.'

'Tell me, Mischa. How is your mother?' Suddenly there was an unexpected change in the air, as if it had been sucked out through the windows. I hesitated because I experienced another dawning, like the lifting of summer mist at daybreak. Jacques looked so sad, so forlorn, so lost, that I was left in no doubt that he had loved her. I averted my gaze because I couldn't bear to look into his eyes.

'She's dead,' I replied and felt his sorrow like a weight on my shoulders. When I lifted my eyes I saw that his were filled with tears. 'Did she know you loved her?' I asked gently.

He nodded. 'She knew.'

'That is why you stood by us.'

'That is why I stood by you, and so much more.' I sensed he wanted to talk about her, so I probed a little deeper.

'How long had you known her?'

'Since childhood.' My mother had never told me that. I had assumed they had known each other through their jobs at the *château*. 'Anouk and I grew up together here in Maurilliac. When she left, I couldn't bear to remain. So I left too, as far as I dared go.'

'Tell me about her, Jacques.'

'Anouk was the girl everyone wanted to marry,' he began and the light returned to illuminate his face from within. 'She was coquettish, mischievous, vain even. She was very beautiful, but she had a wonderful sense of humour. I was fifteen years older than her, but we became friends. We laughed at everything. She had compassion, too, and a vast capacity for love.

'When she turned twenty-one we embarked on a love affair. I had started working for Gustave Rosenfeld's father when I was sixteen. I helped Anouk get a job there when Gustave and his wife, Pauline, inherited the place on his father's death. They were young, with small children. Anouk worked as *jeune fille*, looking after the family, arranging their entertainment. The Rosenfelds were a very important wine-growing family. The vineyard exported all over the world and people came to visit. She was kept busy. But she loved her job and she loved the family, especially the second daughter, Françoise.' He stared into the fire as if he were talking to himself. 'For three years before the war we worked together by day and loved each other by night. I asked her to marry me, but she said she was too young. I said I would wait.' He shrugged. 'Who wouldn't have waited for Anouk?'

'Then the Germans came.'

'First they annexed Austria, then they conquered Czechoslovakia. They took over the Sudetenland and marched into Prague. When Hitler marched his army into Poland, war was declared. We thought we'd beat them. We all believed it would be over in a few days. How could Hitler quash the might of France? It was unthinkable. The 1939 harvest was washed away by rain. The wine was thin, diluted, like dishwater. The peasants have a legend about wine and war: to announce the coming of war, the Lord sends a bad crop; while the war rages, He sends mediocre ones; to mark its end, He sends a rich, bountiful crop. The crop of 1939 was the worst in a hundred years!

'The Rosenfelds remained at the *château*. Since Hitler had come into power a steady stream of Jews had been pouring out of Germany into France and England and eastern European countries. There were rumours of Jews being murdered, but no one believed them to be true. Then in November 1938 nearly one hundred Jews were murdered in a single night.'

'Kristallnacht,' I said and he nodded grimly.

'In spite of this, the Rosenfelds felt safe in France. However, they were desperate to safeguard their wine. They had tens of thousands of bottles in the labyrinth of cellars that lie under the *château*. So Gustave Rosenfeld decided to wall up the best vintages, 1929 and '38, in particular. The children found it very exciting. We supposed it to be nothing more than a precaution. None of us truly believed Hitler would get past the frontier. Gustave and I laid the bricks while Anouk, Françoise and the others ran around with Pauline collecting spiders to place there, so that they would spin webs and make the walls look like they were much older. You see, parts of the *cave* are four hundred years old.'

'Why weren't you enlisted to fight?'

'I was thirty-seven and asthmatic. They allowed me to stay on to run the vineyard. The boys I worked with marched off to war with enthusiasm and arrogance. Not one of them returned.'

'What happened to the Rosenfelds when the Germans came?'

He shook his head, almost bald but for a thin layer of white hair like the webs those spiders had spun over the walls of the *cave*. 'Gustave went off to war. The rest of the family were taken away, never to be heard of again. At the time we thought they would be freed at the end of the war. We worked on with that hope in mind. But they perished in the camps. I cannot bear to think of their suffering. I hope to God the end was quick and painless. The *château* was requisitioned by Colonel Dieter Schulz.'

'My father.'

'He was tall, handsome, upstanding. It is of no surprise to me that your mother fell in love with him. He declared that he wouldn't touch the wine and that he would treat everyone with respect. However, wine had to be sent to Germany by the crate and towards the end of the war, Goering himself

descended on us to choose the works of art to be crated up
and sent back to Berlin on his private train. It is now widely
accepted that he looted some of the most valuable Jewish
collections for himself.'

'Goering stole the Rosenfelds' art collection?' I was
confused. 'Why did he not steal *The Gypsy Madonna*?'

'*The Gypsy Madonna*?'

'It's a painting by Titian. It once hung at the *château*. My
mother gave it to the Metropolitan just before she died.'

'I know nothing about that. As far as I know, Goering
plundered everything. I remember him: a fat, self-important
dandy with blond hair and any number of medals hanging
from his uniform. I bet he spent much of his time looking
in the mirror, gloating. He swaggered about with an
entourage of officers in the most ludicrously extravagant
uniforms, sipping champagne, wandering about the hall as
if he owned it. He chose three or four paintings, a tapestry,
and silver from the dining-room. I don't know exactly what
he took, but Anouk said he pilfered the most valuable things
in the *château*.'

'Did she hide anything?' I asked.

'Besides the wine? I'm not sure, but it wouldn't have
surprised me. Anouk was well-educated and cultured. She
knew a Michelangelo from a Raphael.'

'Did they have other paintings of that value in the house?'

'Goering believed so, otherwise they wouldn't have been
worth taking.'

'And my father?'

'Your mother fell in love, I think, the first moment she laid
eyes on him. He had charisma. He was tall, like you, and
broad-shouldered. Of course, he was an important officer of
the German Reich, he radiated power and that is very alluring
for a young woman. I despised him for stealing my Anouk,
but I concede that he was a gentleman and a kind man. He

fell in love, too. I cannot blame him for that. Everyone fell in love with Anouk.'

'But you continued to work at the *château*?'

'That was my life and besides, to be without her was unthinkable.'

'I went to see Père Abel-Louis . . .'

'May the devil take his soul,' he said venomously.

'I think that is imminent.'

'What could you want with him?' He stared at me almost accusingly, as if the mention of his name was in some way traitorous.

'Because I wanted to torment him. But he is already tortured by the things he did in his past. He told me that he married my parents in secret.'

'Yes, he collaborated too. He traded in human beings, Mischa. Did he tell you that?'

'I assumed . . .'

'It was because of him that the Rosenfelds were sent off to die in the gas chambers of Auschwitz. That those small, defenceless children were denied the right to grow up. Hannah, Françoise, Mathilde, André and Marc.' He fired their names at me like bullets. I was startled. 'He not only betrayed them but every Jew in Maurilliac. Why do you think he lived in such comfort when the whole of France was starving to death? I bet he didn't tell you that!'

'He said he betrayed my mother so that she wouldn't tell people what he had done.'

'And they branded her body like an animal.' I must have looked shocked for he said. 'I bet he didn't tell you that?' He snorted in defiance, then added in a very soft voice. 'Your mother was taken into the Place de l'Eglise with three other women who had collaborated with the Germans. They were stripped naked. Their heads were shaved and they were branded on their buttocks with red-hot irons, like pigs. Did he tell you that? No? Do you know what they branded? The swastika. Your mother would have carried that around with her until the day she died. *Monsieur le Curé* stood by and watched it all happen. By doing so he condoned it. And you? Surely you remember?'

'I remember,' I muttered.

'They would have killed you. I threw myself against them but I was powerless in the midst of so many. The Americans saved you, Mischa, and they saved your mother. If it hadn't been for them you would have both been murdered.'

'And you?'

'I defended you as best I could. After that I was an outcast too, but I never once regretted my actions. I loved Anouk and I always have.'

'You said once that my father was a good man.'

'I meant it.'

'What happened to him?'

'I don't know, Mischa. He left in the summer of 1944 and he never returned.'

'Didn't my mother want to know what had happened to him?'

'Again, I don't know. She never spoke of him. Once he had gone she had to struggle to survive on her own with a small son. I assume he was killed in action. He had wanted to take your mother to Germany. Had he lived, I believe he would have been true to his word.' He looked at me for a long moment, then put down his coffee cup. With a groan he pushed himself up from his chair. He suddenly appeared much older, as if opening the past had robbed him of some of the years he had left. 'I have something to show you.'

He walked stiffly over to a chest and opened the small drawer at the top. He rummaged around until he pulled out the brown envelope he wanted. He ran his thumb over it for a moment before passing it to me. On the front was written

'Jacques Reynard' in my mother's script. My head spun with recognition. It was the note she had left for him the night we departed for America. The last he ever heard from her. With trembling fingers, I opened it and pulled out a neatly folded piece of paper.

Dearest Jacques, Tonight I leave to start another life in America. I cannot bear to say goodbye. I don't think I could leave if I had to tell you to your face. You have loved me for almost as long as I can remember and I have loved you back, although not in the way that you have wished. My gratitude is so great that my simple words cannot adequately express it. Do you remember those days at the château when we laughed in the sun, had picnics on the beach and drank fine wine? Do you remember when we built the wall in the cave and stole kisses behind it? I still visit the dark places in my heart, Jacques, for those are the memories I am most proud of. Do you remember when we hid the Jews in the cellar and smuggled them out of France? Do you remember when you stood by me, branded and bald like an animal on a farm? Do you remember loving my son as your own? Playing with him in the vines? Taking him out on your horse? Do you remember when, in spite of all the pain, the hopelessness, the terror, we had each other and still managed to laugh together? My darling Jacques, I will always remember. Don't forget me and Mischa because we will never forget you. My love, Anouk.

I read the letter over and over until the words were blurred by my tears. I folded it and replaced it in the envelope. Jacques didn't speak, but stared into the flames with sadness. I held the envelope and reflected on her words. The people of Maurilliac had punished her when all the time she had worked for the Resistance, risking her life to save others. She had never told me they had branded her. Perhaps she assumed that I would remember. She didn't know that I remember the horror of my own fate more than hers. If only we had talked about it instead of assuming a common understanding.

'You and my mother rescued Jews?' I asked finally.

'There was a Jewish family in Maurilliac that Abel-Louis hadn't yet informed on. When the Rosenfelds were deported, Anouk feared they would be next. We hid them in the middle of the night and sustained them for a month before we managed to secure their safe escape into Switzerland.'

'You worked for the Resistance too?'

'In my own small way. It started with one family, but grew to be many more. Your mother's code name was *Papillon*. She was a very brave butterfly.' Once again he looked at me steadily, his wrinkled old eyes weary but wise. 'When I said your father was a good man, Mischa, I meant it. He knew we had Jews in the *cave*, but he turned a blind eye. You see, he loved Anouk. He would do anything for her, even compromise his position and risk his life.'

'I remember the names carved on the wall. Leon, Marthe, Felix, Benjamin, Oriane.'

'You have a better memory than I,' he said.

'There is something else,' I added, remembering the young man who had appeared in my mother's album. 'Did my mother have a brother?'

'Yes. He was called Michel.'

'What happened to him? She never mentioned his name.'

'Your mother was a survivor. If she had to close down in order to survive, she closed down and moved on. So it was with your uncle. They were inseparable as children and extremely close as teenagers. When war came, Michel was enlisted and went off to war with the flower of French youth.'

'Was he killed?'

Jacques shook his head. 'No. He discovered Anouk's relationship with your father. He told his parents and they disowned her. They had once been a close family but this drove a wedge between them and the rift would never heal. Michel marched off to war and never returned. When you were born, she named you after him. Mischa.'

'What happened to my grandparents?'

'At the end of the war they moved away. Tarred with the same brush, they could no longer live in Maurilliac. They were devastated by Anouk's public humiliation and you, Mischa, were a constant reminder of her collaboration. They had relations in Italy. As far as I know your mother never regained contact. They must have died without ever having forgiven her. You see, her father fought in the first war. In their view to love the enemy was a terrible betrayal, tantamount to treason. They couldn't understand and they certainly couldn't forgive.'

'Why didn't my mother ever talk to me?' I exclaimed, exasperated.

'Because she wanted to forget the things that hurt her. Why allow them to hurt you too? She loved you more than anyone else in the world. You were all she had. She wanted you to grow up without all that baggage. Now you're grown up, you've found out for yourself and you're old enough to take it.'

'She knew she was dying. There were agonising months of steady decline. Why didn't she tell me then? After all, I wasn't a boy any longer.'

He shrugged. 'I don't know. It was all in the past. Why dig it all up again?'

'Didn't I have a right to know about my father?'

'What more could she have told you?'

'What about the saving of Jews? I could be proud of that.'

'Maybe if she started, you'd ask more questions and she'd

never stop. Anouk didn't like to dwell on things that made
her sad. As I said, she shut down and moved on, that was
her nature. You have to accept her the way she was.'

'And you?'

'I have had a good life and I have been happy. Just because
I loved your mother doesn't mean I denied myself pleasure
with others. I compromised and made do.' He leaned forward
and took my hand. His was small compared to mine but I
suddenly felt like a little boy again. 'But you're my consolation, Mischa. I never had children of my own, but I have
you. Let's not talk any more about the past. I want to be a
part of your future.' He looked at his watch. 'It's never too
early for a glass of wine. Let's drink to your return and to
the future, then I want you to tell me about your life. That
way I can be part of it too.'

33

I remained with Jacques until midnight. We drank together, drowning our tears and our laughter in the wine that is the blood of Bordeaux. I wasn't really fit to drive back to the hotel, but I knew I would meet Claudine in the morning and wanted to be there. We embraced for the last time. I think Jacques knew that he would probably never see me again. He was old and the sands of his life were running out. It would be years before I came back again, if I ever did, and by then he'd be gone. 'Why not settle back here?' he asked in an attempt to keep me nearby.

'My life is in America,' I replied. But he knew the real reason.

'There's been too much unhappiness here,' he said with a gentle nod of understanding. 'Leave it all behind, Mischa. You must move on now, like your mother did. And so must I.' We embraced, savouring the strength of the bond that had enabled us to be close again. He looked old and fragile in the doorway, holding his beret in his hands, turning it around and around. I waved out of the window as I drove my car back past the barns and out into the lane. I caught him in the mirror one last time, then he was gone.

I drove back through the darkness, leaning forward to see past the fog in my head. I had to concentrate. My mind was whirling not only with wine but with all the things Jacques had told me. What had touched me most, though, was the fact that he had loved my mother all those years and held no bitterness. He had watched her fall in love with my father and bear his child. Yet, he had loved me as his own. I realised that true love is unselfish and unconditional. I didn't think I could love like that. I wanted Claudine for myself, no matter what. Yes, I wanted to rescue her from her unhappiness, but I wanted to alleviate my own. I held Jacques in high esteem, for mine was a selfish love.

I managed to reach the hotel without losing my way or falling asleep. The night porter looked surprised to see me as I staggered in, doing my best to walk straight. I smiled at him and greeted him heartily, which was so out of character that he blanched. I made my way to my room and fell on the bed. I thought I'd rest a little before undressing. When I next opened my eyes it was morning. I ordered coffee in my room, threw open the curtains and windows and let in the crisp morning air. The sun blazed with enthusiasm, catching the small particles of ice that floated on the air and making them twinkle. I felt serene. Jacques had enlightened me on many of the mysteries of the past. I felt I understood my mother more and wished that she were alive so that I could discuss it all with her. I believed she had hidden *The Gypsy Madonna* for the Rosenfelds in good faith, expecting them to return at the end of the war. She could not have predicted their fate. I supposed that she had kept it all those years for fear of being accused of theft. It was understandable. How smug she must have felt when Goering preyed upon the house for valuable art. He didn't take the best as he had presumed. I felt proud of *Papillon*.

I showered and shaved. My thoughts turned to Claudine. I waited for her to telephone. When she did, the sound of her voice ignited my longing and I was once again seized with jealousy. 'When can we meet?' I asked with my usual impatience.

'This morning, on the bridge,' she replied. The idea of another walk filled me with frustration but I didn't feel I could voice it over the telephone, so I agreed.

'I missed you,' I said instead. 'I missed you all weekend.'

'And I missed you, too.' Her voice sounded different. I sensed a reservation in her tone that alarmed me.

'Come now. I have so much to tell you,' I instructed. 'I'll be waiting for you.'

I didn't have to wait long. She arrived in her coat and hat, a stripy scarf tied around her neck, brown-stockinged legs in sheepskin boots. She let me hold her, but I felt her body stiffen. 'Are you all right?' I asked.

'Let's sit down,' she suggested, and my stomach plummeted. I followed her to the iron bench where we had sat the morning of our first meeting.

'What's wrong? Are you having doubts? What's the matter?' She took my hand and looked at me steadily. I sensed fear behind the veneer of confidence.

'You were at Mass,' she said. I was astonished.

'I was,' I replied, making an effort to sound casual. 'You were with Laurent. I didn't want to make trouble.'

'But you followed me home.' Again I was amazed. There was nothing for me to do but come clean. I leaned forward and placed my elbows on my knees, rubbing my face in my hands.

'I'm sorry if I was out of order,' I said.

'Why did you follow me, Mischa?'

'I wanted to see how Laurent treats you.'

'Why didn't you ask me?'

'Because you didn't seem to want to talk about him.'

'I don't want him to spoil what we have.'

'His very position as your husband does that.'

'When I'm with you I don't want to think of him.' I was relieved when her eyes shone with tears. I hadn't lost her after all. 'I love you, Mischa. When we're together I can pretend that Laurent doesn't exist.'

I sat back and took her hands. 'He doesn't have to, Claudine. You can leave him and come with me to America.'

'I can't.' She turned away and wiped her nose with the back of her hand. 'You don't understand.'

'Of course you can. Your children are grown up. There's nothing for you here in Maurilliac. It's a desert. We can start a new life together in New York.' She turned to face me. 'You're young and beautiful,' I said, tracing my fingers down her cold cheek. She took my hand and pressed her lips to it.

'I'm afraid,' she whispered.

'Of Laurent?'

'Not of Laurent. I pity Laurent. He can't rest unless he controls the world around him, including me. He has grown into a bitter, angry man. Now he senses me drifting away he is desperate to hold on to me. He never wanted to make love and now he wants me all the time. I'm weary of making excuses.'

'Then who are you afraid of?'

A frown darkened her brow and she looked at me sheepishly. 'I'm afraid of doing the wrong thing. I'm afraid of God.'

'Of God!' I wanted to laugh with relief. Then I remembered her closeness to Père Robert. 'Have you confessed?' She nodded. 'Why, Claudine? You know he'll never condone adultery.'

'I had to. He's been so kind to me all these years. He's been the only support I've had. In the beginning I couldn't stand up to Laurent. He taught me how. I can't lie to him.'

'You can't remain in an unhappy marriage just to keep a priest happy. You have to follow your instincts and put your happiness first.'

'I feel guilty. Laurent is the father of my children. We've known each other since childhood. Shared a bed for twenty-six years. We made vows in church, before God. I am breaking one of the Commandments. I've never done that before.'

'But you haven't done anything yet.'

'The intention is there.' She looked so solemn. I couldn't believe she was taken in by it. Didn't she know it was all a load of rubbish devised by priests to control people?

'For Christ's sake, Claudine, I'm not going to let another priest destroy my happiness.' I took her in my arms and kissed her with passion. 'Let it go. Stop hiding. I can cope with you being afraid of Laurent, or of the future, even of yourself, but don't hide behind the Church. You love me?'

'Yes.'

'Then that's all there is to it. I'm not leaving without you.' She smiled at me with gratitude. She seemed to swell in response to my resolve, as if she had needed proof of my affection. I suppose that, on the brink of leaving all that was familiar to her, she needed reassurance that my love was strong enough not to let her down. Once gone, she could never return.

'I want to make love to you,' she said suddenly. 'I want you to take me, Mischa. I want to be yours.'

'Where?' I needed no persuasion.

'I know a place.' She stood up and took my hand. 'Come, Mischa. Let's start our future today.'

We walked along the river-bank for a while, hand in hand like young lovers. I remembered what it was like in summertime and my heart swelled with nostalgia: the grass verdant, full of crickets; the trees sheltering within their branches clusters of cooing wood pigeons; the scent of pine and rosemary heavy in the air. Claudine represented all those things and I knew that if she came with me to America, I'd take the very best of summer with me. After a while we reached a farm and I put the past away. There were barns and stables but, as far as I could see, not a soul around. 'I used to play here as a child. Do you remember Antoine Baudron?' I didn't remember him but I knew that he was probably one of the boys who had listened, gripped, while I spun my lies of miracles and holy visions in the school playground. 'This was his home. He married and moved away, but his father still runs the farm.' She led me playfully up the concrete road, past buildings, ducking and hiding every now and then, which reminded me of my games with Pistou. At last she pulled open the door of a barn. 'This is where they put the calves in springtime. Upstairs is a hay loft. I bet there will still be some hay there. We can make a nice bed.' She giggled mischievously and beckoned me to follow.

'Some people never grow up,' I teased.

'That makes two of us then, Mischa,' she replied, climbing the ladder into the hay loft.

Our playful mood grew sombre as we lay down together, out of the cold. 'Hold me against you,' she said, pressing her body to mine. 'I need warming up.' We lay entwined in the dim light that filtered through the gaps in the wooden roof and through a small window whose pane was stained with mildew. We began to kiss, slowly at first. I brushed my lips across hers, over her cheeks, her feathery eyelashes and her brow. She smelt woody, like the forest, and I closed my eyes to sharpen my sense of smell so that I could savour it. She burrowed her hand inside my coat and up my shirt. I felt her icy fingers against my skin.

'Your hands are cold,' I said.

'They won't be for long. You're boiling in there.' She inserted the other and traced them up and down my spine. I felt them dwell a moment on my scar before moving on. As our kissing grew more ardent I felt my arousal strain against my trousers. Our breath grew hot and our cheeks flushed cherry red. My hands were warm like dough straight from the oven. I pulled her blouse out of her skirt and released the clips of her brassiere. Her breasts were soft and spongy, no longer the firm breasts of a young woman who has yet to give birth, but I loved her maturity. I loved the marks that time and motherhood had left on her body because they made her real and gave her a pathos that moved me. I wished the children she had borne had been mine. I wished we had grown up together. I buried my face in her neck and lifted her clothes so I could take her breasts in my mouth and feel the texture of her skin on my lips. She let out a low moan and ran her fingers through my hair. She wore a knee-length tweed skirt. I slid it over her hips to find her brown stockings were attached to a suspender belt and she wore silky panties. It excited me to feel the white plains of thigh above the lace. She smiled at me, her eyes shining, her lids heavy with pleasure. I pulled down her underwear and she lay exposed and abandoned, without shame, for me to caress. We made love all morning, pausing to talk, then starting all over again. 'I haven't made love like this since I was a young girl,' she said, blushing with delight. 'I thought I had lost all sensuality in the banal domesticity of my life.'

'You're a feast,' I told her, taking in the beauty of her face. 'Sex suits you.'

'Who'd have thought, when we played with marbles in the Place de l'Eglise, that we'd come to this?' She laughed, climbing on top of me.

'What do you think Monsieur Baudron would say if he found us in his hay loft?'

'I would have to leave Maurilliac for ever.'

'I hope he comes,' I said, turning serious. She stared down at me for a long moment. I wished I could read her thoughts. 'Come with me, Claudine. I can't leave without you.'

'But you haven't found your painting.'

'Yes, I have.'

'You have?' She was amazed. 'Tell me.'

'Not until you promise that you'll run away with me.'

She stopped smiling. 'Do you promise that you'll never leave me? That you'll look after me? That we'll grow old together and love each other to make up for all the years we have missed? Can you promise me all that, Mischa? Because, if you can, I'll run away with you.' I pulled her down and rolled over so that she lay cradled in my arms.

'We might not be young any more, but we've got many years left to share. I promise you, Claudine, that I will love you and look after you until death us do part. I only ask you to trust me because, if you had known me for the last forty years, you would be reassured because I have never loved like this.'

'Where did you get that scar?' she asked.

'In a fight,' I replied, knowing that I would now divulge the full horror of my wasted youth.

'How did it happen?'

'It all began when Coyote left . . .' She listened intently while, layer by layer, I shed my skins. They were tougher towards the outside, like pieces of armour, designed to keep people out, while at the same time keeping me in and out of reach. Now I let them go one by one, feeling lighter and happier as each was peeled away. I told her about Captain Crumble's Curiosity Store; Matias and Maria Elena; the day we were broken into and that heartbreaking moment when Coyote embraced me for the last time; my mother's constant and irritating laying of his place at the table, her unwavering hope, her slowly drifting away and my descent into the world of street gangs and violence. I told her about the theft, the vandalism, the terror I engendered. I wasn't proud of what I had become but I wanted her to know it all. I didn't want to have any secrets from her. If Linda hadn't been able to reach me, I wanted Claudine to delve inside and hold my heart in her hands. I wanted her to have it. It had always belonged to her.

Then I told her about the fight that nearly cost me my life. 'I watched helplessly as my gang ran off into the night, leaving me alone and bleeding on the wet tarmac. It was at that point that I saw my whole life before my eyes. What a waste I had made of it. All because of one man.'

'No, Mischa,' she said, gazing at me with soft, enquiring eyes. 'He triggered it, but he wasn't the reason for your breakdown. You were a damaged little boy. Who knows, you might have done the same thing had Coyote never come into your life.'

'But Coyote rejected me and I carried that burden around like a bag of lead. It just got heavier and heavier until I unloaded it in my first fight. With each brawl it got lighter and lighter.'

'That knife wound probably saved your life,' she said with a smile.

'It made me consider my life. After that I turned it around. I worked with my mother in the store, learned about antiques . . .'

'Girlfriends?'

'Mainly one, Linda. We were together for nine years but to be honest, I never opened up. She struggled from day one to "save me". I think that's why she liked me. I was her project.'

'Did you love her?'

I considered a moment. Now I loved Claudine I realised the difference between love and need. 'I was comfortable,' I replied. 'I needed her. But no, I didn't love her.'

'How did your mother take to her?'

'Not well. She never liked anyone I dated.'

She chuckled. 'That's because she wanted you for herself. You were all she had. I don't blame her.' She traced her finger down my cheek. 'I'd want you all to myself, too. I pity Linda and any other girls you took home. They wouldn't have stood a chance.'

'Do you remember my mother?'

'I remember her as being very beautiful but icy. She always walked tall, with her chin up. She had these incredible cheekbones and flawless skin. I don't recall her smile.'

'She had an enchanting smile, when she wanted to give it. I think she'd have liked you.'

'Why's that?' She was grinning now, unconvinced.

'Because you were the only child who was nice to me. She'd like you for that.'

We ate baguettes that she had brought with her, sitting on the bridge in the sunshine, watching the frost melt. Then, in the afternoon we walked to keep warm. She took me to a little hamlet the other side of the Garonne because her father was buried in the churchyard and she wanted to say goodbye. I left her alone beside the headstone, crouching on the grass, so that she could speak to him in private. I wandered around with my hands in my pockets, toying with the rubber ball, wondering whether my father had a gravestone somewhere in Germany, suddenly longing to speak to him too.

It was then that it caught my eye. A simple headstone, covered in moss and weeds, neglected and left to the ravages of time. I stared at it in astonishment, my heart suspended with my breath. In large letters was the word 'Pistou'. Beneath it, *Florien Roche, 1941–1947, beloved son of Paul and Annie. Always in our hearts*. I knelt down and picked away at the mildew with my finger nails. Pistou hadn't been a figment of my imagination after all, but a little boy of my age who had never been allowed to grow up.

Maria Elena had understood. I had believed in him as a child, when he had come in spirit to play among the vines. He had been there when I had needed him, when I had no one else to talk to. I knew that I would never see him again because the adult world had wrapped itself around me like cement, deafening my ears to his voice. But, as I tended his grave, I remembered him with love, as if he had been a brother. I had no flowers to lay there, but it didn't matter. I spoke to him instead. 'Pistou, my old friend,' I whispered, imagining him there beside me, smiling in amusement as if he had deliberately led me here as a game. 'So you were a little boy like me. I never thanked you for your company when I had no one else to play with. I hope you still run around the fields and down by the river, perhaps with another little boy who needs you like I did. Judging by the state of the gravestone, I should imagine your parents are with you in spirit. If you see my mother, say "hello" for me. And if you're ever inspired and able, make yourself known to me again, one last time, so I can say thank you.'

That evening I packed my case. We planned to leave the following morning. Claudine would come to the hotel and we'd drive to the airport together. It was a simple plan. I couldn't imagine it going wrong. She said she'd leave a note on Laurent's pillow. She confessed she'd find it almost impossible to tell him to his face. I understood. They had been friends all their lives and, although their marriage had grown cold, those years meant something. He was, after all, the father of her children, the man she had shared a bed with for twenty-six years.

I bathed, lying back in the water and imagining our life together in New York. How different it would be with her. I'd clear out my mother's apartment, sort out her post and her papers and move on. I wouldn't be alone any more. We'd have each other, Claudine and I.

Downstairs I ordered a drink in the library, by the fire. I noticed Jean-Luc enter with an anxious look on his face, but I ignored him. I turned my eyes back to the magazine I was reading, sipping a large glass of warm Bordeaux. I felt deeply contented, as if finally all the pieces of my life had come together like a complicated puzzle. I knew where my mother had got the painting from. I wasn't certain about the reasons, but that no longer mattered. My curiosity was satisfied and besides, Claudine had quelled my compulsive searching.

'Excuse me, *monsieur*.' I raised my eyes to find Jean-Luc gazing anxiously down at me.

'Yes?' I replied good-naturedly.

'I was wondering whether you wouldn't mind sharing a table with a very charming guest.'

'Go on.' The thought of having to chat all evening to a stranger was disheartening.

'She's called Mrs Rainey. She's alone and, as she's American, like you, I thought it would be pleasant for her to have some company. She's elderly but very nice and she's a good client of ours.' I was about to decline, but knew it was selfish.

'It would be my pleasure,' I said, wondering how I had suddenly become so agreeable. Jean-Luc's face brightened. 'Thank you, *monsieur*. I will present her to you at eight.'

I returned to my magazine. It was churlish to be irritated at the prospect of having to dine with an old lady, in the light of my impending flight with Claudine. Perhaps she would be a welcome distraction. I hoped she wouldn't be dull or, even worse, one of those enthusiastic women who ask endless questions. I didn't want to talk about myself.

At eight Jean-Luc appeared with Mrs Rainey. I drained my glass, put down the magazine and stood up to greet her. '*Madame*, may I present you Monsieur Fontaine.' We smiled at each other politely until it dawned on us both that we had met before, a long, long time ago.

'Joy Springtoe!' I exclaimed, my jaw falling in astonishment. She hadn't changed all that much. She was just older.

'Mischa?' She was as astonished as I was. She shook her head and her blue eyes shone with happiness. 'You can talk?'

'It's a long story,' I replied.

'I can't wait to hear it.'

'Then you shall.'

'You're American now?'

'We moved to America when I was six years old,' I replied, taking her hand and kissing it in the French fashion. I raised my eyes, my lips still pressed against her skin. 'But I never forgot you.'

34

We sat in the corner, at a round table decorated with candles. 'Oh, Mischa, it's so good to see you!' she exclaimed. Her face was still beautiful. Although the skin was lined, like tissue paper that had been used many times, it was soft and plump. She radiated happiness, and her goodness shone through eyes that now gazed on me with tenderness. 'You're so handsome. I knew you'd grow into a handsome man.'

'What are you doing here?' I asked, astounded that our paths should cross once more. 'I never thought I'd see you again.'

'It's my pink ticket.' She laughed like a girl. 'Once a year I leave my husband behind and come here for a week to remember my fiancé who was killed in the war.'

'I remember. I caught you crying and you took me to your room to show me his photograph.'

'Billy Blake.' She smiled, then lowered her voice. 'You see, Mischa, for me there has only ever been one love. It was a great love. Oh, I've been happy with David. He's a good man. But Billy was my big love and I don't ever want to forget him.'

'Was he killed here?'

'He liberated the town and was the first into the *château*. The following day he wrote me a letter. That was the last letter I ever received. He was killed in action shortly after.'

'A waste of a good man,' I said.

'The best,' she replied. 'But let's not talk about me.'

The waiter came and hovered over the table expectantly. We hastily chose food and wine, eager to continue our conversation. 'What brings you here?' she asked and I felt happy to open up my life and invite her in. After all, she had stepped inside many years ago. For her, I'd always kept the door open.

'It began with my mother. She died of cancer.'

'I'm so sorry.'

'She had been in steady decline for about eighteen months. Typically, she didn't want doctors buzzing around her. She found them intrusive. So she just let her body die slowly, putting her head under the carpet, pretending nothing was happening. We're both like that, I'm afraid. I started going through all her things. She had kept everything. I don't suppose you knew, but my father was a German officer who requisitioned the *château* during the war. My mother had worked for the family who owned it and continued to do so after Gustave Rosenfeld was killed in action and his wife and children were sent off to the camps.'

'They were Jewish?'

'Yes. My mother worked here, hoping they'd come back at the end of the war.'

'Of course, they never did.'

'No. But she fell in love and married my father in secret, and I was born in '41. At the end of the war she was severely punished for her collaboration. It was then that I lost my voice.'

'Now I understand. You poor little boy. What a terrible thing to happen. Whatever became of your father?'

'He was killed in the war.'

'Like my poor Billy.'

'I remember him a little.' I rummaged around in my pocket and pulled out my little rubber ball. 'He gave me this.' She took it and looked it over carefully.

'Goodness me! You've kept it all these years?'

'It's a link to him. I'm a sentimental old fool.'

'Oh, no you're not. I keep things too. I have a whole box of mementoes from Billy. Theatre programmes, bus tickets, flowers he gave me that I've pressed, letters he sent me during the war. I read them sometimes. Like your ball, they link me to him and I feel him close. I'm not afraid of dying because I know he'll be there waiting for me. I'm a little excited by it, to be honest.'

'I think you've got a long time to wait.'

'I'm getting old, Mischa.'

'You don't look old at all.'

'That's because you see through the lines to the way I was forty years ago. I'm pushing seventy. I never thought it would go so fast. Life really is very short.' She sighed and took a sip of wine. 'So, you've come back to wander down memory lane?'

'In a way, yes.'

She looked at me intently. 'Are you happy, Mischa?'

'I'm happy now. It's a long story.'

'I want to hear it. Tell me everything. You see, I have a right to know,' she teased. 'Because I was your first love!'

I chuckled and took her hand. 'You knew?'

'Oh yes, I knew. You blushed every time you saw me and you followed me around like a puppy. You were always hiding behind that chair upstairs. It's still there. You know, I always think of you when I see it – although, you've grown a little too big to hide there now.'

'You were not only my first love but the first woman to break my heart. I was devastated when you left.'

'Oh, so was I. I hated leaving you. You were the little boy I never had.'

'Have you children of your own now?'

'Yes, I have four girls. I never had a son.' She squeezed my hand. 'I always wanted a little blond boy with blue eyes.

Billy was blond. I think we would have had a little boy together. But it wasn't to be. I have grandchildren, though. I'm crazy about my grandsons.'

The waiter brought the starters and we began to eat. 'So, tell me everything. From the moment you left France. I imagine your mother wanted to start afresh in a place where no one knew her past.'

'I think she did,' I replied, although I couldn't help but wonder whether she had to leave because of the Titian. 'She fell in love with an American who came to stay here and we went with him to New Jersey. He was my second love.' So, I told her about Coyote, Captain Crumble's Curiosity Store, Matias and Maria Elena, the break-ins. I didn't mention Coyote by name. I didn't know why at the time, but instinct cautioned me. She listened to every word, fascinated and moved. I told her of my downward spiral into a dark world of gangs, fights, knives and self-loathing.

'What made you change direction?' she asked.

'When you're at the bottom, the only way is up.'

'You just turned it all around, all by yourself?'

I didn't want to tell her about the fight at the parking lot, so I told her of a time a little earlier when I had begun to truly understand my mother's predicament. 'No,' I replied. 'I saw how much I was hurting my mother. I had blamed her for the American's disappearance. I thought it was all her fault. I wanted her to move on, so that I could. Then one night I came home late, drunk, a miserable sight, and I saw her dancing alone in her bedroom to the music she used to play with my father. They used to dance together to the gramophone. I'd watch, clap my hands and laugh. Well, that night she was dancing as if she was with him, her hand on his shoulder, the other in his hand. She gazed up adoringly at his imaginary face, her eyes overflowing with tears. I'll never forget it. I sobered up, slumped on the floor and cried too. For once I didn't think of myself and what I had lost, but of her and the losses she had endured. She was alone. Abandoned by the two men she had loved. Ostracised by the town she had grown up in, disowned by her family. She had endured far more than I, and what's more, she had never stopped loving me. In spite of my anger, the abuse I hurled at her, my rages and tantrums, she had never closed her heart to me, or the door. I awoke the following morning determined to change. I never looked back and I never used my fists again. Neither of us spoke about it, but we became friends once more.'

Then I told her about Claudine. She listened with sympathy and didn't judge me. Instead, she encouraged me. 'If she's your big love, Mischa, then go with your instincts. Life is short. Living a half-life isn't good enough.'

'I'm leaving tomorrow morning.'

'I shall be sorry to see you go. Perhaps we could see each other back home.'

'I would like that very much.'

Again she took my hand. 'So would I.'

That night I lay in bed, too excited to sleep. Joy Springtoe had walked back into my life and Claudine had agreed to come to America with me. As soon as she obtained a divorce I'd marry her. I relished the idea of settling down together. After having been rootless all these years, I'd buy a home where we could grow old together. We had left it too late to have children and that saddened me. I couldn't help but regret that there'd be no one to continue my name into the future. I'd die and leave nothing of myself behind.

Outside the wind moaned as it raced around the corners of the *château*. Rain pelted against the window-panes, thunder roared, and every now and then a flash of lightning lit up the sky. I opened the curtains and sat on the window seat. Black clouds raged in the sky, rolling over one another like boiling porridge. I remembered my grandmother's belief in the wind and recalled the night we had left for America. It had rained then, too, and the wind had nearly blown me across the gardens. It was during a sudden burst of lightning that I recalled the man digging in the garden. I had forgotten him. Now I saw him clearly, kneeling on the ground, soaking wet, forcing his spade into the earth. I heard the rhythmic noise of metal against stone as if it had been only yesterday. Then I had believed him to have been a murderer, burying the body. Now I didn't know. I was inclined to dismiss it as fantasy, but I had dismissed Pistou. I had been wrong then, I could be wrong now. I resolved to ask Jean-Luc if anyone had been murdered. He seemed to know everything about the *château*'s history.

I watched the storm until it passed. The rain continued to fall heavily. The wind still blew a gale. Tomorrow I'd say goodbye to my childhood and put it away for ever. There comes a moment when one has to live in the present or one ceases to live at all. I climbed back into bed and closed my eyes. I hadn't slept so deeply in years. I hadn't dreamed in years either. But that night I had a dream of such vividness, I was tempted to believe it was real.

I was a little boy again. The sun was high in the sky, warm, pine-scented. The river bubbled and gurgled, flies hovered in the heat, crickets chirped in the undergrowth and the yellow-flowered *genêts* swayed in the breeze. I sat on the bank, throwing stones into the water. Beside me sat Pistou. He played with my little rubber ball. We sat in silence for a while, our mutual understanding rendering words unnecessary. A yellow butterfly landed on his hand and he turned to me and smiled. I remembered Jacques Reynard telling me that my mother's code name in the war had been *Papillon* – butterfly. 'So, you see, I'm not a figment of your imagination,' he said.

'I'm sorry. Did you mind?' I asked, throwing a stone into the water and watching it bounce along the surface.

'No. I'm used to it.'

'What's it like in Heaven?'

'Nice. You'll like it when you come. You can eat as many *chocolatines* as you want.'

'That sounds good. Will *le curéton* be there?'

'Abel-Louis is due any minute. They're waiting for him.'

'Will he be punished?'

'Hell is on earth, my friend. You've been there, haven't you?'

'But I want him to suffer.'

'He'll suffer when he looks back over his life and sees what a mess he's made of it. Don't forget the law of karma, Mischa. What goes around comes around. The law of cause and effect. No one escapes it.'

'And my mother?' I watched the butterfly spread her wings and fly away.

'She's here and so is your father.' He handed me back the rubber ball.

'Are they together?'

'Of course.'

'Can I see them?'

'They're always with you, watching over you. Just because you can't see them, doesn't mean they're not there.' He stood up. 'I must go now.'

'Will I see you again?'

'Oh, yes. You'll see me again, if you open your eyes.' He laughed at me in that mischievous way of his. 'You're a cynical old fool!' I, too, stood up. I towered over him. I realised then that I wasn't a little boy at all.

'Thank you for being my friend, Pistou.'

'It was fun, wasn't it?'

'It really was.'

'It still can be. Just don't forget how to be a child.'

'I'll try.'

He walked into the forest. I put my ball into my pocket and turned to the sun. The light was so bright I had to squint. I put my arm across my face and woke myself with a start. The day had dawned in all its glory. The storm had passed, the sky was clear.

I packed the remaining belongings in my case, dressed and went downstairs for breakfast. I was electrified with nerves. Claudine had promised she'd meet me in the hall at ten. We'd climb in the car and drive to Bordeaux airport. From there we'd fly to Paris, then to America, and on to the rest of our lives. I couldn't wait. I watched the clock with frustration. Why, when one wanted the time to pass, did it go so slowly?

I buttered my *croissants* and ate them with jam. The coffee tasted good. I tried to read the paper but the words made no sense; all I could think about was Claudine. After breakfast I wandered into the conservatory to look out over the gardens one final time. To my surprise Joy was standing alone, cup of coffee in hand, gazing out. 'What a beautiful morning,' she said, smiling at me. 'I'm sorry you're leaving today. I'd like to have taken a walk with you.'

'It's a bit cold for that. I'd like to come back in summer.'

'I usually do. This is the first time I've come back in winter. Perhaps it's Fate,' she said, looking at me fondly.

'The garden's still lovely, though.'

'Yes, even after a storm.'

'I couldn't sleep. I sat up and watched it. I remember doing that as a child. My mother said the wind predicted change.'

'Well, perhaps it does for you. After all, you're starting a new life today.'

She looked out over the lawns again and sighed. 'You know, rumour has it that there's a priceless work of art buried there somewhere.' I was stunned.

'Really?' I said, trying to sound natural. I felt my cheeks burn, as if I were guilty of burying it myself.

She spoke in a whisper. 'The last letter Billy wrote me, he said that he and a couple of friends had been the first to enter the *château* after the Germans left. One of them, Richard Quigley, knew something about art and recognised a painting by Titian that hadn't been crated up and sent to Germany on Goering's private train. Apparently, Goering made it his business to steal valuable works for himself. Anxious to save it from ruin or theft, they buried it in the garden. Billy said that if it hadn't been for Richard they would have ruined it themselves by rolling it up the wrong way. You have to roll it with the paint on the outside. They found some lead piping to protect it and buried it like a body with the intention of coming back after the war to retrieve it. Sadly, Billy died shortly after and Richard, poor Richard!'

'What happened to him?' My mouth turned dry and my tongue felt too big for it. The final pieces of the jigsaw were coming together and I didn't think I wanted to see the picture after all.

'He was murdered.'

'Murdered? In the war?'

'No, in about 1952. I read about it in the local papers when I went to stay with my family in Staunton, West Virginia that is. I remember the murderer was sentenced to life in Keen Mountain Correctional Centre. I hope he rotted there. Richard was such a nice boy. Billy wrote of him often. I felt I knew him.' Without looking at her I asked a question to which I already knew the answer.

'What was the name of the third man who liberated the *château*?'

'They called him Coyote.' She frowned. 'I wonder what became of him?'

The world began to spin around me. I sat down and rubbed

my temples with my fingers. 'Are you all right?' she asked, taking the place beside me and putting an arm around my back.

'I'm feeling a little nauseous,' I replied, picturing Coyote in my mind digging up the painting. Now I understood why he had come to Maurilliac and why we had stolen away like thieves in the night. We *were* thieves, or at least Coyote was. I remembered the break-ins and Coyote's disappearance. Did he kill Richard Quigley after he had come looking for the painting? Did he kill Billy too?

I looked at the clock. It was a quarter to ten. 'I'm fine, really. I think it's the excitement,' I said, sitting up. 'Perhaps I'll have a glass of water.'

'I don't suppose anyone will ever know whether it's buried there or not,' she continued blithely. 'It's a nice thought, though. That somewhere in the earth is a beautiful secret. I like mysteries.' She got up and drained her cup. 'Come, let's find you a glass of water. You look awfully pale.'

35

I sat in the hall and waited for Claudine. I needed time alone to digest what Joy had told me. I was desperate. I had trusted Coyote. Now I wondered whether I had ever really known him. I had my suspicions as to his whereabouts during the last thirty years, but I needed to look through my mother's box again to confirm them. Until then I had to forget about him digging in the garden at midnight and possibly murdering the two other young men who knew about the Titian. I had to think forward, to Claudine.

After ten o'clock I began to get anxious. I began walking up and down the flagstones, wandering in and out of the door every few minutes to see if she was coming. I thought back to our first meeting on the bridge. She had been late then, too. I had lost hope and begun to walk back to the *château*. She had finally arrived, as I was certain she would today. I just had to trust her and wait.

Joy returned, filling the hall with the scent of gardenia. I stood up and embraced her. 'You're so big now,' she said with a laugh. 'To me you're still the little boy I lost my heart to all those years ago.'

'We'll see each other back home, I promise,' I replied, kissing her cheek. Her skin was as soft as down.

'I'm so pleased our paths have crossed again. Fate has a funny way of bringing people together, doesn't it? I don't believe in coincidence.' She held my hands. 'I wish you luck with your girl. When you find love like that, hold on to it.

It's rare and priceless. But I don't have to tell you that, do I? You already know.' I watched her leave, momentarily lifted out of my anxious vigil as I pictured her standing in the bathroom doorway in her pretty new dress.

I continued pacing the floor, fumbling in agitation with the little rubber ball I kept in my pocket. Time was running out and Claudine still hadn't appeared. I couldn't believe she had changed her mind. She had been so certain the day before and, besides, she had defied everyone in Maurilliac, even Père Abel-Louis, and become my friend. I knew she was strong enough to walk out of her marriage. I couldn't imagine what was holding her up.

To my dismay Jean-Luc appeared, his hair shining from the wax he put on it to keep it in place. 'So, you leave us today, *monsieur*,' he said, approaching me. He gave a small bow. 'It has been a great pleasure to have you in the hotel. You will come back, I trust?'

'I'm sure I will,' I replied tightly, knowing that I never would. In order to move on I had to bury the past, as Jacques had so wisely said.

'Are you waiting for a taxi?' he asked, frowning.

'I have a car.'

'Are they bringing it around for you?'

'It's ready.'

'Then I will shake your hand and say farewell.' I took his hand. It was warm and soft, the hand of a man who has barely lived. 'I wish you a safe flight back to America.' I watched him hover a few moments, expecting me to leave. When I remained standing, he bowed again and walked away.

I kept my eyes on the clock. I noticed every small movement. Every tick. I began to panic. Perhaps she had got cold feet? Perhaps she had decided to remain in Maurilliac, after all? One thing was for certain, I wasn't going to leave without her. I had promised her that and I had vowed to myself. I hurried outside and climbed into the car. If she wasn't going to come to me, I'd go to her. I stepped on the accelerator and headed down the road into Maurilliac.

It was cold in the car, but my forehead glistened with sweat. Nothing else mattered for me but Claudine. Now I had found her I was desperate to keep her. Laurent rose in my mind. I should have known that he would pose the biggest obstacle to my future happiness. Laurent, my enemy from long ago. I would never forget his words in the classroom: 'Your father's still a Nazi pig!' And I would never forgive him. Not ever. As I raced into town, I prepared myself for the final battle. I expected to fight Laurent; I didn't expect to have to fight God as well.

I parked the car outside her house and remained there a moment, straining my eyes to see through her sitting-room window. I only had to wait a moment before Claudine appeared. She stood facing out, biting her thumb nail anxiously. She looked as if she had been crying. A second later Laurent loomed over her, placing his hand on her shoulder. This time she didn't shrug it off. I gripped the steering-wheel and felt my anger mount. It was too much for me to bear. I climbed out of the car and banged on their door with all the force I could muster. When no one answered I banged again and shouted. 'Claudine! I know you're in there!' Finally the door opened. There, standing before me, was the priest, Père Robert.

'You had better come in,' he said calmly, stepping aside. I towered over them all, like a giant in a playhouse. The room seemed to shrink with me in it. I felt physically powerful but almost crippled with fear. I couldn't tolerate life without her.

I walked past her suitcase to find Claudine and Laurent still standing by the window. Laurent had his arm around her, his fingers gripping her shoulder tightly. He looked at me with that arrogant smirk, as if he had already won. I was filled with such loathing it was all I could do not to lash out at him and floor him with a single blow. I settled my eyes on Claudine. She gazed at me tearfully. I knew what had happened. I could read it on her face. The priest had taken it upon himself to mend the shreds of their marriage. Didn't he know that it was irreparable, like cloth that has frayed too far?

'What are you doing here?' Laurent sneered. I ignored him and spoke to Claudine.

'I'm not leaving without you,' I said bravely.

'You don't even know her,' Laurent interrupted. 'You were six years old!'

'Claudine is staying,' said the priest. 'She has made her decision.'

I turned on him coldly. 'I'm not talking to you,' I said. 'And I'm not talking to you either, Laurent.' I looked directly at Claudine and hoped with all my heart that she would have the strength to walk away. 'I'm not going to beg. You know I love you and that I'll look after you. We've waited a lifetime for each other. Don't make me wait any longer.'

Laurent chuckled cynically. 'You think you can walk into my marriage and suck the life out of it in only a few days. You must be deluded, my friend. Claudine is my wife, or didn't she tell you?' I was determined not to dignify his comments with a reply. I spoke once again to Claudine.

'Life is short, Claudine. Don't waste it.'

I put my hand in my pocket and pulled out the little rubber ball. I threw it into the air and caught it. Her cheeks flushed at the sight of my father's ball and the light of courage returned to her eyes. I caught a glimpse of the toothy little girl who relished breaking the rules and defying her mother. Of the only child who had dared befriend me. She shrugged off Laurent's arm. She turned to him and planted a kiss on his cheek. He froze and his face drained to grey like the colour of the pigs that hung from the hooks in the *boucherie*.

'I'm sorry, Laurent, but we have nothing left with which to repair our marriage.' She said nothing to the priest; she just looked at him sadly and shook her head. He watched in horror as she took my hand, his mouth agape at her audacity, a silent protest on his tongue. I picked up her suitcase and we left the house and Maurilliac for ever.

36

New York shimmered beneath the winter sun. The sidewalks were no longer carpeted with snow, the air was no longer frozen to ice. There was a mildness that hadn't been there when I left. I could smell spring and almost feel the waking earth in Central Park. I was happier than I had ever been. Claudine and I had decided to buy a house together in New Jersey. I'd move my business there and we'd run it together. We didn't talk about Laurent and we didn't talk about Maurilliac. We built our future on today, where the foundations were unsullied.

When we arrived in America, Claudine telephoned her children and told them that she had left their father for me. Joel was surprised but understood that his father was not an easy man. He said he only wanted her happiness and that, in spite of loving him, his father only had himself to blame. Delphine was more difficult. Like most daughters, she adored her father. She worried about who was going to look after him. She blamed Claudine for ruining his life. 'You're both so old,' she said. 'What's the point of running off with someone now?' She raced down to Maurilliac to comfort Laurent and spent a fortnight doing his cooking and washing. She returned to Paris exhausted, her eyes opened to the realities of her parents' marriage. 'When I marry we'll employ a cook and a maid,' she declared to her mother. 'When can I come out and meet this mystery man who's swept you off to the other end of the world?'

After putting it right with her children, Claudine had to reconcile with God. Catholicism was in her blood; it would have been unfair of me to have encouraged her to turn her back on it. She had broken her marriage vows for me; I couldn't expect her to do more. To her delight, she found a local Catholic church with a wise old Italian priest called Father Gaddo. She went to Mass, took communion and spent so long in the confessional that the priest had to ask her to leave in order to give his other congregants a chance to unburden their sins. She returned to me light of step, her toothy grin restored to its full glory.

'I start today with a clean slate,' she said happily. 'My sins are all in the past.'

'What did he say?' I asked in bewilderment. How could a mere mortal wash away the stain of adultery with such ease?

'He said that life is a big training ground and it would be unreasonable if God didn't forgive those who made mistakes.'

'Quite so,' I said, taking her in my arms. 'I like the sound of Father Gaddo. Do you think he'll marry us?' Her eyes filled with tears and she kissed me ardently.

'Yes, Mischa Fontaine, I think he will!'

I finally got around to reading the two letters my mother had kept in her box and to opening her mail. The last remaining pieces of the puzzle began to fit into place.

I sat alone in my apartment. The traffic was a low buzz, like the distant hum of bees in summer. The light was bright as the sun tumbled in with the enthusiasm that belongs only to the morning. I sat on the sofa, a cup of coffee on the table, Leonard Cohen resounding through the rooms. With Claudine I felt complete. I had left New York with nothing and returned with more than I would ever have dared dream. I had wandered back down the years, unravelling them as I went, like a ball of string, discovering along the way the truth about my mother, Jacques Reynard, the priest and the painting. But I had never expected to find myself at the very centre of that ball. All my life I had searched for love. I had found it in Jacques, Daphne, Joy and Coyote, people who had floated in and out of my life like clouds across a sky, and I had found it in my mother whose love had been as constant as the sun. But finally, at the end of my search, I had found it in me.

With a suspended heart, I opened the earlier letter my mother had kept in her box. The paper was neatly folded in the envelope, the words written with great care.

Dear Mrs Fontaine, You may not remember me. My name is Leon Egberg. It is to you and Dieter Schulz that I owe my life and those of my family, Marthe, Felix, Benjamin and Oriane. You gave us refuge in the cellars of the château and organised our safe passage out of France. We settled in Switzerland and later migrated to Canada where we have been living since the end of the war. My children have grown up and married and with each grandchild that is born I say a prayer for your good health. My wife, Marthe, and I will be in New York in May and would very much like to meet you and shake your hand. Forgive me for having tracked you down and for intruding once more in your life. My warmest regards, Leon Egberg.

I was surprised that my mother had never mentioned them, or the letter. She had reassured me as a child that my father had been a good man, but after that she had never mentioned him at all. I recognised the names from the *château* cellar. I had added mine, which I now realised had been highly inappropriate. The letter was dated September 1983. With growing excitement, I opened the other letter. It was also from Leon Egberg, dated May 1984.

*Dear Anouk, it was an enormous pleasure to see you
again and to be able to thank you in person. We were
delighted to hear that you married Dieter Shulz and will be
true to our word and do the very best we can to discover
what happened to him after Liberation. What a consolation
to have borne his son. From his photographs he resembles his
father very much. It is of vital importance that people do not
forget the horrors of war, at least so such atrocities are not
repeated by younger generations. I do hope that we will meet
again one day. Please give your son our best wishes, I hope
he knows how brave his mother was in the war and how
many lives she saved. God bless you, Anouk. My warmest
regards, Leon.*

With a racing heart I flicked through the letters that had
gathered since my mother's death. I was sure I had seen the
same spidery handwriting in the pile. I discarded the bills
and catalogues until I held in my trembling hand another
letter from Leon Egberg. He must have discovered something about my father. I could barely contain my excitement.
I sat back on the sofa, took a swig of coffee and tore open
the envelope.

*My dear Anouk, I hope this finds you well. We have
finally discovered what happened to your husband at the end
of the war. It will probably come as no surprise to you that
Dieter hated the Nazis. He had already proved himself by
saving the lives of Jews like us. However, I'm proud to
inform you that he was involved in the plot to kill Hitler in
the summer of 1944, but saddened that due to its failure he
was sentenced to death by hanging. Life throws up few
heroes, Anouk, but your Dieter was one of them. Had the
plot succeeded so many thousands of people would have been
saved. He was a very brave man to put the lives of others*

*above his own. I hope that by knowing his fate, you are now
able to share it with your son. I know you were reluctant to
drag him back into the past, considering the terrible effect it
had on him, until you discovered what had become of his
father. Now you know the truth, Mischa deserves to know
that his father was a good and noble man, and a hero of the
greatest courage. We honour him in death and wish you good
health. L'hiem – to life! My warmest regards to you and
your son, Leon.*

I sat there, stunned by what I had read. I knew about the
plot to kill Hitler. There were books and television docu-
mentaries on the subject. The conspirators were hanged with
piano wire and filmed while they died. I was devastated to
learn that my father had died this way and saddened that my
mother never learned the truth, because Leon's letter had
arrived too late. I wondered whether she would have shared
it with me, whether she was waiting for Leon's letter before
she told me. It certainly made sense.

So, my father was a hero after all. I had always suspected
as much. My mother would never have loved a man who
sympathised with Nazi ideals. She had respected people too
much, whatever their race or class. She had never been a
warm woman on the outside; I had been one of the few who
had sought refuge in her embrace. But she had believed
everyone had the right to a place on earth and that there was
room enough for all of us. I decided to write to Leon Egberg
and tell him of my mother's passing. I wanted to thank him
for going to the trouble of finding out about my father and
I also wanted to see him. You see, as much as I was able to
walk away from Maurilliac, I could never really sever the ties
to my past.

I returned to my mother's apartment with Claudine. I
wanted her to help me sort out her things. I no longer wanted

to do it on my own. Claudine began in the kitchen, packing into boxes all the pots and pans we had decided to give to charity, while I went straight to her bedroom to do the same with her clothes. We worked all week in the pale wintry light that tumbled in through the open windows. I wasn't sorry to see her things put into garbage bags and taken off in vans. That is what she would have wanted. They were possessions, after all, and she no longer needed them.

I kept various things. Her jewellery, diaries, letters, photo albums, the piano, books and other items that had sentimental value. Back at home I sat down with Claudine to read Coyote's postcards. After hearing from Joy about the murder of Richard Quigley, I decided to do a bit of research for myself. I discovered that my suspicions had been correct: Coyote, known to some as Jack Magellan, was Lynton Shaw. He was married to Kelly and they had three children, Lauren, Ben and Warwick, and lived in Richmond, Virginia. He had, indeed, murdered Richard Quigley and been sent down for life, languishing in Keen Mountain Correctional Centre for thirty years. I presumed he had killed Joy's fiancé, Billy, too, in order to keep the painting for himself. And what of my mother? Had she known the truth and simply chosen to bury it? If not, why hadn't Coyote told us? How could he have let us believe he had deserted us? I hoped the postcards would answer those questions for me.

We lay together on the bed. The room smelt of Claudine's perfume, her bath oils and the vanilla cream she put on her body. I liked the feminine smell of her and the sight of her nightdress that hung on the back of the door. She wasn't tidy like Linda had been. Her clothes were strewn all over the place. I liked it that way. She was earthy and sensual, like the summer in France.

'This one's very touching,' said Claudine, holding it up. '*Tell Mischa I'm in Chicago, the city of gangsters. It's dark and dangerous with men in hats, guns in their belts, skulking around street corners. I know he'll be impressed!'*

'Is that all it says?' I asked. 'Considering how long he was away for, it doesn't reveal much, does it.'

'What about this one: *Tell Mischa I'm in Mexico. I've ridden a white horse across the desert, slept beneath the stars and am sporting a giant hat to keep off the sun and the mosquitoes. The* fajitas *are delicious, the* mojitos *make my head spin. I play my guitar in the squares and women come and dance for me. They're the most beautiful women in the world, but not as beautiful as you, my lovely Anouk. My heart aches for you. Don't forget that I love you and that I always will. I love Mischa too, don't forget to tell him at least once a day. I don't want you to ever forget me.'* She looked across at me and frowned. 'Don't you think that's a bit odd? I mean, it's as if he knew he wasn't coming back.' I pondered on it for a while, reading them over again.

'Have you noticed, Claudine, that he describes the places in clichés. Listen to this, dated July: *Tell Mischa I'm in Chile. It's midsummer. Boiling hot. The sea is freezing cold, too cold for me. I play my guitar at night, the beach is deserted and the stars are much larger here. I miss you both. I'll come home soon. Tell Mischa to look after his mother while I'm away and to practise his guitar. I expect him to play the whole of Laredo when I get home. Lay a place for me at the table, my love, I don't wish to miss dinner.'*

'What's so odd about that?' she asked. I handed her the postcard.

'July is winter in Chile. It's freezing.'

She sat up. 'Are you saying that you don't believe he's been to any of these places?'

'Oh, I'm not saying he never went there. He just didn't go there then. Look at the postmarks.'

'They're all from the same place.'

'They're all marked West Virginia. Do you know what's in West Virginia? Keen Mountain Correctional Centre.'

She stared at me in disbelief. 'Oh God. He was in prison!'

'He spent three decades in prison because he murdered Richard Quigley. I imagine he killed Billy, Joy Springtoe's fiancé, too.'

She put her hand on my arm. 'Oh God, Mischa. Are you sure?'

'Yes. Joy had read all about it in the local papers at the time, so when we got back I did some research myself. Coyote had another life. In fact he wasn't even called Jack Magellan. He was called Lynton Shaw. I suspect he killed Billy during the war because he wanted to be sure that he wouldn't come back and dig up that painting. Then, when the warehouse and our home were broken into, he knew who did it and what he was looking for. That's why he left, to track Richard Quigley down and silence him. For a man so devious and clever, I'm surprised he got caught.'

'You've suspected for some time, haven't you?'

I nodded and sighed. 'It was the only plausible explanation. Why else would he not have come back? What baffles me, though, is why he never told us. We could have visited him in jail. At least I would have known. I wouldn't have felt so let down.' She shuffled through the postcards, scanning every one.

'He might have been a terrible fraud, Mischa. But look at the postcards, they all say "tell Mischa". Every single one. I think the reason he didn't tell you and your mother where he was is obvious. He didn't want to disappoint *you*.' I picked them all up and began reading through them again. She was right. Every single postcard was written for me. 'You had put him on a pedestal. He was this magical man who had given you back your voice and your self-belief. If he had told you the truth you would have lost all trust.

Maybe he thought you'd lose your voice again. I don't know.'

'I loved him like he loved the Old Man of Virginia. He knew what it was like to love an illusion and probably what it was like to lose him, too. He didn't come to my office for the Titian. He came for *me*.' I felt my stomach flip over with excitement. 'He found me because of the painting. Because we had been in the papers. My mother held on to it for all those years, hoping he'd come back for it. That's why it hurt her so much to give it away, because it meant that she was giving up hope he'd ever return to her. When he did, however, it wasn't for the painting. He came back for me and my mother. Don't you see?' I gripped her hand. 'That was what he meant when he said he was "chasing rainbows". You can't bring back the past. We had moved on. My mother had died. He'd rotted away for thirty years hoping to be reunited, but his dreams were nothing but rainbows. Christ! I turned him away.'

'You couldn't have known,' Claudine reassured me.

'I thought he wanted money. But he wanted his son.' I put my head in my hands, my excitement turned to nausea. 'How can I find him?'

'You can't.' She shook her head. 'Unless he finds you.'

That night I sat by the open window and played *Laredo*. I hoped by some magic the wind would take it to him so that he would know I had never stopped loving him. He had been Lynton Shaw, Jack Magellan, a thief, a fraud, and a murderer, but he had been Coyote to me. Coyote with the sharp blue eyes, the mischievous smile, the big loving heart and the voice of an angel.

I was happy to move to New Jersey, for New York had grown into a city of hopelessness. In the face of every tramp I searched for Coyote. Each time, my hope was ignited only to be snuffed out when the eyes of a stranger stared impassively back at me. We bought a pretty white clapboard house with a picket fence and set our roots down with the flowers we planted. I opened a shop and called it Captain Crumble's Antique Store because I secretly hoped that he might come looking for me. I wanted to tell him that I loved him, that I always had. That, in spite of everything, my love was the only thing that had endured.

We settled down, bought a dog and got to know our neighbours. Then one windy August morning I received a package. It was large but light. I recognised the writing. It was from Esther. I tore open the brown paper and pulled out a guitar. My heart faltered a moment. It was Coyote's guitar. With a palpitating heart I read her note:

> *Dear Mischa. This came for you. God knows why you should want it. You don't play, do you? It's hell in New York, too hot, too crowded, too hurried, too lonesome without you. Cheer up! Esther.*

I was too stunned to even smile. I searched among the paper for a letter, a note, anything from Coyote, but there appeared to be nothing. I sat down and started to tune the guitar. My fingers were trembling to such an extent that I could barely keep them on the strings. I could feel him in the notes it played. Hear him singing, his voice carried across the years on the wind that brought him to Maurilliac that late summer day. And then I saw the note, hidden in the body of the guitar. It was small, white, and written in a barely legible scrawl. 'This once belonged to the Old Man of Virginia. Treasure it, Junior, for now it belongs to you?'

I felt my throat constrict and my eyes sting with tears. I strummed with emphasis and sang *Laredo*, just to prove to him that I could.

So we took him down
To the green valley
And played the death march
As we carried him along
Because we all love our comrades
So brave, young and handsome.
We all love our comrades
Even though they done wrong

If you have enjoyed THE GYPSY MADONNA, here is a taster of Santa Montefiore's next novel, SEA OF LOST LOVE, available in hardback in March 2007 from Hodder & Stoughton.

Chapter One

Cornwall, August 1958

As Father Miles Dalgliesh cycled up the drive towards Pendrift Hall, he took pleasure from the golden sun that filtered through the lime trees, casting luminous spots of shimmering light onto the gravel and surrounding ferns and foxgloves, and swept his bespectacled eyes over lush fields of soft brown cows. There was a fresh breeze and gulls wheeled beneath a cerulean sky. Father Dalgliesh was new in town. Old Father William Hancock had recently passed away to continue his work on the Other Side, leaving his young prodigy in the hot seat rather sooner than anticipated. Still, God had given him a challenge and he would rise to it with gladness in his heart.

Today he would meet the Montagues, the first family of Pendrift.

Pendrift Hall was a pale stone mansion adorned with purple wisteria and clematis, tall sash windows and frothy gardens that tumbled down to the sea. Pigeons cooed from the chimney pots and every year a family of swallows made its nest in the porch. The house was large and somewhat shabby, like a child's favourite toy worn out by love. It had an air of contentment and Father Dalgliesh's spirits rose even higher when he saw it. He knew he'd like the family and he anticipated an enjoyable afternoon ahead.

He stopped cycling and dismounted. A sturdy, white faced

Labrador bounded out of the front door, wagging his tail and barking excitedly. Father Dalgliesh bent down to pat him and the dog stopped barking, sensing the young priest's gentle nature, and proceeded to sniff his shiny black shoes instead. The priest raised his eyes to the butler who now stood in the doorway, dressed in a black tail coat and pressed white shirt.

The man nodded respectfully. 'Good morning, Father. Mrs Montague is expecting you.' Father Dalgliesh leant his bicycle against the wall and followed the butler through a large stone hall dominated by a sleeping fireplace and a large set of antlers. The air in the house was sweet with the memory of winter fires, cinnamon and centuries of wear and tear and he noticed an open chest beneath the staircase full of tennis rackets and balls and an old grandfather clock that gently ticked against one wall like a somnolent footman. Classical music wafted from the drawing room with the low hum of distant voices. He took a deep breath.

'Father Dalgliesh, Mrs Montague,' the butler announced solemnly, indicating with a gesture of his hand that Father Dalgliesh should enter the room.

'Thank you, Soames,' said Julia Montague, rising to greet him. 'Father, welcome to Pendrift.' Father Dalgliesh shook her hand and was immediately put at ease by the warmth of her smile. She was plump, with soft white skin, ash blonde hair and an open, gentle face. Julia Montague radiated so brightly that when she was present it was always a party. With large beaded necklaces in pale greens and blues to match her eyes, a laugh so infectious no one was immune – not even that sour-puss Soames – and a sense of humour that always made the best out of the worst, Julia was like a colourful bird of paradise that had made her nest in the very heart of tweedy Cornwall. 'The family are waiting to meet you on the terrace,' she continued with a grin. 'Can I get you a drink before I throw you to the wolves?'

Father Dalgliesh laughed and Julia thought how handsome he was for a priest. There was something very charming in the lines around his mouth when he smiled and behind his glasses his eyes were deep set and intelligent. He was surprisingly young, too. He couldn't have been more than thirty. 'A glass of water would be fine, thank you,' he replied.

'We have some home-made elderflower cordial, why don't you try some?'

'Why not? That would be very nice.'

'Soames, two glasses of elderflower on the terrace, please.' Soames nodded and withdrew. Julia slipped her arm through the priest's and led him through the French doors into the sunshine.

The terrace was a wide York stone patio with irregular steps descending into the garden. Between the stones wild strawberries grew and tiny blue forget-me-nots struggled to be seen. Fat bees buzzed about large terracotta pots of arum lilies and freesias, and drank themselves dizzy in a thick border of lavender that grew against the balustrade lining the terrace. In the garden a gnarled weeping willow trailed her branches into a decorative pond where a pair of wild ducks had made their nest. The family fell silent as Father Dalgliesh emerged with Julia. Archie Montague, Julia's husband, was the first to step forward. 'It's a pleasure to meet you,' he exclaimed heartily, shaking the priest's hand. 'We were very sorry when Father William died. He was an inspirational man.'

'He was indeed. He has left me with the unenviable task of following in his footsteps.'

'Which I'm sure you will do valiantly,' added Archie kindly, running his fingers down the brown moustache that rested on his upper lip like a neatly thatched roof.

'Let me introduce you to Archie's sister, Augusta, and her two daughters, Lotty and Melissa,' said Julia, still holding onto Father Dalgliesh's arm, because she sensed her husband's family could be a little overwhelming. Augusta stepped forward and shook his hand. He winced as she squeezed the life out of it. Large boned and stout with an arresting bosom and a double chin she reminded him of one of her brother's Jersey cows.

'Very nice to meet you, Father.' Augusta's voice was deep and fruity and she articulated the consonants of her words with relish as if each one were a pleasure to pronounce. 'You're a great deal younger than we expected.'

'I hope my age does not disappoint,' he replied.

'To the contrary. Sometimes the old ones have had too many years listening to the sound of their own voices to be sensitive to the voices of others. I doubt you will fall into that trap.' She turned and ushered her daughters over to meet him. 'This is Lotty, my eldest, and Melissa, who has just turned twenty-five.' She smiled at them proudly as they greeted the priest. Dressed beautifully in floral summer frocks with their long hair pulled off their faces and clipped to the top of their heads, they were pleasant to look at and very presentable. However, they were vapid girls, their heads full of frivolities, encouraged by their mother whose main concern was marrying them off to well-bred young men of means. According to Augusta, they were two of the most eligible girls in London and nothing less than the very best would do. She scoffed at the idea of marrying for love. That was a highly impractical notion, not to mention foolish, because one's heart could not be trusted to fall in love with the right man. She herself was a prime example of her theory. She had grown to love Milton Flint over time, though she secretly hoped her daughters would make better matches than she had made. She might have married a Flint, but she remained a Montague through and through.

'This is Milton, Augusta's husband and David, their son,' continued Julia, leading the priest further onto the terrace. Milton was tall and athletic, with thick blonde hair brushed back off a wide forehead and lively blue eyes.

'Good to meet you, Father. Do you play tennis?'

Father Dalgliesh looked embarrassed. 'I'm afraid not,' he replied.

'Dad's obsessed,' interjected David apologetically, 'though he does put the racket down for Mass!' David laughed and Father Dalgliesh was reassured by the presence of a young man of his own generation. Julia let go of his arm and sat down. Father Dalgliesh took the seat beside her and crossed one leg over the other in an effort to look casual. He felt a little nervous. His conviction was as solid as rock, his knowledge of the Scriptures and philosophy unsurpassed, indeed his command of Latin was exceptional – his Achilles heel, however, was people – Father Hancock had once told him: *'it's no good being so heavenly minded as to be no earthly good. You have to learn how to relate to people, Miles, on their level, otherwise you might as well become a monk.'* He knew the old priest was right. The Bishop had sent him out to be among the people to spread the word of God. He pushed his glasses up his nose, determined not to let him down.

'Our young sons are out in the woods with their cousin, Harry,' said Julia. 'The gamekeeper gives them sixpence a rat, if they bring it to him dead. They're getting rather rich, I believe. My three year old son, Bouncy, is down on the beach with Nanny, they should be up soon, and Celestria, my niece . . .' Julia looked around. 'I don't know where she is. Perhaps she's with her mother, Pamela, who's married to Archie and Augusta's brother Monty. She's in bed with a migraine. She suffers from them, I'm afraid. She might come down later. She's American.' Julia hesitated a moment for Pamela Bancroft Montague, as she liked to be called, was extremely pampered, often spending whole days in bed, complaining if the light was too bright, moaning when it was too dark, insisting on being left alone with Poochi, her powdered Pekinese, while at the same time demanding as much attention as possible from Celestria and Harry, and constantly ringing the bell to summon the staff. She doubted whether Father Dalgliesh would meet her at all, as she wasn't a Catholic and abhorred the Church, which she thought a waste of time. 'Monty arrives this evening on the train from London. He's a wonderful character and I hope you'll meet him. You'll certainly meet Harry and Celestria, their children. Harry sings rather beautifully and is in the choir at school.' Julia lit a cigarette and inhaled deeply. Soames stepped through the doors with a tray of drinks. When he handed Father Dalgliesh a glass of elderflower, Julia noticed that the young priest's hands were trembling.

It wasn't long before Wilfrid and Sam, Julia and Archie's young sons, returned from the woods with Harry. Exuberant after a morning building camps and setting traps, they were ruddy cheeked and sparkly eyed. 'We found three dead rats!' exclaimed Wilfrid to his mother.

'How wonderful!' she replied. 'Darling, I'd like you to say hello to Father Dalgliesh.' The three boys fell silent at the sight of Father Dalgliesh's white Roman collar and held out their hands.

'What did you do with the rats?' Father Dalgliesh asked, endeavouring to put the boys at their ease.

'We hung them on the door by their tails!' said Sam, screwing up his freckly nose with delight. 'They're enormous, the size of Poochi!' he added.

'You'd better not hang him up by his tail!' laughed David.

'You'd have to hang Aunt Pamela up with him,' added Archie with a smirk. 'She never lets him out of her sight.'

'Oh you are wicked, darling!' said Julia, eyeing Harry. It was all too easy to make jokes about Pamela without considering her children.

'Where's Mama?' Harry asked.

'She's in bed with a migraine,' Julia replied.

'Not again!'

'I'm afraid she does suffer from them.'

'Not when Papa's home,' said Harry innocently. It was true. When Monty was there, Pamela's migraines miraculously disappeared.

Amidst the idyll that was Pendrift, Monty came and went, arriving on the 7.30pm train from London, in time for a whiskey and a smoke and a set of tennis with Archie, Milton and David. He'd arrive smiling raffishly beneath the brim of his panama hat, his pale linen suit crumpled from the train, a newspaper clamped under one arm, carrying only his briefcase and all the cheerfulness in the world. Pamela's moods would lift like the grey mist that sometimes hangs over Pendrift before the sun burns through, but she behaved as badly as ever, making terrible demands, swinging the conversation around to herself at every opportunity. She was spoiled and self-centred, being the only daughter of a very wealthy American businessman called Richard W. Bancroft II.

The boys took Purdy the Labrador down to the beach to play cricket, just as Nanny returned up the path with Bouncy and Celestria. Father Dalgliesh's lips parted in wonder as he watched the celestial figure of the beautiful young woman walking towards him. To his shame his heart beat accelerated and the colour rose in his cheeks. He hoped it was the midday heat that had caused his sudden agitation. Celestria wore a short red and white polka dot skirt and halter neck top that exposed her midriff. Her blonde hair was loose, falling in waves over smooth brown shoulders and she walked as if she had not a care in the world. He could not see her eyes, which were hidden behind large, white framed sunglasses.

'Ah, Celestria, come and meet Father Dalgliesh,' Julia called out as she approached.

When Bouncy heard his mother's voice he let go of Nanny's hand and ran up the path, squealing with excitement.

'Mummy!' he cried.

'Hello, darling!' Julia replied. When the little boy realised he had an audience he put his hands on his hips and began a funny, jaunty walk, wiggling his bottom and grinning, peering up from under thick lashes. Everyone clapped and roared with laughter. Bouncy was the child that united them all. His mischievous smile, inherited from Julia, could melt an entire winter. He had thick sandy hair and soft brown eyes, the colour of home made fudge. He loved to show off and was encouraged to do so, though it exasperated Nanny that he tore his clothes off at any opportunity and ran around naked. He spoke with a lisp which was irresistibly sweet. Julia and Pamela, who had little in common besides the fact that they had married brothers, discovered a bridge in Bouncy. 'Darling, you're so adorable!' enthused his mother, pulling him onto her knee and nuzzling him lovingly. Celestria followed behind, still laughing and clapping her hands. Father Dalgliesh stared at her as if bewitched.

'This is my niece, Celestria. Harry's elder sister,' said Julia, without taking her eyes off her son. Celestria removed her sunglasses and hooked them into her cleavage, then extended her hand to the priest.

'You're much younger than I imagined. Father Hancock was as old as Nanny!' she said.

'Really, Celestria!' Augusta exclaimed disapprovingly.

'Nanny is as fit as a fiddle.' As the priest's colour deepened, Celestria's somewhat haughty face broke into a warm smile.

'You look like you could do with a swim, Father. The sea's delicious this morning. Cold but refreshing.'

'Do take off your jacket, Father,' said Julia, suddenly noticing the poor man's discomfort.

'I'm fine, really,' he replied. 'I'm used to the heat, having lived in Italy.'

'There's nothing like an English summer,' said Archie. 'Just when you think it's going to be cold and grey the sun comes out and burns you. Unpredictable, that's what it is.'

'I'm going upstairs to see Mama and change out of my bathing suit,' said Celestria, weaving nimbly through the chairs. Father Dalgliesh watched her go and found he was able to breathe again. Celestria's beauty was indeed remarkable. It wasn't so much her thick blonde hair that glistened like the cornfields around Pendrift, or her clear grey eyes that had never been marred by a single moment of unhappiness, or her generous mouth and fine bones that gave her face definition, but the way she held herself. Her poise was cool and confident and superior, nothing so brash as arrogant, it was simply that she was aware of her place in the world and confident of other people's high regard for her.

She was twenty-one and according to her mother, 'balancing precariously on the edge of womanhood'. But Celestria didn't feel at all precarious and if Pamela only knew the half of it, how she had let Aiden Cooney slip his hand into her knickers and how she had felt the hardness through his trousers, she wouldn't have entertained such silly ideas. She was already a famous beauty, well established on the London party scene having come out when she was eighteen. There was many a hopeful man who entertained ideas of marriage. Most looked at her intensely and treated her like porcelain, which she found rather silly, except for Aiden

Cooney, of course, whose eyes were filled with something darker than admiration.

But Celestria was far more than an English beauty. She had something of the exotic about her, which men found irresistible. Concerned for her safety, her mother had taken her to New York when war broke out. They had lived with her grandparents in a Park Avenue penthouse with ceilings so tall she could barely see them and splendid views over Central Park. For six years she was her grandfather's delight. He had long since lost his daughter to Monty and England so he relished having a little girl around the house and showered her with attention and presents that came in boxes, wrapped with tissue paper, smelling of new. He was the father she had lost to the war, the father she could embrace while hers was overseas and in wafer thin envelopes that arrived sporadically to make her mother cry.

Celestria learned to weave her charm and throw it over whole roomfuls of people like a fisherman setting her net, drawing it in little by little until she had ensnared each and every one. She learned to enchant and enthral, understanding very early on what her grandfather expected of her. His applause was addictive and she drank his love and grew dizzy. She was showed off to guests before dinner, presented at seven by her governess with her hair in ringlets, her dress pressed and her shoes shiny and her grandfather's pride was as sweet as candy. She sang songs and duly blushed when they all clapped. It was easy to manipulate them. They thought she was too young to be aware of her charisma, but she knew how pretty she was and it didn't take long to realise that by mimicking adults she could win their admiration. 'What a funny child!' they'd coo. 'A clever little darling!' And the more precocious she became, the more everyone loved her. But no one loved her as much as her grandfather.

Pamela Bancroft Montague seemed incapable of loving

anyone more than she loved herself. It wasn't her fault her parents had spoiled her. She had learned to be selfish, to believe she was the centre of the universe, so there wasn't much room for anyone else. She loved Celestria as an extension of herself; that was a love she instinctively understood. Her husband spoiled her, too. She shone like a jewel and he treasured her as one. She had a captivating beauty, the sort of beauty that struck fear into the hearts of both men and women, for men found such loveliness indomitable, and women knew their own beauty lost its lustre in the light of hers.

Celestria didn't miss her father in those early years – she had arrived in America as a two year old and returned to London when she was seven; she couldn't even remember what he looked like. She had missed her grandfather when she left New York, treasuring the week they spent every autumn at the fairytale castle he had bought as a young man in Scotland to shoot and stalk and the annual holiday at the Bancroft family home on the island of Nantucket. Like her mother, she learned to love herself more. When Monty tried to make up for the years of estrangement with presents, she accepted them gladly, manipulating him with little kisses in the same way she had manipulated her grandfather. Then he gave her mother a little boy: Harry. From the moment Harry was born, Pamela Bancroft Montague discovered that she could love someone more than she loved herself. For Celestria, that was a love she was yet to discover.

When Celestria returned, the family were taking their seats for lunch at a long table beneath a big square sun shade. Father Dalgliesh was placed at the head, Archie at the foot. Julia put herself next to the priest, with Augusta his other side. Pamela's place was discreetly taken away by Soames, who found Mrs Bancroft Montague exceedingly tiresome. Cook's son, Warren, had already been up to her six times that morning, with trays of hot drinks and little bowls of food and water for her wretched dog. He had a good mind to muffle her bell so he couldn't hear it.

Father Dalgliesh made the sign of the cross, then with his head bowed and his hands folded, he said Grace '*Benedic, domine, nos et haec tua dona quae de tua largitate sumus sumpturi.*' As his hands made the sign of the cross for the second time, Celestria raised her eyes and caught those of the priest. He reminded her of a startled fox. She was about to smile at him with encouragement, when Archie invited everyone to sit down with the words: 'let battle commence!'

Celestria was placed between Lotty and David, but she was aware of the priest's attention even though he made an effort not to look at her again. It came as no surprise. Most men found her alluring. It was quite fun catching the eye of a priest and almost tempting to lead him astray for sport. She had had few rivals, but never one as powerful as God. The concept of celibacy fascinated her, especially in a man so good-looking. He had intelligent brown eyes, an angular face with chiselled cheek bones and a strong jaw line. In fact, if he took off those glasses he'd be quite dishy. 'Father Dalgliesh,' she said, concealing a smirk. 'What called you to serve the Church?' He looked startled for a moment and pushed his glasses up his nose, appalled at the effect this young woman had on him. Hadn't his faith and dedication built a resistance to this sort of thing?

'I had a dream as a little boy,' he replied.

'Really? Do tell,' she encouraged.

He raised his eyes and looked at her steadily. 'An angelic being came to me and in the clearest voice told me that my future was in the Catholic Church. It was a vision, a light so powerful it left me in no doubt that God was calling me to serve Him. Since then I have only ever wanted to be a priest.

I have never forgotten that vision and during moments of doubt, I remember it.'

'Like the light on the road to Damascus,' said Archie, chewing on a sausage.

'How miraculous,' exclaimed Augusta, her voice fruitier than ever.

'And how wonderful that miracles happen in the modern world,' added Julia.

'Yes, it is, isn't it,' replied Father Dalgliesh.

'Do you suffer doubts, Father?' Celestria asked to a sharp intake of breath from her Aunt Augusta.

Father Dalgliesh hesitated while he struggled with the impertinence of her question. 'We are, all of us, human beings,' he said carefully. 'And it would be wrong to assume myself super human because of a vision and a calling. God has given me a challenge and at times, it seems great. Just because I'm a priest, doesn't mean I am immune or even excluded from life's obstacles and pitfalls. I have weaknesses like everyone else. But my faith gives me strength. I have never doubted it or my conviction, only my own aptitude.' As he spoke, he grew in stature. He seemed far older than his years, as if he had a maturity gained over decades of experience and yet, somewhere in the darkest corner of his heart, a menacing little seed was sown.

Later, back at the presbytery that stood next door to the Church of The Blessed Virgin Mary, Miss Hoddel brought Father Dalgliesh his tea into the sitting room on a tray. He sat in silence, his eyes far away from the book that rested on his knee. She looked about her, at the heaps of papers and books squeezed onto every available surface and wondered where to put the tray today. With an impatient snort she shuffled over to the coffee table and placed the tray on top of a tower of letters. Father Dalgliesh was shaken out of his trance and rushed to help her. 'I can't clean this place if it's always in a mess, Father' she said, rubbing her hands up and down her wide hips as if to clean the dust off. Father Dalgliesh shrugged apologetically.

'I'm afraid even this house isn't big enough for all my books,' he replied.

'Can't you sell some of them?'

He looked appalled. 'Absolutely not, Miss Hoddel.'

She sighed heavily and shook her head. 'Well, I've left you and Father Brock some cold ham in the fridge and a little salad for your dinner.'

'Thank you,' he replied, bending down to pour the tea.

'I'm taking your vestments home to mend. I've got my trusty Singer, you see, so I can do the job properly. We can't have you looking shabby in Church, can we, Father?' Again, he thanked her. 'I'll be going then. See you tomorrow, bright and early to tackle all that dust. I'll just have to clean around your clutter. It's not ideal but what can I do?' He watched her go, closing the panelled wooden door behind her. He breathed a sigh of relief. Miss Hoddel was a godly woman, of that he had no doubt. The trouble was her ill humour, there was nothing godly about that. Still, no one was perfect, not even he. A spinster in her late sixties, she was dedicated to serving the Church, happy to look after him and Father Howel Brock for very little. People like her were a blessing. He asked God for patience. He also asked God for strength and forgiveness. He hadn't been able to stop thinking about Celestria Montague since the moment he had seen her walking up the garden in her polka dot swimming dress. Once again he pulled his rosary out of his pocket and began to move the beads slowly through his fingers, mumbling in a low voice, ten Hail Marys.